Acclaim for *Love and M...*

"A charming tale of girl meets boy meets gourmet feast. *Love and Meatballs* is a deliciously satisfying read."
—Whitney Gaskell, author of *Pushing 30*

"*Love and Meatballs* is a fun, mouthwatering romp that is one part family, one part romance, one part suspense, one part humor, and all heart."
—Caren Lissner, author of *Carrie Pilby* and *Starting from Square Two*

"*Love and Meatballs* is a hilarious book about the things in life that are most important to me—love, family, and food. Susan Volland writes in a style that will have you laughing out loud and then running to the kitchen to whip up your favorite family recipes. I recommend it highly."
—Nick Stellino, host of the national TV show *Nick Stellino's Family Kitchen*

"Keeps the pages turning . . . quick and witty . . . genuine description[s] of a tight-knit, food-loving Italian family, with personalities reminiscent of the boisterous clan in the film *My Big Fat Greek Wedding.* . . . Gives good food the credit it deserves. . . . It sure conjured up cravings for parmesan-sprinkled Italian fare."
—*Northwest Palate Magazine*

Also by Susan Volland

Love and Meatballs

Cooking for Mr. Right

Susan Volland

NAL NEW AMERICAN LIBRARY

New American Library
Published by New American Library, a division of
Penguin Group (USA) Inc., 375 Hudson Street,
New York, New York 10014, USA
Penguin Group (Canada), 90 Eglinton Avenue East, Suite 700, Toronto,
Ontario M4P 2Y3, Canada (a division of Pearson Penguin Canada Inc.)
Penguin Books Ltd., 80 Strand, London WC2R 0RL, England
Penguin Ireland, 25 St. Stephen's Green, Dublin 2,
Ireland (a division of Penguin Books Ltd.)
Penguin Group (Australia), 250 Camberwell Road, Camberwell, Victoria 3124,
Australia (a division of Pearson Australia Group Pty. Ltd.)
Penguin Books India Pvt. Ltd., 11 Community Centre, Panchsheel Park,
New Delhi - 110 017, India
Penguin Group (NZ), cnr Airborne and Rosedale Roads, Albany,
Auckland 1310, New Zealand (a division of Pearson New Zealand Ltd.)
Penguin Books (South Africa) (Pty.) Ltd., 24 Sturdee Avenue,
Rosebank, Johannesburg 2196, South Africa

Penguin Books Ltd., Registered Offices: 80 Strand, London WC2R 0RL, England

First published by New American Library, a division of Penguin Group (USA) Inc.

First Printing, August 2005
10 9 8 7 6 5 4 3 2 1

NEW AMERICAN LIBRARY and logo are trademarks of Penguin Group (USA) Inc.

Library of Congress Cataloging-in-Publication Information:

Volland, Susan.
  Cooking for Mr. Right / Susan Volland.
    p. cm.
  ISBN 0-451-21524-9
  1. Women cooks—Fiction. 2. Seattle (Wash.)—Fiction. 3. Rejection (Psychology)—
Fiction. 4. Triangles (Interpersonal realtions)—Fiction. 5. Cookery—Fiction. I. Title.
PS3622.O64C66 2005
813'.6—dc22   2005006142

Printed in the United States of America

Designed by Ginger Legato

For Dad

Acknowledgments

Thanks to all of the very talented and overworked chefs of the world. You are true artists. I toast you with an ice-cold beer and a fresh bottle of ibuprofen.

Thanks to the following people for their best wishes and heartfelt support through the tough spots. Critics and cheerleaders all—Ellen Edwards, Jim McCarthy, Karma Fowler, Susan Goodwin, Scott Wellsandt, Kristine Latta, Gwen Hayes, and Bob and Cynthia Burns.

Thanks to the generous folks who offered their expertise and energy— Beverly Volland, Tim and Mayu Jensen, Wally Bivins and the fine folks at Pottery Northwest, Melinda Wellsandt, Shelley Boyce, Jayma Cohn, Arlene Levins and Mark Vinson.

And, of course, this book would have been impossible if not for my own personal Mr. Right, my beloved husband, Jeff Volland.

Chapter One

I'm sitting on the edge of the tub with my feet in the toilet, banging my head with the cordless phone and vowing to make some serious changes in my life. Gaston just called to tell me he is getting married.

"Katie, I'm getting married!" My mouth drops open and my heart races. I swallow air a few times. "What?!"

"I'm getting married! I've been trying to call you all day, but I could never catch you. And this isn't the kind of thing you leave on an answering machine. Her name is Courtney. She's an elementary school teacher. We met a couple of weeks ago at one of Harry's boat parties and fell slam-bam in love, just like that. It sounds crazy." He giggles. "God, who am I kidding? It's the craziest thing I've ever done! But she's amazing. She's different than anyone I've ever met. She's sweet and funny and just the prettiest thing I ever laid eyes on."

I choke a bit, and Gaston manages to snap out of his reverie and hear what he is saying. "Oh, I didn't mean that you weren't pretty or anything. And funny. You've always cracked me up." He pauses a moment, then renews his enthusiasm. "Jeez, Kate, you know what I mean! You'll love her! I can't wait until you two can meet."

Oh, goody, my ex-boyfriend wants me to meet his insta-bride. Knowing Gaston as I do, I can hear a tone of desperation in his voice. He has done something out of character. He is scared to death, and, for some freakish reason, he needs me to tell him it's okay. Somehow I manage to ask all the right questions and be just congratulatory enough.

"Thanks, Katydid. You're the greatest. It's been so crazy. It feels so right, and then when I look at what I've done, I can't help but wonder if I've made a huge mistake. I guess I need you to tell me it's okay."

"Gaston, I think it's amazing that you did something so impulsive and romantic. In fact, I'm a little jealous. She must be some kind of a girl to have you act on a whim instead of graphing out the pros and cons, the odds of success and the long-term consequences of your actions."

"But I did! That's the thing! I did that. And you'll never believe it, so did she! We both did pro/con spreadsheets and concluded that we are perfect for each other. Can you believe it?"

This information inspires the first blow to my head. No longer capable of holding my throbbing skull upright, I let it fall and bang against the shower surround. I manage to croak, "Congratulations. I wish you both the best." And, at first, I do. But once I hang up the phone, I feel the need for a few more blows to the head. Gaston married? To somebody else? Impossible!

I flush the well-scrubbed toilet again, and the cold water whirls around to soothe my aching feet. It has been a brutal night at work, and cooling my dogs in the toilet is a trick my roommate Marissa taught me. The toilets in this house stay busy with a nurse, a chef and a cocktail waitress living together.

I whack my forehead with the phone again. This time it hurts, so I stop. I'm already knocked low from a nasty night at the restaurant where I work. I'm the sous-chef at a hot downtown Seattle restaurant called Sound Bistro. The chef, Nancy Dierbocker, has made the big time. Her grinning mug has been in every food publication printed lately, I swear. I keep trying to convince myself that that's a good thing. It's her turn. Mine will come later, helped along with all of Nancy's good press.

I've seen lots of talented sous-chefs turn bitter and angry. It's a hazard of the job. Everyone knows what a chef does, but not that many folks understand the role of a sous. We're the invisible ass-busters of the industry. Our job is to keep the kitchen humming, the team working together and the food quality high while the chef is busy elsewhere. And Nancy is *always* busy elsewhere these days. In my thinking, the longer a sous-chef can stick out the brutal hours, miserable pay and lack of recognition, the better their own restaurant will be when it's their turn. I'm due for an amazing restaurant someday.

I hired a lot of our crack team, and they're great. That said, it's still the kitchen of a privately owned, fine dining restaurant, which means too little space, too much heat and a lot of ego. When things go well, the entire line works like organic chemistry, but now and then things start to slip, mistakes are made, egos are bruised or customers get crabby, and the place seems like a nursery school with knives. Tonight was a bad night. Nancy, the nation's new little darling chef, was off camera and showed her fangs. She came in right before dinner service and tore through the line, shouting and tossing out pan after pan of prepped food that, today, didn't reach her standards. (Never mind that yesterday the same work would have been praised.) Each of us had a list a mile long to get our stations ready for a busy Saturday night. Deliveries were late, items were missing and in the rush, two full-sized pans of duck confit were burned into very expensive charcoal. While Nancy didn't actually rub the guilty party's nose in the mess, she sure treated her staff like a pack of good-for-nothing dogs.

Just when I thought things were getting better, Cynthia Nims, a local cookbook author and food critic, sat down for dinner with a table of food writers. As if we needed the extra stress. We cranked things up yet another notch and somehow got the job done while Nancy chatted up the writers. Then, instead of jumping in and helping us by breaking down our stations and cleaning up after a hard night, Nancy rewarded us with her wise remembrances of the unbearable situations she had worked through. She knew we could do it. We just needed that extra little push. I'm sure I wasn't alone in my thoughts of things to push through her heart as she fluffed up her clean hair and traipsed off with the owners for cocktails and late-night jazz while we stood sticky and stinking, surrounded by petrified sauce splatters, battered sauté pans and barren prep containers.

And now, cooling my throbbing feet in the toilet and waiting for the ibuprofen to kick in, I'm feeling a rush of the classic sous-chef resentment I have been so good at repressing. I'm pissed. I also can't stop thinking about Gaston's call. Why didn't I marry him when I had the chance?

I dry my feet and pull on my very favorite pair of vintage men's pajamas, the ones with the leaping trout and clusters of cattails printed all over them. Then I go to the kitchen to make a pot of valerian tea. It's late, almost one, but I'm never going to get to sleep unless I have something to calm my overactive brain.

My roommate Iris comes in.

"You're home early." I say, checking the kitchen clock. Iris works as a cocktail waitress at a hipster bar in Belltown, and while she usually gets off a little after two, it's a rare Saturday night when she doesn't finish up the night at an after-hours club.

"Headache."

"Tea?"

"Yeah."

I pour another cup of the slightly skunky herbal tea into a mug and push it over to her. Iris swirls in a spoonful of honey. We sit in comfortable silence for a few minutes.

"Gaston's getting married," I say.

"No way! Did he buy a Russian bride on the Internet or something?"

I groan and shake my head. "Her name is Courtney Davis. She's an elementary schoolteacher, and just the sweetest thing he ever met."

Iris crosses her eyes and sticks her finger in her mouth.

I sigh. "I've had a lousy night. I'm too tired to get as drunk as I want to be. My bones hurt, and I'm thinking about packing my bags and moving to Mongolia. Fermented yak milk is supposed to be delicious once you acquire a taste for it. Maybe I can find enlightenment on the steppes. I can't imagine the working environment would be much worse."

Iris wiggles her nose just like she's done since she was about six. I appreciate the gesture for what it is: restraint. It's her version of biting her tongue. She must recognize that tonight I'm not up for her outspoken assessments of my personal life. "Well, I'm going to go treat my feet to a little eau de toilette and then hit the sack. Sorry about the Gaston thing." She gives me a squeeze. "Don't let it bug you. Gaston's a good guy, but you can do better."

I sit in silence for a moment thinking about Iris's words, both spoken and withheld. She isn't known for her good taste in boyfriends. She's drawn to the artistic and misunderstood. Add some type of addiction, and she's instantly in love. We are the same age and best friends, but our life goals are very different. Iris is still planning on being a rock star when she grows up. Much to her horror, I really like the idea of getting married and having kids.

So, why did I push Gaston away? He was quite a catch: attractive, healthy, intelligent. He loves good food. We had great sex. His family might be a little wacky, but whose family isn't? At least they have a decent excuse—they're rich. Gaston and I were together for about a year and a half, the last few months of which he had tried to get me to wear an engagement ring. What the hell is wrong with me? I scratch my head like a cartoon character. We're still close friends. I still love him, in a way. Why couldn't I commit? Jeez. Women are always complaining that their men aren't ready to commit, and here I had the perfect guy just dying to marry and take care of me, and I turned him down—more than once. His proposals were always quite charming. Twice he very nearly had me convinced, but something just never felt quite right. I insisted I was a square peg and Gaston wanted to jam me into a smooth, round hole. Truth be told, I still have regular urges to dye my hair blue and learn to play the electric bass. Gaston always said that he loved that about me, but I couldn't see him encouraging that kind of behavior once we belonged to a gated community.

Six months ago we really had it out. Gaston declared that my repeated rejections were insulting and unacceptable. I told him marriage isn't something you should be forced into. There was shouting and door-slamming, and we broke up. The following morning Gaston came back with flowers and a well-rehearsed apology. We held each other and cried. I told him I still loved him but that maybe we needed a break, and it's been good. I haven't been dating; I don't have time for that. But I have been flirting with the produce delivery guy. His name is Kurt. He's got great legs and a quick smile. He has this untamed, wolfish energy that makes me wonder what he's like in bed. He also dishes the best restaurant gossip in town. That's as hot as things have gotten for me in the past few months. But sitting here in the middle of the night, I have a suspicion that the produce guy isn't going to offer me the happily-ever-after I've always hoped for.

Gaston was probably my one and only chance at a fairy-tale ending, a life filled with heirloom roses and silk pillows. I glance down at my tired, pajama-draped body. I'm slumped at the kitchen table, my right cheek squashed in my cupped palm and one aching foot tucked up underneath my butt. Gaston offered me a life of comfort, riches and adoration, and I said, "No thanks." I'm such an idiot.

I rub my tired eyes and try to remember my reasoning. I didn't want to marry Gaston because I thought he was too regimented. His future seemed all charted out from birth. The most impulsive thing he ever did before this stupid engagement was move to Seattle, and his mother had his condo picked out and decorated before he ever got here. I remember feeling like he was rushing into marriage because he wanted to check it off his life list. Six months ago, this sounded like a reasonable complaint; tonight, I have to wonder.

If I'm honest with myself, I'll admit to having a list, too. Well, less of a list and more a collection of grandiose wishes. First and foremost, I want a useful and productive life. I guess, since I have chosen to be a chef, that means creating the very best food possible, perhaps in a cele-brated, cutting-edge restaurant similar to Sound Bistro. I would like a handsome husband. I'll even settle for someone best described as interesting-looking as long as he is my best friend and an adoring father to our perfect children. The kids will grow up in a home just busting with love and warmth and creativity. That's the best-case scenario. If for some reason that doesn't happen, I'd be happy with paychecks that accurately reflect my hard work and expertise, and the occasional weekend off. But why not dream big? How about a weekly shiatsu massage, too? I stretch and yawn, letting my imagination run wild. What would my life be like if, on a whim, I could spend my days sunbathing naked on a sailboat in the tropics or picnicking barefoot on the grassy banks of the Loire? My head falls back on the chair. Boy, I could use the fairy tale right about now.

I squeeze my eyes closed and sigh. Gaston's little quirks that used to drive me crazy seem so miniscule now. It used to bug me that he used too much mayonnaise and that he has this obsessive-compulsive need to organize things in lidded plastic boxes. There is also that hollow clicking sound he makes with his tongue while he sleeps. But what's that compared to his kind heart? He was always supportive, even when he didn't really approve of my career path. I smile remembering how he was always trying to nudge me into the corporate world and get me to make long-term goals. At the time, I felt like he was bullying me, but I see now that he was just looking after my best interests. Is it possible that some other woman might understand and love Gaston the way his doting French mother and I do? Can an elementary school teacher make the pan-fried sole and caper butter he loves so much? It is crystal-clear what I need to do. I am going to win Gaston back.

Chapter Two

I'm up first, at about ten. No surprise there. Iris doesn't show her face much before noon most days, and since Marissa, the nurse, fell in love, she is more of a specter than an actual roommate. Most of my contact with Marissa involves reading the notes she leaves on the fridge or noticing when her mail has shifted. She works two jobs and crashes at her boyfriend's house a lot. She pays her rent so she can use her room as storage and as a cover for when her parents call. They are deeply religious, and she isn't ready to tell them that she's living with her boyfriend in a less than virginal state.

I practice my normal Sunday morning routine. I brew a pot of coffee, invite Norah Jones to join me for breakfast on the CD player and go out front to pick up the soggy newspaper. I poke around the kitchen looking for something to eat. Finding nothing enticing, I grab a sheet of frozen puff pastry from the freezer, brush it with melted butter and sprinkle it with chopped, toasted filberts, sugar and cinnamon. After cutting the pastry into strips, I give them a few twists and pop them in the oven. It isn't the most nutritious breakfast in the world, but I want something hot and sweet to soothe my bruised soul.

I grab the phone. I'm going to call Gaston and tell him point-blank that he can't get married. I want him back. I run through a few conversations in my head. Each ends with sweet tears and passionate declarations of our eternal love. Our reunion becomes choreographed in my imagination. I cradle the phone tenderly near my neck until I push a button with my chin and the dial tone snaps me out of my reverie.

If I'm going to win Gaston back, my first action has to be extreme. I take a big gulp of coffee, wipe the sleep from my eyes and with bravado punch in the familiar numbers that will, I hope, change everything. I call Gaston's mother.

"Allo?" I wait a second to speak until I hear her exhale. Adele Lambert never fails to take a deep puff on her cigarette the moment she answers the phone.

"Adele, it's Kate," I reply, steeling myself against the kitchen table, ready for her barrage of histrionics. We haven't spoken much since the breakup.

"Kate! What have you done? My boy calls me and tells me he is getting married to some coquette he just met? He is engaged before he even introduces this girl to his own mother? Is that my sweet Gaston? No. No. That is a brokenhearted, empty and desperate man."

As I expected, Adele isn't interested in small talk or catching up. She gets straight to the point. I wince, but remain quiet.

"And it is *you* I blame, Kate Linden! Why would he do such a thing? Because you ruined him, that's why. You, with your clean, fresh American looks and French palate, how could he ever resist you? But you tore out his heart, squeezed it dry and threw it in the dirt. And now some horrible girl will turn him against me. Already I can feel it. She will finish him off. She will steal away my angel!"

After that tirade, I half expect her to spit on the floor. Adele Lambert is a piece of work. She is a Parisian living in Vancouver, BC, as a sacrifice for love. She met Gaston's father when they were both students in New York. She was a drama student—no surprise there; he was in international business. They were both young, rich and attractive. They flirted together at the A-list parties. Adele's dream of being on the London stage was rerouted as she found herself knocked up, married and then, much to her horror, the mother of an *American*-born son. I'm pretty sure she is happier as a beautiful, albeit slightly tortured ex-actress and mom, but you wouldn't know it to hear her.

Gaston's father is from an old lumber family in British Columbia. I've seen the pictures and heard stories of his joyful, party-filled youth, but today Graham Lambert's steady heartbeat rarely increases unless you're willing to discuss the soft woods market. He spends a lot of time abroad, working out international trade contracts. The few times we met, his face seldom materialized from behind the financial section of various international newspapers. I sometimes wonder how Gaston will act when he has his own children. The ideal scenario would have his stern, industrious father and dramatic, meddling mother melding into enthusiastic adoration and a firm, consistent resolve.

Adele is hard to ignore. She's like a very determined fruit fly gunning for your wine. At times, I have been tempted to swat at her for getting in my face, but right now I have some groveling to do. I've got to get her back on my team.

"Yes, Adele. I'm so very sorry. I agree about everything. That's why I'm calling."

"Calling to remind me that soon my boy will be dead to me? Stolen away by some cunning fox? You break his heart, break *my* heart, and then you walk out of our lives. You know, I loved you like a daughter, and still you don't even call or send a card. Not even for my birthday."

Ouch! Her words sting. Forgetting Adele's birthday is a high crime, unforgivable for actual family members. But I think there is hope. It sounds like I might still have Adele on my side. If Adele Lambert were now on Courtney's team, it would be like battling the wind and the tides. Adele is a strong force in Gaston's nature.

I take a deep breath and play the part that is expected of me. "Adele, I'm so sorry. I've been terrible, horrible to both you and Gaston." She is silent. I can almost hear her nose in the air, her cigarette poised as she awaits more kowtowing. "I've been selfish and unthinking. That's why I'm calling now. I want Gaston back. He can't marry someone he just met. You need to talk to him."

Those are the magic words. "Oh, my sweet! Can it be true? You also see that this marriage is doomed? You see that you and Gaston are meant to be together? My dear, dear Kate."

Phew! "So, you'll talk to him?" I squeak. My fingers are crossed.

"Impossible," she barks. "I'm not talking to Gaston now."

Argh. My hopes are dashed. Adele continues. "He *calls* from Seattle. His family is merely a few hundred kilometers north of him and he *calls* to say he is engaged to a *stranger*? No, I cannot speak to a son who treats his mother like that. He meets this girl and instantly he forgets the good manners that he learned all his life? I won't stand for it. I don't know her. You don't know her. We know nothing of her family. I will not speak of her until we are properly introduced. *Finis!*"

My heart sinks. I plead with her. "But I need your help, I can't do this alone. I should never have let him go. Gaston was the best thing in my life, Adele."

"Yes, yes. Of course he was. I'm so glad you finally see that."

"We've got to break up this engagement."

"Yes." She thinks for a while, and we are silent while she lights up another Gauloise. "Just go to him and tell him of your mistake."

That's plan B. It will be much nicer if I can convince Adele to introduce the idea to Gaston, and then I can just swoop in and start where we left off. I try her again. "He sounds pretty smitten with this Courtney girl."

"Phsss. He wants someone to hold close because you are gone. Simple as that. She means nothing to him."

"Let's hope so."

"Kate, you and Gaston would be together right now if you didn't work so much. If you want to win my Gaston back, you must always put him first. You must think of him before anything else. Gaston said you rarely saw each other except for sex. Sex is good, but he has other needs too. Cook for him. Make yourself pretty for him. He is a special boy who needs special care." I roll my eyes at Adele's familiar words.

"Stop working so hard to fill the bellies of strangers and start taking care of the man you love. If you worked even half as hard on your relationship as you did at your job, we would never be having this conversation. You would see the truth. What woman could ask for a better life than to love a man like Gaston?"

Amidst her maternal babble I see a kernel of truth. "Of course! *It's my job.* The *restaurant* caused our breakup," I say, flabbergasted. My long hours and fervent dedication to Sound Bistro made me emotionally unavailable. Why didn't I see this earlier?

"Yes, dear. Of course it's your job. What else could it be? He never seemed to mind how you dress."

The familiar insult doesn't faze me. "You're right, Adele. Of course! You're so wise. Why didn't I call you earlier? It all makes sense now."

"I accept your apology." Apology? What apology? She continues, "If you are serious about this, you will need more of my help. You must come see me. Today? No, I have plans with a friend. Perhaps tomorrow."

Adele always acted like Vancouver was practically next door, never mind the hours of driving (inevitably in peak traffic) and the international border crossing. "But, I have to work. . . ."

She is irritated. "Kate, what did we just speak about?"

"I need to put Gaston first."

"Yes. And that means seeing his mother and working together to get rid of this Courtney woman. You simply must make the time." With this declaration, Adele hangs up.

I nod obediently into the phone. I know from experience that she isn't being rude. Well, no ruder than usual. Adele leaves the room or hangs up the phone whenever she feels her point has been made. She likes to have the last word. After I disconnect, I ponder our conversation. Gaston and I never had what might be considered a "normal" relationship; my schedule never allowed it. We spoke often, but often only met a few times a week for late dinners or an elicit lunchtime rendezvous. A quality relationship requires selflessness, time and commitment. Selflessness isn't something I excel at. And as for time and commitment, all of mine are used up in Nancy's damn kitchen.

Now that I understand the root of the problem, there is no reason I can't make this work. If I want a fairy-tale life, I'd better not wait around for a flying godmother. I need to shed my slave girl persona and start acting like a proper princess. When was the last time Gaston saw me in makeup, wearing something other than fleece or flannel? I'll tell him I want him back and then get a new job, a *normal* job, to show him how much I'm willing to sacrifice for his love. I'll work nine to five for a while, in a bank or an insurance office. I'll send him off in the mornings filled with a good breakfast. We'll eat dinner together every night. We'll go to the movies. Ohmigod! We can actually watch prime-time shows together! I can see some of this reality television everyone has been talking about.

My enthusiasm swells as the house fills with the aroma of buttery pastry and hot coffee. Iris makes an appearance in her tattered silk dragon robe, boxer shorts and huge, plush Shrek slippers. A cigarette dangles from her lips. I avoid all eye contact and hand her an oversized mug of milky coffee. I'm not exactly a morning person. The first rays of sunlight make me more angry than inspired. The only thing worse than an alarm clock is a well-rested individual who loves to start the day with a smile. Iris is not one of those people. You don't talk to Iris until she is on her second cup of coffee, and then you use a soft voice. I have seen big, tattooed bikers run in fear the morning after a date with Iris; not just because she looks like hell, but because she's as mean as a trapped weasel.

Iris and I have known each other since we were kids. My mom and her dad are both local artists. We lived in the same neighborhood, but Iris went to private school. We ran around at art shows together, and we both have older brothers who rebelled against the artsy-fartsy lifestyle and took a more conservative path: Mine is a lawyer in Portland, hers is on Wall Street.

Iris is what you might call an honest-to-god badass. She has been playing in bands for almost as long as I've known her. She's got her own style and can rock with the best of them. Her present band, Lipstick and Lithium, is a rowdy, all-girl thing. The name is quite apt. Their music is pretty bipolar: Iris can sing songs so sad they will make you moan in pain, and then on the next set, she'll have the whole place jumping and flailing frenetically. They haven't been playing together long, but they're great and getting pretty well-known in the area. Someday soon, she may be able to quit her cocktail job and play full-time.

When the pastries are brown and crisp, I move them to a cooling rack and drizzle an orange glaze over the top. Instead of washing it out, I hand the sticky bowl to Iris, who cleans it up with her forefinger while reading the weekend magazine section. I wait until she is well-caffeinated and all sugared-up before I announce, "I'm quitting my job."

She smiles and raises her mug in a toast. "That's awesome. Good for you! Did you get another killer offer?"

Over the years, I've had some decent job opportunities. I've interviewed with highbrow restaurants and enthusiastic foodies with inflated bank accounts. But the restaurants demanded relocation, a complete gutting or a good dose of pure magic. The best offer I ever got fizzled once it was clear that the aspiring restaurateur didn't have an attention span long enough to write a proper business plan. In retrospect, I wonder if my reluctance to take a job as head chef might be linked to my fear of commitment. I shake the thought from my head. I don't have to worry about that anymore. I'm going to marry Gaston.

"I'm going to get out of the kitchen altogether. I'm going to get a real job. I need a change."

Iris doesn't buy it. "Yeah, right."

"I am! I think maybe I'll work at a bank."

"I can see it now. Kate Linden, up at first sparrow fart, dressed in panty hose and pumps, headed for the office." She laughs, inhales a crumb and has a coughing fit.

"Why not? I have more talents than just cooking, you know. I was almost a marketing major."

"Yeah, well, you were almost a lot of things."

It's true. During my brief stint at the University of Washington, I declared my major three times, once as history, once as English literature and once in psychology. Then, I spent a summer backpacking through Europe, dropped out of college and decided to go to cooking school. I'm pretty sure that, in the long run, it was the most usable degree of the bunch.

Iris takes a huge bite of pastry, and in between chews says, "Nancy's a bitch. You had a bad night." She swallows. "But let's face it, Kate, you couldn't leave the kitchen if you tried. Cooking is like oxygen for you:

You'd die without it. Besides, you're too anal. You'd drive everyone crazy by polishing their staplers and reorganizing the filing system. And when was the last time you worked only forty hours in a week? You'd go completely nuts."

"I'm not anal, I'm just organized. A forty-hour workweek sounds like a dream. We can get a pet. I can work in pretty clothes and take coffee breaks. I can find out what a 401K is, and have someone else pay my medical insurance. And it's not like I'll have to give up cooking altogether. If I only work five days a week, and in the *daytime,* I can cook normal dinners for my friends and family. I can make Gaston a proper cassoulet."

"*Gaston?* This is about Gaston?" Iris asks.

"No, of course not." I turn away and start sponging the countertop so Iris can't see me blush.

"Are you wigging out about Gaston getting married? Is that why you're all freaked this morning?"

"I'm not freaked, I'm just planning ahead. You think I'm going to be happy as Nancy's sous-chef all my life? No way."

"Yeah. And becoming a banker is the perfect solution." Iris shakes her head in frustration and disbelief. When she sets her mug down deliberately, I can tell she's getting ready to lecture me, so I choose to make my exit.

"Well, I gotta go. I promised Mom I'd help her out today. See you later!"

She shouts after me, "We need to talk about this!"

I grab my keys, jump into Mabel, my ancient brown Mercedes, and drive to my mother's studio.

Chapter Three

My mother, Lauren Linden, is a ceramic artist. She made her name long ago with what she refers to as the "bread-and-butter line." It is classic tableware, carved and decorated with images inspired by the region: pine needles and cones, ferns, beach pebbles. She also does a popular line with fish, berries and mushrooms. Not long ago she hit gold again with her espresso mugs. She created four glazes that closely mimic popular coffee drinks: black, mocha, latte and creamy breve.

Now and then, Mom builds a wonderful, one-of-a-kind piece. But most of what goes on in the studio is more production than fine art. That's where I come in. I've known how to use a pottery wheel for as long as I can remember, and I still help her out by working the clay, throwing basic pieces, and loading and unloading the kiln. If Mom says she needs two full sets of bread-and-butter and a dozen latte mugs, I know the weight, shape and texture. I inherited Mom's hands, so the pieces come easy to me. Now and then, I work on a few of my own sculptures. I'm into a neo-archeological thing right now. I make plaques with impressions of twigs, leaves, bones and the occasional Hello Kitty figurine in the layers. I can't imagine what it all means, but I'm having fun.

Art has always been an important part of our lives. To Mom and Dad, being creative was almost as important as proper hygiene and basic math skills. It doesn't matter what the product is, it's the process that counts. I'm sure I was drawn to cooking because of the creative and sculptural aspects. I'm happiest in the kitchen when I am given a bounty of raw materials and the opportunity to create something truly magnificent—a beautiful plate of perfectly balanced aromas, textures and flavors. That is my art. Well, that *was* my art. In reality, these days it is more common for Nancy to hand me ten pounds of rutabagas, some frozen pork neck bones or yesterday's cod and tell me to come up with a creative special for the night. I won't miss that.

When Gaston and I get married, I can spend my evenings making wonderful dinners just for him. On Saturday mornings, we'll wander through the Pike Place Market. I'll carry our purchases in a handmade shopping basket with a bouquet of fresh-cut flowers, a baguette and a tousle of carrot fronds peeking from the top. At home, I'll blow some cooling breaths at a spoonful of my simmering sauce then gently ladle a taste between Gaston's eager lips. He will clasp his hands together and moan with delight, then embrace and kiss me. I'll laugh and push him away. After dinner, we will work side by side at the sink, cleaning up the dishes and discussing our plans for the following day. Shall we plant bulbs in the garden or peruse the shops in Fremont? My feet and shins won't ache, my legs will always be shaved, my face and hair will be vibrant and grease-free. It will be perfect. I sigh with contentment, turn off the loud diesel engine and walk into Mom's Georgetown studio.

"I'm quitting my job and marrying Gaston," I announce to my mother.

Mom hums as a reply, "Mmm, hmm." She is concentrating on the intricate pattern she is scraping into a plate. I walk closer to her and repeat my declaration. Finally she looks at me, but her response isn't much changed. "It's Sunday, isn't it? You always want to quit on Sundays."

"No, I really mean it this time! I'm done with the restaurant business. I'm going to go work in a bank, or maybe do something with computers." I hand her a couple of pastries I've brought from home. She slaps her hands together to knock off the clay bits and digs right in. "So, I take it Nancy went on another rampage last night?"

"Yeah. But that's not why I'm quitting. I'm used to that." Within minutes of my arrival, Mom has me questioning my motives. Am I just pissed off at Nancy? I grab an oversized sponge from the sink and start wiping up the newest layer of dust from the counters, shelves and bins while I put my thoughts together. I tell her about last night at the restaurant, about how I think it's time to work someplace where people deal with nonperishables and speak to each other in proper sentences instead of screams and expletives. Then I sidle up to her and tell her the whole truth.

"And then Gaston called and told me he's getting married to some sweet, perky grade-school teacher named Courtney."

"Aww, honey. I'm so sorry." She wraps her dirty arms around me and gives me a good, squashy maternal hug. The kind that makes me feel like nothing can ever hurt me. But the sensation only lasts a second. She has never coddled me. She tells it like it is, and expects me to make my own way in the world. Maybe that's why I am craving the easy life. I can't recall a single time when she made warm cookies for us when we got home from school. I've worked all my life. When Gaston and I have kids, they'll have the best cookie mom in the whole school. I'll make fancy jam sandwich cookies and cream-filled Florentines just like on the cover of magazines. And when it snows they'll get real *chocolat chaud* made with bar chocolate and cream.

Instead of backing me up in my new life plan, Mom dismisses it as ridiculous.

"You just need some rest. You work too hard and you never leave any time for fun." She looks over at a pile of junk near the loading dock. "Jerry's probably got a joint tucked away somewhere in all his stuff. I can go dig through it if you want. That might mellow you out."

I decline. Jerry is Mom's old hippie studio partner/assistant. A couple of weeks ago he stopped coming to work. Turns out he is feeling artistically "blocked," so he is moving to a Mexican beach town to study tile-making.

I look around. "Did you find a new studio assistant yet?"

Her eyes sparkle. "Yeah. I hired this guy, Sam Guerra. He might stop by today, so you can meet him. He just moved here from Albuquerque. He seems really nice, and he certainly has a lot of diverse talents. He's looking for a place where he can have his own studio space. He's doing some pretty neat stuff. I'm giving him the back room, the one Jerry used for storage."

I shrug, feigning interest. I'm still too consumed with my own life to care. Mom holds the plate she is working on up to the light. She tilts her head a few times and squints at it, then starts carving again. "Tomorrow, Nancy will probably be down on her knees apologizing and praising you. As for Gaston, let's just wish him the best and hope he's finally found someone who is right for him."

"*I'm* right for him!" I shout. "Haven't you been listening?" I glare at her.

Mom looks up, shocked. "Good Lord! This isn't your normal Sunday blues, it's a full-blown life crisis, isn't it? Over Gaston?"

I nod.

"Honey, Gaston's a sweet guy. But you had your chance and turned him down. A bunch of times." She reaches out and strokes my back. "Maybe he just seems more attractive now because you can't have him? Maybe you're feeling a little lonely?"

"That's not it at all. His engagement got me thinking. I was too selfish. I never made any kind of sacrifice or even really put any effort into making things right between us. I was too busy at work, too busy making fancy food for strangers when I should have been cooking good meals at home." I'm about to share the romantic market fantasies I had in the car, but when I look over at my mother, I change my mind. Her face is screwed up in disbelief. I defend myself. "I never stopped loving Gaston. He's practically my best friend. We were taking a break, that's all. I thought I needed a little more time. I mean, who would have guessed that he would run off and meet someone else? They met at a boat party last month. What is he thinking? It will never work!"

Mom shrugs. "Well, there you go. This will never work out for Gaston. So, when it's over, you two can fall into each other's arms and live happily ever after in the suburbs. Your career and extraordinary skills be damned."

"*Mom!*"

"What? What am I supposed to say here? I'm sorry you're hurting. I'm sorry you had a lousy night at the restaurant. I've been telling you for years that Nancy takes you for granted. You work harder than anyone I know, and you do it for a pittance. You love cooking, and it would be a shame to see you throw it all away because your boss is a tyrant and your heart aches. I agree that maybe it's time for a change. So, take some time off. Pass it on that you're looking for a new restaurant. You shouldn't have any problem finding a job as executive chef somewhere. God knows, you've paid your dues. But I *don't* think the answer is trashing your career. And I sure as hell don't think the answer is getting married. I want to see stars in your eyes when I hear that, not grim determination."

Mom knows about true love. She and my father were like newlyweds from the day they met. It used to embarrass me horribly. My father died seven years ago when his motorcycle was T-boned by a drunk in a pickup truck, but I have little doubt that Mom loves him just as much today.

She flicks off a few curlicues of leather-hard clay in irritation. "Now, I've got a lot of work to do and I need some stock thrown. Why don't you go on back and get your hands dirty for a while. That always makes you feel better. And you do those big bowls better than anybody."

"I thought you said I worked too much," I say, just to bait her.

She gives me a nasty look. Our little standoff is interrupted by a crash at the back of the building. Recently, a homeless man has been sleeping on the old covered cement loading dock. I've never seen him, but Mom says he and the Angel of Death might be on a first-name basis. We run to the back door, expecting the worst. What we find is not an elderly bum in the throes of death, but a muddy tangle of limbs and machinery emitting kitchen-quality curses. Mom laughs. "Hey, Sam."

A young man extricates himself from his crashed mountain bike, pushes his helmet back, and a bright, contagious smile lights up his mud-streaked face. "Hi, Lauren. Sorry about that. My plan was to glide smoothly to the studio door and expertly dismount, but I got a cleat jammed. Damn these new shoes."

"Are you okay?" Mom manages to ask between chuckles. He does a quick damage inspection.

"I'm good." He goes on to explain his disheveled appearance. "I wanted to try the ride, to get the route from home figured out, you know? It's going to be great, except for that last bit, south of the stadiums. Those huge container trucks on the waterfront are seriously territorial. I got edged off the road twice. The second time, I swear this guy wanted me to go swimming. He pushed me into a puddle the size of a small lake. Since I was already a mess, and you weren't expecting me at a specific time, I figured I'd do a little off-road exploring. There are some pretty cool paths all through the scrub under and around the freeway and bridges. People live in there. Did you know that?"

Mom nods. She looks him over and says, "If that's the route you plan to take every day, maybe we should scrape off that mud you're wearing and load up the clay reclaim bucket. We may really cut down our material costs."

We all laugh. At the sound of a third voice, Sam looks over at me, just now registering that Mom is not alone.

"Sam, this is my daughter, Kate." We nod. "Kate's a chef—she's amazingly talented. She's also a great potter. I think I mentioned that Kate helps me out now and then. She knows everything about this place. If you ever have a question and I'm not here, just ask Kate."

"Nice to meet you. If you're anything like your Mom, I'm sure it will be a pleasure working with you." His eyes spark as if he just remembered something, and he slaps his helmet and shouts, "Oh, crap!" He pushes his bike forward and removes the rubber straps holding down a mud-soaked duffle and a crushed, soaking-wet paper bag. "I forgot about the muffins!

I brought you some of these awesome muffins from a great bakery near my place."

I grimace. No muffin could have survived his off-road adventure. I look to my mom, hoping she knows the proper social response to a gift of filthy muffin crumbs. Sam lifts the flattened bag from his bike and peels the wet paper back. He peeks through a hole in the side of the bag, then moans and looks away in horror. "They're dead! I killed them!"

Mom crosses herself, then steps up to Sam and in her sweetest voice says, "I'm sure they went quickly." She lifts the bag from his hands, hums a funeral dirge and drops the remains in the garbage.

Sam clasps his chest with despair and looks into the waste bin. "They were so young, so fresh. What have I done?"

"There will be other muffins someday, Sam. Maybe even doughnuts." She leans toward him and whispers, "For the record, I like a good cherry Danish."

The joke isn't all that funny, but they laugh like old friends. Sam will be a welcome addition to the studio. I'm thrilled to see that Mom has found an assistant she can have fun with. Jerry was a real downer, always talking about political and ecological gloom and doom. I leave the two of them to their fun and head back to the big plaster table to gather up my clay. Mom loads the CD player with her folksy music, and Sam walks over to the deep work sinks to scrub off some of the unwelcome mud.

I load a plastic tub with balls of wedged clay. As I turn to go to my favorite wheel, I can't help but notice Sam. He's stripped down to bike shorts and an undershirt. After six years of working with hairy Jerry, I find Sam's good looks worthy of a double take. His arms and legs are long and lean. His skin is a dark golden color from the New Mexico sun. His hair is a mass of thick, sun-bleached curls. He leans over the sink to wash his face, and his shoulder blades slide and pucker under his shirt. I am mesmerized. Some women are all about square chins and hair. Some judge a man by his beefy pectorals, steely six-pack abs or tight ass. I am a shoulder girl. The summer Olympics, with all that rowing, swimming, throwing and gymnastics . . . ooooh. It's about the only thing that made me consider splurging on cable TV. Sam looks up and catches me staring at him. We are both flustered.

"Oh, I'm sorry. I wasn't uh, . . . I was just thinking of something. I've been kind of distracted lately. A lot on my mind." I skulk to my pottery wheel and get busy. Sam pulls on an old garage monkey suit with the name ALAN sewed on a breast patch, then joins Mom in the glazing room to discuss techniques and formulas.

The hours fly by. I throw six big, shallow bowls, three pitchers and a couple of dozen mugs. Mom is right, getting my hands in the muddy clay and focusing my energy does take my mind off my problems. I put the wet pieces on a sealed rack to dry a bit yet stay pliable enough for Mom's finishing work.

I go to the glaze room to say good-bye. Sam and Mom are once again laughing together. They look as if they have been friends forever.

"I'm finished for the day, unless you need anything else done."

"Nope. That's all. Thanks for your help." She smiles at me, flushed from all the laughing. Sam smiles too. His eyes are a twinkling blue, and his skin is smooth. "Nice to meet you, Kate." He lifts his hand from his knee in a casual wave.

Mom looks from me to Sam and then back again. She sits up straighter and gets an impish gleam in her eyes. Uh-oh. I try to scoot out the door, but I don't move quickly enough.

"You know, Kate, you and Sam have a lot in common. Instead of rushing off, why don't you two spend some time talking? You can tell him all about our different lines. Or, better yet, Sam, maybe you should go with Kate? You two can grab a cup of coffee or maybe a pizza." She jumps off her stool and shuffles to her desk. "Let me give you some cash. It'll be on me." Sam and I glance at each other with similar expressions of horror. We chase after her.

"*Mom!* Stop it," I whisper through my teeth. "I know what you're doing."

She tries to play innocent. "What do you mean?"

Sam has picked up on Mom's blatant matchmaking as well. He stutters a minute and then says, "Lauren, I'm sure Kate has all sorts of things she can teach me about the business, but I think we should keep things, uh, professional, you know?"

I hiss at my mother, "The last thing I want to do is date your studio partner." Sam might be attractive and funny, but I know all about ceramic assistants. I've had a lifetime of experience with these losers. No doubt Sam is just another former stoner turned potter because it was the easiest class to pass in high school. And, if you were sneaky, you could even make your own drug paraphernalia. Thanks, but no thanks.

"And what about what we talked about earlier? How could you forget about Gaston?"

Mom winces and whispers back, "Oops. That's right. Gaston. I forgot. Sorry, Hon. It's just that Sam is so . . ."

"Unavailable," says Sam with determination. Mom and I blush, unaware that he could overhear our words. His handsome face is contorted in a pained expression similar to the one he used for the destroyed muffins. His look and tone are dismissive as he says, "Kate, I'm sure you're great, but I'm just not interested."

My jaw clenches. I blurt, "Well, that's a relief." I have no interest in this guy, but for him to be disgusted is a blow to my ego. Sam and I lock hostile eyes. We all fidget a bit until I grab my purse. "I'm outta here. Bye, Mom."

Chapter Four

My awkward moment with Sam at the studio gives me a new burst of determination. I call Gaston as soon as I get home. I'm giddy with excitement as the phone rings. I can almost taste the heartfelt words and romantic lines in my mouth. I'll tell him straight up that I love him and think he's making a huge mistake.

I go cold and hang up when his phone is answered by a sweet, female voice. Gaston doesn't have caller ID, so I will remain anonymous. At least he didn't *used* to have caller ID. He didn't *used* to have a fiancée named Courtney either, so what do I know?

I put my feet up on the back of the couch and look around the living room. That's another reason to love Gaston. He lives in a classy Magnolia condo and yet never complained about spending time in this wacky house.

We live in a pretty nondescript street in Ballard, a neighborhood most famous for its Scandinavian fishing heritage. Over the past few years a younger, slightly funkier crowd has moved in. Our house belonged to Iris's favorite aunt, who died of AIDS. (I know Iris loved her, and it is a sad story, but the death of her aunt has been a benefit to me in many ways. First and foremost, her aunt's demise taught Iris the importance of safe sex. Without such a grueling lesson, I can only wonder what kind of shape my horny little friend would be in now.) Iris's parents kept the house, thinking it might be a good way to boot the kids out of the nest. It has been. Her brother and his college buddies beat the shit out of the place for a few years. Now it's Iris's turn. But I don't think this is a temporary residence for her; I get the feeling she's here to stay.

When she first moved in and started scraping off the top layer of guy grunge, she unearthed a goldmine of glorious retro decor; cork flooring, gold foil wallpaper, wood paneling. Instead of covering it all up with cheap IKEA camouflage, she has embraced kitch as a design component. She is now a connoisseur of fine thrift store art. There is a bamboo pod chair swinging amongst many beaded macramé plant hangers and owls perched on driftwood. One wall is an homage to Margaret Keane, filled with portraits of big-eyed children and animals. She scored a few years back when she found two original Keane canvasses at a flea market. She loves to inform visitors that these paintings, once sold as reproductions at Kmart, are now worth a small fortune. I look around again. The place is crazy, but it's home. I'm comfortable here.

I wallow in self-pity until I get hungry. I make tomato soup and pop-corn for dinner. It's my dirty little secret, but many of my solitary meals are like this. I like Jif peanut butter and grape jelly on soft white bread and lots of sugar-crusted cereals. I have a new thing for Hot Pockets. When I'm shopping for this junk, I'm always tense. But I can't seem to give it up. I must look like a chipmunk in the supermarket, all twitchy and nervous, hoping no one recognizes me as I load my cart with cans of ravioli and frozen potpies. If I'm jonesin' for fast food at a national chain, I hunker down in my seat and use the drive-through window. When I have my own top restaurant, I don't want inflammatory Internet photos circulating of me, sitting in a plastic chair, sucking down a stack of chalu-pas. I'd die.

I sink deeper into the couch, feeling sorry for myself. Good thing I'm going to leave food and marry Gaston. If I were a *real* chef, I wouldn't like this crap. If I were a *real* chef, I would have been motivated enough to find a way to finance my own restaurant by now. I look over at the stack of food and trade magazines that arrived in this week's mail. I often spend Sunday evenings trying to catch up on the newest culinary trends. I go through every page, taking note of new ingredients, flavor combina-tions and presentations. Tonight, it doesn't seem worth the effort.

The next morning I'm feeling much better. I blame yesterday's foul mood on a bad case of Sunday blues maybe paired with a little PMS. I wash up, pull on some casual clothes and a ponytail thingy, and drive to the restaurant. Mondays are supposed to be my day off, but that just means I don't have a specific time to arrive and I'm not scheduled to work the hot line. If I don't put in one full day organizing the stores and keeping tabs on the vendors' stock and prices, it won't get done.

When I took the job of sous, it was agreed that I would work a maximum of 50 hours a week, get regular breaks and be added to the medical plan. It's been four years, and none of that has happened. Long ago I stopped doing the math that exposes how close to minimum wage my salary hovers when I break it all down. Money isn't a problem when you don't have any free time to spend it.

The kitchen crew looks sullen, and there is whispering. They must still be fuming from Saturday night. I call them together for an impromptu pep talk.

"Hey, guys, listen up, okay?" I speak loudly so everyone can hear without having to leave their work. "I just want to take a minute and tell you that you did a great job the other night. For those of you who didn't work on Saturday, I'm sure you've heard by now that we had a pretty rough night."

Craig Spooner, a talented but loudmouthed sauté cook, replies, "Tell it like it is, Kate. Saturday totally blew. We were in the fuckin' weeds by four-thirty in the afternoon, and just when we thought we might catch up, things went totally to shit. Expediting? My ass. Nancy was just in the fucking way."

I have to laugh. Craig has translated my thoughts into perfect chef talk. I smile and almost nod in agreement, but try to keep my professional composure. I don't want to start a mutiny. Well, no. I don't want to be *accused* or *connected* with starting a mutiny. A mutiny sounds just fine.

Gloria Pendergras, our elaborately tattooed salad and cold appetizer diva, speaks up. "Nancy was, like, totally out of line. Who does she think she is, prancing in here at service time and acting like she's the queen of the fucking universe? She treated me like I was a total idiot! I *knew* the chives were bruised and the radishes needed to be redone. But, God! The things she went off on were hardly a priority. I mean, Friday's rush left me with only two orders of salmon, and I was totally wiped out on all my vinaigrettes. And she goes ballistic about the fucking chives! Christ!"

When my soft-spoken lead, Frank Sato, clears his throat, I know there is serious trouble. Frank is the kind of line cook that most chefs will sell their soul for. He's not fast or flashy, but he's a true pro. He shows up on time, does his work well and he's got a family that depends on his paycheck. When he finds a job he can live with, he sticks with it. And that is priceless in an industry where cooks skitter from job to job like water bugs. Frank has been working with Nancy longer than anyone here.

Frank continues to pay close attention to his work as he speaks. "I don't know what's gotten into her. I'm used to her yelling, but she's usually tuned in enough to jump in before things get ugly. Lately she's never around, and when she *does* show up, it's just to wreak chaos and yell. That duck confit thing was pretty messed up. It's not your fault, Shorty. You got steamrollered."

Corey "Shorty" Hanson is a culinary student doing his externship with us. He's young and a little goofy, but he has a lot of potential. He was the one who was supposed to keep an eye on the duck, but a lot of people loaded him up with extra work because we were so behind. That, combined with a faulty timer, could be blamed for the burnt duck. Corey is the one who really got plowed with The Wrath of Nancy Saturday night.

I look at all of them. I wonder if, like me, their work is messing up their personal lives. We all need a break. The last few months have blessed us with some good national press, which in turn cranked up the reservations and invited still more critics to our doors. It's the classic restaurant catch-22. These guys have clearly pushed themselves close to the breaking point. If something isn't done soon, we'll start losing talented cooks.

"I just want you to know that I'm proud of you. Saturday night was brutal, and yet we got through it with the food looking and tasting about as good as ever. You were beat, but you didn't cut corners and you didn't make excuses. If you have some ideas of how to make things run a little easier around here, let me know. I'm going to suggest to Nancy that we hire a couple more people. I know she hates the idea of relying on prep cooks, but if we get a couple of eager, cheap students in here, it can't be any more expensive than paying the overtime you've been working lately."

"Fuckin' A!" says Craig, in what I assume is approval.

"We'll get through this, guys. You're great!" I succeed in convincing not just my crew but myself as well that things are going to get better soon. Hiring more staff will give me a chance to take a few weeks off. Then maybe I can win Gaston back and still feel useful. I won't have to leave cooking altogether. I am needed here.

Just as I finish my pep talk, the delivery door opens and Nancy herself arrives. Speak of the devil. She struts in with her crumb-and-oil-stain-free Coach briefcase and new Ferragamo shades. There are no windows in the kitchen at Sound Bistro, and I'm tempted to run into the dining room to see if it really did get sunny outside or if she's just showing off the glasses. I bite the inside of my cheek instead. Nancy is not the enemy;

she just had a bad night. I should practice the golden rule and give her a break.

Nancy whips off the shades and blesses us with one of her million-dollar smiles. Rumor has it that her grin has landed her an invitation to try her own cooking show.

"Hi, guys! How are things going?" She's everybody's best friend today. She turns to me. "Hey, Kate. Good. I was hoping I could catch you. When you get a second, can you meet me in my office? We need to discuss a few things."

I breathe a deep sigh of relief. Mom was right, as usual. Nancy is going to grovel and apologize for her behavior. She'll remind me of how important I am to the success of the restaurant and maybe send me home with a couple of bottles of wine some local purveyor has given her. Today might even be a good time to talk to her about scheduling.

Before I meet with Nancy, Frank and I talk about tonight's specials. The weather has turned cool again after a long Indian summer. We are both eager for the hearty, warmer dishes of autumn, but Nancy has very specific rules for dinner specials. Sound Bistro entrées must be creative, seasonal and include at least "five elements." Meaning, there must be a minimum of five unique components to each dish. A special sauce can be considered one element, but at least two items on the plate must add height or modern drama to the presentation. Nancy is militant in her insistence that the specials at Sound Bistro never hint of "comfort food." Roasted chicken and mashed potatoes might be tolerable for a staff meal, but to serve that to paying customers is a sure sign of laziness and lack of creativity. Tonight, Frank and I deconstruct a classic Belgian carbonnade of beef. It's a little tricky, because the dish smacks of classic European peasant food, and it's a short leap from "peasant food" to Nancy's forbidden "comfort food." We decide that instead of stewing chunks of meat and vegetables we will slowly braise beef short ribs in brown ale. The sauce will be reduced to a nice rich gloss, and the meat served with chèvre *pommes duchesse,* a tangle of julienned, candied carrots and turnips, a cluster of fresh peppery watercress and two long batons of toasted bread slathered in spicy mustard. I peel a dozen potatoes for Frank and put them on the stove to simmer before I wander back to the office for my session with Nancy.

She is sitting back in her office chair, reading an article Iris saw in the Sunday paper about her home kitchen.

"There you are. Come in." She sets the paper down. "Did you see this silly thing? As if people care what my kitchen looks like? I mean, I can see hiring me to do some design consulting or something, but just taking a sneak peek like that? Why bother? Why don't you close the door?"

A closed-door meeting? This is serious. She's probably going to cry or get down on her knees and beg for my forgiveness. I close the door and dig a chair out from beneath a pile of paperwork.

Nancy pulls her chair close to her messy desk, makes a triangle out of her arms and balances her chin on peaked fingers. "So. I thought maybe we could talk about Saturday night."

I practice my poker face. "I think that's a great idea. I appreciate your making the time."

"Well, I only think it's fair. After all, I'll always give you the benefit of the doubt: You're my right-hand gal."

"Hmm?" That sentence doesn't seem to be phrased quite right.

"Well, I thought I'd give you a chance to explain what happened, give you a chance to apologize before I write anything permanent in your file."

My mouth falls open and I make a few grunting sounds before I can form words. "Uh, er, excuse me?" I would suck at poker.

Nancy puts her arms down and clasps her hands. She leans over with a big, fake smile, and with each word she pats my thigh as if she were my coach getting me ready for the big game. "You're. Just. So. Gooooood." I'm horrified. What's going on here? She continues.

"I can't ignore it when things get so out of control. The staff was so far behind it was ridiculous. You know how I feel about the importance of the details, and the little stuff, like the finishing prep, looked like it hadn't been touched." Is Nancy actually blaming me for Saturday night?

"It's my *name* at stake here, Kate. I can't let stuff like that slide. I've put you in charge because I've always felt you understand what it means to work hard, and I *thought* I could count on you to keep the quality level as high as I demand. But I'm starting to wonder. I pulled it together in the end on Saturday, and we didn't have any major mistakes other than the burned confit. But what if I had been out of town or at some benefit? It could have been a disaster. Thank God that table of writers didn't seem to notice that the kitchen was in total chaos. Cynthia Nims sent me an e-mail asking about that salmon special you made. She said her dinner was super-fabulous, so I think we squeaked through that little nightmare."

All of my body heat transfers to my skull. My head throbs with hot rage. Nancy, of course, assumes it is embarrassment. She pats my thigh again. I want to scream.

"I know you still care, Kate. That's why I thought we could talk. I figure you just need a gentle reminder about the level of professionalism I expect from my crew. I'm sure you won't disappoint me again."

I am speechless. I do my best to keep my wits about me, rubbing my face with my hands to mask the anger in my eyes, running my hands through my hair instead of tearing it out. Nancy uses my silence as an invitation to talk more.

"And, jeez, the crew is downright hostile these days. It's like a war zone every time I step out of the office. As a James Beard Award–winning chef, I can't just turn a blind eye to these things. I thought you understood that, Kate."

I have to leave right now. If I hear her refer to herself one more time as a "James Beard Award–winning chef," I am going to officially lose it. "I think I've heard enough." I stand up and grab the doorknob. Nancy finishes her informative discussion the wrong way. "As for all of that duck that was ruined, I've decided to take the cost out of the kitchen's tip allocation. I won't make them pay retail, only ingredients and labor."

That pushes me over the edge. I spin and stare at her. "You must be joking," I demand.

She throws her hands up, like it's out of her control. "I'm trying to run a business here, not win any popularity contests. I can't just let that kind of waste go unnoticed."

I can no longer hold my tongue. "Let it go unnoticed? I swear, if you had been any louder the *guests* would have come in to apologize."

"Don't overreact, Kate. I'm just doing my job."

"Your job? Correct me if I'm wrong here, but you're the *chef* of this restaurant. Doesn't that mean that in addition to posing in front of the camera, you also have a role in the *kitchen* of this establishment?" I point to the hot line. "You're a *stranger* out there. You freak everyone out and mess up the rhythm of the line by fiddling with everything. The only time you step up to the stove is when you storm in to throw tantrums about the quality and precision of food that, I swear, you don't even know how we make!"

She gasps, clearly hurt by my words. "Are you seriously questioning my abilities? I'm a James Beard Award–winning chef! I've been named a top chef in this country repeatedly. Does that mean nothing to you?" I have pierced her very soul. She is wounded. She is also my boss. I look up at the ceiling, count to five and try another tack. It's my turn to sit on the edge of the chair and look caring and sincere.

"Nancy, I know you're a great cook. You've got talent and speed and an amazing palate. Maybe that's part of the problem: We don't ever see it anymore. When you join us in the kitchen, you don't cook, you criticize. We've come up with some pretty damn incredible food lately. People have noticed. And it really sucks to read all of those interviews and press releases you do, and never once see you acknowledge your team. All we see is *you* getting the praise for *our* hard work. We see our original recipes in the papers and magazines with your name on them. *That's* why the kitchen is hostile. Did you ever stop and wonder if maybe you had spent some time helping and not just yelling at us, last Saturday night wouldn't have been such a goddamn nightmare?"

She has been sitting stock-still until my last sentence, then she jumps to her feet and points an accusing finger at me. "So you admit it! Saturday was out of control."

I agree, "Saturday night sucked."

We glare at each other for a minute, but I remember my place and avert my eyes first. "I've got to go check on my potatoes." I leave the office. The staff has heard the shouting and they are oddly silent on my return.

Five minutes after our confrontation, Nancy shows up on the line, dressed in her whites and carrying her knife roll. The crew collectively grimaces, but I can't help but grin. My words have struck home. We might just have our chef back.

While Nancy inspects the fresh food in the walk-in refrigerator, I drain the boiled potatoes and spread them out in a shallow hotel pan to dry in the oven. I have made a light, creamy béchamel sauce to blend into the pureed potatoes with a good spoonful of soft goat cheese. I plan to pipe them into rosettes, glaze them with egg and brown them in the oven for a crisp and creamy accompaniment to the rich "stew." Nancy steps up next to me as I am spreading the potatoes out. She asks, "What are those?"

Considering our earlier conversation, I should explain my intentions for the spuds with a straight answer and serious tone. But I can't help myself. "Potatoes, Nancy. These are boiled potatoes."

She isn't amused. Her face turns red, she takes a breath and then explodes, right in my face, "Boiled russet potatoes? At this time of year? You're not making mashed potatoes, are you? Our shelves are full of French fingerlings, German butterballs and the prettiest Chioggia beets, and you *boiled* russets? What do you think I run, some kind of comfort-food bistro from the nineties? Can't you think of anything *good*?"

At just that moment I bump my forearm onto the hot stove and burn a strip of tender flesh. I jump back and the potatoes in their pan crash to the floor.

"FUCK!" I shout." Fuck, fuck this fucking bullshit!" I pick up what is left of the pan of potatoes and fling the whole thing against the oven. The sound of metal on metal resonates through the tiny kitchen. Lumps of fluffy, steaming spuds take flight, and the pan clatters to the ground. The staff stands in silent shock until a few valiant folks lean down and start picking up my mess.

"NO! Don't touch those fucking potatoes!" I shout at them. "You've been doing Nancy's dirty work for too damn long. I'm not going to let you clean up after me, too."

Nancy bellows, "Kate! That's enough."

I kneel down and start scooping up the hot potatoes with my bare hands. The burn on my forearm is less noticeable with my hands on fire. "It's enough of what, Nancy? Enough of the truth? Enough of me getting fed up with your condescending, Hollywood bullshit? Or maybe you're concerned about wasting these potatoes. Do you want to take that out my paycheck, too?"

"Kate, stop it. This is a professional kitchen."

I feel as splayed and raw as the meat in the cooler. This isn't what being a chef is supposed to be like. This place is the center of my universe, and it really sucks. I'm sick of it all and I'm not about to be silenced.

My voice is softer now, but the words are still intense. "Professional? I work here sometimes eighty goddamn hours a week with no breaks and no overtime pay because I was stupid enough to agree to my pathetic salary." I get down on my knees and crawl around collecting wayward potatoes. "You think bankers and lawyers and other *professionals* go home to their loved ones smelling like fish and garlic and lamb fat every night? Is this country run by people whose biggest pleasure is going home to an empty house, making a cup of tea and soaking their feet in the fucking toilet?" I throw the crushed, steaming potatoes in the dented pan then sit back on my feet and point to the mess around me.

"I'm crawling around on a disgusting, wet rubber mat picking up food I just threw across the room. Do you think this is normal, professional behavior, Nancy?" I look up at her with tears in my eyes, trying to see if she understands how screwed up things are. How screwed up my life is. I've worked so hard and where has it gotten me?

She grits her teeth and spits out her reply. "No, Kate. It's not. You're fired."

Chapter Five

Iris calls at about seven that night. "Did you really get fired?"

"Yeah," I grumble, then I sit up straighter. "How do you know?"

"Pleeze! It's all over town. Our bartender, Sasha, is good friends with the manager at Lark, whose pastry chef used to date a waiter at Sound Bistro. Everyone knows."

"Great."

"Did you really get up on the counter and throw potatoes at Nancy?"

"No!"

"I didn't think so. That kind of sounded out of character. But hey, that gives me a great idea. How about we get a bunch of people together and go pelt her place with baked potatoes later tonight? She totally deserves it. She's such a bitch!"

"No! Don't do that. You don't even know what happened."

"So what are you doing now? You should be out celebrating!"

"Celebrating? I don't think so."

"What, are you just sitting in the dark, brooding about how your bitch of a boss was right and that you deserved to get fired, even after you've worked yourself half to death for her for the past four years?"

Yes, that's exactly what I'm doing. I stay quiet.

"Well, get over it! You've got a night off! So why don't you get off your boney ass and come down here so I can buy you a drink? Oops, the GM is glaring at me, I gotta run." I spit out my refusal just as she disconnects.

I weigh my options. I can continue to sit in the dark feeling sorry for myself, but to do a proper job of it, I will require at least a pound of miniature peanut butter cups. Or, I can go out and drink with the beautiful people at Iris's bar. My sad story might be worth a few pity drinks from the bartender, but the music and festivity sound as appealing as gum surgery. I poke around in our own booze cupboard, but the pickings are mighty slim. Tucked behind the Chinese cooking wine and some fruity, neon schnapps left over from girls' night, I find a miniature bottle of Grand Marnier that has a tablespoon or two left in it. I rifle around for some chocolate. I often have a chunk or chip of some kind tucked away for baking. I find nothing. Iris must have found my stash.

Iris might be in charge of the living room decorations, but the kitchen is all mine. Every bit of space that isn't taken up with pottery creations is filled with cookware. If you dare open the cupboard or look in the fridge door shelves, you will see that I am a victim of that popular cook's affliction, "condimentia": the need to surround oneself with every possible variety of vinegars, chili pastes, mustards and chutney. I rattle through the jars in the fridge. There isn't even any hot fudge or chocolate syrup. I must have somehow, somewhere, managed to piss off my guardian angels.

To distract myself from my chocolate yearnings, I grab the ancient yellow dial phone on the kitchen wall and call Gaston. No answer. I plod back to the couch, feeling utterly alone. I want a big furry cat to magically appear so I can have something to coo and cuddle with. Iris and I agree that a house is hardly a home without something warm and furry. Marissa is on the fence. But after long, heartfelt discussions, we were forced to admit that none of us is around enough to spoil a cat or dog. Now that I'm unemployed, I might be able to get a pet. Now there's a good spin. I perk up for a moment until I remember that Gaston is allergic. So much for furred creatures. I'm sure Iris wouldn't mind an iguana or a snake, but I can't see myself getting snuggly with a reptile. What else is there? How about a fish? Surely Iris and I can manage to take care of a fish? It's not a pet that I can cuddle with on the couch or that will greet me at the door when I get home, but I had a friend in college who had angelfish that kissed her fingers when she fed them. I could live with that.

I am jerked from my introspection when the front door bangs open. Marissa hurries in, carrying a gym bag and a huge paper coffee cup. She flips on the lights.

I squint and cover my eyes. "Hey."

My greeting startles her. "Hey. I thought I'd take a quick shower between shifts. What are you doing home? You're never home on weekdays. Are you sick?"

"I got fired."

She stops cold. "Nancy fired you? What happened?"

"I went a little nuts and told her the truth."

Marissa makes a face. "God, Kate. You should know better by now."

"Yeah. And guess what else. Gaston's getting married."

She cocks her head in astonishment. "To someone else? Who?"

"Some school teacher named Courtney Davis." I sink deeper into the couch cushions, and my lower lip starts to quiver. Marissa slips back into nurse mode. "What can I get for you? You need tequila? Percodine? Valium?"

I manage a halfhearted smile. Marissa is always generous with pharmaceuticals. "Got any chocolate?" I ask.

She rummages through her giant handbag but finds only a Kit Kat wrapper, a few spearmint LifeSavers and a pillow pack of extra-strength Midol.

I take the Midol. I try again to find the silver lining in this hurricane. "I've been thinking about looking for a new job anyway."

Marissa peeks at her wristwatch, torn between her desire to help and her tight schedule. "I've got to get in the shower. Are you going to be okay?"

I nod. If I speak I will start to cry.

Ten minutes later Marissa comes running up the stairs carrying a different set of scrubs. She throws me an ancient chocolate Easter bunny with the ears bitten off. "It's pathetic, I know, but that's all the chocolate I have stashed. I'll swing by after work with more if I can." She leaves, but before she closes the door all the way, she pokes her head back in. "You know, if things get really bad, Cedar Heights is always looking for kitchen help. I can put in a good word for you."

I can't hold back a snort of digust. Cooking for a nursing home isn't my idea of a career upgrade. Marissa catches my look and pretends to be hurt. "What? You got a thing against pureed chicken and all the pudding you can eat?" I manage a laugh. Marissa blows me a kiss and runs out the door.

By ten o'clock the next morning, I have decided that Nancy has done me a great favor. Losing my job at the restaurant is further proof that leaving the business and getting married to Gaston is my destiny. I've got enough money in the bank to pay the rent for a while, and now I can focus all of my attention on winning my true love away from some life-sucking, elementary-educating lamprey.

I establish a plan. First, I will call him and tell him in my most pathetic voice that I have been fired. That will draw him to my side as a caring friend. When we are together, having a serious conversation about my future, I will proclaim my undying love to him.

I whistle a little tune as I punch in the number to the downtown financial firm where he works as an analyst. Desiree, the chatty receptionist, answers. "Wheton-Lofton, how may I direct your call?"

"Hi, Desiree, it's Kate. Is Gaston around?"

"Hey, Kate! How's it going? I haven't talked to you in ages."

"I guess I don't have many reasons to call these days."

"Personally, I don't know what Gaston is thinking. I like you so much better than this little Miss Courtney. She calls here all the time. Sure, she's kind of sweet, but I never trust people who are permanently perky. With you, there's no guessing where you stand. You tell it like it is."

Well, that is true. And look at where it has gotten me.

"Is Gaston around?" I ask.

"Hold on, I'll transfer you. Glad to talk to you, Kate, don't be a stranger!"

"Hello, Gaston Lambert speaking." I get goose bumps at the sound of his familiar voice. If that isn't love, what is? I return to the role of miserable waif. I sniffle and with no enthusiasm in my voice, say, "Hi, Gaston, it's me, Kate."

"Hey, Katie. You sound funny. Is everything okay?"

"Not really. Nancy fired me."

"Oh, my God! She fired you? What happened? Are you all right?" This is just the reaction I am hoping for. To Gaston, getting fired is the ultimate humiliation, an unforgivable smear on the all-important résumé and a malignancy on the five-year life plan. I take a staggered, painful-sounding breath of air and whine, "I'm not sure what happened. I'm just so upset. It's all kind of a blur. I don't want to bother you. I know you're busy these days with the wedding and all, but I don't know where else to turn."

"Oh, Katie. I'm here for you, of course. What can I do? Do you need to talk about it?"

"I don't want to be a bother." I sniff.

"You forget about that, Little Missy." (That's a pet name I haven't missed.) "I'll just tell my boss that I'm taking a long lunch, and we'll go talk. I can't believe you got fired. Poor girl! You must be devastated."

I do a quiet little dance while we make arrangements to meet.

We agree to have lunch at the Brooklyn Oyster Bar on Second Avenue. It was the site of our first date and a favorite, late-night haunt. We used to slurp briny oysters and drink flinty wine or microbrews with the nice crowd at the bar. Today, I bypass the cheery bar and choose a secluded and cozy booth in the back of the restaurant. I'm tempted by the aromas and debate ordering a couple of appetizers, but decide that I will look more miserable if I let Gaston coerce me to eat something rather than have him arrive and find me scarfing on a plate of fried squid. I order a beer. Drinking before noon is a top-notch display of despair.

I adjust my shirt so it drapes just right. I'm not much of a clothes person. My career hasn't demanded a well-crafted ensemble or clever accessorizing. Today's outfit took me all morning to select. I wanted to look dejected and depressed, but still stunning and desirable. It's a standard overcast Seattle day, so I went with a pair of skinny jeans and some sexy boots I found in Marissa's closet. My long, mousy brown hair is down, carefully tousled, with one side tucked behind my ear instead of pulled back in my traditional work ponytail. Gaston likes it this way. I lean back into the corner of the booth and feel quite comfortable and relaxed. I'm staring into my beer, daydreaming about my new life, when Gaston rushes in.

"Kate. Sorry I'm late. I got stuck on the phone." He holds his arms out, and I scoot out of my hole for a warm embrace. He's a bit shorter than I am, and I am reminded why I don't own many shoes with heels. His hair is due for a cut, but I like it best this way. Chestnut curls are forming at the nape of his neck and around his perfect ears. I tuck a lock of hair back and look into his warm hazel eyes. I press my cheek against his sandpaper stubble and breathe in the familiar scent of Gaston. No way can someone else have this. This belongs to me.

We sit, and I tell him all about my last few days at the restaurant and how everything came about. He is enraged.

"You need to fight it! She can't just fire you like that. She has to give you written and verbal warnings. There's a procedure. And you've got your whole team to back you up. All you need to do is talk to the owners and explain about how you burnt yourself. I'm sure they'll understand. You've done so much for them over the years. Nancy can't just throw all that away."

I nod in agreement to everything he says and look for the right opening to declare my love. His words are distracting me. How do I tell him about the revulsion I feel at the idea of going back to Sound Bistro? I had been toying with the idea of finding a more traditional career just the other day. Now, I don't want anything to do with Nancy or the restaurant. "The thing is, I don't think I *want* my job back. Everything I've been working toward, everything that used to be important to me feels like a dead end. Sure, I can find another job, maybe even an executive chef position somewhere. But then what? I'll spend even *more* hours at work." I look up from my beer with my heart on my sleeve and my eyes pleading. "I'm tired, Gaston. I'm done cooking for a while. I want to have fun again. You know, like when you and I were together."

Gaston doesn't hear my words as a reunion plea, but as a career problem. He has his boardroom face on. He's all business. "You know how I feel about the whole private restaurant gig." Gaston has almost made a hobby out of keeping track of failed restaurants. He doesn't like the profit patterns of most privately owned places, and has urged me to work in a big hotel or resort so I can work my way up the management ladder. "You're in shock right now. You need a little time to readjust, then you'll be dying to get back in the kitchen."

Here's my big chance. "I don't think so. I want out. I want something better." I gaze into his eyes, ready to spill my guts and tell him how much I love him, how I was wrong and I think we should get married right away. But the words get caught in my throat. For the first time, I consider the possibility of rejection. What if Gaston doesn't want me back? I couldn't take it if I got fired from my job and then cast off by my one true love, all in twenty-four hours. I turn away. "I'm thinking about getting a job at a bank."

He laughs. "That's funny."

"No, really! I want to see what it's like to work at a normal job—to get up and go to an office and take a sack lunch. I want a normal life."

"You're serious?" He perks up.

I try again to think of what to say, to recall the romantic lines I practiced in the car or some new way to test the waters. The best I can come up with is, "I'm serious, Gaston. I'm ready to change."

"That is so great, Katie. If it weren't for getting yourself fired, I'd even say I'm proud of you. You're taking charge of your life. Moving on."

I nod. I'm inspired by his confidence in me. "You were right. You were right about everything. I was wrong. I was a fool." Is he getting this? Maybe not.

He slaps the table top with gusto and says, "C'mon, Katydid, don't be so rough on yourself. You know, you need to be more like Courtney. I swear, she can put a good spin on everything. She's the sweetest thing—a human sugar cube. I could eat her right up." He goes on to explain how Courtney never has a bad day at work. She loves kids, loves teaching. I try to move the conversation back to me, back to us. But Gaston is on a roll.

"Oh, Katie. She's just so amazing."

I drum my fingers on the table and inspect the fabric of the booth until he is finished gushing about Courtney. Then I say, "She sounds a little too good to be true, if you ask me."

He laughs. "No, no. Don't get me wrong. She's not perfect."

"Really?" I ask in my most sarcastic tone.

"Just between you and me . . . she's a terrible cook!" He whispers the last bit, then grins. I stare at him in horror. "What the hell are you doing with this woman?" I holler.

He chuckles in response. "I know, I know! I dated a chef and now I'm engaged to a woman who can't cook anything without a can of Campbell's soup. Who would have guessed? It's crazy."

"Dated a chef? You *proposed* to me, remember? You said I was your soul mate. Your one true love."

Gaston chuckles again. "Yeah. If you told me last year I would be engaged to someone else, I would have laughed right in your face. Amazing how things change, huh?"

The way I see it, he is, in fact, laughing in my face. I try again to muster up the courage to denounce this engagement and proclaim my undying love, when he looks at his watch. "How did it get to be so late already? We didn't even order, and I've got to get back to work." He jumps up from the table and throws a couple of twenties at me to cover the bill.

"Get yourself something to eat. This was great, Katydid. We need to do it again, soon!" And he is out the door.

My plan has gone awry. I didn't perform my rehearsed speech. I never got to fall into his arms in misery, letting him nurse my tears away. He left acting as though this were a fun lunch meeting. As though we should get together every week and chat about how miserable I am and how dreamy Courtney the sugar cube is.

I kick myself all the way home, trying to figure out how I could have reworded my conversation. I am thrilled when I check my messages and hear Gaston's enthusiastic voice on the answering machine. "Kate! I think I got you a job! Call me right back!"

Gaston found me a job? Probably the deli in his building is looking for a new sandwich maker. Or maybe he wants to hire me to teach Courtney how to cook. I scrunch up my nose in distaste, then call the office. I get Desiree again.

"So, is it true? Are you going to be my replacement while I squeeze out the latest Anderson child?"

"Huh?"

"Gaston said you might sit in for me during my maternity leave."

My cluttered, self-absorbed mind tries to process this information. "I am? I will? You're pregnant again? What is this, the third?"

"Yeah, can you believe it? And we've got ourselves another boy. As if there aren't enough smelly socks and pee droplets in the bathroom already. . . ."

Eww. Time to change the subject. "Is Gaston around? He left me a message."

"He's right here. He's been hovering around my desk all afternoon. I can't get rid of him. Hang on."

"Kate, isn't this great? I didn't think about it until I got back to the office. Desiree's taking three months off, and Marsha Lofton was going to hire a temp. I told her you're looking for a city job, and she gave it the okay. You can train next week and start whenever Des is ready to leave. How perfect is that?"

It's unbelievable. Gaston found me a job in his own office? That means that rather than humiliate myself, begging him to come back to me, I can win his affections with my proximity and natural charm. Gaston will never be able to resist the new, professional me. Once he sees me every day and notices the changes I am willing to make, he will drop that Courtney skank like fuzzy butter. It's the first really great news I've had in days.

"I asked Marsha if she wanted to set up an interview or anything, but she just laughed. I'm not sure what that means. Maybe you should talk to her. I can have Desiree patch you through now if you want?" I agree.

"Hi, Marsha. It's Kate Linden."

"Hey, how're you doing, Kate?"

I stammer, "Uh, okay I guess. Sort of. Well, things could be better."

"Yeah, I bet. I've been hearing a few things. Gaston says you might want to sit in for Des. Is that for real?"

"If it's okay with you. I'm looking for a change."

"Of course you can have the job. I was going to hire a temp. We'd be thrilled to have you. But don't expect too much: Someone with your talents might find it a little dull."

"You're forgetting that my special talents include a knack for pan sauces and the ability to bone out a chicken in less than three minutes. Outside of the kitchen, that doesn't do me much good. I only hope I can live up to your company's professional standards."

"No worries there, kiddo. Can you really take the bones out of a chicken in three minutes?"

"Is that going to be part of the interview process? If so, I can bring my knives."

Marsha laughs. "I think I'll trust you on that. And why don't you leave your knives at home until I'm more confident about how you and Gaston are getting along. Since he's the one who suggested you take the job, I guess you two must have it all figured out?"

"What? You mean his engagement? You thought I might be bothered by that?" I force out a lighthearted chuckle. "How ridiculous. We're all adults. And friends. That's what this is all about, friends helping friends in need." And what I need is to get this job and win Gaston back. We agree that I should start in two weeks but come in a day or two early to train. I ask her to transfer me back to Gaston.

"I'm in! I'm starting in two weeks. Isn't that great?"

"Good for you, Kate. You're taking this seriously."

"Of course I am. But I've got a long road ahead of me and I sure would appreciate your help. Maybe we can get together tomorrow and talk about my new career goals. I could use a hand with my résumé, and I guess I should think about doing one of those five-year plans you always talk about."

It's like bees to honey. "Really? You mean it? You want to do a five-year plan?" I can hear him thumbing through his calendar. "Tomorrow's no good; I promised Courtney we'd go to a lecture."

"But, Gaston, I can't plan my future without you."

He is quiet for a minute, but I can hear him anxiously clicking his pen in the background. "Oh, heck. I'll do it. I'll just call Courtney and explain. She'll understand. Where do you want to meet?"

"My house, of course. I'll make dinner."

"It's a deal. I'll see you at six."

I sign off with a distinct increase of heartbeat. Gaston's ditching Courtney to come to dinner tomorrow. I dance a little jig. I'm going to have a real office job! I will sit in a chair with wheels in a carpeted room and win back the heart of my Prince Charming. Life is good.

Chapter Six

I feel like a superhero. I am finally taking charge of my life. I call Gaston's mom and tell her of my success. "I did it, Adele! I got a job at Gaston's company. I'm going to be the receptionist for Wheton-Lofton and see him every day."

"That is magnificent, Kate. Marvelous. And did you tell him you still loved him?"

"Well, no. But I did convince Gaston to cancel a date with Courtney and join me for dinner tomorrow. I made up some line about discussing the details of my position and getting started on the wording of my new professional résumé."

Adele gets right to the meat of the matter. "What will you cook? You must make something very special. And wear something nice, sweetheart. Throw those horrible jeans of yours away and wear something pretty for a change. Ooh, ooh! Now that you will have a real job, you can finally wear *parfum*. I know just the scent. Gaston will love it!"

I'm not sure who is more excited about my new career, Adele or me.

"You simply must come see me. If you leave right now, you can make it before the rush hour."

"God, no!" I blurt.

"But you must, darling! Gaston's father is in China or Korea or someplace horrible for who knows *how* long. Gaston and I aren't speaking, and my friends have all flown south for the winter. I've been thinking about spending the month at Miraval or Canyon Ranch, but what kind of mother would I be if I left my dear boy alone while he's in the midst of such a serious life crisis?"

Uh-oh, I think to myself. Adele's bored. That could mean trouble.

"So you see, darling. You simply must come see me tonight. We'll go to Tojo's. I know how you love his tuna."

"Tojo's?" At the mere thought of my very favorite sushi bar, I start to salivate. I know this is a trap. I debate the pros and cons of the trip. Sure, I'll have a fabulous dinner, but I'll also have to spend an entire night with Adele, alone. I'm weakening, on the verge of agreeing to visit, when I remember Gaston's wise solution to situations like this. He figured out a way to fulfill his mother's demands for attention without ruining an entire day or weekend.

"How about if we meet halfway? We can have a nice dinner in Bellingham and catch up." To sweeten the deal, I offer her a perk she can't refuse. "Maybe you can give me some fashion tips? You know, some ideas about clothes to wear at the office."

Adele gasps. "Fashion tips? Did you say fashion tips? My darling, I am so proud of you. I would *love* to help you with your wardrobe. Yes, yes, we'll meet tonight for dinner. I'll see you at Anthony's at seven-thirty." And she disconnects.

Bellingham is a little bit farther for me, but I don't have to mess with the international border crossing. Adele doesn't mind. She'll fill up her tank with cheap American gasoline and stock up on liquor and cigarettes at the duty-free stores. Jumping from one country to another for an evening event makes her feel European again.

As I drive the ninety miles to Bellingham, I think about my odd relationship with Gaston's mom. I don't enjoy extended visits with her, but I do like her company. I've learned to accept her insensitivity and selfishness as harmless dramatics. Adele and I called a truce early on. One day, she told me the sweater I was wearing looked as though it had been used to wax the car. Instead of getting all sensitive about it, I told her she might rethink her lip shade. Her present tint brought out the natural greens in her skin. She offered me a smoke, and we polished off a plate of fresh sardines and a bottle of pastis. We were good.

I leave early to avoid traffic, so I have time to spare. I get off the interstate after Everett and drive the state routes through the Skagit Valley. I stop at a few produce and smoked-salmon stands. Because there aren't many tourists at this time of year, I take the scenic route, Chuckanut Drive. The road is narrow and winding and can be terrifying on crowded or rainy days, but there are lovely views of the Puget Sound. My old car purrs now that we are away from the stop-and-go of the city streets. I pat the dashboard and promise Mabel an early oil change as a reward for good behavior.

I arrive at the restaurant early and take a walk among the pleasure boats docked nearby. When I get cold, I go to the restaurant bar and enjoy the view and the old Northwest feel of this bustling port and college town. The night is clear, and the moon glimmers on the choppy water. I sip a perfect Hendricks martini. Thirty minutes later, my empty stomach insists I beg a bread basket from the bartender. An hour after our agreed meeting time, Adele shows up with a flourish.

"Allo, allo, Kate, my darling." She gives me multiple cheek kisses, and I smell her expensive perfume mingled with cigarettes. Before we are even seated, she orders two glasses of Champagne and a dozen oysters. As always, she looks beautiful.

"Adele, you look great. It's nice to see you." And I mean it. Adele is the most glamorous person I know.

"Thank you, Kate. Yes, I'm very pleased with my most recent chemical peel. The aesthetician had a steady, assertive hand. Water is the key to beauty, you know. Kate, you really must drink more water. It will give your skin a dewy, fresh glow."

I try to recall if I've ever seen Adele drink something that wasn't caffeinated or alcoholic. She must do her water drinking in private.

A valet enters, his arms laden with shopping bags. Adele gestures to him. "Over here. Bring them right here." She helps the valet arrange the bags around her chair and starts rifling through them as she talks.

"I didn't have much time, so I just threw some things together, some old jewelry, belts and handbags. They might be of no use to me, but for you, they will be fine. If you weren't so big, I could have passed on some of last year's pieces. Oh, well, I did what I could. I made a quick stop on Robson Street and found a girl about your shape. I dragged her around for a while, trying to find some basics, but darling, I just can't do it without you. It's like starting from scratch. I know you like your blues and grays, but I thought with your coloring and the season, we should bring in some autumn shades, you know, plenty of nice gold tones and rich browns. I managed to find a couple of very simple black dresses. Even though you're so mousy, you can't go wrong with basic black."

"Adele, I don't know what to say. This is unnecessary."

She doesn't agree. She pins me with a look and says, "Well, that's all a matter of perspective, isn't it, dear?" She continues picking through the shopping bags. "There was some nice lingerie on sale." She holds some tiny purple panties up for my approval. "Aren't these just adorable?" I about die of embarrassment. "I threw a few items in for Gaston as well.

You'll make sure he gets them, won't you? Just because we're not speaking doesn't mean I must abandon him entirely."

"Adele, this is too much; you really shouldn't have."

"Darling, I've been dying to get you properly dressed for ages. If you would just write down your measurements, we can get the job done right."

"No, no. You can't—"

"That's the wonderful thing, dear, I *can*! But not with a mere hour's notice. Next time you call me, pleading for help with your wardrobe, you must give me more time. You can't expect miracles."

The waiter arrives with our Champagne and oysters. Adele reaches for the Champagne but refuses the shellfish before they even land on the table. She says to the waiter, "Oh, dear. I forgot to mention that I *cannot* eat oysters that have been anywhere near cocktail sauce. The poor things see that ketchup and simply sour with embarrassment. Take these back and bring us a new plate. Is Jonathan here tonight? He is? Then have him make one of those nice mignonettes we discussed last year. And have him make it with a good fresh shallot and Champagne vinegar if he has it. Tell him it's for Adele."

She takes a sip of her Champagne and starts right back in with her purchases.

"I brought you some French magazines too, dear. Of course, with your kitchen French, you won't be able to read them, but there are pictures. And I threw in half a dozen or so nice scarves. You know how mad I am about scarves!"

Adele often wears expensive, colorful silk scarves as an accessory. I like the look on her, but when I tie a scarf around my neck, I look like a flight attendant or as if I'm getting ready for a sock hop.

"I couldn't decide on the perfect scent for you. My first choice would be Alluriance, but there are others. I can't remember what half the bottles on my dresser smell like or why I bought them, so I just threw them in a bag for you. The duty-free shop had a good price on Chanel, so I got you some bath powder—it's always nice to have around when you want a quiet evening at home."

It has always irritated Adele that I don't wear perfume. She never understood that perfume interferes with my palate. She would just pout and wail when she saw my dresser or luggage devoid of poufs and vials. Gaston never complained about my aroma or lack thereof, but I'm quite sure he will appreciate the change. I can see him right now, walking through the door and becoming intoxicated by the scents of good food and a sexy woman. He will swoon. They say smell is the most powerful of the senses; the one most connected with memory. Once Gaston takes a whiff of me, he will become awash in emotion and forget he ever met Courtney.

Adele reaches into the bread basket and makes a face. "Tsk, Tsk. I don't like the color of this butter. Is it salted? It's a bit warm, wouldn't you say? She lifts her left arm, jangles her bracelets and hoots, "All-looooo" to a busboy carrying a heavy tray of dirty dishes. Our waiter sees her and rushes over. He replaces the butter with chilled, unsalted pats and recites the evening specials.

I order first. "I'll have the salmon special."

"Ooh, that does sound good, doesn't it, dear? I'll have that as well." She hands the waiter her menu, as if her decision has been made. I know better. "But instead of the Israeli couscous, can I have some nice sliced tomatoes? Vine-ripened, of course. And if you insist on serving only Roma or plum tomatoes, will you at least peel them? The skins can be so tough. Now for the fish, I don't want the spicy apricot glaze that it comes with. I can't imagine what you Americans see in all of those sweet sauces. Horrible, I tell you. So why don't you substitute the tarragon butter sauce from the halibut special? It sounds much nicer. And rather than pan-seared, I'd like my salmon poached. Make it a center cut piece, please."

As usual, I am torn between utter embarrassment at her behavior and pure joy at being on the receiving end of a customer's special requests for a change. I can think of only a handful of times I've seen Adele pleased with her meal. Even then, she will send back her food for one reason or another. Often she returns the plates of everyone else at the table as well.

Our oysters arrive, and the talk changes to food. We toss around ideas for the perfect menu to woo Gaston. It's no secret that his free will is accessible through the belly. He will walk on broken glass for a lamb chop or perfectly seared duck breast. Dip them in béarnaise sauce, and he might gobble up an entire deck of playing cards.

I decide that the cold, early November weather is perfect for a crisp endive salad with pears and *soupe l'onion gratinée*. She agrees. Classic French dishes such as these have Gaston drinking wine with abandon and then sitting back, feeling flushed and happy with the world. The soup takes skill to make, but it isn't fancy and it doesn't require a lot of last-minute prep work; I can focus my attention on Gaston, not just dinner. Adele keeps repeating the importance of putting Gaston first.

After dinner, we move back to the bar for cigarettes and late-night espresso. I sometimes smoke when I'm with Adele. I mean, why not? Inhaling the air around her is almost as bad as having one yourself. The coffee and cigarettes counter the lethargy I feel after the meal. I'm wired when we say good night in the parking lot.

On the way home, I again think about Gaston's mother. I've never confused my relationship with Adele with my relationship with Gaston. I think she respects me because of that. I tolerate her bossy ways, but don't let her steamroller me. In turn, she likes knowing that her darling boy is being watched over by a competent woman who will keep her beloved satiated with good food, wine and plenty of sex but not too much coddling. That's her role. Her constant doting on Gaston is kind of pathetic. His spine seems to disappear when he's around her, but that's not my business. Family can be complicated.

I'm unloading the many bags that Adele loaded into my car when Iris comes home. "What's all this?"

"Adele agrees that I should get back together with Gaston. She seems to think that throwing money at an ugly duckling might turn me into a swan."

"Excellent! Let's see the goods!" We open boxes and unwrap tissues and unearth quite a bounty. Among the many accessories, there are two very classy black dresses. One is too formal to wear to work, but the other will be perfect for my new job. Unfortunately, both of them are too big. Iris pins me into one of them, adorns me with a myriad of accessories and then directs me to a mirror. We both start laughing. I look like I borrowed my clothes from a rich aunt.

People never guess my size right. I'm a big girl—tall, but quite thin. I guess my fondness for loose, comfortable clothes doesn't flatter my girlish shape. Exchanging this stuff is out of the question, unless I'm willing to haul it all back up to Vancouver. Iris offers to do some tailoring, then pokes around in one last bag and is perplexed by the neckties and boxer shorts she finds inside. "What's this? Are these for me?"

"Adele said she added a few things for Gaston."

"Well, you can't give them to him, so why don't you give them to me?"

"Huh?"

"You know I'm always going to back you up, even in this horrible Gaston plan of yours. But if you do manage to break up this engagement, how do you think he'll feel when he finds out you and his mother have been in cahoots? He'll feel betrayed."

I think about it for a minute, and brush off the idea. "Naw, you know how Gaston and his mother are. He'll do anything to please her. That's how I know this engagement isn't really right. Gaston would never go against his mother's wishes, and Adele wants us together. He'll be glad to please her."

Iris makes a querulous face.

"Trust me, I know what I'm doing," I say. But when I get to my room, I stash the underwear and ties in their boxes with my summer clothes, way back in my closet, just in case.

Chapter Seven

I go all Martha Stewart over the details for my dinner with Gaston. I stash the collection of miscellaneous junk that has gathered on the dining room table and arrange two place settings with seasonal elegance. Without realizing it, the neighbors have been generous and volunteered a few late flowers and some greenery for a centerpiece. I iron my best oversized French linen napkins. (Gaston loves using real napkins instead of paper. I wonder if sweet, little Courtney has figured *that* out yet!) With a rush of optimism, I pull on a pair of the tiny silk panties that Adele bought me. They are scratchy, but my alternatives are pretty utilitarian. I'm going to wear the sexy dress I bought last Christmas. It's a flattering Michael Kors halter dress in winter white. It's classy but still comfortable. I wore a sheer black wrap with it at Gaston's company party, but tonight I'm going to reveal plenty of skin. The dress shows off my long slender neck and collarbones. The flair skirt is flirty, and the hemline makes my legs look a mile long.

I pull the dress from my closet and give it a once-over. I meant to get it to the dry cleaners after the party, but it slipped my mind. I dab at a tiny stain until it is unnoticeable, then put it on. I look at myself in the mirror. The dress looks great, but it's kind of formal for an early dinner at home. I experiment with scarves. I decide on a long, narrow, sheer silk number in vivid coral. The color makes my brown eyes look almost exotic, especially when I wear my hair up. After tying knots that would make a boy scout proud, I give up and leave the ribbon scarf in a simple loop. I let it go snug around the front of my neck but drape down my bare back. It looks quite sexy. I set my one pair of nice high heels by the front door. I won't put those on until I have to.

Just before Gaston is expected, I sauté up a little garlic and thyme in butter and wave this savory potpourri right by the front door. As soon as he enters, he will get hit hard with a sensory blast, right where it counts. It works. Gaston enters the house and says, "Wow, it smells great in here! What's for dinner?" I beam at him, feeling radiant. He takes in my outfit. "You look amazing." He pecks me on the cheek and asks, "Are you wearing perfume?"

Instead of hopping up and down in glee, I manage a demure pose and say, "Why, yes, it's called Alluriance. How nice of you to notice."

"How could I not notice? I *love* Alluriance. That's what Courtney wears." He leans in, takes another deep breath and gets a dreamy, far-away look in his eyes. "It's like she's with us right now!"

I jump back. This perfume is getting dumped in the toilet, tonight. After he opens his eyes and stops fantasizing about stupid Courtney, Gaston hands me the heavy shopping bag he's been carrying.

"I brought some books. I thought you might find them helpful." I look down and read a few titles: *What Color Is Your Parachute? The One-Minute Manager.* There are a couple of motivational books written by media moguls and sports stars. I had forgotten about Gaston's collection. This bag is stuffed full of books, and I know it didn't make a dent in his personal-improvement library. I thank him and plant another tender kiss on his cheek. When he starts to sniff me again, I pull away.

I gesture to the table. "Make yourself comfortable. I have a few last-minute things to do in the kitchen. I'll get you a glass of wine." I go straight to the sink and attempt to rinse off the stupid perfume. Having Gaston smell Courtney every time I step near him is not on my agenda. I break off a sprig of fresh rosemary from a potted plant and rub the bruised leaves on my wrist and neck. The scarf keeps falling forward, getting in my way. I stuff it in the back of my dress to keep it secure while I cook.

I fill a heavy earthenware casserole with bread, ladle on the rich beef and onion soup from the soup pot, then top it with lots of cave-aged Gruyère cheese. I prefer family-style terrines of French onion soup instead of individual servings. I like the way the bread, cheese and broth marry together slowly in the oven rather than just bubble and brown under the broiler. And, if it's as good as I want it to be, it's best if I don't dictate the serving size.

I set an electronic timer and look around at my outfit for a place to pin it. I'm not wearing pants, so it can't go where I usually put it, on my waistband. I don't want to ruin the flow of the dress, so I clamp it on the narrow band of fabric near my neck and arrange the scarf to cover it. I pour two big goblets of wine and go back into the dining room to see Gaston. He is thumbing through the books, marking pages with Post-it notes. "I thought I'd mark a few chapters that I found inspiring or helpful."

"Do we have to get right down to business, Gaston? You just got here."

"Yeah, but you're all dressed up. And aren't those your good shoes by the door? I figured you were going out after dinner. You must have a hot date."

The shoes! I forgot to put on the shoes! Oh, well, too late now.

I bat my lashes as I hand him his wine. "I *do* have a hot date. With you!"

He laughs. "Ah, Katie. You always know just what to say. You think I'm going to miss my freedom, maybe yearn for the wild days now that I'm engaged. But believe me, I don't miss them one bit. Once you meet Courtney you'll understand. She's pretty much everything a man could want in a woman. That doesn't mean I don't appreciate the effort. You're a real pal. You know how to make a guy feel good."

I manage to resist the temptation to whack him across the back of the head with a rolled-up newspaper. Instead, I try once more to seduce him. In my sultriest voice I say, "Of course I know how to make you feel good. It's what I do best." Lowering my voice like that makes me have to cough a bit. To make sure he gets my point, I saunter behind him, dragging my index finger along the back of his neck.

He responds immediately to my touch. "Oh, yeah. Now go a little lower and to the left. I've got a pimple back there that's really starting to itch. How did I forget about your awesome back-scratches? Courtney's nails are long and pretty, but kind of hard. Since you bite yours, they're perfect for this kind of thing. You know, all squishy and soft, so they get the itch but don't make the pimples bleed."

I give up on my seductive poses and make a childish monster face at the back of his head. Then I consent, and scratch his back with my "perfect nails." At least we're touching. He moans with delight and directs me around his back to the spots that need attention. After a long, thorough scratching through his shirt, he sighs with contentment. I move my hands up to his shoulders and lean my body forward to whisper in his ear. I'm not sure if it is the movement, the coughing or just gravity, but the electronic timer falls from my halter strap into a fold of scarf material. The weighted scarf drops fast and hard, right into Gaston's Pinot Noir. I bolt upright at the clatter. We both reach for the tipping glass and catch it before it crashes. We manage to save the wine, but the Pinot Noir–soaked scarf swings and lands with a wet slap on the bodice of my beautiful dress.

"Ooh. That's going to leave a stain. You'd better take care of it right now. Courtney told me how to get red wine out once. I can't remember what she said. Lemon juice? Hair spray? Let me give her a call." Before I can object, Gaston reaches into his pocket for his cell phone and speed-dials the number. Courtney answers so fast it's as if she is sitting by the phone, eagerly awaiting Gaston's stain-removal questions.

I shake like a wet dog and stomp to my bedroom to change. I'm not keen on standing in my bare feet and ruined dress, listening to Gaston chat about his day with another woman. I peel off the dress and change into something comfortable.

When I return to the dining table, Gaston is still talking to Courtney. He looks up from the phone and says, "Soda water! Courtney says soda water works on red wine. I knew it was something like that." He goes back to the phone. "Okay, sugar dumplin', I better get off the phone now. The sooner Kate and I finish this, the sooner I can come home to you. Yeah, I miss you too. No, *you're* the sweetest. No, *you* are. I'm sending you kisses! Smooch smooch, num, num num."

Oh, good God! So much for our romantic evening together. I guess I'm doomed to spend the night actually listening to Gaston read the canned career advice he loves so much. He gets started by telling me about his new favorite motivators, and I manage a minimal amount of eye-rolling. I catch myself before I ask if he has anything entitled "How to Be the Best Sheep in the Flock." I have always mocked Gaston and his career guides. I think real work involves muscles and sweat and dirty hands. I used to scoff when Gaston complained of his long, hard days at the office. I can see him now, flat on the couch in his starched shirt and loosened Italian silk tie, exhausted. He might have had a stiff back from sitting all day, perhaps a tender ear from contact with the phone receiver. Sometimes, I would go to his house after my shift and he would plead for a shoulder rub—he was in *meetings* all day. As if meetings should be considered for Olympic status . . . Meanwhile, as I rubbed his shoulders, my work clothes would be on their way to the laundry service for industrial-strength bleaching. I would be peppered with small burns and cuts, my feet, shins and lower back soothed only by a handful of pills.

But what do I know? I've never had an office job. I guess if I'm going to win him back, I'll have to accept that people who sit in ergonomic chairs in professionally decorated offices are actually working. I half-listen to Gaston's lecture on how to get ahead. He has the lingo down. He dishes out dozens of bon mots on leadership, managerial style, communication and teamwork. I flip through some pages. I guess these books have never appealed to me because what I do isn't quite on the professional map.

And there it is. I feel like I've been run over by a freight train. I have been *fired* from a basic service job. I've always been so proud, so cocky about my highfalutin talent and fierce work ethic, but in the end, what am I? I'm a cook, a laborer, the hired help. Cooks are everywhere! High-school dropouts get work as cooks. Homeless shelters and prisons are full of ex-cooks. My glorious gift, my sanctimonious sweat, produces something that is chewed, churned around in the guts and then eliminated. Food and cooking, my life, my work: It's all shit!

I start to hyperventilate. Gaston is reading aloud, but I can't hear him. I am deafened by the blood coursing through my skull. I was always trying to get Gaston to loosen up. He used to wave a best seller in my direction now and then and read motivational quotes, but I would tease him. My God! How had Gaston ever tolerated my artistic temperament and lowbrow ways?

He looks up from the book when he hears me moan. "You okay, Katydid?"

"No. I'm a disaster." I claw a few loose strands of hair off my face. "I always thought of myself as such a hard worker, but . . . I was just kidding myself. I never got my degree at the university. I don't finish anything. Jeez! I quit college to go to *cooking school*? I've worked for four years as a *sous*-chef. Who does that? If I had real talent, or any ambition at all, I should have my own restaurant by now. My God! I'm twenty-six years old and what have I done with my life? It's only a matter of time before I start spending my days on the couch with a bong, a box of Froot Loops and the *TV Guide*!" I jump up and pace the room.

Gaston scratches his head. Of course, I take his silence as acknowledgment of my failure. I point an accusing finger at him. "You've known this all along! You've waved these books at me and tried to get me to improve myself for years. Why didn't I see it before? Why didn't I listen to you?" I reach for the nearest book. Gaston takes my hand.

"Kate, calm down. Take it easy."

I jerk my hand back. His touch is like fire. "Everything in my life that made sense is turned upside down, and you want me to calm down? You want me to take it easy? Give me that pad of paper over there. I've got to start writing some of this down."

Instead, he starts gathering up the books and putting them away. I grab *Good to Great* and *Success Through a Positive Mental Attitude* out of his hands.

"No, Katie. I don't think this is a good time. You're not ready." He tries pulling the books from me, but I yank them back.

"Not ready? What are you talking about? I've never been *more* ready. I *need* these books. You can't just dangle *Who Moved My Cheese?* in front of me and then snatch it away. I need to know who moved my cheese!" I am shouting, close to hysterics. We tug at the books until the timer for the soup chirps. Gaston's gaze darts back and forth from the kitchen to me. His determination crumbles at the thought of a ruined dinner. He hands over the books.

"Okay, you win. They're all yours."

I gather my spoils and arrange them in a tidy stack next to me. I pat and caress the top cover a bit. Here is my salvation, my ticket to the professional world, a blissful marriage to Gaston and a life that might feel normal. I breathe a deep sigh of relief and return to the kitchen to dress the salad and retrieve the soup.

Dinner is served. We both fidget at the table for a few minutes. Gaston makes all the prerequisite noises and small talk about how everything looks and smells delicious. It hardly registers. I'm still trying to sort through the flood of emotions I am experiencing.

Gaston looks concerned when he says, "You're going through a lot of stuff right now, Katie. It's gotta be tough."

"I'm fine," I croak. I wipe a thread of melted cheese from my chin and clear my throat. "Well, I will be fine. These should help." I pat the stack of career-coaching books. "These should get me back on track." I look at Gaston, my white knight. "But I can't do it without you." He is shoveling a large chunk of hot bread from the bowl to his mouth. He waves his hands and makes monkey faces to try to cool down the huge, steaming mouthful. He tries to ease the burn and talk at the same time. "You know, I didn't bring those to . . . I didn't think . . . I mean . . ." Finally he slurps some wine to cool the fire. "You're a great person just the way you are, Katie. I just thought you might want a little polish. It's not like you need a complete life makeover or something."

Well, that's a relief.

"You're no slacker. If anything, you push yourself too hard. Nothing in that pile is going to teach you anything about how to work hard. That's something you have deep inside."

I am soothed a bit by the comforting food and kind words. Gaston continues. "But you've got to think of your future. Are you using your talents in the right arena? I've said it before, but you need to think about redirecting all of that energy. You're never going to get ahead until you step away from the stove and start managing your career.

"That's why I think this receptionist job is so perfect for you. You'll get a chance to see that people can make a living without pounding themselves into a jellied mess each day. Getting out of the kitchen will give you the chance to experience an environment where a scathing memo might be your only work hazard."

I smile. Gaston puts his soft, office worker's palm over my chapped and scarred hand, and my whole body tingles with recognition and memories. He looks in my eyes and explains, "It's like I keep telling Courtney. Hard work alone never made anyone rich." Then he spends fifteen minutes explaining how devoted Courtney is to her second-graders, spending her weekends working on math games and bulletin board cutouts.

My smile melts into a grimace. Damn!

Before he leaves for the night, Gaston admits slipping a special book into his stack, just for me. "I hope you don't take this the wrong way. You know I've always loved your casual, funky style, but I thought it might be helpful." He hands me a book called *Attention to Detail: Social Graces, Manners, Conversation and Charm for Today.*

I grit my teeth and see that Gaston's face is screwed up funny. It's as though he is expecting me to freak out or throw a tantrum. Instead, I try out the new professional demeanor I am determined to live by (at least until we're hitched) and thank him.

"How sweet. I've been thinking a lot about what I'll wear to the office. I'll read this tonight and go shopping tomorrow. You're the best, Gaston. Courtney's one very lucky gal."

Ugh! He doesn't get my subtle innuendo about how *I* want to be the lucky one. All he hears is the "C" word, and before he leaves, he spends ten more minutes telling me a funny thing one of her students said to her at school that day. To stop him, I insist I need to get started on my reading and shoo him off the porch.

Hours later, Iris's hysterical laughter wakes me up. I'm on the couch, surrounded by self-help books. Iris has picked up my extra-special gift book on style and grace, and she is reading it aloud in a Miss Piggy voice. I groan. Iris strikes a tortured pose, holds out her cigarette like an old-time movie star and in a husky voice says, "Oh, dear. I'd better tell the girls in the band that we're doing it all wrong. How are we ever going to make it in the rock and roll business without a neat, well-groomed appearance and the proper hemline?" Tonight, Iris is wearing a classic boys' private school uniform complete with the wrinkled striped tie. The pant legs are cut short and frayed. Vintage daisy and peace sign patches are sewn onto the elbows and butt, and a pot leaf has replaced the school crest. I groan. I don't want to be awake, but I know the house rules. Falling asleep on the couch means you are still "up."

I don't feel like explaining my night to her, so I change the subject. "How do you feel about goldfish?"

"They're okay. I like the plain orange ones better than the Parmesan."

"No, not the crackers, I mean the swimming kind. I know it's only been a few days, but I get lonesome around here when you're gone. We need a pet."

"Cool! Why don't we get a cat?"

"Gaston's allergic."

She sighs and makes a face of pure tolerance. Then her eyes light up. "Ooh, a puppy then! There's a guy I know at the bar who's got the cutest puppies. The dad's been in a few fights, but the momma's only bitten one person, and I guess they were totally asking for it."

"No! Jeez, Iris. Are you crazy? I don't think going from pet-free to owning potential fighting dogs is the smoothest transition. Let's just start with a fish, okay? I'm going to the pet store tomorrow." I look over at the wall clock. "I mean today."

"Cool! Can I come with you?"

Chapter Eight

I'm amazed, but Iris is still interested in going shopping with me even after she sees my list.

"I just want to have it on the record that I do not approve of this. You're not going to go downtown and spend real money on a generic office wardrobe, are you? Sweater sets? Pearl studs? Panty hose? *Fake nails?* Are you out of your mind?"

I'll admit, the nail thing is a little scary to me too, but after the back scratching incident, I've had to rethink my objection to long fingernails. Pretty hands are the first things to go on a chef, and nail polish is utter taboo, since flecks of polish can find their way into the food. But if I get plenty of conservative, golf club clothes and nice long nails, I might magically become a lady. It's worth a try.

"If I'm going to make a new start of things, I need to have the right stuff. Dress for success they say."

Iris pretends to hold back a barf.

"You're the one who's always complaining about what a disaster my wardrobe is. I thought you would back me up when I told you I was going shopping."

She's serious for a moment. "I'm disgusted with your clothes because they are just sooooo boring! Let me at a few things with my scissors and sewing machine. I can add a little something."

Few pieces of clothing make it into Iris's closet without being attacked and altered in some unique way. I'm sure she has grand ideas on how to turn my old blue jeans into power suits and my sweaters into bejeweled fashion spectacles. Right now she's a big fan of old-fashioned fringe, extra zippers and decorative silver chains.

I head to Nordstrom, prepared to max out my credit card. Iris runs into an old boyfriend selling ladies' shoes and flirts with him while I wander upstairs. I march up to a sales clerk in my standard uniform of jeans, T-shirt and hooded zip-up sweatshirt. I'm not wearing makeup; a plastic clamp holds my sloppy hair off my face. "I need a new professional wardrobe, can you help me?"

Like Adele, this woman seems thrilled that I am asking for help.

"Absolutely. What are you, an eight, tall?" I nod, and she starts whisking clothes off racks. She runs back and forth from the dressing room with item after item until I have a simple yet stylish new wardrobe. When I do the math, I realize that my new clothes might cost more than I will make during my temporary stint at Wheton-Lofton, but my visit with Adele has convinced me that winning back Gaston's heart is worth any expense.

Iris finds me just as I am handing over my credit card. She freaks out when she sees the total. In a decidedly un-Nordstrom style, she hollers, "Are you fucking nuts? I could buy a brand-new Neumann microphone for that much money." I look dumb, so she puts it in terms I can better understand. "You could rent a villa in Italy with money like that, and you're going to waste it on . . . this?" Iris doesn't want to even categorize the conservative business attire as clothing. "What are you thinking?"

She snatches my credit card from my personal shopper, clamps on to my arm and pulls me away from my well-dressed future. I yell to Pamela, my wardrobe consultant, "Hold that for me, I'll be back!"

"Like hell you will," Iris murmurs. Women whisper and stare as Iris forcibly walks me out of the store and back to the car. She directs me to a couple of her favorite consignment shops, and I manage to find a couple of nice, professional pieces that are "lightly worn" and a great bargain. Then I make myself go shoe shopping. Unlike some women, I don't think of the shoe department as a candy store for grown-ups. I have big, sturdy, square feet that hold up my tall frame for twelve to fourteen hours a day. When I'm not standing, I'm walking or reclined and shoeless, so I gravitate toward very practical shoes. Narrow, strapped and beaded sandals have never fit into my life, and they sure as hell don't fit on my feet. Me wearing a pair of Manolos is like serving a slice of pizza in a Limoges eggcup.

I end up with some low pumps and a couple of pairs of rather cute high heels for a more formal, sexy look. If I'm going to be a lady of leisure, I better train my dogs to heel.

Iris and I finish our retail extravaganza at the pet store. We want to take home every living thing with fur, scales or cute brown eyes. In the end, we buy a single fish, as planned. We make a pact that if we can keep the fish alive until Christmas, we can move on to something a little more demanding. None of the goldfish dazzles us, so we select an electric-blue Siamese fighting fish—a betta. Ours puffs up his gills and strikes a ferocious pose when anyone comes near. We like that. Our fish has attitude. We name him "Spike," and for the rest of the afternoon fuss over his bowl, colorful gravel and single frond of aquatic plant life. Iris swears Spike is already learning the command "stay."

Our fish worship is interrupted by the telephone. It is Gaston.

"Kate! There's been a change of plans. Desiree went to see her ob-gyn, and I guess her blood pressure is getting too high. They want her to lay low for a couple of weeks. We're going to need you to start earlier than we thought. How about tomorrow?"

"Yes, yes! I can be there tomorrow. What time?"

"Six-thirty? Will that be okay? I know you're not much of an early bird. . . ."

I wince at the early hour, but I did a stint as a pastry chef once, and I know it is indeed possible to get used to early mornings. With my new "gung-ho" career attitude and professional enthusiasm, I'm quick to agree. "Six-thirty it is! I'll be there."

"Oh, yeah, and lucky you—since it's Friday, you don't even have to worry about dressing up. It's casual day." He should stop there, but he doesn't. "That doesn't mean jeans, you know." I grit my teeth. I might be a complete idiot when it comes to the professional world, but I don't need Gaston to remind me how to dress . . . again.

I reassure Gaston that I will arrive in proper attire. I hang up the phone and turn to Iris. "They need me tomorrow! I get to start tomorrow!"

"Oh, yippee." She twirls her finger in the air with fake enthusiasm.

I ignore her sarcasm. "Ohmigod! I'm not ready. I don't have a proper briefcase or any panty hose, and I need to get my hair done!"

Iris grabs my shoulders to stop my pacing in circles. She gives me a shake. "Enough already! You can buy nylons anywhere. And you're going to be answering phones, you dingbat! Why do you need a briefcase to answer phones? Are you going to carry around your own copy of the yellow pages?"

"But my hair!"

She looks me over and agrees, "Yeah, your hair could use some work."

I scrunch up my nose and stick my tongue out at her. I was counting on Iris to tell me my hair was just fine.

"I'll call Cindy." Cindy is the drummer in Lipstick and Lithium. Her day job is at a trendy barbershop in Fremont, where she does a lot of buzz cuts and "fauxhawks," but she can do a straight-ahead trim and color, too. Iris makes the call. "Cindy can't do it, but her cousin can. We've got practice tonight and she said she'd bring the cuz along. That'll be cool. You can listen to us jam while you get your new do."

Adrienne, the cousin, is quite a sight. She has big teased hair, dramatic, sparkly makeup and an eclectic arrangement of piercings and tattoos that ornament the many fashion styles she wears at once. I know better than to judge a book by its cover or a hairdresser by her personal cut. The band is already jamming, so I use shouts, sign language and facial expressions to communicate. I point to Iris and explain my connection to the band. I pull my long, mousy locks away from my head and chop at them with finger scissors. I point to the plastic bag I've brought from the pharmacy that holds, among other things, a bottle of lustrous-copper hair highlights, a couple of pairs of cheap panty hose and some new makeup. Adrienne nods and seems to understand. She sets me down on a tall stool and wraps a plastic tablecloth around my neck.

The band sounds great. I sip a beer, close my eyes and slip into a music coma. Adrienne handles my head with authority and has the aggressive comb pull and confident snip of the scissors that only true hair professionals have. That's why, when she finishes and hands me a mirror, I can't hold back the scream. My hair is bright orange and sticks out in a dozen different angles. The band hears my shrieks and stops playing. I dash into the practice space with the tablecloth still tied around my neck. "Smokin' hair, K! I'm loving it!" is the consensus from the band. I look at Iris in a panic. She can't hold back her laughter.

"That's not helping! What am I supposed to do now? It's eleven at night and I have to be at work in a stuffy office at six-thirty tomorrow morning!" I am not with a sympathetic crowd. They tell me I am making a good statement about the oppression of the financial world against creativity and personal liberty. Iris wraps her arms around me and in between giggles says, "You're saving their ass, Kate, remember? They called you at the last minute because they need help. They aren't likely to fire you because of your hair color." She holds me at arm's length to take another look. "Uh, but you can always borrow one of my hats."

I bury my face in my hands. Iris teases me until my weeping becomes a tortured laugh. Turns out, Adrienne doesn't speak much English. She's visiting from Berlin and assumed from my gestures that I was there for a punk-rock cut and color like the rest of the crowd. It didn't help matters that my pharmacy bag held an enticing combination of peroxide, hair color and cranberry juice concentrate. Sure, I used to threaten to do something crazy to my hair, but that was when I spent my days and nights deep in a windowless kitchen.

I drive home and scour my head half a dozen times, hoping some of the fresh color might rinse out. In the end, I think I just made it a brighter shade of tangerine. I steal the sharpest scissors in the house from Iris's sewing basket and chop and snip at my head until I have a style that looks almost intentional. I debate running to the all-night pharmacy to buy another bottle of hair color, but I'm afraid if I add yet another chemical to the mix, everything will fall out.

I toss and turn all night in restless anticipation of the alarm clock. At 5 a.m. I trudge through a shower, make a pot of superstrong coffee and start applying my new makeup. (I tie a towel around my orange hair so I don't have to look at it.) With a little help from Iris, one of the new dresses Adele bought now looks like it fits. I attach some conservative earrings and spritz on another perfume Adele gave me called Pheramonium. She swears it will drive Gaston wild. I tear my first pair of panty hose on the rattan laundry basket. It's okay. I have extras.

I grab my battered purse, newly stocked with sharp pencils and two almond streusel tea loaves. I pour more coffee into a vacuum to-go cup and dash to catch a bus. I feel very organized and professional. My heels make very grown-up percussive sounds on the hard kitchen floor. My mascara-coated eyelashes feel long and luxurious. I can feel and smell the moist glaze of my new makeup. It's kind of weird being all dressed up when the sun hasn't even risen. It's just like you see in the movies. I can do this! This is going to be my new life. I grab my things and strut out the door, catch my heel on the doormat, spill hot coffee down the front of my new dress and rip my panty hose to shreds when I fall against the iron porch railing.

I swear a lot and run back to my room to change. My new consignment store clothes are still crammed in the bottom of plastic sacks. The iron is in Iris's room, and I don't dare set foot in the rabid she-bear cave before the morning turns to double digits. I tear through my closet and settle on a sleeveless summer dress with a cotton cardigan thrown over the top to make it more seasonal. So much for my calm, confident demeanor. I'm a raving maniac by the time I find the bus schedule and discover my chariot left three minutes ago. I will gather my composure while I drive.

It takes me forty-five minutes to get to the financial district, a trip that takes twelve in the light of day. I know about evening rush hour, but what the hell are all of these people doing on the road before six o'clock in the damn morning?

Because I refuse to pay a month's rent for a spot in the building, I park six blocks down the hill in a cheap lot I know. As soon as I leave the protection of my car, it starts to rain. It's not the refreshing drizzle or mist we Seattleites love, it dumps buckets. I hoof it up the steep downtown hillside with my purse balanced on top of my head like an umbrella. I ignore the odd looks I get from people in the elevator, and manage to sneak unnoticed to the Wheton-Lofton bathroom.

I look bad. It's worse than I imagined. My orange hair is plastered to my skull in dripping wet tendrils. My makeup looks like it was applied by a hallucinating cubist. My new shoes are bleeding dye onto my heels, and my feet already have blisters. There are mud splatters sprayed up the back of my legs and skirt, and I have the distinct impression that I don't smell as fresh as I did an hour ago. I consider running back to my car for the duffel bag that holds my studio clothes. I will at least feel comfortable in the clay-smattered jeans and oversized man's dress shirt. It *is* casual Friday.

I try to remember a few of the motivational phrases I read with Gaston and give myself a pep talk. "*Enthusiasm begins with a positive attitude. Keep your face to the sunshine and you cannot see the shadows. You are what you eat.*" Oh, good Lord. That might be bad. What did I eat last night?

At six-thirty-two, I have managed to reconstruct my face and clothing. (There is nothing to be done about the hair.) I am ready to face the office. Gaston is in the lobby awaiting my arrival. "Whoa! Katie."

I cover my face with one hand and try not to burst into tears. Crying is not allowed. I've never cried at work before and I will *not* start now that I'm a real professional. I pinch myself hard to fight away the tears and stumble in Gaston's direction. Damn these shoes!

"Good morning," I mumble. I look into his eyes, trying to telepathically convey to him that he should pull me into his arms, cover me with kisses and tell me to go home and have some cocoa. My valiant attempt at a life change and obvious misery will inspire him to have my things moved into his condo this very night. Gaston will take care of me.

He blurts, "Good grief, what happened to you?" and I almost collapse into a heap of embarrassment and shame. He averts his gaze, inspects the carpet and tries again.

"Uh, good morning. It's nice to see you."

I pull myself together and try to find my voice. "I, mmm, had a difficult morning."

"Yeah, I guess so. I'm guessing that Iris helped you get ready?"

I wince and nod. I look down at my miserable clothes and try to explain. "I had on this great new dress, but I got coffee on it. And my other new stuff was wrinkled and I couldn't get the iron, so I had to wear this." I tug at my sweater. It has grown three sizes since this morning. "It kind of got stretched out from the rain." It's no use. I stop making excuses and admit defeat. "This isn't how I wanted to start my new job."

"Yeah, okay, but what happened to your hair?"

I pull at my hair again. "There was a little chemical mix-up. Do you want me to go buy a hat or a scarf or something to cover it up?"

He gives me another inspection, then smiles. "You crack me up, Katydid. I never know what to expect from you. For future reference? Maybe bright orange hair isn't the best look for your first day in the financial world. But you'll make it work, I know you will."

His confidence renews my own. I take a few deep breaths and face the reception desk. I *will* make this work. "So, tell me what to do. I'm as ready as I'll ever be."

Gaston walks me through the office and introduces me to everyone. I'm braced for some strange reactions to my appearance, but no one says anything. They are all too busy to be bothered by a new, albeit very colorful, temporary receptionist.

When we get back to the front desk, Gaston gives me the rundown on my responsibilities.

"Well, I guess the place to start is, uh, with your vocabulary."

"Vocabulary? But I did really well on my SATs."

"That's not quite what I mean. This isn't a kitchen, Kate. You're going to be talking to a lot of different people, so you might want to curb your swearing. Clean up your language, you know?"

I'm embarrassed and promise I will make an effort. "Ixnay on the kitchen English. Gotcha."

"Desiree said she would try to e-mail you a job description and a detailed list of her schedule." Gaston turns to the phone. "Well, I wish I could tell you how this puppy works, but I'm afraid it's a little more complicated than the extension I have in my office. Hopefully when Des calls she'll tell us where she hid the instructions."

I laugh. "I mastered the telephone way back in junior high school, Gaston. I think I can handle it."

"Yeah, but this isn't your ordinary home phone. I'll keep looking for the instructions, but Marsha says we can route calls through voice mail today."

"Voice mail? Why do you pay someone to answer the phone when you have voice mail?"

"It's just the way things are done. A professional greeting is always more personal than talking to a machine. A lot of our clients are old-school, and they want to talk to someone when they call, not just punch in an extension. It's also important that we have someone greet people when they visit."

"So, I can just sit here and file my nails until someone stops by, and I'll still be doing my job?"

"Your nails?" He guffaws. I sit on my hands. "You might be able to take it easy today, but this job is trickier than it looks." The phone rings.

"It's a telephone, Gaston, how hard can it be?" I look down at the flashing lights, buttons and digital screen. There is no receiver. I panic for a moment, then see the headset. I put it on (not worrying at all that it might mess up my hair), push the button next to the blinking light and in my sweetest voice say, "Thank you for calling Wheton-Lofton, how may I help you?" I flash Gaston a smug smile. He shoots me a thumbs-up and heads back to his office. That's good, because I'm talking to a dial tone.

I ignore the bleeps and rings from the console, and call my personal hairdresser to book an emergency appointment for tomorrow. Then, once I manage to get another dial tone, I call the studio. I need a few words of encouragement from my mother.

A young man answers, "Linden Studios."

"Sam? It's Kate Linden. I need to talk to my mom."

"She's a little busy right now, can I take a message or have her call you back?"

Huh? I'm irritated. Who is Sam to screen my calls to my own mother? "It's important. Kind of a personal emergency, in fact. Do you think she can make time for that?"

"Jeez! An emergency? Why didn't you say so?" He shouts to my mom. "Lauren, Kate needs to talk to you right away!" He comes back on the phone. "Are you okay? Is there anything I can do? Your mom's mixing glaze right now, so she's wearing the clean suit and her respirator. Give her just a second." He is alarmed. I hear clunking in the background. I shout into the phone, "No! No! Sam! It's not really an *emergency*. Tell her I'm fine. I'm just, well . . . having a serious hair crisis."

"A hair crisis?"

"Yeah."

The phone is silent for a second. Then Sam shouts back to my mother,

"Lauren, I'm sorry I have to break this to you, but your daughter is having a *hair* emergency!"

Mom is silent as she processes this information, then she shrieks in mock terror, "Call the paramedics! Send out the SWAT team!"

Sam comes back on the line. "What is it, Kate? Split ends? Bed-head?" He gasps. "Don't tell me it's . . . dandruff!"

Mom is yukking it up in the background. I'm not nearly as amused.

"Go ahead and laugh. It's short, it's neon orange and I'm calling from my new receptionist job downtown."

"No *way*!" Sam bursts into even louder hysterics, and I hang up on him.

I pivot in the big chair, not knowing what to do next. I'm not the kind of person who can sit idle while everyone around me is overwhelmed with work. I go to the lunchroom, slice a loaf of tea bread and arrange it on a plate. I make a fresh pot of coffee and tidy up the kitchen. After I pester her long enough, an office assistant gives me some papers to collate and envelopes to address.

When that is finished, I try again to work the phone. Some of the buttons make the lights and digital readout do different stuff when you hit them once, twice or hold them down. A loud double beep blares from the console. On a lark, I push the button next to a new light. It's Gaston.

"Um, Katie? I just got a message from Steven Baxter. He says he's been having a little trouble with our phone system. Is everything okay out there?"

As I accept Gaston's call, I knock another button. A couple of little blinking lights go out. "Everything's fine, no problems out here!"

"Great, Kate. I'm sure you're doing fine. But don't forget, no one expects you to learn the phone system in one day. It's complicated. Maybe you should leave it alone until you get proper training."

"Pshaw, what are you talking about? It's the phone, for God's sake! Gotta go, another call is coming in." At least I sound efficient and competent. I press a button next to a green light and say with zest, "Wheton-Lofton, how may I direct your call?"

"Uh, Katie, it's still me." It is Gaston.

I press more buttons. Gaston is gone. So is the other caller. Oddly, there are no lights anywhere, and the screen has gone blank. This can't be good. I creep away from the desk and slice up the second cake.

Chapter Nine

After work, I can't wait to get out of my horrible outfit, so I wriggle into my art gear in the front seat of my car. I'm eager to get to the ceramics studio. I'm craving a comfort zone, where I will feel safe. I throw my bag into a corner and get ready for work. Sam inspects my orange hair. He shrugs. "It's not that bad. You're pretty enough to pull it off."

His words make my heart melt. That may be the first spontaneous compliment I've had in weeks. Sam's eyes are animated and warm. Did I underestimate his intelligence the last time we met? I notice his teeth are very nice. He has full lips and a great smile. I guess I'll give him another chance.

"I thought you were a chef. Why are you working in a downtown office?" asks Sam.

There are a lot of *wrong* ways to answer this, so I try a few versions out in my head before I speak. "I needed a little more structure in my life so I decided to do the professional thing for a while. I'm working at a downtown financial firm with my boyfriend, Gaston." Oops, I didn't mean to say that. That doesn't sound quite as impressive. I was doing so well, too. I backpedal. "Well, Gaston isn't actually my boyfriend anymore; he's sort of engaged to someone else right now. But not for long." It's time to stop talking. I wave him off. "It's complicated."

His blue eyes have lost their warmth. They go icy. He says, "It sounds insane," and walks away.

The warm, homey feeling of being in Mom's studio wanes when I see that things have been reorganized. Tables and shelves that have stood forever in the same spot have been moved. I feel edgy and irritable. I walk to the big plaster table to prepare my clay for the night.

"Ugh! This table is a mess. Who scraped it like this? Don't you know that bits of plaster in the clay can explode? That could ruin days, maybe weeks of work. Where's the scrub brush? I swear, no one ever cleans up around here."

Mom is on the phone, but Sam hears me. "Yeah, sorry about that. I wedged up a bunch of clay yesterday and put in the back. We're trying to decide if we're going to break this old table up and pour a new one or just give it a good scrape and scrub."

Oh. I gather up the clay I need and walk to my favorite wheel. My stool has been replaced with a rickety old chair. I shout, "Where's my stool?"

Sam is quick to admit his guilt. "Oops, sorry. My fault. I used it as a step stool to clean up that top shelf in back. I'll get it for you."

"And my tools?" I demand. "I like my wire cutter right here on this bolt above my wheel. You're not using my tools, are you?"

Sam whisks away the chair and exchanges it with my precious stool, then points to a tub of scrapers, sponges and needles arranged within easy arm's reach. My favorite tools have been scrubbed, gathered together and made easily accessible.

"Oh." Okay, I'm officially an idiot.

Sam looks down at me with an expression of obvious distaste. "Are you always this confrontational, or are you just short on meds? Did you forget to visit your pharmacist this week?"

I know I deserve it; I've been acting like a spoiled, whiny child. But his words are like lighting a match around pure dynamite. I'm still fretting about my disastrous day at Wheton-Lofton. I wanted today to go well; I wanted to dazzle the business world with my diverse talents, not offer comic relief. I hate that I couldn't work out the damn phone system. I hate feeling like a stranger in my mom's studio, and right now, I really hate Sam Guerra. Who the hell does he think he is, all level headed and organized? That's *my* job around here! I am just about to explain this to him in glorious detail when Mom extricates herself from her long phone call. I shoot a poisonous glare at Sam. He sneers and disappears into the back room.

"Kate? Just look at you! Let me see." Mom pulls up the glasses she keeps on a chain around her neck and spins me around to look at my hair from all angles, tugging at stray locks and giggling. "Tell me again the chemicals she used on this? Maybe we should try them in a new glaze."

We chat for a while about my new job and the changes here in the studio. She explains that while the new arrangement should be more efficient, the move has made her fall behind in her production schedule.

"And Sam isn't confident in his throwing skills yet, so there's a ton of work to be done."

"I don't mind coming in the evenings. But why did you hire Sam if he can't even throw?"

"He can throw; it's just not his specialty. He learned with the traditional pueblo potters of New Mexico, so he's more of a hand builder and a chemist. He really knows his base materials. I feel like he'll add some good energy around here, and . . . I just have a feeling about him, you know?"

I shrug. "I don't see it."

"You will."

She is determined. Mom's "feelings" are pretty good, but not perfect. She had a "feeling" that the weird boy across the street from us would mature into a powerful, successful young man. He's now a local porn king. Was she wrong?

Mom takes off to meet with a buyer and then go home. She kisses my cheek, waves good-bye to Sam and leaves. He and I keep to the edges of the studio and sidle along like a couple of lobsters in a tank. Our claws are unbound, and the room ripples with tension. Who will attack first? We keep our distance and feel each other out for a while, until I spy some ancient templates.

"Since you're out of practice, you might find these helpful." I point to a cupboard. "There are some good calipers in that first drawer. You might want to start on the tapered mugs. They're by far the best seller, and they're a good size to get your hands and rhythm back."

He mumbles, "Thanks," then gathers up the tools. We never make eye contact, but some kind of truce has been formed, so we can get to work. We sit side by side at the wheels, throwing Mom's bread and butter. He does remarkably well. The first few mugs have bases that are a bit heavy, and he doesn't get the rims quite right. But as his hands become more familiar with the moisture and viscosity of Mom's stoneware, the pieces turn out more consistently. He doesn't seem to need much help, so I do my work in silence. As usual, the spinning wheel, the warm, muddy water and the familiar feel of producing pottery calm me down. There is an unfamiliar CD playing on the stereo, so I decide to offer him an olive branch and ask, "What are we listening to?"

"Seriously?" Sam replies.

"What? I'm supposed to know who this is?"

"I thought your roommate was a singer in a band."

"Yeah, so?"

"You live with a girl singer and you don't even recognize Marianne Faithfull? What, is your roommate some kind of Britney Spears wannabe?"

My serenity evaporates. This jackass needs to be put in his place. I stop my wheel. "Who the hell do you think you are? I ask you a simple question, and you turn it into some kind of personal attack on my roommate? On my musical taste? Let's get something straight. I am in charge here, and I deserve your respect. You have done little more than flip me shit since the moment we met." It feels really good to tell someone off, to be the boss again, so I run with it.

"You just don't get it, do you? You're just another set of hands. A bit of muscle. There are dozens of aspiring ceramic artists who are dying to get paid to work with a successful potter, and they don't need a refresher on how to throw a basic mug. So why don't you try a little harder to keep your clever comments to yourself? Try and be civil."

Sam doesn't cower or even spout apologies. Instead, he spits back with equal vehemence. "Civil? Is that what you're being?" He whistles with sarcasm. "Funny, if there are so many other perfect candidates out there, why do you suppose I got the job? Did you even think about that?" He doesn't give me a chance to reply. "I don't know what the hell is wrong with *you*, but I think your mom's great. She's talented and funny and a pleasure to spend time with. We get along just fine, and frankly, I don't think she's going to fire me because you're having a little hissy-fit power trip." He continues, "Why don't you just chill for a while? I don't need your uptight, clenched-ass superior attitude. I get it that you're in a weird place right now. You're losing your job and freaking out about your future and all. But can't you just give it a break while you're here?"

"You're giving me advice? You don't know anything about me!"

"Oh, please. You're a woman. That's all I need to know."

What arrogance. "That proves it! You're fucking clueless." I turn back to my wheel, ready to ignore this jerk. He's not worth my time.

He stops his own wheel, and I can feel his eyes drilling into me. His words almost bowl me over.

"Let's see. You're smart, but what's more important is that you've got a lot of common sense. You're a great chef, not just because you work damn hard, but because you can make quick decisions and are a born leader. You don't get out much because you work too many hours. But then, other than your roommates, you don't have many real friends. You're loyal, but bored, which is probably why you're doing this crazy office thing. You're stubborn and hotheaded; you get that from your father. Oh, yeah, you're also supposed to make the world's best walnut shortbread cookies. I'd like to try them someday."

I can't speak. I can hardly breathe. I stare, open-mouthed, at Sam for a second. He looks away, perhaps ashamed of his inappropriate, very personal comments. "Your mom's been worried about you. She talks."

My brain is spinning. I don't know anything about this asshole, and he has just given me a rundown of my entire life. I want to storm out, slam doors, but I am covered in wet clay. I leave my stool and pace for a while, waving my arms and trying to think of a comeback. There is nothing to say. I give up. I scrub my hands and arms raw as Sam tries to apologize.

"I'm sorry," he says. "That was maybe a little harsh. My life is complicated right now, too. I didn't mean . . ."

He stops talking when I return to the wheels. I look him dead in the eyes and flick all of the wet mug bodies he has produced off the table and onto the floor. As they hit the ground they make a very satisfying wet splash. I leave my mess at the wheel for him to clean up, and exit the studio. I'll admit I'm a little disappointed when I hear not cursing and threats of retaliation, but a big, booming belly laugh.

It's only eight-thirty, but I am utterly exhausted.

Chapter Ten

My hairdresser, Angie, can't stop laughing. She says the dye job is brilliant considering the circumstances and the mélange of ingredients. It's the cut that shocks her. It looks like someone attacked my head with a pair of kitchen shears. I keep quiet. She poured a few foul-smelling potions on my scalp, and now I'm a brassy strawberry blonde. I leave Angie's chair with a short, funky haircut and a couple of new products designed to keep it that way. It's a new look for me, but I like it. The short hair shows off my cheekbones, and the color brings out the copper and greens in my brown eyes. It's still pretty wild, but it looks intentional, and I think it suits my present mood.

I get my nails done, too. I have always had a fear that the nail professionals of the world will shriek in horror at the sight of my hands. My nails are flat, paper-thin and maintained daily by my teeth. For years, my hands have been elbow-deep in some gooey mess most of the time and then scrubbed to oblivion every day. Nails and nail polish seem like a blaring declaration of my liberation from the kitchen. Perhaps I am lightheaded from the fumes, but I sit and grin stupidly as the nail technician grinds, sands, glues and polishes. I leave with ten perfect, squared-off, pearly-pink fingernails. Twice I almost drive off the road because I can't stop admiring my wiggling fingers.

When I get home, I buzz around the house moving things from here to there for no reason. I stop myself after rearranging the couch pillows for the third time. I sit and take three long, deep breaths to slow down and focus. It's been a hell of a week. I deserve a break.

I call Mom and tell her I'm not going to make it into the studio this weekend, but that I will make up the time next week. Truth is, I just can't stand the idea of facing Sam. I acted like a baby last night, and in the end, it's Mom who will pay for my tantrum in less inventory. I decide to make a double batch of walnut shortbread cookies as amends.

Making the cookies leads to culinary inspiration. I end up spending the whole weekend in the kitchen. I fill the fridge and freezer with cookie dough, pastries and a bunch of soups and rich pasta sauces. If I can't dazzle Gaston with my office skills, I will have to cook my way back into his heart.

Cooking is different with nails. They keep distracting me. I feel the need to watch my hands as I use them. With new grace, I peel GROWN IN WASHINGTON labels from Johnnygold apples and unwrap the butter cubes for an apple cake. My pinkies rise with formal charm as I pour crème fraîche into quiche batter. I test the timbre of every surface by rapping mixing bowls, measuring cups and countertop with my new, strong talons. It takes me three times as long to get things done, but I feel glamorous. I should be wearing pearls and a frilly little apron like Mrs. Cleaver.

I am well rested and filled with determination when the alarm goes off on Monday morning. I manage to get to the bus stop without ruining my outfit, and arrive at the office twenty minutes early. I make a pot of fresh coffee in the lunchroom and set out the warm apple cake I tormented my fellow bus passengers with this morning. (I'm lucky to have made it to work alive.) I greet the staff with a smile. They don't seem to notice my new, improved haircut or nails. They see only the cake and tear into it like buzzards. I'm pleased when Gaston moans with delight after his first bite.

I slide into Desiree's chair, take a sip of bad office coffee and then, once again, the phone starts ringing and my day goes all to hell. Arrangements have been made for Elizabeth Branson to spend the morning training me. Elizabeth used to fill in for Desiree when she was an intern. These days she's buried in work, like the rest of the firm, but she has agreed to spend a few minutes working with me. She punches buttons, enters numbers and sends callers flying at cyber speeds. Elizabeth shows me how to recognize the order of calls, pick up a line, put calls on hold, enter the extension, buzz the intercom or page the recipient. She explains that when things get busy, you have to stack up callers and keep mental notes about who is going where. She warns that transferred callers are often cranky and need special attention. She writes down a list of frequently requested extensions, explains the speed-dial settings and gives me her own laminated sheet of the names, numbers, schedules, cell phone and pager numbers and e-mail addresses of everyone in the office. Elizabeth is a willing and patient teacher, even though I know she has no time to spare. Now *that* is professional.

She makes it look so easy. I take lots of notes, attach multicolored sticky flags to the buttons, arrange my cheat sheets and agree that I'm ready to go it alone. I do okay at first when the calls come in one at a time, but then the whole console lights up with bleeps and rings and multicolored lights, and my stupid fingernails bash into all the wrong buttons. I can't remember whether it's John M. or John S. who works on the PugetCo account, and my color-coded notes and sticky flags just confuse me more. It gets ugly.

I'm trying to track down the financial reporter from the *Seattle Times*, whom I just lost, when the phone rings again. I sputter out my harried greeting, "Good morning, Wheton-Lofton. How may I direct your call?"

"Hi! Is this Kate?" The voice on the other end is faint, but enthusiastic. She has perfect diction. It's *her*.

"This is Courtney. You know, Gaston's fiancée? I am just so thrilled to finally talk to you! Gaston has told me so much about you!"

Courtney's inflection is contagious, and I catch myself returning her chitchat in a similar singsong. "Hi, Courtney, aren't you just the *sweetest* thing? I've heard a few things about you, too!"

She makes a fuzzy-kittenish sound, like she's giving me a big hug over the phone. "Oooh, I think it is just so great that you and Gaston can be such good friends. But that's just like Gaston, isn't it? He's such a sweetie! And he says nothing but nice things about you. We'll probably end up as best friends! Wouldn't that be something?"

My smile feels glued on.

"I guess you're about the greatest chef in the whole world! Gaston is always talking about the fancy food you can make, stuff I can't even imagine, let alone pronounce. He's so much more sophisticated than me. His mother's from Paris, did you know that? Of course you do. What am I thinking?

"Anyways, you really should send me some recipes, or give me some lessons or something. I'm not much in the kitchen. Oh, I can make a few things like tuna hot dish, taco salad. Gaston seems to really like my Tater Tot casserole. He asks for it all the time."

I hold back a chortle. I know exactly what Gaston thinks of her mushroom soup–laced casseroles. If he *asks* for something made with Tater Tots, her other specialties must be horrendous. The phone continues to ring, but I ignore it. If the callers deal with the automated voice mail system, there's a better chance they will end up at their destination.

Courtney continues to talk. "Mostly he likes to go out. I swear, he spends so much money taking me to all of these fancy restaurants! You know how he is."

Well, actually I don't. When I wasn't working, Gaston and I ate something I whipped up at home or we went out for the dishes I craved.

"That's actually why I'm calling," she says. "It was a half-day at school today, so I thought I'd ask him *not* to make dinner reservations. I want to make him a home-cooked meal. I'm thinking about doing a meatloaf and au gratin potatoes. Hey, since I'm talking to you, maybe you can give me a few tips? I've already got a box of potatoes, so that's done. But do you have any favorite recipes for a really good meatloaf? Something that Gaston will just love?"

Her sweet, innocent voice disarms me, and I find myself answering her honestly, without menace or forethought. "Uh, well. I haven't made a meatloaf in a while. But we had a pretty good one for staff meal at the restaurant awhile back. It was kind of Greek—you know, ground lamb with lots of garlic and chopped fresh mint. It was great. You can serve it with warm pita and *tzatziki*."

"Ooooh! Lamb?" It seems impossible, but her voice gets even squeakier. "I don't think I could eat a lamb!"

Of course. Who did I think I was talking to? Lamb is cute, therefore icky. I lower the bar and suggest something generic. "You can always do it the old-fashioned way—use a combo of ground beef and pork sausage. Add some hard-cooked eggs and maybe top it with strips of smoky bacon for extra flavor."

"Hmmm. That sounds okay. But sausage can be so fatty. Do you suppose I could substitute something else? I read somewhere that Stovetop stuffing mix works in meatloaf. And Lipton's soup mix, what do you think about that? I think I'll use ground turkey instead of beef. I try not to buy bacon. I just love it, you know. And if I keep it in the house, I just end up eating it all up! Yum, yum, yum." She makes pretend gobbling sounds.

I stare at the phone in disbelief. This woman can't be for real. Have I really felt threatened by this lunatic? Gaston could never fall for someone who considers turkey meatloaf and instant potatoes a real home-cooked meal. I can no longer hold back my joy.

"Courtney, I can't tell you how great it's been talking to you. You've made my day."

"Ohhh. That is so nice of you to say! I've really loved talking to you, too. Finally! It's funny. I've tried to call Gaston a bunch of times, but I can't seem to get through."

"Hmmm. Well, we have had some trouble with the phone system." I smile diabolically. "Let me transfer you to Gaston right now! Bye-bye, Courtney!" This time I disconnect her on purpose.

Last week I would have laughed in the face of anyone who suggested that answering phones might be exhausting, but at the end of the day I am wiped out. My body is drained, my mind weary, and I haven't done a darn thing but sit and push buttons. I don't feel like going to the studio, but I know Mom needs my help. I can't put off facing Sam forever.

I nudge open the door and creep into the studio. The only person I see is my mother.

"Hey, sweetie. Look at you! I love your hair. It's very different, but it suits you."

"Thanks." I look around for signs of her evil assistant, lurking behind the kilns or slithering around the loading dock.

She watches me for a while then says, "Sam's not here. I kicked him out. He's worked twelve hours a day every day since I hired him. I think he's out playing ball with his roommates."

I am more relieved at his absence than I care to admit. I hold out the tin of cookies and say, "I might have been a little rude the other night, but I don't like him, Mom. I don't like him one bit."

Her smile is gone. She shakes her head in disappointment. "Yeah, I got that. I don't understand—I thought you two would really like each other and yet . . ."

"Did he say something? What did he say?" My memories of the other night have festered. I keep thinking about my hollow threats to have Sam fired and about all of the mugs I ruined.

Mom opens the tin of cookies and peeks inside. She looks at me with suspicion.

"Cookies, huh? Are these some kind of peace offering? An apology, maybe?"

"It depends. What did he say?"

"He said you're a great teacher. You gave him the materials he needed and then left him alone to make and correct his own mistakes. He watched what you were doing and then tried to duplicate your techniques. I'm impressed. His work is much better than I expected."

Mom walks me over to a rack and uncovers three dozen mugs resting on work boards next to the larger pieces I threw. Sam must have stayed late and finished up whatever he thought should be done, because the moisture content is the same as in the work I had completed. She touches a couple to test the tackiness of the clay. "A few of them are a little heavy. They're not as nice as yours, but they're no worse than what Larry produced at times. Some will take a little trimming, but they'll be fine." She replaces the plastic sheeting. "He said you had a little disagreement about the music. He seemed worried that he might have pissed you off, but I told him there was never any question. If you were mad, he would know it. I'm guessing by the cookies that there is a little more to the story." With an earnest, almost pleading look she says, "I hope you two can work it out. I like him. And let's face it, the kid knows clay."

"He seems to know an awful lot about my life, too." Mom is surprised, then embarrassed. I continue, "Do you suppose you could keep the details of my pretty messed-up personal life out of your conversation with complete strangers?"

"I'm sorry, honey. He's just so easy to talk to. I'll be more careful."

"I know you like him, and he seems to think you're just great, too. But you have to remember, I don't know anything about him, and he seems to know *everything* about me!"

She gets the message, and I let it go. It's nice working with Mom. We pull handles for the mugs and pitchers and pack up a couple of boxes of finished pieces for shipping. I talk about my new job and tell her about my conversation with Courtney.

"She is such a ditz! You wouldn't even believe it." I mimic Courtney's horror at the suggestion of eating lamb and her yum-yummy sounds when she spoke of bacon. Mom laughs. I go back to the loading dock to empty a trashcan into the Dumpster and pass Larry's old storage room. A shiny new padlock bolts the freshly painted door.

"What's in here?" I gesture with my elbow.

Mom looks up. "That's Sam's studio."

"He keeps it locked? What, he thinks you're going to steal his ideas?"

"Oh, no, nothing like that. He's just a little spooky about his own work. He thinks if people see what he's doing, they're going to mess him up or interfere with his vision. I think it's a good idea. He's got some pretty expensive equipment in there."

"What kind of equipment?"

She closes her mouth, tightly shut.

"Mom! You told him everything about *me!*"

"Yes. And I'm sorry about that. But you're my daughter. It's a mother's right to talk about her children." I object, but she shushes me.

"I apologized. And I promised to be more careful. But I won't tell you about Sam's work. This may be his job, but that's his art. If he wants to share it with you, he can. I'm not about to mess around with someone's artistic juju. If he wants it to be a secret, I'll keep his secret."

No amount of pleading or coercion works. Mom's mouth is sealed as tight as the studio door. That doesn't stop me from rattling the lock and peeking through the cracks every time I walk by.

I'm starving by the time we're done for the night. On my way home I stop at the Ballard Market and pick up some shrimp, spinach and baby bok choy. I stir-fry it all up with plenty of spicy XO sauce, and with each bite, feel the vitamins rushing to revitalize my tired blood. As I am washing up, the phone rings. I answer, "Wheton-Lofton, how can I . . ." I catch myself before finishing the automatic greeting. "Uh. Hello?"

"Kate? Is that you?" It's Nancy. I go cold at the sound of her voice.

Her voice is quiet and subdued. I remain silent, and she starts to cry. "God, I am so sorry about what happened last week. Oh, Christ, has it only been a week? I'm screwed. I was such an idiot! I can't believe I fired you. Jesus, you were the only thing holding this place together. I understand that now."

I can't believe my ears.

"The kitchen crew hates me. Craig walked out tonight, after calling me a useless motherfucking food princess." She sobs a bit more and then gulps air. "And I *am*! I *am* a food princess! I've been spending so much time running around the country promoting the restaurant that I can't even get the ordering right anymore. I don't know the menu well enough to get the plates timed right. The whole place is falling to pieces."

It is as though a symphony of angels is singing in my ears. Her words are music. I might be a chef, but that doesn't automatically make me a loser. I was a valuable, talented lead at a premier restaurant. Even more important, I was *right*! In my heart I am screaming with joy, but somehow I manage to make my new, practiced phone voice sound sympathetic. "Oh, it can't be that bad, Nancy. Surely you just had a tough weekend." Tee-hee-hee.

"It was a complete nightmare. We had to eighty-six half the items from the menu and then comp desserts for practically every table because things took so long. There is nothing left in the walk-in or the stations. I lost my fastest sauté cook. I'm totally exhausted, and it's only Monday! You've got to help me out, Kate!"

Frankly, I am shocked to hear that things went so bad so fast. My first instinct is to rush to her side. The restaurant means a lot to me. I devoted most of my time and energy to its success over the last four years. I know the moods of the crew, the quirky equipment and every last nuance of the menu.

"You've got to come back." Nancy's sobbing subsides, and her bossy tone returns. "I admit I made a mistake. I shouldn't have lost my temper like that. Let's just move on. The important thing is that we pull it all together before the press finds out. I can spin a few bad nights, but if this lasts much longer, it might damage my reputation."

"I can't, Nancy."

She is perturbed. "I said I was sorry. I was *wrong*, all right? I'm back on the line cooking and it feels right. But I can't do everything. I need you to back me up."

"I told you so" is on the tip of my tongue, but I keep quiet.

"Do you have any idea how hard it was for me to make this call? Oh, I get it. It's the money. Well, I can't promise anything, but I'll try to get you a raise. Things are pretty tight, but I'll do what I can."

"It's not the money. I just can't come back. I already have another job."

"Damn it! Did Josef finally snag you? Or was it Tom? I swear they've been sniffing around Sound Bistro for years trying to steal you."

Two of the top chefs in town were interested in hiring me? This is the first I've ever heard of it.

"No. I'm not cooking anywhere. I took a job downtown. I'm working for a finance company."

"Oh! Well, that's different." She blows out a sigh of relief. "That'll be easy to get out of. Just tell them you made a mistake and you're taking your old job back. It happens all the time. So, do you suppose you could be here by ten tomorrow?"

"No, Nancy. I'll be at work."

"Goddamn it, Kate! I get it, all right! I was a bitch. I embarrassed you in front of the staff. I got a little hot under the collar and spoke too soon. But now *you're* being a bitch! Whatever happened to loyalty? To the concept of working as a team? I can't believe you're thinking of *yourself* at a time like this! What the hell are you doing working for a financial company anyway? You belong in the kitchen. Are you just trying to punish me?"

I'm not sure if it is a testament to my devotion to that restaurant or the fact that I am a softhearted sap that I even considered going in and helping her. I lose my sense of charity when she starts screeching and accusing me of trying to ruin her.

"I've got to catch an early bus tomorrow, so I'd better hit the sack. Good night, Nancy." I finally get to use one of my new, professional skills. With an artful flick of the wrist, I hang up on my old boss.

Chapter Eleven

I bring cardamom scones with grapefruit marmalade to the office for breakfast and stash a pot of smoked chicken and sweet potato chowder in the fridge. In addition to enticing Gaston, the food is a peace offering to the office. I have a suspicion these folks are getting tired of lost calls and irate clients.

The work doesn't get easier. In addition to what I assume is a freakishly high call volume, I also have to deal with a bunch of fancy-pants clients who keep dropping by for scheduled meetings. It's a bitch. I am thrilled when the lunch hour arrives. I go to the back room and heat up two paper bowls of soup in the microwave, one for me and one for Gaston.

Elizabeth, my patient trainer from yesterday, walks into the kitchen just as the soup is warm. "That smells good. Did you bring it from home?" she asks, breathing in the savory aromas.

"Uh, yeah. There's more in the fridge." I look down at the two bowls of soup in my hand. "Why don't you take this one? I'll heat up more."

She eagerly accepts, as do the next six people drawn to the kitchen by the sounds of activity in the break room and the luring aromas of home cooking. I spend most of my lunch hour heating and distributing bowls of soup to a hungry and thankful crowd. It feels good to be doing something helpful for these busy people. Near the end of the hour, Gaston wanders into the break room with Marsha Lofton. They must have been in a meeting.

"What's cookin', good lookin'?" sings Gaston. "It smells great in here."

"You're just in time. I'm almost out of soup. Who knew how desperate this crowd was for a little home cooking?"

"No kidding?" asks Marsha.

"They were like a pack of starving wolves. But I managed to set some aside just for you."

I fill their bowls extra-full. I don't need to eat. I spy some crackers in the cupboard. I'll snack on those at my desk later on. Gaston and Marsha make contented sounds as they savor their lunch. Now seems like a good time to bring up Courtney and her cooking.

"How was dinner last night? Did Courtney make meatloaf?"

Gaston winces. "Yeah. I guess you could call it meatloaf. I think it was more bread and salt than anything else." I grin with pleasure. "I guess that explains why I've been so thirsty today."

Marsha finishes her lunch. I catch her eyeing the bottom of the bowl, perhaps considering a quick lick, but she pushes it away and says, "So, Courtney's not much of a cook, huh? That must be tough, especially after growing accustomed to Kate's great food." Hooray for Marsha. I will make her more soup soon to reward her excellent timing and choice of topics.

Gaston nods. "I'd be lying if I said I didn't miss Kate's cooking." He looks over at me with those loving brown eyes. My heart beats in double time. "But then again, I didn't get it all that much. I had to go to Sound Bistro if I wanted more than Sunday brunch or a late-night dinner. In fact, I think Courtney cooks for me more than you ever did, Kate. The food isn't great. Who am I kidding? It's terrible. But she loves to set the table and sit down for a family style dinner. It's just so sweet." He spoons up the last of his soup and sighs. "She'll get better. God, I *hope* she gets better." I grit my teeth and silently pray for Courtney's milk to sour and her dry goods to get weevils.

I smile. "Well, even *she* should be able to toss together a good soup now and then. That's easy enough." I don't bother to mention that their lunch required two trips to the supermarket, a triple-strained, homemade stock and dirtying every pan I own. I pick up their bowls, grab a handful of crackers and say, "I'd better get back to work!" I return to the dreaded telephone.

At two, Marsha Loften stops by my desk with some co-workers and graciously invites me to join them for coffee. I leap at the offer. Not only am I thrilled to be leaving the phones, this will be my first official coffee break! I will sit with my co-workers, sip a hot beverage and get paid for it! I manage to curb my enthusiasm and not look too much like a raving maniac as I gather up my mug and handbag. I figure we are headed back to the break room to sip at the Boyd's that has been simmering since early this morning, but it seems they have other plans. We take the elevator down to a boutique roaster in the lobby, and people start pulling out their frequent-buyer cards.

Marsha turns to me and says, "My treat today. What'll ya have?"

"Black is fine for me," I answer.

Marsha shakes her head in obvious disappointment. "No, no, no, Kate. We don't come here for *coffee*. We come here for . . . COFFEE." She gestures boldly with her hands. As a food professional, I know all about the differences between Sumatran and Colombian, Kenyan and Costa Rican. Marsha knows my background. Is she suggesting that I might not be able to order my own espresso?

She waves me away. "Don't worry, I'll take care of it."

The team orders half a dozen elaborate drinks. Marsha hands me a huge paper cup that looks more like an ice cream sundae than a cup of coffee. It's brimming with whipped cream, chocolate shavings, squiggles of caramel sauce and what looks like toasted almond flakes.

"What's this?"

She licks her lips. "A Mars latte. It's my present favorite. It's a caramel mocha with a splash of toasted almond syrup." She nudges me and whispers, "After a couple of these, they'll start popping up in your sexual fantasies."

I laugh with her and start to head back upstairs, but Marsha touches my arm to hold me back. "How about we have a little chat?" She maneuvers me to a table in the building's lobby, tucked in a corner behind a pillar and a ficus tree. She pulls out a seat and gestures for me to sit. I sit. I swirl and ponder my drink. It is ridiculous but delicious. Marsha is right, this isn't just coffee. I look up from my beverage and am about to say something when my breath leaves me. There, standing in front of the security desk, wearing a crisp, policelike uniform, is perhaps the most beautiful man I have ever laid eyes on.

Marsha whispers to me, "That's Victor."

He is tall, with thick, dark, wavy hair, broad shoulders and a perfectly tapered torso. I gasp a little, then whisper back, "He's beeeeautiful!"

Marsha stirs her coffee. "Of course, I don't condone any kind of behavior that might treat workers in this building as sex objects or discriminate according to appearance. That would be very unprofessional. I merely join my co-workers here for an afternoon cup of espresso to promote teambuilding and camaraderie. I have a decided interest in the security of this building, that's all." Marsha licks whipped cream from her tiny straw and fills me in on the details. "He used to work the swing shift, but got transferred to days when old Frank retired. He's not wearing a ring, and I've sent Dylan, from across the hall, to sniff out whether he lives somewhere over the rainbow. So far so good."

"Marsha!" I pretend to be shocked. Gaston always made Marsha sound like a hard-ass, but she's just a brilliant, organized woman who takes her job very seriously. I am quickly becoming one of her biggest fans.

"Not that *I'm* interested, of course. I couldn't ask for a better husband than Don. He's a mighty fine cook, too, did I ever mention that?"

I shake my head. We take a few sips of our drinks and admire the view. Then she says, "Kate, I'm afraid this receptionist situation isn't working out. A temp who is familiar with our multiline, computerized system will be starting tomorrow."

I don't get what she means at first. I'm relieved that I'll have some help with the phones.

She pats my hand, tilts her head and smiles. "I'm so glad you're not taking this personally, hon. You know I think you're great, but let's face it, phones just aren't your thing. It's my fault, really. Desiree makes the job look so damn easy. The way she gabs to her friends and family all the time, I figured just about anyone could do it. Turns out, when I called the agency, they say there aren't many temps who are fully trained in this kind of system. Luckily, they have someone available to replace you."

"Replace me?" Did I hear her right? My eyes well up and my chin quavers. So much for handling it well. "You're firing me?" I manage to croak the words past the lump in my throat. Fired? Again? It can't be possible. How will I win Gaston back? I'm on the verge of hyperventilating when Marsha explains.

"Goodness no, Kate. I'm not *firing* you, exactly. I'm hoping you might be interested in a different position, one better suited to your special talents. I want you to cook."

I am nanoseconds from exploding into heaving sobs. I gulp and clear my throat a few times. I take a sip of my ridiculous sundae/coffee drink. I can't trust my voice yet, so I just look at Marsha for more information. She manages to explain before I freak out.

"It hit me earlier today, after you told me about the crew lapping up that fabulous soup. They've been working so hard and things are going to get worse instead of better. We've got some big, big projects to finish between now and Christmas. I've been racking my brain trying to figure out a way to help motivate them, to keep them working smart, not just hard. And then it dawned on me—I can feed them. Nutritious meals are about the first thing to go when my schedule gets crazy. And judging by the sheer quantity of paper soda cups and Subway sandwich wrappers scattered on desks around here, I'm not alone.

"When I was studying at the London School of Economics, I did an internship at a firm that served proper lunches every day in the corporate dining room. Instead of wasting their time going out for a decent restaurant meal, executives were served poached salmon fillets and asparagus tips in their own office dining room. It was worth the money to keep people focused, and the chef was so good that clients begged to have lunch in-house. I want to do something like that."

I'm listening, but not ready to speak yet. She continues.

"I'm hoping, since you're in kind of a transitional period right now, that I might persuade you to do some private chef work for a while. I'm thinking a nice soup, like you shared today, with maybe a salad. Say, three times a week? I know we can't pull off the whole dining room thing. And unless you're some kind of a whiz with a coffee maker and microwave, you'll have to do the cooking at home." I am stunned. I think Marsha is salivating. She swallows and continues the negotiations.

"I can't expect you to work your wonders on the salary we agreed upon earlier. You're a professional, after all." A guffaw almost escapes from my lips, but I manage to restrain myself. "How about if we estimate a per person cost, bump up the hourly wage and round it off to a set amount each week? It's only temporary. Let's say until Christmas, okay? I can probably finagle a parking spot for you, but that's it for benefits." Marsha does some figuring in her head and spits out a number that makes my jaw drop. She looks over at me. "Is that going to be enough?"

I find my voice. "Maybe. I'll have to crunch the numbers." I read in one of Gaston's books that you should never jump at the first offer. I'm trying to play it cool and not leap up and dance around the room in elation.

Marsha taps a pencil on the table. "Now, there's another little thing I could use your help with. I hope you don't think this sort of thing is beneath you. Of course, you can say no—don't think that you're obligated or anything. It's just that I've been a little worried about my dad. My mother died last year, and I don't think he's eating very well anymore. I was wondering, if I tag a few more bucks onto that weekly check, will you do a "meals on wheels" kind of thing for my dad? He's not eating enough vegetables, and I want someone to fill his fridge now and then with something other than eggs and lunch meat. I've been meaning to do it, but I just can't seem to find the time."

Right now, I'd do anything for Marsha Lofton. She just handed me a new, perfect life. She's actually going to *pay* me to cook for *Gaston*. She is my hero. I will decorate a special seat at our wedding with silk ribbons and cabbage roses, just for her. I hum and look up at the ceiling for a minute as if I'm considering things, then accept her offer.

Chapter Twelve

After my meeting with Marsha, I phone Gaston's mother to share the good news. I duck down in the office chair and whisper my words into the desk drawers, to be discreet.

"You won't believe it, Adele! Gaston's boss just offered me a job *cooking* for the office. Instead of answering these stupid phones, I'm going to be here in pretty clothes three days a week making his favorite dishes. He will be mine in no time. Isn't that great?"

Adele doesn't share my elation. "It's good, Kate, but it isn't enough. Yes, it is fine that you will feed him and be near him, but he will still be spending his nights in another woman's arms. You think you will break up this engagement by making his life comfortable? Gaston likes an easy life. You must know that to fill his belly and be there as his friend during the day only to send him home to this Courtney woman is to seal your fate. Gaston is a dear, but the boy needs sand in his shorts to make him move out of the sun."

"And that's me? I'm the sand?"

"Yes, darling. You must start an irritation, a level of discomfort that makes him aware of his potential to burn, and then become his savior. You must be both the sand and the sunscreen."

Of course, Adele is right. I need to become the ultimate beach kit, not just the picnic lunch. "So, what do I do?"

Adele takes a long time before she answers, and I'm not too keen on what she finally says. "My dear Kate. You cannot pretend that you are too innocent to fix this. You know you are like a daughter to me, and that is because you are not always an angel. I know there is fire and a cunning mind behind those warm eyes. You will find a way. Tell him again and again that you were a fool to let him go. Remind him that you are the one his mother loves. Don't let pride hold you back. Don't be afraid to cry or beg. Don't be afraid to tell him how miserable your life has become without him."

Adele is pushing it. I've had a difficult week, but I'm not a quivering mess. In fact, I'm feeling pretty good about life today. I don't think groveling at Gaston's feet dripping crocodile tears is the way to spiff up my future. I should be able to convince Gaston that we should be together without humiliating myself. I am gracious and compliment Adele on her wisdom before I say good-bye.

After disconnecting, I pick through Adele's rock pile of advice for hidden gems. One thing I'm sure she's right about: If I concentrate exclusively on feeding him, Gaston will have the best of both worlds and settle into a new level of comfort with Courtney. I must become sand.

Marsha urged me to go home early and leave the phones to voice mail. She is just so generous. I collect my things, but before I leave, I stop by to talk to Gaston. I knock on his open office door.

"Gotta minute?" I ask. His nose is almost pressed against his computer screen. He looks up and blinks a few times. His eyes take a moment to focus.

"I met with Marsha today," I say.

Gaston's pained expression tells me that he is aware of the office buzz. Folks are less than pleased with my performance at the front desk.

"No, it's okay. We've worked out a new deal. I probably shouldn't tell you; she might want to announce it herself. She's hired me to cook for you guys for a while. I start on Friday." I explain that my cooking is meant to be a motivational perk for his team. Gaston is thrilled.

"Your food? Three times a week? Are you kidding?" He's like an excited puppy. If he could wag his tail, he would.

"And breakfast treats when I have the time." That isn't part of the deal; I just throw that in on a whim.

"That is so awesome!"

I'm not clear if he is most pleased with my career move or my proximity, or if he's just eager for some decent lunches. Now seems like a good time for me to practice being "proactive" and to "move it forward," like his bossy books suggest.

"Maybe we can get together after work and talk about some menu ideas? You know the people around here and my food. You can help me out."

"That sounds good! Oh, wait. I can't tonight. I promised Courtney we would go to the Olive Garden." I grimace. He doesn't notice. "Why don't you join us? That would be great! I want you two to meet, and to-night will be perfect. You can help us with the wedding plans."

My grimace deepens. Gaston assumes it is the restaurant. "Oh, right. You wouldn't be caught dead in a chain restaurant. I guess we'll have to do it another night: Courtney has her heart set on those breadsticks."

I can't let this chance slip through my fingers. I can do this. "The Olive Garden sounds delightful. I've never been there. It'll be something new for me."

He's stunned. "Okay then, we're on! Courtney likes to eat early, so how about if we meet at 5:30?"

After the bus ride home, I have just enough time to change clothes, freshen my makeup and fix my hair before it's time to go. I question my sanity as I pull into Seattle's god-awful northbound traffic. I'm doing this so I can eat dinner at the mall? I'm a few minutes late. I pray they have found a table way in the back where no one can see me. No such luck. Gaston and Courtney are seated by the front window. They wave.

She looks nothing like I have imagined. I pictured her as a petite blonde with high-maintenance hair, a button nose and dimples, but Courtney is tall and lithe. Her dark brown hair is cut short and bounces with the kind of body and shine I have always yearned for. Her dark eyes are framed with natural lashes so long they might have come off a camel. Her skin is pale and clear except for a few freckles dotting her cheeks and nose. Only her clothing betrays her tendency toward sweetness. She is wearing a chocolately corduroy skirt, a tan turtleneck and a home-sewn vest, appliquéd with autumn leaves.

They both rise to meet me. The moment we are introduced, I start babbling incessantly. Too much coffee, no doubt. "Courtney! How wonderful to finally meet you. You're tall! And . . . uh. I guess since Gaston has all those fantasies about Pamela Anderson, I kind of figured you might be a short, busty blonde. Oof." Gaston elbows me in the ribs.

"Nope—not me," replies Courtney, in that same perky, little girl voice. "I'm just a Montana ranch girl." She and Gaston sit almost on top of each other. They kiss and touch and whisper to each other as if they have been separated for weeks, not hours.

"Soooo," I sing. "You met at one of Harry's boat parties, right?" I lean halfway across the table and feign interest. I nod so much I must look like a bobble-head doll. In between kisses, Gaston explains the magic that brought them together. "Harry's new girlfriend has one of those scrap-booking stores, and Courtney is always going in there for her school projects. The two of them became friends and . . ."

I slap Gaston on the arm and interrupt. "You remember that one party on Kevin's boat last year? Matt brought all of those hot sauces, and you were both determined to try every single one. And you were drinking those pepper vodka shots, too. Remember? Ohmigod! Before the coals were even hot on the barbecue, you had your clothes off and were demanding that someone hose you down, you were on fire. Then you did the dirty towel dance on the top deck." I try to make my laughter sound as realistic as possible.

"You guys did so much puking over the rails that night, Anthony said you might raise the water level and cause climate changes." I take a quick peek at Courtney. She seems unfazed, so I ramp it up a notch. "Wasn't that one of the times you proposed? I remember hauling you up the stairs to your apartment while you shouted to the whole world that Kate Linden was your one true love, the only woman you could ever be with." I flash a confident smile to Courtney, and then try to look concerned. "I hope he wasn't drinking when he proposed to you. When Gaston has a few, he'll get down on one knee and proclaim his undying love for the valet."

Gaston gives me a stony look, but Courtney's pleasant smile remains. She tilts her head and says, "I seem to remember having a glass of wine, but it wasn't . . ."

It's Gaston's turn to interrupt. "I was drunk all right, but not from alcohol. I was drunk with love the moment I laid eyes on her." Courtney giggles, and they rub noses. I manage to control my gag reflex and look around for our waiter.

We peruse the slick menus. Gaston inspects a table tent of feature items.

"Hmmm. The lasagna special sounds good," says Gaston.

"Ooh." Courtney purses her lips, shakes her head and makes a disapproving clicking sound. "I'm sure it is delicious, but are you sure that's what you want? It looks like there's a lot of cheese and maybe something creamy in that picture. That's not very good for you. Maybe you should think about something a little lower in saturated fat? They say tomato sauce is really good for the heart. I don't want to tell you what to order, but I do want my Pooh Bear to be around for a long, long, long time."

Good grief! I am astounded when Gaston puts down his menu and says, "Why don't you order for me, Pumpkin? I'll have whatever you want me to have."

After we order, they chirp and coo a bit more, and I ponder what lovebirds might taste like, maybe baked with shallots and rosemary. When

Gaston nibbles on Courtney's fingers, I get a glimpse of her engagement ring. The flash from the stones hits me like lightning. How dare this woman wear Gaston's ring? My jaw feels locked tight, my lungs constricted, but I manage a friendly tone as I say, "Oh! Your ring. Let me see."

Courtney holds out her hand with pride. My voice seems odd. I hear myself bark, "This isn't the same one you bought me, is it Gaston? What did you do, get it resized? Heh, heh." I take Courtney's hand, which miraculously is still hanging in the air. I pull it close, as if I'm having trouble seeing the stones. "Oh, no. This is different. Mine had that one big stone and yours has all these little tiny ones. It's lovely. It suits you."

Good Lord! I'm not just sand, I'm an infestation of beach lice. I'm a rogue wave littered with medical waste. I better tone it down or Gaston will have me thrown out.

For a split second, Courtney's eyes lose their sparkle. They hold mine and a chill shoots down my spine. She says nothing until she pulls back her hand and admires her ring. Her face is alive again. "It's perfect. Absolutely perfect."

I nod and murmur, "Yeah, I hope you don't get too much Play-Doh in it. I'm sure that stuff can dull the shine." She is deaf to my words. That appliqué vest of hers must have a Kevlar lining. Or maybe she's just dim.

Our food arrives. While I'm prepared to hate everything, I'm quite content with the soft, hearty food. (Not that I'm willing to admit that to Gaston or Courtney. When they ask me how my pasta is, I just shrug and say something dreamy and knowledgeable about real San Marzano tomatoes and the boutique olive oils of Tuscany.)

"Speaking of food, we were hoping you might give us some ideas for our wedding," says Courtney, wiggling in her seat with excitement.

"Of course I will! Gaston and I have such a history together, it would be horrible if I didn't help out." I gasp, as if struck with a brilliant idea. "How about if I tell you some of the ideas Gaston had for *our* wedding. That should make things easy. And, of course, we can't forget to include Adele. She must be so excited. She's probably calling and drilling you every day about your plans, isn't she, Courtney?"

"Adele?" Courtney asks.

Gaston squirms and then explains, "My mother." At last I think I've found a chink in their armor.

Courtney squeals. "Oh, of course! *Adele Lambert!* I keep telling Mr. Silly here that I want to meet his parents. Gaston always has us running off somewhere, so we've never even had a chance to chat on the phone."

"Oh, *really?*" I pretend that this is new information, and focus an inquisitive look at Gaston. He tries to change the subject.

"How about dessert? Anyone want coffee?"

"That's so surprising to me. As a rule, Mr. Silly won't blow his nose without calling his mom first."

"C'mon, Kate. That's not true."

I raise my eyebrows at him. It *was* pretty much true. At least before he met Courtney. I wonder what it is about her that has given him this new independence. He hasn't even mentioned Adele's silent treatment or displeasure with the engagement. He seems to have grown a backbone overnight. I look over at Courtney and say my first uncontrived sentence of the night. "Adele's a piece of work. You might be better off making your wedding plans without her." Courtney is about to object, but Gaston rubs her shoulder and adds an almost imperceptible nod.

The pasta hits me like a tranquilizer bullet. I need to leave. "It's been a long day. I'm beat. How about if we talk about the wedding plans another time, huh?" I push myself out of the booth. Courtney jumps up and gives me a sorority girl hug: butt out, kissy neck bob, tiny shoulder squeeze and another squeal. It's just like the ones Iris and I perform as a joke.

"Kate, it's been so incredible to finally meet you. We will definitely get together again, *soon*. You know my Gassy better than almost anybody. I can't wait to pick your brain for wedding ideas." My lips spread over my teeth, but it doesn't quite feel like a smile. My head starts to throb.

Back in the sanctuary of my car, I slump against the wheel. It's barely seven. I am tempted to go home and crawl into my dark bedroom, but I know I will just lie there going over and over the day's conversations. I consider heading to Iris's bar and getting hammered, but in truth, I threaten to get drunk way more often than I actually do it. Adding a hangover to my heartbreak sounds heinous. I pass up the exit to Ballard and head toward Mom's studio. I'll meditate over clay.

Mom's van is gone, but the studio lights are on and the music is cranked. Sam must be here. I think about leaving; I'm not in the mood for another fight. I'll be nice, I tell myself. It shouldn't be too hard. I've been so nasty and sharp-tongued tonight, I have no poison left. I trudge into the studio. Sam is working at the shipping table, packing orders. He doesn't hear me arrive. I watch him for a minute, remembering his laughter and pleasant demeanor the first time we met. I recall his fine, bare form at the sink and feel flushed. I can be nice. I don't have quite such a chip on my shoulder tonight, and dredging up our past differences seems juvenile.

I drop my bag on Mom's desk. It startles Sam. I shoot him a sideways smile and a lame wave. I shout so he can hear me over the music. "I just thought I'd get a little production work done. Zone out, you know? Don't mind me."

He acknowledges me with a nod. I sit in Mom's chair and stare at nothing for awhile. I think about Courtney and Gaston. She is so different from me. How can they be so attracted to each other? She must be thinking the same thing right now. She's probably wondering if Gaston really asked that insensitive loudmouth to be his bride. I look for similarities in our personalities but come up with nothing. Finally, I battle my inertia and get up to sift through Mom's work clothes, looking for something to cover my own.

The CD ends, and Sam goes to the stereo. He's looking at me funny. His brow is furrowed. He's sending me a weird vibe. I swear under my breath. I must have put on a work shirt that is now used exclusively for glazing. Or maybe, by sitting at Mom's desk for five minutes, I disturbed a new filing system. I sigh in irritation and ask, "What?" I'm ready for one of his sarcastic comments, so his kind words surprise me.

"You okay? You look kind of down." Sam's face shows honest concern. He must be a terrible liar; his eyes are too expressive. They shine when he laughs and when he talks with my mother, flash with ice when he is angry, go blank when he dismisses me as a waste of his time. Right now, they are intensely focused. It is as if they can drill through my flesh into my very soul. It is like he's performing a medical procedure, a scan for potential emotional cancer. I feel naked and vulnerable. He recognizes my discomfort, looks away and changes the subject. "I just made some Mexican hot chocolate. You want a cup?"

I nod. I want a cup of hot chocolate more than anything in the whole world. He fusses by the microwave for awhile and brings me a mug of the cinnamon- and almond-laced cocoa. One sip and the world seems like a gentler place. Instead of returning to his work, he hops up onto a worktable near me and takes a drink from his own mug.

"You're here late. Are you working on your own stuff?" I ask.

"Not today. I can't do much on my own until another delivery gets here. I'm working late because I took the afternoon off and went to the beach with the boys. I thought I'd come in tonight and finish up the day by loading the kiln and finishing up some packaging."

I cock my head. "The boys?"

"Yeah. Ziggy, Jake, Scoop and Micky. You know, the animals I live with. My roommates."

I seem to remember Mom mentioning something about Sam's room-mates, but I don't remember much. "How'd you hook up with these guys?" I ask. "Did you live in Seattle before?"

"How did I find my place? My sister lives here. She works with the guy who had my room before me. He just got married, so the room opened up. It seemed pretty perfect for me right now. Sure, it's kind of crazy sometimes, but I don't mind."

I think about Iris and Marissa. "Yeah, I know all about roommates. I don't know what I'd do without Iris. She's nuts, but she's my best friend."

"Ziggy's turning out to be like that. The moment we met, we just had this bond, you know? He's a nut. He's a social disaster, but I just love him."

That's nice to hear. I've eavesdropped on the occasional drunken "I love ya, man" slurred from one late-night tavern buddy to another, but it's rare to hear such honest affection between male friends.

"So Ziggy's kind of a wild man, huh?"

"Nah, he's mellow, unless there's a pizza around. He's just huge and he's got a couple of looks that'll scare the shit out of strangers. Between you and me, the only thing you have to be afraid of with Ziggy is his gas. Man, when he farts, he can clear a room, and fast!"

I laugh. "Doesn't sound like the first guy I'd choose to share a desert island with."

"The Zigster's awesome."

I feel more comfortable with Sam now that he fits the role I first at-tributed to him: a sun-loving party boy. For some reason it's much easier to be around him when I can just write him off as another goofy assis-tant. I listen attentively as he describes more members of his household. His buddies sound like a bunch of hyperactive frat boys. But who am I to judge? My house isn't a *Better Homes and Gardens* showcase.

"Cy's a control freak. He's been there the longest. I guess that makes him the boss. I hear he's had more than his share of fights. No doubt: He's a scrappy little bugger. But I figured him out pretty quick. Give him a little weed and turn on some nature shows, and he'll just melt into the couch.

"The only one I'm having trouble with is Dieter. He's new. His girl just left for Germany, so he's bored and unbelievably *loud*. I can't under-stand half of what he says, and I can't shut him up. I'm tempted to sic Cy on him. He's getting on my nerves."

"Maybe we should hook Dieter up with Adrienne, my freak hair-dresser. It seems like a match made in heaven."

Sam agrees. "That's a brilliant idea. Get me her number, will ya?"

It sounds as if there is always a group just hanging out at his place, either trying to bum a ride to the beach or looking for a pickup game of soccer or Frisbee in the park. Sam's buddies seem to me like your typical twentysomething underachievers. I have no interest in meeting any of them, but Sam is fond of the whole crew.

My cocoa is long gone, and Sam's talk has been a soothing tonic after my abrasive dinner with Gaston and Courtney. I could sit here all night and listen to stories of his fun, friend-filled life. I'm almost disappointed when he stretches his neck and shoulders, looking tired.

"Why don't you go home, Sam? I can finish up here."

"No, that's okay. I got the shipping done, but I can help you throw for a while." His offer is tempting. He's been good company. But he's had a long day and must be worn out.

"Naw, I'm good. I don't need any help." After he leaves, I load up the CD player with a few of his discs and spend a couple of hours challenging my potting skills. I try to make the most perfect pieces I can in as few movements as possible, then I fool around with some new container shapes and lid knobs.

My brain feels scrubbed clean by the time I lock up. I have spun out my worries, and I'm eager for the new challenges of tomorrow.

Chapter Thirteen

Stacks of cookbooks and the current issues of *FoodArts*, *Saveur* and *Gourmet* surround me at the kitchen table. I am armed with a pen, a pad of paper and unbridled culinary inspiration. What shall I cook first? I have a world of recipes, almost unlimited access to ingredients, a sweet budget and a half-starved audience. If I had some decent professional equipment, I'd be in chef's paradise.

The only downside to the plan is the limited schedule. I tried to convince Marsha that I could cook five days a week, but she felt that was spoiling her team. She did agree to let me start right away, but still, I have only one meal to prepare this week. It's Wednesday morning, and my first performance isn't until Friday's lunch. That's more prep time than even I can kill. It doesn't help that I still have a fridge and freezer full of the stuff I made last weekend. I have decided to devote the day to creating the perfect soup and salad menus to woo Gaston. Oh, yeah. And the twenty-three other people who work at his office.

I call Marsha. "So, what are my parameters for these lunches? Do you have any employees with allergies or restrictive diets who I need to consider? Are there picky eaters? Any meats or ingredients I should avoid?"

She is definitive in her reply. "Hell, no! Don't you worry about that one bit. The minute I survey my team and ask them what their likes and dislikes are, you'll have twenty-four different meals to cook. I just want a pot of soup and a salad—good food made with good ingredients. If someone doesn't see what they like, they can go out and get something else."

Marsha comes through for me again. That's just what I wanted to hear. "How about you? Do you have any favorites?"

"Darling, I like it all. I didn't get this big eating birdseed. I never had a bad meal at Sound Bistro. I'm sure if you make it, I'll like it."

"What about your father? What should I make for him?"

"Why don't you call him and ask? Better yet, let me call him right now and set up a meeting. You two should get together. He's a great guy."

Marsha's directions lead me to a modest house in the Ravenna neighborhood. The door is opened by a wiry old guy with reading glasses balanced on the tip of his nose.

"Mr. Wright? I'm Kate Linden." I know Marsha's dad is in his midseventies, but he looks younger. He's wearing the standard Northwest uniform of blue jeans and a flannel shirt, but instead of hiking boots, he's got on comfy moccasins. His face is weathered and wrinkled in that handsome, rugged manner that makes some women want to just suck on a Botox syringe and die with envy. I can tell the moment I see him that he has an original REI co-op card tucked in his wallet. He's got the look of someone who has shopped at Seattle's mecca for outdoor gear since day one.

He leads me into the living room. The walls are decorated with photographs: views from various mountaintops, glorious island sunsets, deep river canyons. An oak display case is filled with rocks. Marsha explained earlier that her dad is a geologist, a professor emeritus at the university. His friends call him Skip, but, in addition to being Marsha Lofton's father, he is a formidable man, and I can't bring myself to address him with such a familiar nickname. I'll settle for Mr. Wright.

He is formal, but still warm. He offers me beverages and snacks. I refuse. We make a little small talk about the photographs, then sit down. I pull out a notebook and pen. I have some questions written down.

"So, as you know, your daughter has hired me to cook for you. I thought maybe we could talk a little bit about what you like to eat."

He waves an arthritic hand at me. "That Marsha. She's a sweetheart, but she doesn't need to worry so much. I'm fine. She's the one that's always busy. Lucky thing that husband of hers likes to cook. Come to think of it, they're the ones who need a private chef, not some retired old fuddy-duddy like me."

"I will be cooking for Marsha and her staff, but she's concerned that you haven't been eating enough vegetables since your wife died."

Mr. Wright agrees. "Yeah, she's probably right. I look at the vegetables now and then, when I'm in the store. But I'm not sure what to do with them."

I return to my notebook, ready to get down to business. "I need to know if you have any dietary restrictions. Are you diabetic? Potassium-sensitive? Are you watching your cholesterol or sodium?"

"Hell, no! I've got the digestion of a goat—I could eat rusty nails if I wanted to. And I'm proud to say my cholesterol has rarely been higher than my IQ. Comes from scrambling around mountains all my life. Or, maybe it's just good genes. Too bad Dori wasn't so lucky."

"Dori?"

"Mrs. Wright. Marsha's mother. She loved good food. Was a hell of a cook, too. But she inherited a bum ticker. Her heart gave out a year and a half ago, after a couple of pretty nasty years. We ate all sorts of that heart-healthy crap back then. I've had my fill. Marsha complains that I eat too many eggs, but I figure I'm just catching up for lost years."

I write "N/A" beside my question regarding dietary limitations and move on.

"What about likes and dislikes? Would you describe your favorite dishes as traditional? Simple? Are there certain ingredients you would like me to avoid?" My pen is poised. I expect Mr. Wright has a pretty standard American palate. He'll like meat with lots of gravy, potatoes and "regular" vegetables like carrots, peas and green beans. No "weird" stuff like fresh cilantro or eggplant.

I remember looking through my grandmother's recipe cards. She was always remembered as a great cook, and yet the majority of her recipes were for Jello salads and bar cookies.

"Don't you worry about me, sweetheart. You make whatever you like to make, and I'll eat it. Don't fuss." I breathe a sigh of relief. This gig would really suck if he ate only white foods or didn't like garlic.

I'm glad to hear he isn't picky, but I still need to know his preferences. I'm being paid good money to fuss. I rub my eyes and try another angle. "So, would you consider yourself an adventurous eater? Do you like to try new things? What do you think of ethnic foods?"

"Like I said, I'll eat just about anything. Dori and I did a lot of traveling after the kids moved out. She was a real gourmet. She'd spend weeks figuring out which restaurants to visit and where to try local specialties. I found myself in all sorts of crazy places eating all sorts of wild stuff." He thinks for a while, and I'm blown away by what he says next. "I wasn't real crazy about the grilled guinea pig we had in the market down in Ecuador. And you know that Kobe beef in Kyoto that everyone is always raving about? It's good, but too damn expensive. If you ask me, nothing beats a good Omaha rib-eye cooked on a backyard grill."

He leans forward and points to my pad of paper. "You can make a note that I'm not a fan of those rubbery cheese slices in plastic. They call it American, but I don't know how it's any more American than a slice of good, sharp Tillamook Cheddar." He looks over at me, as if sizing me up, then he whispers, "Truth be told, I just plain don't like beets. I know they're good for me, and I've eaten plenty in the name of keeping the peace around here. But I wouldn't mind a bit if I never saw another beet as long as I live."

I laugh. "Okay. No beets." I write this down. Now we're rolling. "Why don't you tell me about some of your favorite meals?"

He shakes his head. "Oh, no. You couldn't cook anything like that."

I take that as a challenge. "Mr. Wright, I'm a pretty amazing cook. I don't think there are many things I can't make." I mean it. Sure, he's eaten at some famous restaurants, but it might be really fun to dazzle him with my home-cured gravlax or handmade *agnolotti* with shaved white truffles. "What do you remember as the perfect meal?"

He thinks about it awhile. "The perfect meal? I don't think there's any doubt in my mind: that would be breakfast."

"Oh." I'm a little disappointed. "Well, that's simple enough."

He looks over his glasses at me. "It's the simple stuff that's always the best, don't you think?" I shrug. I like scrambled eggs, but I don't consider them to be the world's best food.

He glances at what I assume is an early photograph of his family. "I'd get up early and drop a few flies in a stream or maybe an alpine lake and catch me a nice trout. I swear, Dori knew before I did when I caught a fish. She'd have the fire going and the coffeepot on. There'd be onions cooking in bacon grease in the big black skillet. I could smell it as I walked back to camp. She'd throw in a handful of diced potatoes and then fry up that trout till the skin was brown and crisp. If she did it just right, the tail would be brittle and salty, kind of like a potato chip. I'd have coffee in a tin cup, and Dori and I would find a log, or move our chairs to where the morning sun peeked through the pine branches. We'd sit there and eat our breakfast and listen to the kids shout and scramble around the deer paths, exploring the woods."

I can practically smell the forest and the campfire. I am lost in my own memories. He leans back into his well-used easy chair. "Yep, I think that's about the best meal a person could ever ask for. You think you could pack up a few dozen of those in my freezer?" He laughs.

I am humbled. No chef in the world can make a meal that good.

Chapter Fourteen

Thursday morning, I call my mother and ask her out to lunch. She is blown away by my invitation.

"Lunch? With you? Really? My goodness, that would be wonderful, Kate."

"I need to borrow a few things from the studio and then pick up some ingredients in the International District. I thought you might want to get out for a while."

"It sounds marvelous! What time to you want me to be ready? I can go anytime." It's as if I asked her to fly to Rome for the weekend.

"Mom, it's no big deal. It's just lunch."

"But it's lunch with *you,* darling. And how often do I get to do that? I like this new life of yours. You don't look as tired, you're taking more care with your appearance, wearing such nice new clothes, and you know how much I love that haircut. You're such a pretty girl, and now people can really see your face."

I roll my eyes at the phone and smile. The littlest things get her all *mommish.* I'd better start asking her to do more stuff or cut her off entirely. This "once in a blue moon thing" is making her giddy. I arrange the equipment I'll need for lunch tomorrow and double-check my shopping list. I'm going to borrow one of Mom's handcarts and maybe some boxes or crates for transporting the food. I'll grab a few platters and bowls from her most recent line. If someone at Wheton-Lofton shows an interest in them, I'll take orders or sell them on the spot. No harm doing a little guerrilla marketing while I'm hanging out downtown with the moneyed.

Mom jumps up from her chair the moment I arrive. "Okay, all ready!" She is wearing fresh lipstick, clearly eager to go. Sam is looking over some paperwork at the desk.

"Hey, Sam. How's it going?" I say.

"Good. How about you?"

Mom is pleased with our simple interchange. She looks back and forth at both of us, beaming. I catch myself in a social faux pas. "Oh, Sam! Did you want to join us for lunch? I didn't mean to leave you out of the loop. We're just going for a quick bite. You're welcome to come."

He shakes his head, still smiling. "No, thanks. You two go ahead."

Mom joins me in the invitation, but she doesn't sound convincing. "Yes, Sam, of course you're welcome to join us."

Sam refuses. "Thanks, but no. I have three sisters, remember? I know a few things."

We both look at him, perplexed. He explains. "My sisters taught me a lot. As a kid, I learned the basic ballet postures and a few tap dance moves. As a teenager, I discovered that chin pimples are the hormonal equivalent of a red flag alerting men to either disappear or carry lots of chocolate. And as an adult, I understand that when a mother and daughter say they're 'going out for a nice lunch' it is, in fact, a secret code for serious girl time. I brought a sandwich. You two go and have fun."

"Brilliant! He's brilliant, I tell you," shouts my mother. "And he's just so cute. Are you two sure you're not interested in dating?"

I groan, grab my mother's hand and pull her toward the door. Sam rubs his forehead and grins. Mom persists, "Perhaps a drink? Dessert and coffee?" She's laughing now.

I holler back to Sam. "I'll keep her for as long as I can stand it, but then she's all yours."

Mom pipes in again. "How about a nice walk on the beach? A moonlit ferry ride?" We're all laughing at her silliness now.

Sam says, "Have a good time. Don't hurry back!" And we're out the door.

I park just east of Seattle's Chinatown. It's a neighborhood sometimes referred to as "Little Saigon" for all of the Vietnamese restaurants, grocery stores and jewelers packed into the intersection of 12th and Jackson. It's another good example of why this area is often called the International District rather than simply Chinatown. Since Seattle was first settled, this neighborhood has been home to waves of immigrants— Japanese, Filipino, African American, Chinese and Southeast Asian. The most recent influx has been a flood of techies. A couple of big computer giants have built slick high-rises nearby, and my favorite tiny restaurants and shops now have lines of hungry white-collar lunch patrons, waiting for cheap rice bowls and two-dollar pâté sandwiches.

I stock up on produce at an outdoor stall and visit a restaurant supply store. Mom peruses the pottery aisle for inspiration. I see her sketching covered Japanese soup pots and rice servers in the tiny notebook she keeps handy. I buy two ladles, a portable butane burner and a couple of inexpensive stockpots to warm up soup in the Wheton-Lofton break room. We walk to a good restaurant I know of and settle in for a lunch of crisp Vietnamese rice crepes and sweet iced coffee.

"I'm going to Portland this weekend. Since you have all this time off, why don't you join me?" says Mom.

My face scrunches up in distaste before I can stop myself. Mom is defensive.

"Really, Kate. The baby's changed so much since you last saw him. Danny is a proper little man now. You wouldn't even recognize him."

I know I should go to Portland with her. I haven't seen my brother, Jack, or his baby in ages. When my sister-in-law, Frances, first got pregnant, I was thrilled at the prospect of becoming an aunt. Then I met little Danny. He was cute enough when he was sleeping, but he was what you might call a *seriously* high-maintenance baby. It was an epic case of colic. He was a little screaming gas machine. Poor Frances went off wheat, dairy, eggs, nuts, chocolate, beans, soy, everything, but Danny's guts just wouldn't work right. When he grew out of the colic and started to sleep through the night, his teeth came in. The boy was a sticky, stinking, crying mess. After our first few meetings, it didn't break my heart that my schedule prevented more visits. I wonder if my unexpected revulsion at this squirming, gurgling bundle of joy had anything to do with my reluctance to settle down with Gaston.

"I think I'll stay home," I say. "I've got to get everything all planned and prepped for my first week of cooking."

Mom is enjoying her meal too much to be bothered. She wraps another bit of shrimp-filled crepe with fresh herbs and a lettuce leaf and dips it in the spicy fish sauce.

"I think your brother and Frances might be coming up for Thanksgiving. You can see Danny then."

"Thanksgiving! I forgot about Thanksgiving. What are we going to do? I don't have access to those free-range turkeys at wholesale price anymore. I can see if the co-ops have anything left, or maybe call and see if that farm up in the Skagit Valley has any heirloom birds that aren't spoken for. The weather has been wet but mild, so there are still some late chanterelles. I can make a wild mushroom and hazelnut stuffing, or maybe I should just roast them in butter as a side dish."

I feel an almost imperceptible stiffening. Mom looks and sounds normal, but a daughter knows these things. I'm prepared for the worst, but she tries to soften the blow.

"That all sounds delicious, Hon. But, you know what? I've made some other plans. You've had such a crazy fall, how about if you just take the holiday off? You don't have to cook anything at all this year."

"Take the year off?" I ask. Has she gone mad? Thanksgiving is a holiday devoted entirely to food and eating. I've never even considered taking the day off.

"You don't mind, do you? You've been cooking so much already and helping me out at the studio. Why don't you just take a break? You can sit back and play cards with Aunt Virginia. If Jack and Frances really do come up, you can spend the day with Danny. You can be Auntie Kate."

"Great. Thanks." My response is automatic. I'm still in shock. Mom and Dad cooked Thanksgiving together when I was a kid. Dad did the turkey and sweet potatoes, Mom made the stuffing and pies. My brother and I helped some, but spent most of the day on a blanket of newspapers in front of the TV, watching football and fiddling the seeds from pomegranates. I took over Dad's jobs the year he died, and then edged Mom out of her kitchen altogether. Maybe she just feels like cooking. I can't deny her that.

After lunch, we roll back into the studio, stuffed to the gills with good food. Mom lends me her collapsible cart/trolley, a couple of handy plastic crates and a wonderful assortment of new serving platters and dishes.

"I guess I should take you to lunch more often," I say.

"It's a deal! There's a Malaysian place I keep hearing good things about."

We make tentative plans for the following week. It's been a long time since my mother and I spent time together outside of the studio. It was fun.

When I arrive home, Iris is sitting at the kitchen table, inspecting our fish in his bowl. "I think Spike's depressed. He has this bored expression and he's stopped doing his tricks."

I drop my things, rush over to her side and look in the bowl. "You know, I've been thinking that same thing. I just didn't want to say it out loud in case you thought I was crazy. He's got no spunk. What do you think we should do? Do they sell fish toys?"

"Let's go find out!"

We dash to the nearest pet superstore and fill a shopping cart with fish supplies. We pick out a neat plastic tank with tunnels, a filter kit with a bubbling treasure chest and a forest of plastic foliage. I hold up two boxes for Iris. "What do you think he would like better? The scuba diver or the pirate?"

"Is it a girl scuba diver?"

I inspect the tiny figure. "It could be, I guess."

"Let's get that. He might need to get his groove on."

"I can relate to that," I say. She agrees. While I peruse the fish tank statuary, Iris discovers a small freezer tucked in next to the gurgling tanks of tropical fish. "What's this for?" She peeks inside. "Omigod! Tiny fish TV dinners!" She holds up plastic trays filled with miniscule cubes of brine shrimp and other fishy delights. "Oooh, oooh. Frozen blood-worms. I bet Spike would *love* those!"

We end up spending a ridiculous amount of money on our beloved fish, with no regrets. We have scrubbed and sanitized everything and are acclimatizing Spike to his new digs when Iris says, "How about a pizza? I'll buy." Without even waiting for my reply, she speed-dials our local delivery service and orders a large pie.

"I thought you had a gig tonight," I say.

"We did. But the club got its liquor license pulled last week for serving the underaged. I'm kind of relieved. The place was a pit, and the girls have been acting weird this week. Something's off. I can't put my finger on it."

We watch Spike in silence for a few minutes more.

"So, how're things with you?" she asks.

I think about it a minute before I answer. I'm well-rested, well-paid, cooking my own food, meeting new, interesting people, and spending time with my friends and family. "I'm feeling pretty damn good. Things are great."

Iris sits up, claps her hands and cheers, "Hooray for Kate!"

"The only thing I need now is Gaston."

Iris stops her applause and blows a raspberry, which ends our conversation.

Friday morning, I can't sleep. I'm too busy planning my first Wheton-Lofton lunch. I get up at five-thirty and start making fortune cookies. The idea came to me in the middle of the night. I will make a batch of my favorite buttery, tuile cookie batter but substitute sesame seeds for the almonds. They will be perfect with the Chinese-style lunch, and I know just the message to write and tuck away in Gaston's cookie.

The cookies are, in fact, a royal pain in the ass. It takes a lot longer than I expect to write out clever sayings and fold each warm cookie into the traditional shape. I rush to get everything finished so I can keep an hour free to shower and primp. In the end, I cut my grooming time short by thirty minutes. I still manage to look pretty good, and it gives me time to load up the car with the crates of food, dishes and equipment.

The cooking for these lunches is going to be a breeze, but I underestimated the other work. Without a restaurant behind me, I'm also responsible for the shopping, packing, hauling, service and cleanup. I have a new appreciation for the industrial dish machines and hardworking dishwashers of the world. I will think twice when I use a pan or a dish now that I have to wash everything by hand.

Because Gaston is a sucker for duck, I roasted a couple of Chinese-style ducks. I pulled the rich meat from the bones and tossed it with lots of crunchy vegetables. At the office, I'll dress this with a hoisin-ginger vinaigrette and serve the salad with wedges of chewy scallion pancakes. This, combined with my authentic hot and sour soup and the homemade fortune cookies, should knock Gaston off his feet.

After everything is ready, I take a moment to package Gaston's picture-perfect cookie that has a strip of paper inside saying, "You're making a terrible mistake. I still love you." I wrap this precious gift in a nest of paper towels and settle it in a safe corner of my handbag.

The Wheton-Lofton break room has been scoured and rearranged for my arrival. The messy lunchroom tables are now covered with lengths of floral oilcloth. Stacks of inexpensive bowls and plates have been purchased. I'm relieved to see that my precious food won't be relegated to disposable paper products.

I toss the salad and reheat the soup, checking it for seasoning. I crisp the scallion pancakes in the toaster as people arrive. The lunch is a huge hit. Marsha is ecstatic. Instead of secreting themselves away in their offices and cubicles with fast food or scattering around the city, the team has gathered together. They talk and laugh. In less than an hour, the entire office has bonded over a wholesome meal and become rejuvenated. Ah, the magic of good food.

I am so busy accepting compliments and answering questions, I don't get the chance to give Gaston his cookie until much later. He comes back into the kitchen to congratulate me while I'm cleaning up.

"That was incredible, Katydid. Everyone loved it." He joins me at the sink and dries some dishes. He gathers up the ceramic platters and bowls and stacks up the extra kitchen chairs. I've never known him to be so helpful. It's time for the magic cookie. I'm giddy with excitement.

"I think it went well. And you know what? That's not all. I have something special, just for you."

"Oh, yeah?"

I search for my handbag. I swear, I set it on a chair right over there. My sweet moment goes sour when I see my purse strap peeking out between the seats of a stack of plastic chairs. I pull on the strap, peek in my handbag and whimper when I find a crumb-filled wad of paper towels.

"So, what is it?" he asks, eager for his surprise.

I reach into my purse, tempted to hand him the buttery crumbs and wrinkled message, but I can't do it. I go back to the crates, grab a couple of misshapen cookies from a box I had stashed, in case of emergency, and hand them to Gaston.

"I have a few extra cookies. I thought you might like them." I can't look at him. I'm too miserable.

"Thanks, these were great." He cracks a cookie and reads the fortune out loud.

" 'Live long and prosper.' Like in *Star Trek*. That's clever."

I'm staring at the sink, trying to figure out a way to rescue the fortune and stuff it into one of the mutant cookies. In between bites of his next cookie, he says, "Maybe you can help me out. I want to do something special with Courtney this weekend. It's our three-month anniversary. Do you have any ideas?"

My chance for a romantic moment has passed. I give up and fall into a chair at the table. I thump my temple with my finger to make it look like I am really pondering his question. "What have you come up with so far?"

"I'm thinking about taking a road trip to Winthrop. I hear there are some nice, remote lodges around there. You can stay way out in the woods and rent snowshoes and sit by the fire, or stay in town for shopping. It sounds pretty nice."

It sounds great, but not for Gaston and Courtney. For him and me!

Why didn't Gaston ever come up with these charming, romantic getaways when we were going out? Our one vacation together was preceded by a couple of months of arguing and trying to coordinate our schedules. We ended up in a cheesy resort in Mexico where we had lousy food, got ripped off by a tour guide and ended up sleeping and drinking the week away. The only cozy fires and leisurely meals we ever shared involved me in the kitchen and Gaston reading the *Wall Street Journal,* calling out for drink refills. I'm peeved.

"Winthrop is all wrong. It's too clichéd, too impersonal." The words are coming out of my mouth before I can think them through. "If you want to impress Courtney, you need to open up and let her into your life."

"What do you mean?" He looks concerned. I have an idea.

"How is she supposed to get to know you if you hide behind such a beautiful mountain backdrop? How is she supposed to get inside your head and your heart if all she can see is snow-covered paths and charming candle shops?"

"I see what you mean."

"You need to share something personal. Does she know about your models?" Ever since he was a kid, Gaston has loved to build model airplanes. When the weather gets bad or work is slow, he will buy a new model, obsess for a while sanding, gluing and painting it, and then add it to a collection of similar projects he keeps in a trunk. Once or twice a year, he will think about the trunk and haul out his planes. He likes to talk through every detail of the assembly, and sometimes he'll even fly the crafts around the room, making jet sounds at takeoff and landing. It's beyond geeky.

"Take her to the hobby shop and pick out a model, just for her. Or better yet, take her to the Museum of Flight. You can each pick out your favorite plane, and then maybe find a model to go with it." This is the kind of date that Gaston loves and I despise. Gaston can spend an entire day at the Museum of Flight. I swear, he looks at every rivet in every plane. I don't see the appeal. I walk in the door, see a roomful of planes, think for a minute or two about how they got them all in the building and then look for the coffee shop.

"That sounds perfect, Kate. Perfect!" says Gaston.

I'm proud of myself. I may not have gotten my cookie message to him, but I have ruined all chances for Courtney's romantic weekend.

Chapter Fifteen

Saturday morning, I pour myself some coffee and slump at the kitchen table. Now what? I have no idea how to entertain myself. It's been ages since I had two real weekends in a row. My most pressing task is to woo Gaston, but I planted a seed yesterday and need to let it germinate. I drum my fingers on the table. Iris had a late night last night, so she won't get up until dinnertime. Marissa is working, and Mom has gone to Portland for her monthly visit to her beloved grandson. I should have gone with her. Perhaps this time I might see past little Danny's face, slimy with strained carrots, and like his doting grandmother, become deaf to his screams.

I go to the kitchen and open a few cupboards. I could make a run to Mr. Wright's. I look out the kitchen window and squint at a glimmer of rare November sunshine. I tug at my jeans. They are binding around the hips. Two weeks of relative inactivity, combined with an unending supply of homemade cookies, is catching up with me. I change into some workout clothes and drive to Green Lake. I'm going for a run. I was on the track team in high school, so even though I haven't done any real running in a lot of years, I still consider myself an athlete. After about half a mile, it is clear that I am not.

I walk the remaining miles around the lake. As I pass the sports fields, I scan the ragtag group of coed soccer players and spot Sam's curly, wild hair. He's wearing a pair of ancient red sweatpants and a torn gray Henley over a vintage T-shirt. A bandanna is tied around his forehead. I should alert the local fashion police. I laugh when I think of what Adele would say.

Sam is playing defense. He hangs back with the goalie, laughing and goofing around with the other fullbacks while the ball is upfield. A teammate kicks it out of bounds. The opposing team throws the ball to a tall, strong woman. She races straight at Sam. His playful attitude disappears. His energy intensifies, and he hunkers down into a posture of attack. Sam lurches toward the woman, arms flying and legs kicking. She makes no attempt to avoid him. They tangle. She does some fancy footwork, makes a half turn, juts her hip and leaves Sam flat on his back in the dirt. His nemesis dashes free of the scuffle, kicks the ball to her teammate and they score.

Sam's earlier good nature turns ugly. He refuses the woman's hand up and cries foul. His teammates pull him back to his feet and slap his back in mock sympathy. Minutes later, a whistle blows and the game is over.

I stand, watching the camaraderie and backslapping until Sam finally sees me.

"Hey!"

"Hey," I reply, a devilish smile on my lips.

"What are you doing here? Getting some fresh air? I was beginning to think you were allergic."

I pretend to laugh. "Yeah, you're my role model" is my witty reply.

I hear a woman's laugh to my left. It is the soccer player who flattened him. He's still irritated with her, but he introduces us anyway.

"Mandy, this is Kate Linden, my boss's daughter. Kate, this is my sister, Amanda."

"Nice to meet you, Amanda." I remember now that Sam said his sister lives in town. "Well done on that last play. I like how you creamed Sam."

She grins and bumps Sam with her hip. "You liked that?"

"I loved that!"

Sam defends himself. "She's like Dr. Jekyll and Mr. Hyde. Mandy may look sweet now, but don't let her fool you. When she gets on a soccer field, she turns into some kind of savage. She played in college, you know."

Mandy makes a pouty face and says, "Aww, poor wittle Sammy got knocked down by a big, mean girl." She dope-slaps him on the side of the head, and her smile broadens into an intoxicating grin. I like her immediately. Even better when she turns to me and says, "I'm starving. You want to join us and go get something to eat?" I jump at the offer. We pile into Mandy's VW and go to Red Mill for green-chili chicken burgers and Babe's famous onion rings.

I learn more personal information from Mandy in the ten-minute car ride than I've learned from Sam since we met. Mandy is Sam's twin, older by fourteen minutes. "And there are two more sisters, one older and one younger. Dad traveled a lot for work when we were kids, so Sam basically grew up in a house full of girls. That's why he sometimes acts like he knows everything there is to know about women."

"I hear you there!" I nod with enthusiasm, remembering some of his cheeky comments.

Sam responds, "I know *everything* about women. Why do you think I'm still single?" The twins nudge each other and share a knowing look. I'm perplexed. When Sam told Mom he was unavailable, I assumed that meant he had a girlfriend.

Mandy says, "I'll admit he knows more than most guys. We made sure of that. He was always getting stuck in the car or at the dinner table while we compared sports bras, boys' butts and PMS remedies."

At this memory, Sam slaps his forehead and looks disgusted. I have a vision of him at eight years old, making that same face and wishing he were invisible during similar sessions of gossip and girl talk.

"What brought you to Seattle, Mandy?" I ask.

"I moved here a couple of years ago. I work at a biotech firm near Lake Union. I like Seattle, and it's the place to be in my line of work. But last year I was pretty lonely. I miss the sun and the desert and my family. I'm just so glad Sam's here now. We've got that twin thing going, you know? So, he can't stand being away from me for long." She does a cute nose wiggle and makes a cheesy smile, right in Sam's face.

He grins back and pinches her nose. "In your dreams, Sis." He leaves the table to check on our order, and I get to hear some dirt.

"I don't know who did whom a bigger favor. He's here now to keep me company, but I gave him the chance to get the hell out of Albuquerque and patch up his life."

"Patch up his life?"

"You probably can't tell, since you haven't known him that long, but he's distant and moody these days. He's got this attitude, you know? Like there's a chip on his shoulder, and that's not like him. As a rule, he's the nicest, funniest guy in the world. That she-devil sucked the life right out of him."

Ooh, this sounds good. I urge Mandy to continue. "She-devil? Tell me more."

"He didn't tell you about Selena? Typical!" She bangs the table. "Sam moved to Seattle to escape a real bitch of an ex-girlfriend."

I lean in to hear everything.

"Since he was just a kid, Sam had a crush on the prettiest girl in school, Selena Gutierrez. Never mind that she treated him like a stain on her favorite blouse. His loyal and trustworthy sisters repeatedly informed him that she was a two-faced, stuck-up princess, but there was no stopping his blind devotion. Well, a couple of years ago, after Selena had slept her way through a long list of handsome and shallow boy toys, she and Sam run into each other. She discovers that in addition to growing into quite a stud, Sam is about the greatest guy on the planet, so she agrees to go out with him.

"It was sickening how she got her claws into him. No matter what we said, he wouldn't hear a harsh word against his sweet Selena. She was the only woman he was ever meant to be with. He had known it since he was a little kid. Blah, blah, blah. It was all a bunch of romantic horseshit, if you ask me."

Sam returns with trays of food and hears what we are discussing. "Jeez, Mandy! What the hell? This isn't any of her business."

I raise my eyebrows at Sam's comment. "Imagine that. It must be very unsettling when a trusted family member spills the beans about your private life." I give him the eye. He drops the trays in defeat. I return my attention to Mandy. "Go on." Sam ignores us and focuses on his sandwich.

"I'm sure you can guess what happened next. Sam, in his blind, love-addled way, refused to listen to us. It wasn't until he walked in on Selena and another guy getting it on that he finally got a clue and broke up with her." Mandy is still angry about the whole affair. Maybe madder than Sam himself. "And can you believe she had the nerve to try and get back together with him? For months she called him, crying, begging him to forgive her. She worked out some story about how she had had too much wine at a friend's bridal shower and she was feeling vulnerable and abandoned that day. According to sweet Selena, he was the first guy she ever cheated with."

"He was!" Sam insists, but his mouth is too full of food to elaborate.

"Oh, wake up, Sam. You think we concocted some kind of conspiracy to keep you single and miserable your whole life? Selena is a manipulative tramp. She always has been. Deal with it."

From her tone I have a sneaking suspicion that Mandy might have been burned by Selena a few times, too. Perhaps a stolen boyfriend? Mandy looks over at Sam. "It's important that your friends in Seattle know about this. So they can protect you." She turns back to me. "Selena would do anything to get him back. If she knew his number in Seattle, she'd try to patch things up just for the fun of ripping out his heart again." Sam squirms a bit but remains quiet.

Mandy gasps, "Oh, my God! She *is* calling you!"

Sam answers, "Don't worry about it, Mandy. We're not getting back together."

"She's still calling you?" Mandy seethes. "After everything she put you through?"

"Just drop it, okay? We talk now and then, that's all. I can take care of myself. How did this even come up?" He redirects his irritation to me, as if it is my fault his sister has exposed his dirty laundry. "Did you learn anything from this, Kate? Here's the lesson if you didn't catch it: No matter how perfect you thought it was, once a relationship is dead, it's dead for good. Women who whine and moan and try to patch things up are just wasting their breath."

That stings. Mandy looks confused. Sam is eager to explain.

"She's just like Selena. She had a decent guy who loved her. He wanted to marry her and spend the rest of his life with her, but that wasn't good enough for Kate. And now, when that guy moves on and tries to make something of his life, she wants him back. She's changing her story, trying to patch it all up with a bunch of sweet talk and lies. It's pathetic, really."

Mandy's vicious glare is now focused on me. I sputter in my defense. "But I'm not . . . I never . . . That's not how it happened at all!" I try to explain, but my protestations sound feeble. We sit in frustrated silence and concentrate on our food.

Mandy breaks the silence with a welcome change of subject. "So, Sam says you're a cook. That's cool. I've always wanted him to open a restaurant." I look incredulous. "He's a fabulous cook. Didn't he tell you? If he weren't so into his art, he would open a restaurant for sure."

Sam objects. "I *like* to cook, but I'm no chef. I don't have the kind of training and expertise Kate has. She went to chef school and everything."

"You could totally do it." Mandy polishes off her last onion ring. "But, for the record, I think you're on the right track. Does Kate know about your project?"

"No."

"Are you going to tell her?"

"No."

My heart races. They're talking about the locked studio. I plead with Mandy. "You've got to tell me what's in there! My own mother won't even tell me. C'mon, Mandy, give me a hint."

Sam gives her a cold look, and she shakes her head. "Sorry, Kate. I'll tell you about the time when he was four and rolled up the page of a

Golden Book and stuffed it up his nose. I'll tell you all about his screwed-up love life. I'll even give you my take on why he's turned into a surrogate parent or mother hen for that Animal House he lives in. I think he's got some nurturing issues. But I won't tell you about his art."

"What's the big secret? We create art together all the time. I see it, and he still manages to produce good work." Sam looks quite pleased with my slip of a compliment.

He starts to explain, but his big sister takes over. "You're going to have to trust me, Kate. Sam's brilliant. And I'm not just saying that because he's my brother. His work is just amazing, so if he wants to keep it a secret, I'll humor him. I think he got all this superstition from Mama Rose. She's the one who taught him about clay, and how to cook. That all seems to be working for him, so let's just let him be a temperamental, quirky artist."

I try one last plea. "But think of his health! If you really cared about him, you would insist he open that door more often and let in some fresh air. He's used to long days and desert sunshine. Just think of the gray Seattle winter we're headed for. It even makes us natives crazy sometimes. Haven't you ever heard of seasonal affective disorder? He'll never make it locked up like that."

Her laugh is back. "Excellent angle, Kate. Going for the sisterly sympathy is a valiant effort. But he's got plenty of light in his studio. And now that he's close, I'll keep an eye on him and do regular fungus checks." She grabs his ear and looks behind it. He swats her away and pokes her in the ribs. They play-fight and laugh like best friends. I watch their horseplay with envy. I wish I had someone to goof around with like that. I yearn for the camaraderie of the kitchen. Maybe Mom's right, I'm lonely.

I shake off the thought and ask Sam, "So, you can cook, huh?" Again, Mandy answers for him. I don't mind. I get more information when he keeps quiet.

"He's awesome! He's the only one who can even come close to making Mama Rose's red chili." She explains, "Mama Rose was our neighbor and babysitter, but she was more like a grandmother. We all went to her house after school. She had granddaughters, so we girls would all play together. She taught us stuff, too, but since she didn't have any sons or grandsons, she liked Sam the best."

Sam waves away her suggestion of favoritism. "Nah, we just liked each other, that's all."

"That's another reason I finally talked Sam into moving here. Mama Rose died a few months ago."

"I'm sorry," I say. Sam nods and then stares past us. There is pain in his eyes, as if the loss of his beloved Mama Rose still causes his heart to ache. I know the feeling. I still miss my dad. If his sister weren't here, I would reach across the table for his hand or give him a hug. Mandy rubs his shoulder and gives him a kiss on the cheek. It makes me feel awkward, like an outsider.

We've been sitting looking at our table full of scraps for too long. It's time to go. We pack back into the VW, and Mandy drives me to my car. "Cool car! I love those old chrome-covered Mercedes."

"Yeah, those old diesels are really great for the environment, too" is Sam's mouthy addition. I roll my eyes and look over at Mandy, my new friend.

"It was great to meet you. I feel much better knowing Sam has a sister to check that attitude of his, on the soccer field at least."

She gives her twin a one-armed hug. "Aw, he's not so bad. Give him a break. He's had a lousy year."

Chapter Sixteen

Sam and Mandy entertained me during the day, but my Saturday night is a bust. Here I am, a young, healthy, attractive single woman, and I spend my night off not dancing the night away, but on the couch with a cup of herb tea, making lists. I'm determined to and clear my wobbly mind. I've got to focus, to pull things together. As a chef, long prep lists managed my days. I might not be able to write the five-year plans and organizational charts that Gaston likes, but boy, can I make lists.

I gather a few manila file folders and a couple of the free notepads Marissa gets from pharmaceutical companies. In one file I collect menu ideas, recipes and magazine photos I've torn out for the Wheton-Lofton lunches. Another file has an inventory of clothes, perfume samples ripped from magazines, some makeup tips and a few ads for upcoming sales. I'm still expanding my wardrobe to help entice Gaston. The final folder is thin but the most interesting. I am determined to come up with a whole bunch of ways to entertain myself. I'm sick of this sad sack routine. I don't want to spend my new, leisure-filled life racking my brain for things to do or running to my mother or Sam in search of companionship.

When Gaston and I get married, I'll have lots of time on my hands. I'd better learn how to use it, or I'll end up like Adele, living from spa visit to spa visit to counter the effects of shopping, drinking and smoking myself to death. After I think about it, I scratch "visit Adele" off my list of things to do. The lists and files have helped. I feel organized.

I watch Spike in his new luxurious habitat for awhile, drop a few granules of food in the water for him and document the feeding. Iris and I have promised to keep careful logs of what we feed Spike so our adoration doesn't kill him. Marissa hasn't been home to pick up her mail in a few days, so I nab her *Sunset* magazine and go to bed early.

Sunday morning is crisp and clear. Inspired by my lists and the Western living magazine last night, I pull on some old jeans and a padded jacket, and spend the day pulling weeds and giving our miserable little yard the makeover it deserves. I splurge on masses of tulip bulbs at our local nursery and plant them in clusters along the house and walkway. I almost giggle out loud when I think of how Iris will react when the goofy, bright colors appear this spring. Cleaning up the garden is very satisfying. It gives me that feeling of instant gratification I get when I cook. It's nice to stand back from a day's work and see what has been accomplished. Perhaps that is what made the receptionist job so hard for me; the beginning and the end were dictated by hours, not accomplishment.

I am flushed and happy from my time in the brisk air. After prepping tomorrow's lunch, I take a long, hot shower and fluff my hair. I grab dinner at a taco van I've always wanted to try, and then take myself to a movie. I arrive at the multiplex just as an animated family film is about to start, so I go to that and laugh so hard I have to wipe tears from my eyes. It's about the best evening I've had in years, and I spent it alone. Imagine that.

Monday, Gaston almost floats over to me as I'm unpacking the crates that hold his gourmet lunch. He hands me a tangle of weeds tied with string.

"What's this?"

"Courtney made you a doll out of Indian corn. Isn't that sweet?"

I'm not quite sure *what* it is.

"Your idea was dead-on, Katydid. We never could have shared such a wonderful weekend together if we went to some silly mountain lodge. Turns out, Courtney's favorite grandpa was a pilot in Korea. He used to spend snowy afternoons showing her his war memorabilia and telling stories. They would pass the day looking through books and pictures together. She hadn't thought about it in years, and yet she knows every last detail of every story he told her. I learned so much!

"We bought a model, then went online and found some pictures so we can duplicate the old bird exactly. She's thinking about working out a study plan to teach her kids about the history of flight. She's so excited. It's adorable.

"I know it sounds corny, but while we looked at the private jets on

Boeing Field, we pretended we were shopping. Like we were picking one out for our very own, to go somewhere exotic. I suggested we zip off to Tahiti or the Caribbean. And do you know what she said? She said, 'Gassy'—that's what she calls me sometimes—'there's nowhere I'd rather be in the world than right here with you.'"

I think I'm going to be sick.

"We had so much fun at the Museum of Flight, we're looking into having the wedding reception there." He sighs and puts his hand to his heart. Lucky thing I left my knives at home, or I'd slit my wrists.

Gaston pulls himself from dreamland but maintains his delirious grin. "So what are we having today? Smells good!"

I look over at the avgolemono soup, Greek salad with grilled shrimp and homemade dill crackers I have prepared, and feel like a fool. Adele was right. This is no way to win him back. Thinking of Gaston's mom gives me an idea.

"So, what does Adele think about all this? Has she met Courtney yet? I can't imagine *what* those two would talk about." Bingo! Tiny beads of sweat form on Gaston's brow.

He searches for the right words. "I *meant* to get them together right away. I was tempted to drive straight to Vancouver the night Courtney and I met. I wanted to share the great news. But the first few days were a blur, you know? We were just so happy. And then the time just slipped by. I didn't really notice how long it had been. I'm pretty sure I told Mom about her. She says I didn't even mention her name until we were engaged, but I'm pretty sure I told her I had a new girlfriend."

There is a diabolical cackle building up inside me, just dying to get out. I slap his hand as he grabs for a cracker, just to show some authority. He continues, "I'm not quite sure what I'm going to do about it now. It's turned into a real mess. Mom's not speaking to me. She'll listen on the phone—I can hear her smoke, but she won't respond."

I am dripping with mock sympathy and understanding. "But you and your mother are so close. Why is she so mad?" As if I don't know.

He squares the napkins and straightens the cutlery. "I'm sure she's pissed off because I didn't involve her enough. I didn't show her the respect she feels she deserves. And let's face it. She wants me to marry you, Kate." Gaston's words sound almost practiced. He is clearly parroting his mother's lines. It gives me new hope. If Adele is still this engrained in Gaston's psyche, Courtney hasn't won yet.

I step close and caress Gaston's upper arm. "This must be killing you.

I can't imagine what your life would be like if your wife and your mother were sworn enemies. It would just rip you in two, wouldn't it? If Adele and Courtney can't get along . . ." I make a face of impending doom. Gaston goes white. The very concept makes him ill. That's when I light up with a brilliant idea.

"How about if I call her? Will that help? I'll call your mom and tell her how you're not yourself these days. You're so confused by this crazy love affair that you're not thinking clearly." I reach for Gaston's hand and make sure we have eye contact. "You're so smitten with Courtney that you've been unable to see how your actions might affect the ones who truly love you, the ones who have always been there for you."

Gaston looks back at me with honest adoration. By George! I think I got through to him! His eyes are a little glossy. He breathes a deep sigh of relief. "I must be the luckiest man in the world. Not only am I engaged to the woman of my dreams, my ex-girlfriend is willing to smooth things over with my mom and help with the wedding. It's too good to be true!" He squeezes my hand, grabs a cracker and heads back to his office. When he is gone, I strangle the Indian corn doll.

I call Adele that afternoon. "It's not working."

"What do you mean it's not working?" she demands.

"I don't know how to get through to him. I've done everything except whack him over the head with a frying pan and tell him that Courtney's all wrong for him. I mean, I've come close, but I'm afraid if I'm much more obvious, or too tough with him, I'll push him away."

Adele is not pleased. "There you go again, thinking of yourself. Have you forgotten what we are working for? We are trying to save a *family*. This is about *Gaston*. My *angel*. If this continues, we will lose him forever."

"I'm trying, Adele. But it's like he's living on the moon. And this Courtney girl, I tell you, she's bulletproof. I think she believes that I'm happy for her, that I'm really interested in planning her wedding. It's crazy. I don't know what else to do."

Adele is angry. Her voice is stern. "I thought I could count on you, Kate. I thought you loved Gaston enough to see what needed to be done."

"I've *tried*, Adele. No one wants to break up this relationship more than me. But they're impossible."

"No, Kate. Nothing is impossible when it comes to love. I guess only a mother can truly understand that."

"It's not that I don't love him, Adele. It's just . . ."

"No, no. Say no more. I thought I could count on you. I thought you were a capable and smart girl, but obviously I have asked too much of you."

"What do you mean? I'm not giving up. I'm just out of ideas. I can do it, Adele, I know I can. I just need more time."

"Time is something we just don't have, do we? As each day passes, I am losing my son to a stranger. The child I carried in my loins for nine months and suckled at my breast has found another. And I won't stand for it!"

Ick. I pull the receiver away from my ear and make a face. "You okay, Adele? You're kind of creeping me out. He's engaged to Courtney, not being birthed by her. It's not like he's dying or something. He's still living the same old life, he's just engaged."

"I'm losing him!" Adele wails. "She's got to be stopped!"

"Uh, yeah. Okay. Well, I'll keep working on him, but maybe you should think about breaking your silent treatment and talking to him yourself."

"Yes! It is time."

Hallelujah! She's ready to step in. I'm eager to get off the phone. Adele is someone best taken in small doses. "Well, best of luck to you. I'll call if there are any changes on my end."

"There will be changes, my dear. Rest assured, there will be changes soon."

I shudder, and the tiny hairs on my neck stand on end. It becomes crystal clear to me that Adele has been playing me like a fiddle. She's been sweetening me up so I will do her dirty work. She wants me to punish Gaston for acting spontaneously, for thinking for himself. She and I had a decent relationship, but this new "I love you like a daughter" stuff has been a little hard to swallow.

I pack up the cooler and head to Mr. Wright's.

"Hey, there, young lady," he welcomes me.

"I brought you some food."

"Thank you, dear. Come on in."

I fill his freezer with little bags of fresh, blanched veggies in various sauces. Then I explain how the entrées are meant to be served. "This citrus and sesame mixture should be sprinkled on the soy and orange-braised lamb shanks after you heat them up. You should eat that with this edamame salad. Just toss these vegetables with a container of this dressing. The root vegetable cakes are best if they are crisped a little before serving. You can do that in a skillet with a little butter. Serve them with a spoonful of this tomato chutney. This is a kale and bacon strata. You need to cook it in the next twenty-four hours. You can have it for break-fast, or whenever. I know you like eggs, and this way you can get a few extra vitamins and minerals with them. I put detailed instructions on the container. You just need to pop it in a preheated oven for twenty to thirty minutes. Then top it with this little container of grated myzithra cheese. It's all written right here."

Mr. Wright nods mechanically. "It looks wonderful. You've done far too much." His words sound right, but I get the feeling he's not really paying attention to my instructions. He doesn't seem impressed. I must not have guessed right when it comes to his tastes. He's going to be a tough nut to crack.

He fills the kettle. "I was just about to make some tea. Do you want a cup?"

I don't, but I want to get a better feel for what he likes, and I also want to make sure he understood how the food is meant to be served.

"Do you play cribbage, Kate?" he asks.

"Sure." My Aunt Virginia is rarely seen without a deck of cards. She had me playing cribbage as soon as I could add.

"Wonderful. My neighbor, and cribbage partner, left for Palm Springs last week, and I'm already missing our daily games. I hope I can interest you in a match now and then?"

"I've got time right now. How about it?"

"You're on!" Mr. Wright brews a pot of aromatic blackcurrant tea in a chubby brown teapot. He pulls half a package of vanilla sandwich cookies from the cupboard, and we settle in for what turns out to be a great game. The cards are kind to me and I take an early lead, but he is cunning, and I fall into some of his pegging traps. I win the game, but only by a few points.

As he shuffles the cards for a second game, I ask him for more food memories.

"You ever go geoduck hunting?" he asks. I shake my head. I've heard tales of battling the giant beach clams, but I've never found one myself. It's a funny thing. Here in the Northwest, you pick berries, dig clams and gather oysters, but for some reason, geoduck and wild mushrooms are listed among the critters that are "hunted."

"Hoo, boy! They're a lot of fun. We used to go over to Hood Canal and canoe out to the sand flats at low tide. The kids would sneak along the beach, spotting the siphons. If you rattle around too much, the geoducks just pull their necks into the ground and disappear. But the kids were quick. One of 'em would grab the neck and the other two would be down on all fours in the wet sand, digging for all they were worth. Sometimes, I thought the big ones might take a kid down with it.

"Most of those battles, the clams won. Dori and I had a system: She'd spot them, and then I'd surround 'em with a thirty-gallon drum with the bottom cut out. If you press a big cylinder into the ground, you can dig down deep without the sand collapsing all around you, filling in where the clam neck used to be. It's still a race. We'd dig sometimes two feet or more before we would bring those buggers up. When we got back to the cabin, I'd hose the kids down and Dori would cook up our catch. Once, we got one that weighed nearly six pounds! Oh, that was fun."

"Cook?" I ask, surprised. "Most of the geoduck I've had is raw as sushi or sashimi."

His expression is of obvious distaste. "I guess you could eat it raw if you wanted to. But have you ever taken a good look at those things? They're *ugly*! I'm not so sure I'd have much of an appetite for raw geoduck."

I laugh. The neck of the clam is so long that it never fully withdraws into the shell. No one can deny that the protruding, wrinkled neck of a geoduck looks just like a huge, limp, yellowish-gray penis.

"Once you cook it, I'd say a good geoduck beats a lobster any day. The meat is sweet, and oh, so rich. The kids liked the chewy bits, breaded in cracker crumbs and fried as clam strips. The tender, sweet foot we'd save as our own. Dori would slice it up and fry it in butter and maybe a little lemon. Oh, you've never tasted anything so good."

"I can do that. I can do that right now, if you want. It sounds great."

Mr. Wright looks up from the cards, startled. "Oh, now. Don't be silly. I'm just an old man, reminiscing. You gonna go dig us up a geoduck just 'cause I say they're good?"

"No. But I can buy one. I'd love to taste geoduck like that. And I've never cooked one before. Do you know how to clean them?"

He nods. I grab my coat and my keys. "Then what are we waiting for?"

I drive Mr. Wright to Uwajimaya, the premier Asian market in Seattle, where I know they sell live geoduck. We pick a fat clam from the live tanks. It's outrageously expensive, but I remember hearing that geoduck pirates have been known to sneak in during the night and devastate the local crop using illegal dredging equipment. We make sure the fishmonger squeezes out the excess water from the huge clam before he weighs it. I buy butter, lemons and saltines alongside the giant clam, and we hurry back to Mr. Wright's house. We spend the rest of the afternoon talking, laughing, cooking and eating. I have to agree. This is some mighty fine seafood.

I find myself thinking out loud about different recipes and presentation ideas. "I bet geoduck would be great with mushrooms. Wouldn't it make an incredible deluxe surf and turf, with a slab of seared foie gras and a drizzle of white truffle oil?"

The mystery of what Mr. Wright thinks of my food is about to be solved. He is irritated by my suggestions.

"What the heck's wrong with the way we just had it? Why do you have to go and mess it up with all those fancy ingredients? You chefs. You're always putting mangos on halibut and strawberries on steak, fiddling with good food, rather than just leaving it be."

I'm shocked. "We're trying to make it better. Trying something new."

He is embarrassed by his outburst. "I know, I know. I'm sorry. You're an artist. You need to create, to make things original." He scratches his chin and explains, "You asked me last week about my favorite meals, and I guess it really got me thinking. The way I figure it, the best meals I ever had were made by people who wanted to share something with me— sort of like what we shared today. I've eaten at a lot of fancy and famous places, but I can tell you, straight up, that not one of the best meals I ever ate required a suit jacket or sorbet spoon."

I try to object, but when I think about it, I have to agree.

"I remember when a colleague from Spain invited us to his family estate in Andalusia. His father cooked us a genuine Valencia paella over a fire of grapevine cuttings. It wasn't anything fancy, just rice with some chicken. Or maybe it was rabbit, now that I think of it, and some spicy sausage and vegetables. We sat on this bluff, overlooking an ancient vineyard, and ate it straight from the pot with wooden spoons. That was a heck of a meal."

"Yeah, but you were in Spain. It was the setting that made it good, not just the food."

"I see what you mean, but I'm not so sure you're right. Some of my all-time favorite meals were served right here at the kitchen table. One of my favorites was when we made an entire meal of potato salad. Dori made the best potato salad. She always cooked them just right, and she never made it too creamy or gooey. She added a little pickle juice to the dressing, I think. Oooh, and nothing beat her wild blackberry pie. We knew a place where the little tiny ones grew along the ground right around the Fourth of July. She never bothered with the big fat blackberries you see all over the place. She only picked those tiny native berries that have all the flavor. And she used lard in the piecrust. It was so flaky, it nearly blew away at every bite."

I'm stuffed full of geoduck, but my mouth still waters as he describes his wife's wild blackberry pie and how good it was served warm with a scoop of vanilla ice cream. I'm finally convinced. I had my head in the clouds when I thought we were making the nation's best food at Sound Bistro.

Chapter Seventeen

It's taken only one week for word to get out that the Wheton-Lofton break room serves the best free lunch in town. Marsha boosted the numbers every day last week. Business associates have been calling her and arranging to "drop by" at lunchtime. Last Friday, I made soup and salad for thirty-four. Today she asked if I could make Wednesday's lunch a pre-Thanksgiving feast for forty-two. I don't mind. I make more money with every hungry visitor, and I'm used to cooking for a lot more.

Marsha is thrilled not only with the attention she is getting but also with the increased productivity. I'm getting a tiny taste of the celebrity that Nancy had and it's intoxicating. Being the belle of the building also makes me look good in front of Gaston. And I must say, I am looking pretty good these days. My eyes aren't as puffy, and the lines on my forehead don't seem as deep. Last weekend, Marissa and I went shopping downtown, and I got a mini makeover at the cosmetic counter. I also bought some new, flattering clothes and dangly earrings. I'm looking great.

But I'm not putting my appearance before the food. Right now, I'm back, sweating over an electric griddle, flipping tiny grilled cheese sandwiches. I'm serving spicy tomato bisque with wee sandwiches to float on top as croutons. For the salad, I tossed grilled onions and endive with bitter greens, and topped it all with thin slices of cold, marinated flank steak and shredded fresh horseradish. A peppery red-wine vinaigrette is served alongside.

As usual, Gaston offers me a hearty hello and proprietary pat on the back when he enters the break room. He helps himself to the food, then sits down with the office computer guru, who, much to my amusement, asks him in a loud whisper, "Whatever happened between you and Kate? I can't believe you let such an amazing woman get away. I mean, not only is she an incredible cook, she's beautiful, too. What else were you looking for?"

Gaston replies, "Yep, Kate is something special, all right. We'd probably be married right now if she would have had me."

I spin on my heels, almost pouring a ladle full of hot soup on a woman standing near me. My heart is beating quickly. I want to shout out, "I'll have you! I'll marry you right now!"

Gaston finishes his thought. "I'd be dying inside if it weren't for Courtney. She's not much of a cook, but she's a real sweetie pie. And she loves me to pieces." He takes a bite of salad. "Kate's still my best friend, and I get to see her here for lunch all the time. It's the perfect situation."

Argh. Adele was right. Cooking for Gaston is just making his life more comfortable. I haven't been acting like sand lately. I storm out of the kitchen and volunteer to watch the phones so the temp who replaced me can eat. I'd rather sit here and pick up the occasional phone call than hover over everyone and scowl if they reach for the salt. The phone rings. I pull on the headset, punch a button and say, "Wheton-Lofton, how may I direct your call?"

"Kate! Is that you? You've got to help me!" It's Courtney. I sort of grunt into the phone. She's the last person I want to talk to right now. "Gaston's *mother* is coming to town."

I perk up. "She is? That's great!" I rethink my words. Maybe that's not the reaction Courtney is looking for. "I mean, she's not all that bad once you get to know her."

"What do you mean? I'm sure she's a sweetheart!"

I let out a spontaneous and loud "Ha!" then excuse myself as if it were a sneeze. I envision Adele pulling off Courtney's limbs one by one, like a cruel kid with a spider.

"I'm planning a dinner so we can really get to know each other, and I'm not sure what I should cook. Gaston's being a big meanie and won't let me prepare a traditional Thanksgiving dinner. He says because Adele lives in Vancouver, she celebrated Canadian Thanksgiving back in October. Isn't that crazy? And he's been making all of these elaborate plans. I really had to put my foot down and insist that we have at least one dinner at my apartment. It's not a big place, but I've done it up so warm and cozy. It will be like our first dinner as a real family!"

Courtney is living in a nursery rhyme. She's traipsing in the woods with a song in her heart and a basket full of goodies. She has no idea

Adele Lambert is more hungry wolf than meek old granny. It will be a massacre.

Courtney continues, in blissful ignorance. "I mean, she's going to be my new *mother*. What kind of daughter-in-law would I be, taking her to some stuffy old restaurant instead of welcoming her into my home?"

I feel the same way. The difference is that at my house, the food is on par with that of the best restaurants in town. Courtney's Tater Tot casserole and taco salads aren't going to warm Adele Lambert's cold heart. I have not seen Courtney's apartment, and I might be off-base about her decorating style, but I can't help but picture her tucked in the back of a suburban dollhouse complex, overlooking a strip mall. Gaston's parents live in a chic, waterfront palace.

I have a spark of hope. Maybe this relationship will self-destruct after all. The rules are changing now that Adele's stepping into the game. I can stop being the irritant and try to be helpful, to play the hero. I offer Courtney some valid menu-planning advice.

"Adele has very sophisticated tastes, but don't try too hard to impress her. Keep it simple." I'm hearing Mr. Wright's words as I speak. "Most people mess up their dinner parties by trying to cook something fancy and unfamiliar. The best meals are often things your family used to share. What did your mom make for special occasions? Sometimes the dishes that seem boring or easy to you might be charming and unique to other people."

"Well, food isn't really what I remember about growing up. My mother wasn't your typical American housewife. She was sick a lot when I was young, so it was just my dad, my uncle and my granddad. We lived in a work cabin on the ranch and didn't get to the store much. We ate a lot of canned stew and Campbell's soup and pancakes. Every once in a while my dad gathered the hands, and we would have a big barbecue. That was always good."

Oh, dear. Her words have inspired the beach in me. Courtney will be mincemeat when Adele and I are through with her.

"A barbecue sounds *perfect*. Maybe you should do burgers, or how about barbecued ribs?" I try to keep the snicker from my voice. Adele hates sloppy or sticky foods. She is adamant that the only thing that should be eaten with the fingers is a croissant. And, like many French, Adele is baffled by Americans' love of sweet or fruity flavors with meat. I can see her toying with a rib if she was vacationing in Texas and there were a lot of tight-jeaned cowboy waiters, but to eat such fare for a family holiday would be an abomination.

Courtney makes happy-mouse sounds. "That will be so yummy! I can buy some potato salad and baked beans, and we can pretend we're having a real summer picnic. Oooh, oooh, I just came up with another idea. How about sloppy joes? My dad always loved my sloppy joes."

"Don't forget the corn on the cob!" I say with glee. You can pick it fresh off the stalk, cook it to perfection, slather it in hand-churned butter and put diamond-crusted picks in the ends, and Adele will still shun corn on the cob as cattle fodder.

Courtney is overjoyed. "It will be a real American holiday, just like the Fourth of July! Thanks so much, Kate, you're the best!"

I'm feeling flush and smug when the temp comes back from lunch. I go see Gaston in his office. His belly is full, so he is looking happy with the world.

"I hear Adele is coming to town."

That yanks him from his gastronomic serenity. At the sound of his mother's name, his eyes start shifting and he gets a nervous, twitchy look.

"I guess I should thank you. She called and said you two talked. I guess she's ready to meet Courtney."

"I'm sure it will be fine. Courtney is very sweet."

"She's the best, but you know Mom."

"Why don't you have her call me when she gets to town? If she has some free time, maybe we can go have coffee or a drink."

"Uh, if you don't mind, I don't think I will. Mom's still a little pissed off that it didn't work out between the two of us."

"Tsk. I guess you're right. You need her to focus on Courtney this weekend." I sit down in a chair and put my feet up on his desk. "How do you think that's going to work out?"

"Frankly, I'm a little worried. Courtney's tougher than she looks, but you know Mom. She doesn't do sweet." Gaston now looks as if his lunch hasn't settled well.

His discomfort swamps my confidence. I am racked with guilt. I am a saboteur. Courtney just wants to make a nice family meal, and I've set her up for potential emotional slaughter.

"Gaston, you need to talk Courtney out of cooking dinner."

"I've tried. Believe me, I've tried. But she has this romantic Norman Rockwell vision of the holiday. Thank God, I managed to get out of the classic Thanksgiving dinner. I can't even imagine the damage that girl could do to a turkey." He shudders. "I think I have everything figured out. I'm taking them to Ray's the first night. We'll have a good regional dinner with a nice view, on neutral ground. I'm hoping that's all it will take for them to get to know each other and hit it off. But I'm not counting on it. Mom can hold a grudge, you know."

I pretend to be surprised. "Really?"

He explains how he's planned the whole weekend with things they can do together without having to communicate much. He's booked long spa treatments and purchased theater and symphony tickets.

"Then, while Courtney's busy cooking, I'll take Mom shopping downtown. If Courtney can make something edible for dinner and I can keep an eye on Mom's wine intake and convince her to smoke outside, everything will be fine. It will be fine. It'll be fine." He keeps repeating that over and over again, clearly trying to convince himself.

It's time for me to sit back and watch. I can't add much to what will be a weekend of pure chaos. I pack up my gear and take the leftovers to the studio for Mom and Sam.

The studio is open, but I don't see anyone around. Mom's van is gone. I hear some movement coming from Sam's locked room. I bang on the door.

"Chow's here!"

Sam and I pretty much called a truce after his sister spilled the details on his personal life. He and Mom seem to have stopped their archeological exploration of my life. I'm getting used to the new, efficient studio systems, and can appreciate his organization rather than resenting his familiarity. In turn, he's beginning to understand that I'm my own person, not Selena or one of his sisters. We've even worked out a decent routine. I like the mind-soothing spin and tactile feel of the wet clay, so I concentrate on production. He prefers the alchemy of dipping and firing, so he works in the glaze and kiln room.

The door to his studio opens, and I try to get a peek inside, but a thick black curtain shields my view. He comes out of his lair, and all I get is a glimpse of boxes and an array of electrical cords. He runs his long fingers through his thick hair. He looks grateful for a break.

"How's it going in there?" I ask.

"Okay. I got some new equipment that I'm not too familiar with. There's a lot of reading to do and technical information to absorb. I feel like an engineer again."

"An engineer?" I hand Sam a container of the steak salad.

He pulls two bottles of seltzer from the fridge and hands me a drink. "Lime, right?" I nod. He sits down on a stool. "Yeah, but this is a lot more fun than the Dilbert days back in Albuquerque."

I can't figure out what he's saying. My expression must reveal that.

"Didn't your mom tell you what I did before I came to work for her?"

"She said you worked with the pueblo potters."

"Yeah, sure. But not as a job. I was a civil engineer. I worked at a con-crete company. I had to wear a tie and work in a cubicle. My boss even had a pocket protector." He acts as if it's no big thing, as if all of my mother's studio grunts might have had engineering degrees. He takes a few bites of salad. "This is great. What's in the dressing?"

"Fresh horseradish. You're a civil engineer? Why did you quit? Why on earth are you working as an assistant in a pottery studio when you could have . . . a real job?"

He looks up from his food. "I love this job. It's great. I hated engi-neering. I mean, I liked the study and the science behind it, but I hated my job. I worked as a glorified buyer. I was on the phone all day talking to the good-old-boy network about sand prices instead of building any-thing. This is way better." He waves his fork around my mother's studio, then tucks into the salad again.

I point to his studio door. "So, what are you doing in there, building bridges?"

He laughs. "Yeah, maybe. Sort of. Among other things."

I look over at the closed door and then watch him with amazement. Who the hell is this guy? And what am I going to find out about him next?

Chapter Eighteen

Marsha asked for a Thanksgiving-style meal for Wednesday, but I don't want folks to overdose on turkey. I make curried squash soup with chive crème fraîche and candied pecans, red apples hollowed into cups and filled with ham salad, and a slaw of spiced carrots, peppers and celery root. I spend hours rolling out and baking paper-thin sheets of pumpkin-seed flatbread. Since there are more guests than dishes, I spend all day dashing back and forth serving plates and bowls then washing them up. It feels like real work.

Thanksgiving morning, Iris and I lug Spike's new aquarium setup to the table so he can have breakfast with us. She puts on a Marianne Faithfull CD. (I'm not about to admit it to Sam, but I've taken a few notes on the music he plays and bought copies of the stuff I like for home.)

Iris has had a very bad week. I keep my head low and the coffee coming.

"The band is doomed. Cindy fucked Denise's boyfriend and now they hate each other. They refuse to be in the same room together. All that's left of the band is that weirdo, Lola, and she's always high these days. I swear, she's either so cranked she only wants to play the fastest shit, or too wiped or paranoid to leave her rat-hole apartment." I pour two more bowls of Lucky Charms. "I thought this time it was going to happen! I thought by getting rid of the testosterone we might be able to work without all the juvenile bullshit. But no, those bitches are as bad as the guys.

"What am I supposed to tell Rex, our new engineer? He's *so* cool. He had it all set up so we could burn a new demo disc. He knows just tons about music and he's got an amazing ear. I just *know* he's going to get snapped up by one of the big studios and move down to L.A. and I'll *never* get a chance to work with him." She looks into Spike's fish tank. "Hey there, Spike? Can you play the bass? The drums?"

We sit and brood over our coffee for awhile. I try to lighten things up. "It's Thanksgiving," I say. "We're supposed to be thankful today. Let me get a piece of paper. We'll make a list."

"Oh, goody! And can we make paper bag turkeys, too, Sister Mary Catherine?"

I ignore her sarcasm and get her to help me with the list.

Kate and Iris are thankful for:

- Having great roommates who are also your best friends in the world and the fact that we can live together without stealing each other's men or driving each other crazy (even though Kate makes Iris do these lame lists now and then)
- Having the best fish in the whole world
- Good, real coffee
- Gibson electric guitars
- Le Creuset casserole pans
- That Marianne Faithfull survived her drug-addled youth to record such cool stuff later on
- Having families that are cool enough that we don't mind having holiday dinners with them
- Pagliacci pizzas—delivered
- Mascara that doesn't get clumpy
- Lemon verbena soap
- Glitter glue

Even though Iris complains a lot at first, we both feel better after taking an inventory of good things. Iris is even peppy enough to don her special Thanksgiving outfit. It's basically a tiny black skirt and white shirt with big, black army boots, lots of buckles and a contrasting, demure pilgrim's hat. I pull on jeans and a few comfortable layers. Thanksgiving is not a formal affair at the Linden house.

Iris grabs a couple of cans of olives from the pantry. That's her contribution to her giant family potluck. As she heads to the front door she says, "Tell your mom hi for me." Then she remembers something. "I forgot to tell you—your mom called a few days ago. You were off making a delivery or shopping or something. She wants to set me up with some guy she works with. What do you know about Sam?"

I'm stupefied. "Sam? My mother wants to set you up with Sam? You must be joking."

Iris adjusts her hat. "He's not so great, huh? I kind of wondered. She made him sound pretty cool. Nice-looking, an artist. But if he's really all that, you would have snapped him up by now."

I'm horrified by the idea of Iris and Sam dating. So against it that my head is spinning and I'm short of breath. This baffles me. "Sam isn't your type at all."

She laughs. "I guess not—he's got a job." She reaches for the door. "But if you're not into him, maybe I'll give him a call. I've been dealing with too many women lately and I'm hankering for a man. I want some stubble and sweat to rub up against, you know? I'm craving a good dose of rough, muscle-laden man-meat. What does this Sam guy look like? Is he hot?"

"I don't think he's the kind of guy you're looking for. You can hardly see him—he's got this curly blond hair that is totally out of control. He dresses like the homeless. He's always working." I'm not being fair. Sam doesn't deserve to be trashed to someone he hasn't even met. I try and think of some nice things to say. I scratch my head and think.

"He's tall. He has nice eyes. His skin is a great color, kind of golden brown. He rides his bike and plays soccer, so he's fit. He's smart, too. I just found out he was an engineer. He's sarcastic, but he can be nice. He remembers how I like my coffee and knows which seltzer flavor I like best even though I never told him." I think some more about how to describe Sam. "I guess some girl back in Albuquerque did a number on his heart. Poor guy."

Iris looks at me funny. "Okay. I get it. I'll leave him alone."

"Yeah. That's probably a good idea. Don't get me wrong, he's not *that* bad. He's way, way, *way* better than any of the guys you usually bring home. He and my mom are, like, totally bonded. He's just a little . . . delicate right now. I don't think he's up for the whole Iris dating treatment. I mean, what man is?"

"Say no more. He's all yours, sister." And she's out the door.

"Mine? No, that's not what I'm saying. . . ." I run to the door to make sure she doesn't have the wrong impression. "I'm not interested in Sam at all! We fight all the time. He lives with a bunch of loser guys. It's Gaston I want. Gaston, remember?"

Iris starts her purple Toyota pickup truck and shouts, "Happy Thanksgiving, sweetie!" and drives away. I stand on the front steps for a while, hoping my words got through to her. Me and Sam? Forget it! Sure, Sam's attractive. He's not afraid to speak his mind. He knows how to work hard and he is a talented artist, but he's just not my type. Even if he was, he's not interested in me at all. I learned that the first day we met.

I should probably hook him up with Iris. A shudder goes down my spine. Why does that idea bother me so much? I try to think it through logically. Iris is my best friend. She deserves a good guy. Sam is a good guy. Sam and Iris should get together. "No!" the voice in my head shouts. Sam can't date Iris because he's on the rebound. Iris will fall for him and get hurt. No, that doesn't sound right. Iris will dazzle Sam and then dump him when she's bored. It's Sam who will get hurt, and I don't want to be in the middle of it. But what if they like each other? What if it is a perfect match? I get a sweaty, nervous feeling again. It would be crazy to have my mom and my best friend both in love with Sam. It would be too much. I try and shake all thoughts of Sam and Iris from my head. I go back inside and get my handbag. I might as well take off, too.

Sitting in my car, I can't help the feeling that I am forgetting something. It doesn't *feel* like Thanksgiving Day. I don't have a trunk or backseat full of groceries, and there is only a mild ache and pulsing in my feet from working the day before. Arriving empty-handed seems impolite, so I stop at the local supermarket and buy a bouquet of fresh-cut zinnias for Mom and a floppy little stuffed bunny for Danny.

I pull into the driveway of my old family home. When I was a kid, there was a small lawn that held the wooden play equipment my dad made. Once Jack and I moved out and Dad died, Mom got rid of the toys and replaced the grass with hearty, low-maintenance greenery and native plants. My old house is roomy, but the upright design and cedar siding make it look naturally nestled in the surrounding evergreens. The big deck, front porch and various foliage are dotted with assorted outdoor art: wind chimes, bird baths, feeders and metallic whirligigs. Today's early-morning showers have the yard looking at its best: The rhododendron bushes, licorice ferns and salal are a miniature rain forest of vivid greens.

I walk up the familiar slate path and wooden steps to the front door. I am greeted by a wave of the most wonderful aromas. Mom's cat, Raku, rubs affectionate figure eights around my ankles. As usual, my Aunt Virginia and our family friends, Barbara and Gary Pinkerton, are in the living room, sipping vodka gimlets and bickering over which jigsaw puzzle to start. Aunt Virginia is my mother's wacky aunt. Perhaps I'm immune to Adele's dramatics because I grew up with Aunt Virginia's theatrical personality. She also sweeps into any room she enters. Her clothes are often original pieces made of hand-loomed cloth or tribal weavings. She wears huge beaded necklaces and must own two dozen pairs of eyeglasses in every color of the rainbow. But unlike Adele, Aunt Virginia isn't overly self-absorbed. She has a loud, easy laugh and a quick, sharp wit. I adore her.

The Pinkertons live down the street in a conservative, meticulously landscaped colonial. Over the years they have loosened up and become a lot more fun. They're much happier now that their kids are gone. Their troublemaking sons made the local news a few times for their bad decisions. I think that's why Barbara and Gary prefer to celebrate with us.

I say my hellos and receive my annual cheek-pecks and personal growth and beauty assessment. My short hair is scrutinized before it is approved.

When she hears that someone has arrived, Mom comes out of the kitchen, wiping her hands on a dishtowel. I give her the flowers. "Aren't these lovely! Thank you, sweetheart." I wipe a smudge of flour from her cheek.

"It smells great. Different," I say. "What are you making?" I peek into the kitchen and am bowled over to see Sam wearing an apron and shaking something in a hot skillet. Mandy is standing near him, picking through fresh herbs.

"Sam's cooking?" I'm not sure if my words are a question or an accusation.

"Didn't I mention that? I've been so excited, I can't believe I didn't say something. We're doing everything different this year. Sam's been talking about all the foods he loves from New Mexico, and the more we talked about it, the more we just had to have it. He doesn't have much of a kitchen at his place, so I came up with this idea to make Thanksgiving a real American feast: chiles, tomatoes, corn. He got his mom to ship him a bunch of special ingredients from Albuquerque. You should see some of the stuff he's got in there!"

"Yeah." I wander into the kitchen to watch the activity. I'm irritated. I feel left out of the loop. Once again, Sam is treading on my sacred territory, pushing his way into my private life whether I like it or not. In this particular instance I don't mind that I often make recreational chefs nervous when I'm in the kitchen. I like watching Sam squirm. I look around and see piles of red and green chiles, corn husks and bowls of colorful pastes and powders. I know my way around a lot of ingredients. In a pinch I could concoct something out of all of this, and it might be tasty, but it wouldn't be authentic. Sam handles everything with authority.

He looks different. I guess I'm just used to him in his trademark, thrift store coveralls or muddy soccer kit. Today he is wearing khakis and a nice shirt with real buttons down the front. His hair has been combed and treated with some kind of magic potion. It falls in perfect ringlets and seems to have less electrical charge.

I am desperate to take over, to stir something or dip my finger in a sauce. I want to offer my help, but I know from experience that I would just be getting in his way. I grab a can of ginger ale from the fridge and leave the kitchen murmuring, "Call me if you need help with anything." The words dribble away behind me. Sam looks relieved to see me go.

Back in the living room, it has been determined that the puzzles all look too complicated and they will play cards. When my lack of kitchen responsibilities is made clear, I am roped in for a game of pinochle until my big brother, Jack, and his family arrive. My petite, usually charming sister-in-law, Frances, pushes sixteen-month-old Danny toward his gushing grandmother and runs to the bathroom.

Jack explains, "I guess there's no keeping it secret now. Frances is pregnant again."

Mom and Aunt Virginia hoot like it's New Year's Eve and cover Jack with congratulatory kisses, as if a guy who's gotten his attractive, young wife pregnant has performed some kind of magic trick. While everyone fawns over Danny, Jack wraps his arm around my shoulders, squeezes tight and ruffles my short, coppery hair. It's his traditional greeting.

"Hey, Kiddo. I like the hair."

"Thanks." I manage to withhold a wisecrack about his hair, or lack thereof, and tickle his softening stomach. He instantly releases me. It feels good to be with family. Jack shakes Sam's hand and they share a few words. Then my brother grabs a beer and checks out the action at the card table. Frances staggers from the bathroom looking pale and miserable. Her apple-red cheeks have turned to green. She is still holding back her glossy black hair. "Hi." Her greeting is sickly. "If you don't mind, I'm going to take a few minutes and crash in the back bedroom. Can someone watch Danny for a while? I need every precious minute of silence and rest I can get." We all offer to help.

My eyes lock on to Danny. It's hard to believe that this walking, jabbering, adorable little boy is the same being I met before. His hair has come in curly. His pudgy cheeks have the rosy glow of his mother's (usually). There's a hint of goo near his lower lip, but for the most part, he's clean. And he's *smiling*. I can't help but grin stupidly as I watch him toddle around the house, chasing the cat and testing every piece of furniture for mobility. I remember the stuffed bunny in my purse and run to get it, hoping I might win some of his attention. I wave the toy at him, and he laughs. It's not just a giggle, but a deep, uninhibited child's belly laugh. It is perhaps the purest sound I have ever heard. Danny gallops across the living room, grabs the bunny, squeezes it tight, waves it up and down a few times and squeals with delight. I see my dad in his sparkling brown eyes, and I am instantly and utterly in love.

I turn to my mother, who is on her knees in the grandmother's pose of worship. "Don't you have something to do in the kitchen?" I ask. She jumps up and heads back to work, and I have Danny all to myself. I lead him into the family room, where we sing silly songs and make a fort out of the couch pillows. We play bouncy games with his new bunny, compare our shoes and do some rolling around on the floor, laughing together. We are having so much fun, I forget all about the action in the kitchen. I'm almost disappointed when Mom calls us for dinner.

Back in the dining room, Jack and Frances scoop up Danny and perform acts of parental efficiency. I inspect the table with a critic's eye. It looks kind of bare. I'm used to seeing a platter of carrot and celery sticks or at the very least the prerequisite bowl of jiggling cranberry sauce, pushed straight from the can. I guess those things don't go with turkey tacos or whatever the hell Southwestern Thanksgiving food might be.

When we are all seated, Mom presents a huge platter of steaming tamales. Sam follows with a terrine of aromatic, brick red sauce. We help ourselves. Unwrapping the corn husk package reveals soft, fluffy masa wrapped around rich stewed turkey. Alone, the tamales are so sweet and mild that Danny gobbles his up as fast as his parents can get them cool. With a spoonful of Sam's red chili sauce, the earthy ingredients are transformed into an explosion of contrasting flavors.

This isn't the Taco Bell dinner I expected. Mandy is like a kid, bouncing in her chair and repeating over and over again, "Mama Rose's tamales and red chili! Tamales and chili!" What has, at first, looked like enough food to feed Australia dwindles to a modest pile. We all take turns cursing the fire in our mouths. We weep and choke from gluttonous bites of the hot sauce, only to gulp down a cold drink and repeat the glorious, painful experience.

Sam is seated next to me. (Surely that was Mom's doing.) When I'm willing to leave my mouth free of food for a moment, I lean over and bump his shoulder with mine. "Well done. Mandy is right, you really *are* a great cook."

He beams with pride. "Thanks. The sauce came out just right. And I found some fresh young corn at the last minute to stir into the masa. That makes them moist. You really like it?"

I nod and scrape up the residual tamale crumbs and last smudge of sauce on my plate. "I've tried red chili sauces before and they always taste kind of raw, like there's a flavor or seasoning missing. I guess I just never had it done right. This is amazing." I am about to reach for my third tamale, but Sam stops me. "Don't eat too much. There's lots more food to come."

Sam, Mandy and Mom go back into the kitchen and return with a huge tureen of hominy soup and perhaps a dozen bowls piled high with accompaniments.

"Posole is a traditional Christmas dish, but I couldn't wait," Sam explains. "Lauren, hand me your bowl and I'll serve you." He ladles the soup into Mom's bowl. Her open adoration of him is apparent to everyone. I'm willing to admit I like Sam a lot too, but not in a romantic way or anything. Maybe I'll let Iris date him after all.

Sam continues, "I like mine pretty plain, with just a spoonful of extra chili and a squeeze of lime, but I gathered up every condiment I've ever heard of so you can experiment and create your own masterpiece."

I go a little overboard and pile my bowl high with fresh cilantro, avocado, radishes, tomatoes, and a crumbly white cheese. The second bowl I top with finely shredded cabbage, olives and pickled jalapeños. If anybody misses turkey and gravy, they don't make a peep about it.

It's strange. When we first sat down at the table, I was uncomfortable. I felt as though I was the mom and these kids were just playing house. I would be gracious and choke down the weird food with a smile. Next year, when Mom got over her whim to screw up Thanksgiving, I would step in and make it all right again. But it isn't working out that way. This food is great. It is, in fact, better than any Thanksgiving I can remember, and that kind of sucks. Once again, I am left questioning my role in the food business. My discontent is brief. As I fill my belly with warm, well-seasoned food, I feel taken care of, not underappreciated. My holiday is calm and nurturing instead of harried and ridden with performance anxiety.

In classic Thanksgiving style, I swear there is no room left, but I still manage to polish off a puffy fried sopaipilla drizzled with mesquite honey and a sliver of pumpkin pie.

Danny is his father's son. After dinner, their few bites of turkey hit them hard. They are asleep, snuggled together on the living room couch. Frances curls up in a chair with a stack of magazines. Mom plays another round of cards with Virginia and the Pinkertons. Sam, Mandy and I drape ourselves on the couch and family room floor and halfheartedly watch a DVD of *The Wizard of Oz*.

I can't help myself. Sam's head is just so close, so touchable. I reach out and finger one of his perfect curls. Mandy watches me. I get the feeling Sam can feel it, but he doesn't even flinch. I pull the curl tight then let go and sing, "Boing."

Mandy smiles. "Did you read *Ramona the Pest* when you were a kid?"

I nod. "It was one of my favorites." But it wasn't until she mentioned the story that I realized what might have inspired my actions. She reminds me of Ramona's curl-pulling compulsion, and we talk for a while about our favorite children's books. Sam exchanges *The Wizard of Oz* for the original, animated version of *The Grinch Who Stole Christmas*. I'm embarrassed when he gets up and I realize I have been absentmindedly fondling his curls as Mandy and I talked.

"So, what are you making for Christmas dinner, Sam?" I ask, trying to distract him. I smooth the spots I might have messed up in his hair. "Since your food is so good, I think I'm going to retire."

He laughs. "You can't do that. I pretty much tapped out my repertoire tonight. I'm a one-trick pony, so it's your turn. Everything you make is so amazing."

I'm not feeling like a star chef tonight. I might be capable of great food, but I haven't been performing up to par these past few weeks. Also, Mr. Wright has me questioning my definition of what good food really is. It might be nice to lay low and let other people cook for a while. "You've never even had my *good* cooking."

"Yes, I have. You're always bringing me those containers from the office."

"Those are just leftovers. That doesn't count."

"What do you mean?"

I'm not sure how to explain myself. If Nancy Dierbocker heard such praise for my recent break room buffets and meals on wheels deliveries, she would pee her pants laughing.

"It's soup and salad. I warm up the soup, toss the salad, then scoop and serve for an hour and a half. It's glorified comfort food. A fancy church lunch."

He turns and looks at me with concern, then shakes his head with dismissal. "I don't understand you, Kate. You have a real talent, a gift. Knowing how to cook is one of the proudest achievements of my life. And it's not like I can make anything fancy. I cook how Mama Rose taught me. But it's just so amazing how people respond to good food, even the simple stuff. If you can cook, you have the power to make people happy. You might not change anyone's life, but at least you can give somebody a great moment, a pleasant mouthful. What more do you want out of life than that?"

I'm quiet for a moment, then have to admit, "Wow. That actually makes sense." I look to Sam, my new culinary sage. "Maybe you're right."

Mom's cat crawls onto Sam's lap. After a chin scratch, Raku flops on his side and looks as if he might turn himself inside out with pleasure. I watch them both, wishing I too could get so comfortable and feel so loved.

Chapter Nineteen

Mandy is the first to move. She pushes herself up from the couch and says, "I'm gonna go home and call Mom. You coming?"

"I called her this morning. But, yeah, I still need a ride."

I agree, it's time to go. We say our good-byes. I kiss little Danny on the forehead as he sleeps and promise Frances I'll visit soon. In the driveway, I surprise myself by volunteering, "Mandy, if you want to go straight home, I can give Sam a ride. He's not too far from my place."

"Really? That would be great."

Sam piles into the passenger seat of Mabel the Mercedes. The silence is uncomfortable. We shift and squirm for a while, not knowing what to say. I played with his hair! What was I thinking? Once we get on the freeway, I make up my mind. I will hook him up with Iris. He's a good guy. She's my best friend. It seems like the right thing to do. I swallow the lump in my throat and ask, "Are you still unavailable? I mean, are you over that Selena thing and interested in dating again?" I keep my eyes on the road. I don't want to mess this up with accidental expressions. I can feel his pale blue eyes questioning me.

"What do you mean?" His voice is nervous. I need to word my request with care. I know Selena hurt him. He is delicate. I don't want to pressure him into anything and, let's face it, a blind date with Iris needs to be preceded by an honest assessment of her personality.

"I have a . . . friend. She's funny and artistic—a real character sometimes. And she's kind of found herself with a little extra time on her hands. She's not interested in a serious relationship or anything; she's had some trouble with men before. But don't get me wrong, she's a lot of fun. There's even a good chance you might get lucky. She loves sex . . .

and I just thought you two might want to get together sometime. Maybe go have a drink or something." I blow out a breath of air. I thought that was going to be awkward, but it came out all right.

"I don't know what to say. I'm flattered. Let me think about it." We are silent as I drive the familiar route to Ballard, then proceed north to the Crown Hill neighborhood. Sam directs me to a parking lot on a main intersection.

"Right over there is fine."

"In that parking lot?" I look around. The nearest house is half a block away, and it looks way too well-kept to board Sam and his frat brothers.

"I can take you all the way home, you know. You don't have to be embarrassed."

"Huh?"

"You don't have to get out on the corner and walk home. How bad can the house be? This is a much better neighborhood than I *thought* you lived in."

"What are you talking about?"

"Your roommates. Ziggy, Cy, Dieter. The Animal House you always refer to."

Sam sputters a minute, then bursts out laughing.

"What?" I ask, getting irritated. He can't answer. It takes him a minute to catch his breath. There are tears in his eyes from laughing so hard. "Kate, you crack me up. C'mon in. I want you to meet my roommates."

He gets out of the car and goes through the parking lot to a back gate of the nondescript professional building. Everything falls into place when I read the small sign next to the gate. CROWN VETERINARIAN HOSPITAL. PLEASE RING BELL FOR DELIVERIES AND DROP-OFFS. The moment Sam's keys start to jingle, the place goes wild with barking.

"You live with real animals," I say, shocked as a dog the size of a pony pushes his way through the door and leans into Sam. The door shudders and thuds with each thump of the huge dog's tail. Sam sweet-talks and scratches the beast.

"Hey, Zig. Did ya miss me?" The mastiff responds by rearing up on his hind legs, placing one huge paw on each of Sam's shoulders and licking his chin. One lick with a tongue like that might constitute a bath for some people. Sam nuzzles the dog's enormous head. "I missed you too, big guy." Sam looks over from his intimacy and introduces me.

"Kate, this is my roommate and best friend, Ziggy." The dog takes one step closer to me and sticks his nose in my crotch.

"Yeeowww!" I shriek and hop.

Sam chuckles. "I think I mentioned it to you before, but the Zigster here doesn't have much in the way of manners."

"But Ziggy's a dog!"

"I can't believe you didn't get that. I know I sometimes call these guys my roommates, but I didn't realize I was quite so guilty of anthropomorphizing. I wasn't trying to fool you or anything, honest." He laughs again, and his eyes and straight white teeth are mesmerizing. I smile along with him. This guy keeps blowing me away.

What is this weird feeling I'm having around Sam? I like him. He's fun to be with. I would have flirted with him if I had met him a few months ago, but not anymore. I know what I want now. I want Gaston, a nice house, beach vacations and the whole happily-ever-after package. I want a man with a grown-up job and a future. What I'm feeling for Sam must be just physical attraction. He's a very good-looking man. My insides do a similar pitter-patter when I see movies starring Johnny Depp or Clive Owen.

I decide that it's healthy for me to be drawn to Sam, especially since I have been so focused on relationships. My current obsession with Gaston and marriage and my future is obviously whacking out my hormones and sex drive. Seeing my adorable nephew must have my uterus working like a homing beacon. Bleep, bleep, bleep—virile sperm straight ahead— all systems ready!

"So what about Cy and Dieter and the rest of them? Is anybody human?"

He shakes his head. "I get free rent in exchange for being a live body around here when the office is closed. The vet who owns this place, Dr. Boyce, got tired of getting his pharmacy stripped by addicts and found having a lodger is a great deterrent. It's not expected of me, but I like to give the dogs some exercise and keep an eye on the sick cats.

"Ziggy showed up right after I got here. It was fate, I guess. I needed a friend, and there he was. Some rich couple got him because they thought it would be regal having such a large and expensive dog decorating their home. But they never bothered training him and left him locked up in a kennel most of the time. I wouldn't doubt it if they gave him up because they couldn't take the gas. Ziggy here's got a pretty sensitive stomach. He can clear a room mighty fast if he eats the wrong thing. The drool is just something you learn to live with. But I guess his original owners weren't fond of slime on their suede pants and silk furniture. They didn't even bother looking around for a home for him.

They just dropped him off with a check to have him dealt with." Ziggy sniffs at me again, decides that I'm nothing special and goes back to Sam's side.

Sam says, "You wanna meet everyone else? We've got extra pens here and take in boarders. I've been gone all day, so I'm sure they're dying to get out." He leads me into the back room. I can hear the dogs next door in the kennel, but a one-eyed cat is barring the way, looking pissed off.

"Let me guess. That's Cy," I say.

"Yeah, he's mad that his dinner is late." The cat is blocking the door into the rest of the clinic. Ziggy won't go near him. The huge dog lies down a few feet from the door and whines until Sam picks up the cat and walks into the other room. I guess Sam was right: Cy's the boss around here. Sam pours some cat food into a bowl on a countertop, and points out his tiny apartment. Then he goes back to the kennels to release the small pack of dogs that have been left as boarders over the holiday weekend. I follow Sam and the dogs into a fenced exercise yard, and finally get the dose of pet attention I've been craving. Spike might be good for a laugh now and then, but a fish can't give you love like a dozen attention-starved mutts.

Dogs of all sizes chase and wrestle with one another, excited to be free and energized by gathering as a pack. Retrievers go straight for the loose tennis balls and drop them at our feet. Sam and I throw balls and Frisbees. We squeak tiny plastic pork chops, hedgehogs and barbells for the terrier mixes. The hounds bounce and play with the other dogs but are most interested in sniffing corners and crevices. I get down on my knees and use my strong, fake nails to give thorough back and tummy scratches to the homesick mutts.

Ziggy decides that I might be worth getting to know, once I convince a few of the smaller dogs to grab a knotted rope for a game of tug-of-war. He muscles in beside them and gives the rope a yank. I'm pulled off my feet and thrown into Sam. We both crash into a heap on the hard ground. I'm sure glad that Sam has been diligent about clearing the steaming land mines.

"You okay?" Sam asks me.

"I'm fine, but you must be crushed. I landed right on top of you." I roll off him and brush my hands on my jeans to remove the grit and rubble. Ziggy barks an alarm. He is standing over Sam with his head cocked, looking very concerned. Sam and I laugh at his expression.

"I'm okay, buddy. She didn't hurt me. I can handle it." Ziggy barks again. Sam hams it up. "You're right! She's an intruder! Let's get her." He gets up on his knees, wraps his hands playfully around my neck and pretends to choke me. "See? I've got her. I'm safe." I shriek and moan and flail my arms in dramatic agony and then fall down dead. A second later I can feel Ziggy giving my face a sniff. A warm drizzle of drool lands on my cheek. I grimace and open one eye. "Eeew!" Sam leans over me, and wipes my cheek clean. He is looking at me funny. I grin to let him see I'm just fine, and then he kisses me. It's a chilly evening, I'm lying on the cold ground and yet my every corpuscle goes white-hot.

"Uh, excuse me. What was that?" I ask.

"You couldn't tell? I must be out of practice. Here, let me do it again and maybe you'll recognize it." I should object or resist, but it feels so good. I kiss him back this time.

"Did you recognize it that time? It's a kiss." The dogs are standing around us, wagging their tails and panting. They are watching to see what we will do next. I'm curious, too. I push myself upright.

"Yeah. Okay. *That* was definitely a kiss." It was a kiss that has my toenails melting and my personal bits feeling very hot and bothered. The repetition of the word "kiss" sets off Scoop and Micky, a pair of fat corgi brothers. It is a command they are familiar with. They rush over to us and cover our faces with licks. The rest of the pooches seem to like this idea and join in. I try to push them away, but I can't stop giggling, and my laughs encourage them.

"He licked my tongue! Eew! For the record, I definitely prefer *your* French kisses." I reach out my arms for help, and Sam pulls me upright. I'm a mess, but I haven't had so much fun in a long time. I'm still giggling when Sam brushes away a few stray wisps of hair that feel like they have been pasted to my cheeks and forehead with canine saliva. I look up at him, and what feels like a bolt of lightning passes between our eyes. I look away. What the hell is going on? I'm horny, that's all. And he caught me by surprise with the food, the moonlight, the animals and the kiss. I step away, flustered. I need to set things straight.

"That was nice, but I don't want to mislead you. I'm still unavailable. You know that, right? I'm in love with Gaston. We might not be together right now, but we will be, soon."

He looks devastated. He scratches his head and stutters, "But you said . . . In the car you said . . ."

"You think kissing *me* will help your chances with Iris? Honey, she's a big girl. If she wants to kiss a guy, believe me, she just does it. She doesn't expect me to give them a test run." (Although I intend to pass on the word that Sam is a mighty talented kisser.)

"Iris?" His expression is pained. Again, I am confused by Sam.

"Yeah, Iris. My roommate. She's . . . Oh, my God! Did you think I was talking about myself?"

He shakes his head. "No, of course not . . . I was, uh." He can't pull off the lie. "Jeez, Kate! What do you expect me to think? Your 'friend' is funny and artistic with a lot of spare time on her hands and past boyfriend troubles? Who else could it be? I thought it was a little strange that you were referring to yourself like that, but hell, sometimes you can be kind of strange."

"Argh!" I groan. I feel all twitchy and weird. I wag my hands and pace. "It's Mom's fault. I guess she called the other day and told Iris you were some hot item. Iris's band just broke up, and she's been feeling kind of down. She wanted to know more about you, and I thought . . . uuhh. God, I'm so sorry. I knew I should never have brought it up."

Sam and I are both embarrassed. We walk around the courtyard picking up dog toys and avoiding eye contact. I know I should leave, but I don't want to abandon my new furry friends. I kneel down and scratch a golden retriever. "I should go."

"You don't have to go. It was my mistake. I'm sorry. I knew about Gaston and everything. It's just that you haven't said much about him lately and . . . I shouldn't have assumed . . . Let's just forget it, okay? Why don't you come in and have a cup of licorice tea? Mama Rose always made us licorice tea after a big dinner. And besides, the dogs seem to like you. You can give them their evening treats. I give them a biscuit after we play and a chance to mellow out on the carpet in the waiting room. It helps them wind down."

I'm torn. I feel as if I should go home, but a roomful of warm, lovable pets and a cup of tea with Sam sounds much more inviting than my empty house. I follow Sam inside. His voice is a little forced, but he manages to keep up his lighthearted banter.

"I keep thinking about it. Did you actually think I lived with a bunch of guys? You thought I hung out with a group of hungry losers who just waited around for a ride to the beach or park?"

"Well, yeah. Everyone assumes I know everything about you. But remember, I don't spend all day gossiping in the studio like you and Mom. The way you talked—'Ziggy is a big lovable lunkhead, Cy gets into fights and likes weed . . . '" I look around. "Which one is Dieter? Did you finally get rid of him?"

My question is answered as we step into the waiting room. There is an ugly squawk and the sound of metal banging. I look up to see a gray parrot bobbing his head with excitement. "Hello. *Dieter ist ein hübscher Vogel. Deiter will ein Kegs haben. Kegs haben. Kegs haben.* Squawk. Hello."

Sam has still not warmed up to Dieter. "You ever get that phone number from your hairdresser? His owner is delayed. She's having trouble getting her work visa, and it would be great if we could find this guy another home." His words are tough, but he knows the parrot is starved for attention, just like the dogs. Sam steps close and wiggles some of the toys hanging from the cage for the bird's entertainment.

"Dieter *ist ein* loud bird," he says. "Dieter *ist ein* pain in the ass." He chats with the lonesome bird awhile, then disappears into the back office. He returns with a couple of fresh sugar peas and pokes them through the wire into the bird's dish. While he watches the bird work on the peas, I watch him. Since he came back with the peas, he's been holding his stomach funny. I wonder if he doesn't feel well until I see his shirt bulge and wiggle. He pulls his shirt collar away from his neck and looks inside. A tiny dog head peeks out and looks around.

"You ready to play now, Trixie?" He unfastens a few buttons and releases the teeniest dog I've ever seen, a toy fox terrier puppy with a broken leg.

"She's a trooper. She's just three months old and a scooter tagged her last week. We thought for sure she was a goner, but she's doing great. She should be able to go home this weekend."

Trixie romps and plays with the big dogs, seemingly unaware of her lame leg. The dogs are very gentle with her, somehow knowing they could snap her in half. Sam hands me a tin of dog biscuits, and I pass them around. I sit on the carpeted floor and nuzzle ears and scratch bellies. When they all have been loved, Sam herds them back into their kennels. Only Ziggy and Cy remain loose.

"Oh! Tea. I forgot to make your tea. C'mon back."

Sam leads me through the office to a tiny kitchenette and laundry facility near his room. He plugs in an electric kettle, and grabs two mugs and a couple of teabags from the cupboards.

"This place isn't designed for entertaining guests. At least not the two-legged variety." He pulls out two padded break room chairs from under a small table and hands me a steaming mug. Then Sam makes himself at home. He kicks off his shoes, and pulls the shirt he's cooked in all day over his head and throws it in the laundry hamper. And there they are again: his naked shoulders, covered with only a narrow strip of sexy white T-shirt. Sam is once again flashing me with my ultimate aphrodisiac.

He reaches for a sweatshirt from a basket of clean laundry. The action causes his left shoulder to ripple and dimple in a way that makes me feel drunk. If I were standing, my knees would buckle. I can't help but notice how his narrow waist swivels under the T-shirt. His long arms lead to elegant wrists and strong, graceful fingers. My eyes take in the whole upper package, then wander down his khakis.

My lusty thoughts remind me of our earlier kiss. I am hungry for more. It doesn't take me long to rationalize my impulses. Sam knows I'm in love with Gaston. He understands that I'm not looking for a relationship. If we fool around a little, it's not like I would be unfaithful to Gaston. After all, he's probably having sex with Courtney right now. In fact, sleeping with Sam might be *good* for my future relationship. When Gaston and I get back together, we'll be even.

Sam turns around and sees me staring at him. Our eyes lock. Once again, there is an electric energy passing between us. I push myself out of the chair. Without ever breaking our gaze, I walk over to him, grab him with both hands and kiss him with determination. He kisses me back. This isn't like our playful smooch with the dogs. This kiss could light a fire.

"This is probably a bad idea," Sam murmurs. He's being a gentleman, giving me a chance to change my mind, to back out, but his words are contrary to his actions. He isn't pulling back.

We kiss some more, and my hands start to explore his marvelous body. I nibble at his neck and explain, "On the contrary, I think this is a very *good* idea." We start reaching for buttons and zippers. "I've had a lot of tension in my life lately. I need a release."

He agrees. "Tension, yeah. A release." We continue to kiss and peel off clothing. I swear there must be smoke coming out of my ears, I feel so hot. Sam pulls back for a moment, and his eyes clear as if he's going to say something. I distract him with a touch. He moans and his eyes go out of focus again. He grabs me, and our bodies meet, not as tender lovers, but as mountain animals in the early spring, starving beasts desperate to mate. We are pulling and writhing, sucking and biting. We stumble toward his apartment in our underwear. Then he stops. He pulls away from me as though I am poison.

"Oh, Jeez. No . . . Kate, we can't do this . . ." He slams his hand against his forehead in frustration. Well, so much for my tension release. I

stand there in my underwear and socks, quivering. Ziggy and Cy are staring at me, awaiting my next trick. I am trying to decide if I should talk
to Sam some more or just put my clothes back on and head home while
I have a shred of dignity left.

"I don't . . . I didn't . . ." he stutters for a minute, looking for the right
words. I save him the trouble.

"No biggie, Sam. You don't have to make up an excuse." I am half-
naked, obviously horny and being rejected in front of a couple of curious animals. This isn't my finest hour.

His arms flail until they find his hair. In a desperate voice he says, "It's
not that! I don't have any condoms! I threw them all away when I
moved! I never thought to buy some in case . . . in case. I mean, who
would have guessed I would want a condom tonight?" He pulls at his
crazy Einstein hair. It is my turn to laugh.

I go back and find my purse, pull out my small, beaded "girly bag,"
and sure enough, there are half a dozen condoms, all of them designed
"for her pleasure." I spread them out in my hand like cards. "Do you
think six ought to do it?"

Sam's mouth drops open. He grabs for the condoms, lifts me into his
arms and carries me to his tiny bedroom. "I just want you to know how
much I respect and appreciate a well-prepared modern woman like yourself." He tosses me on the bed like I weigh nothing, then kicks the door
closed, locking out all furry voyeurs.

Sex with Sam is marvelous. He is so different from Gaston. He is
strong, tall and limber. His skin is smooth and relatively hairless. His legs,
arms and torso are lean and muscular. Instead of closing my eyes and letting my body drift away in a sensory cloud, I leave the light on and keep
my eyes wide open. I want to see and explore every inch of Sam. He
smells of cooking oil, spices and musk. He tastes sweet.

His skin prickles with excitement. Tiny tremors and goose flesh ripple
like waves along his torso. I watch his muscles flex and his frame bend
and sway. I watch my own long, strong legs reach out and cling to him. I
run my fingernails up and down his back, pull handfuls of his thick hair
and bite those wonderful shoulders. I listen to his sounds and hear my
own in harmony. Our bodies melt together with tender liquidity, then
turn rigid and forceful. We flex and writhe and sweat and then roll apart,
satiated and gasping for air. I am awash in contentment. It is as if my
veins and arteries have been rinsed with effervescent spring water and my
tired, old blood replaced with warm, spiced honey.

"Wow!" he says.

"Well, I guess I'll have to add sex to my list of things to be thankful for," I say.

Sam grins. "It's a nice addition to the holiday."

I lie still for a moment and drift off to sleep. I awake with a start, now wrapped in Sam's arms. I try to convince my bones to straighten and my nerves that they might have a few synapses left in them to move me out the door. Sex with Sam was a whim. It's not something that requires postcoital cuddling. It was an act of sensory indulgence after a nice day; a release, an exercise in independence and liberation. Sam looks over at me and, as usual, reads my mind.

"So, we're still good, right?"

"Huh?"

"You're okay?"

"I'm great, actually. Thanks."

He stares at the ceiling. "So, we're, everything's . . . okay?"

"You afraid I changed my mind? Think I might have buyer's remorse?" I peek under the covers at his merchandise. "Nope. I'm good."

He snaps the sheet down, embarrassed. "I just want to make sure things are cool. It's been a while, you know. And when things got going, maybe I wasn't thinking so clearly. I want to make sure we don't have another misunderstanding. I know you're into Gaston and you know about Selena. Neither of us is looking for a relationship right now."

I'm not about to let him know, but my feelings are bruised. *I'm* supposed to be the one saying this. I'm the one who wanted to remind *him* that this was just a casual thing. I laugh it off. "Let's just think of it as . . . a good workout. Maybe a very special spa treatment. Can you imagine all of these rich women going to the desert and waiting around in their robes for their turn in the orgasm treatment room? I wonder what kind of aromatherapy candle would be best for that?"

He laughs with me and pulls me close. It feels good, but again, I feel like I should go. "I didn't sign up for the all-night treatment. I should probably go."

"I wasn't trying to get rid of you or anything. I was just thinking out loud. I like you, Kate. But maybe we should just be . . ."

"You want to be friends, right?" I blow out a sarcastic sigh. "Oh, please. Spare me the tired old line."

He is exasperated. "I *mean* it."

I roll my eyes. Somehow his hokey line about still being friends cheapens what we did. "But that is such a breakup line. That's what you say when you're trying to detach yourself from a sticky relationship and still maintain a facade of honor. You don't have to be gallant. I'm as responsible for tonight's lovemaking as you are, if not more so. I'm not about to get all clingy. It was good. It was great, in fact. Can't we just leave it at that? I'm comfortable with you, Sam. I like you. Why can't we keep things the way they've been without having to declare a formal *friendship* just because we had sex?"

"Jeez, Kate, you make me sound like a real asshole. I'm sorry if it sounded like I was dishing you a tired old line or trying to wriggle out of any attachment. That's not what I was trying to say at all." He's silent for a while. "It's just that I don't *do* this. I'm not like you; I don't carry condoms everywhere I go. I was a geek in high school. I had a few short-term girlfriends in college, and then Selena. In fact, I think I can say that I've never *asked* a woman to be my friend. I don't need female friends. I've got three sisters! But you're different. I like spending time with you, and to top it all off, I've just had about the best sex in my life. That's kind of big deal for me. It means something.

"I know you're still into Gaston, and that's okay, because I'm still a little shaky from the whole Selena thing. I guess what I was trying to say was, I don't have much to offer you except an open invitation to repeat this evening's fun and games whenever you feel the need, and my friendship."

I look into his eyes and know he means every word. I wrap my arms around him and kiss him. "Okay, Sam, I get it. I would love to be your friend." We kiss for a few minutes more, and then I clear up one tiny misconception.

"I don't want you to get the wrong idea about me. I'm not as experienced as you think. I've always carried condoms. I don't have a choice. Instead of a tooth fairy, I have my own prophylactic fairy. Her name is Iris."

I was about twelve the first time I found a strange, crinkly package in my backpack. I was mortified, and as soon as I could, I flushed the condom, package and all, down the toilet. The next day, I found another. For about a month, I had no idea where these "gifts" were coming from. When, in the middle of algebra, a Trojan fell out of my pencil case, I just about lost it. I scooped up the package, tucked it in my pocket and ran home to my mom, crying. Mom connected the deeds to Iris and explained that Iris's aunt was dying of AIDS and that, unless it embarrassed me to death, it might be a good idea to support Iris in her campaign. In high school, it got out that I carried condoms, and I became a very popular girl. It wasn't because I was labeled a slut (I often wonder why no one ever assumed I *used* the things), but because I saved a lot of horny teenagers an embarrassing trip to the pharmacy.

Iris hasn't slowed down. She volunteers and does talks and presentations at local youth groups. She insists that women take charge of their safety, and has been known to do random purse searches of her friends and band mates to make sure they are carrying condoms. I have accepted it as a fact that every few months Iris will restock my tampon carrier with a supply of fresh, often whimsical rubbers. And they have, quite honestly, been very handy. Like right now, when it seems like a good idea to test a new variety.

Chapter Twenty

At home, late the next morning, I lie in bed pondering. Did I really jump into bed with Sam just because it sounded like fun? I'm not a vixen. What's gotten into me? I stare at the ceiling. I'm not sure about anything anymore. When I stopped goofing off in college and went to cooking school, I knew who I was and what I wanted. I was a chef and aspiring restaurateur. I had a crystal-clear vision of my goals. How did everything get so murky? How would I define myself now? I'm a part-time cook, craving a husband and family with a man I turned down, a man who is engaged to someone else. I had spontaneous sex with my mother's pottery assistant. Jeez, who the hell *am* I?

I reach over and grab one of Gaston's self-help books that are stacked on the bedside table. I need some life coaching. I thumb through the pages but find most of the information oversimplified and trite. There are no chapters about what I really need to know. How do I get Gaston back? What does "good food" mean? What on earth am I going to do next?

I roll myself out of bed, make a pot of coffee, play a few hands of solitaire and roast off a turkey breast. Sam's New Mexican feast was awesome, but it won't be November without a few turkey and potato chip sandwiches on white bread. Once again, I find myself content with trashy food. I should stop calling myself a chef.

Iris calls. "Do you think you could move my wet clothes into the dryer? I'm not going to have a chance until later. I'm at the recording studio with Rex. I called him last night and told him the band broke up. I tried to cancel our session, but he asked me to come by myself. He is so nice! I guess he figured since we had the time booked, I might as well use it."

"Yeah? So what are you working on?" I ask. I'm happy for her. Iris sounds more excited than she has in months.

"All sorts of stuff. I thought we were just going to do some sound checks, but he keeps digging up all this ancient sheet music, and we're jamming. Rex is *amazing*."

"He's not the only one. You're talented, too."

"You know, it's weird. I'm playing and sounding better than ever. It must be his equipment."

Iris comes across as ballsy and bold, but she's got all sorts of insecurities. She's never been able to take compliments, and she's always underestimated her skills. I'm almost glad the band broke up. Working alone with this guy Rex might give her a good boost of self-confidence.

I do a few loads of wash, feed Spike and think again about adopting a pet. I can't remember if Gaston is allergic only to cats or if dogs get to him, too. Maybe I'll just load him up on antihistamines and get an animal anyway. I loved having all of those pets around yesterday.

To distract myself from more disturbing thoughts, like sex with Sam, I throw myself into a fit of housekeeping. I rearrange all the cupboards and scrub the floor of the broom closet until Marissa calls and offers me another option.

"Kate! Great, you're home. I have a favor to ask. Do you have anything planned for today?"

"Not really, why? What's up?"

"You remember I told you the nursing home where I work is always short on kitchen staff? Well, today they're screwed. You know how the holidays are. I guess the cook got into it with his ex-wife's family last night and he's cooling off at the King County jail. His assistant is snowed in up at Snoqualmie Pass. We need someone to bang out the dinners. I know it's not your thing, but are you up for it? Just this once?"

"Will I have to wear a hairnet?"

"I won't tell if you don't. I think they'd let you wear a tutu as long as these people get fed."

I search my head for a good excuse, but can't come up with one. I blow out a sigh of exasperation. "Okay. I'll be there in a few minutes."

I pull on some chef whites and pack up a small knife roll, then drive to Cedar Heights Nursing Home. I walk up to the reception desk and introduce myself. The building has the unpleasant smell of industrial cleaners and medical adhesives.

"Hi. I'm Kate Linden. Marissa Ruiz called me and asked if I could help out in the kitchen." The woman behind the desk gives me a blank look. I try again. "I guess you're missing some cooks? I'm here to fill in?"

The woman blinks slowly a few times more, and I have to wonder if she has been sampling some of the patients' sedatives. Finally, she speaks. "I don't know anything about that. You'll have to talk to my supervisor. She's on a break right now, so why don't you wait in one of those chairs in the lobby?"

I chew the inside of my cheek a bit, trying to decide if I will hunt down the kitchen myself or try again to break through this woman's apathy. My problem is solved when I hear my name.

"Kate!" Marissa shuffles quickly toward me down a long hallway. "Thank goodness you're here!" She steps behind the reception desk, pushing the indifferent woman aside as if she weren't even there. She pages an orderly.

Marissa is too busy to give me the tour, so she introduces me to a huge man named Glenn. He greets me and leads me downstairs to a big, sterile kitchen. He points to a blue paper calendar taped to the kitchen window.

"Here's the menu. It says that tonight they're supposed to have vegetable soup, pork chops with applesauce, green beans and yellow cake with chocolate icing. I have no idea where anything is kept, so you're on your own in there. There's a list on the wall next to the fridge about the special-needs folks. Some need everything pureed, some just need their food chopped up. I'll be here at 4:55 to start taking trays upstairs. Call the front desk and have me paged if you need me."

I look around and get familiar with the layout of the kitchen. I peek into the freezer, walk-in refrigerator and storeroom looking for ingredients. I guess the ordering wasn't done, because I can't find half of what I need. I see a list of purveyors taped next to the phone. Many of them are familiar to me. I make a call to the produce company and request an emergency delivery.

I find a couple of cases of pork chops and sear them to a nice golden brown. I deglaze the pan with a bunch of tiny cans of apple juice, some hot water and a few crumbled chicken bouillon cubes. I sprinkle in some ancient ground sage and black pepper that looks as if it might add more sandy texture than actual flavor. I whip together a basic cake batter I learned in school. As I finish loading tins of pound cake in the oven, the produce arrives. I'm pleased to see the cases of green beans and apples carried in by Kurt, my favorite delivery guy—the one with the nice legs.

"Kurt! How're you doing?"

I get the feeling he was planning on dropping off the stock and running but at the sound of his name, he looks up. He seems to register my face as familiar, but out of place. I can almost see the gears moving in his brain as he tries to figure out who the hell I am.

"It's Kate, Kate Linden. From Sound Bistro."

The lightbulb goes on. "Kate! I've been wondering what happened to you. Nice to see you again." He gives me one of his sexy, wolfish appraisals. He looks around, registering where I am. "What the hell are you doing here?"

My heart sinks when I remember Kurt's most appealing trait after his fine legs; his unending supply of restaurant gossip. I should never have stopped him or announced myself. Now every kitchen in town will know that Kate Linden has fallen low. She's cooking for people who can't even chew. I try to explain.

"Uh, my roommate works here. There was an emergency. I'm just here for the day."

Kurt bobs his head like he understands, but his smile is shifty and smug. What did I ever see in this brute? "Yeah. Okay. Whatever you say. Nice to see you, sweetheart. Don't be a stranger." He heads back to his truck. I imagine him going straight to his radio, sending word to the dispatcher and alerting the entire city that I'm now pureeing pork chops for a living.

The potential for gossip torments me. I create all sorts of horrible scenarios in my mind as I peel and slice apples then sauté them in butter with sliced onions. I am staring into space, lost in thought, topping and tailing the green beans, when Lucinda, the cook's assistant who was trapped in the snow, rushes in. She drops her stuff and ties on an apron as she explains her predicament.

"I'm so sorry! I went to Yakima for Thanksgiving. I thought I could make it home in time, but—" She stops short and stares at the prep on the table. "What are you doing?"

I lift my hands and look down, concerned that I am doing something wrong. I guess they like their beans French-cut. Or maybe pork chops are always served with yellow wax beans.

Lucinda looks around in confusion and sniffs the air. "It smells different in here. . . ."

"I saw the menu and just started cooking." I show her what I have done so far. I lift the lid from a mélange of ingredients I scavenged from various shelves in the freezer and fridge. "Vegetable soup." I have removed the seared pork chops from their braising liquid and placed them on a sheet pan while the remaining sauce reduces and thickens with sautéed apples and onions. "Pork chops. Applesauce." I point to the boiling water and the fresh vegetables I am almost finished prepping. "Green beans." The loaves of pound cake are cooling a bit more before I drizzle melted bittersweet chocolate chips over the top. "Yellow cake. Chocolate icing."

"Oh, my God!" is Lucinda's reply. "Mrs. Schmidt is going to totally freak out."

"Mrs. Schmidt?" I ask.

"And Mr. Foster and Mrs. Fogel. Everyone." She looks nervous.

I'm a little irritated. My food isn't going to kill anyone, and they are at least getting fed. "Mrs. Schmidt and Mr. Foster will just have to live through one day of somebody else cooking."

"Are you kidding? You better have an exit strategy planned, or they'll tie you up and make you stay forever!" Lucinda pulls back a hand truck that has been tucked in a corner. I hadn't noticed it before. She grabs a couple of number-ten cans off the loaded cart and drops them on the table. She pushes them toward me so I can read the labels. "Vegetable soup." She pushes two more big cans at me. "Apple sauce. Low-sodium green beans." She returns to the storeroom for two big, generic boxes. "Yellow cake. Chocolate icing."

"Oh."

"Damon buys bags of fresh vegetables for some of the lunch salads, but that's it. I never knew you could make vegetable soup from scratch. How did you get those pork chops brown? They look moist, too. I cook them just like Damon tells me to, but they're always gray and dried out."

Damon is the incarcerated chef. The more I learn about him, the more I am convinced he was trained in a work-release program. Lucinda doesn't know much about food either. She's just a kid and she has a baby of her own. She's happy to have regular work. She does whatever Damon tells her to do, but I find she is eager to learn more. I explain about browning meat and cooking it slowly with plenty of moisture instead of just plopping the chops on a pan and roasting them to death.

We chat as I plate up the regular dinners, arrange them on trays with plastic covers and slide them into rolling carts. Lucinda chops and purees those dinners for special-needs patients and then distributes milk and juice to the trays. I'm ladling the steaming soup into tiny bowls at the last minute so they will stay hot, when Glenn, the orderly, and his assistant arrive for the carts.

I guess Damon isn't much for clean-up either, because Lucinda is blown away by my offer to help clean and prep for the next day. We are leaning on a worktable, discussing how she can spruce up tomorrow's fish, when I hear an elevator ping down the hall. Lucinda looks up and whispers, "Uh-oh."

A stooped old woman with huge glasses and deep, furrowed frown lines is hell-bent for the kitchen. She uses her sturdy, four-footed cane like a third leg, and she's moving darn fast for someone with such obviously decrepit knees.

"What the hell is going on down here? Where's that no-good bastard Damon?" she demands, pointing a threatening, rather crooked finger at Lucinda.

I mumble out of the side of my mouth, "Mrs. Schmidt, I presume?" Lucinda nods. She is trying to become invisible.

"Who are you? What are you doing here?" Mrs. Schmidt interrogates me. I open my mouth, but before I can introduce myself, she waves a long, cold green bean in my face. "This is a green bean!"

I nod in agreement. This poor woman is deranged. She doesn't know what she is doing or saying. I'm about to run for help, to call Glenn the orderly, when Mrs. Schmidt steps right next to me and tilts her head up so she can get a good look. She squints through her thick trifocal lenses, her frown deepening. I can see by her sharp gaze that this lady is not, in fact, addled or confused. She's old and small, but I can see in her eyes why Lucinda might be nervous. This is a woman who is not afraid of confrontation. She's ready for a fight. I'm concerned now about that stick of hers. A crack to the ankles with that thing would really smart.

"This is a *fresh* green bean," she repeats.

Again, I nod.

"Do you realize how long it's been since *real* food has been served in this geriatric prison?" I shake my head. After hearing a little about Damon's work ethic, I'm going to guess it's been a very long time.

The elevator bell dings again, and a skeletal, formerly tall man steps out and holds the door for a tiny, genteel woman in a pink sweatshirt. She is pushing a walker with bright yellow tennis balls attached as bumpers to the legs. I want her to move faster: I'm not sure the man could hold back the elevator door if it moves, and I don't want to see them both squashed.

The woman with the walker calls to my interrogator in a tiny voice. I think it's her version of a shout. "Mildred! The soup was hot! Glory be, I nearly burned my tongue. The soup was actually hot."

"Yes, dear, I noticed," says Mrs. Schmidt. "I'm trying to get to the bottom of it right now." She turns back to me and once again demands, "I asked you before. Who are you? What have you done with Damon? I'm an old lady; I don't have forever, you know."

The two new visitors make it to the kitchen, and I introduce myself. "I'm Kate. I'm a friend of Nurse Ruiz." They eye me suspiciously. "Damon is, er, indisposed, and Lucinda here had some road trouble. Marissa asked if I could help out."

Mrs. Schmidt looks over at Lucinda. "Damon back in the pokey?" Lucinda nods.

"Let's hope they keep him there this time!"

"I'm sorry if things seemed a little different today. I'm not familiar with the normal procedures." I turn to the woman with the walker. "I hope you didn't burn yourself on the soup."

"Oh, my. No, but I don't think I'd mind one bit if I did. They serve everything lukewarm around here, even the coffee. I don't know how many days this year I've wished for a cup of hot soup." She introduces herself as Dolores Fogel.

There is a snort from Mrs. Schmidt. She holds up the bean for me again. "I think this might be your basic pole bean. I don't think it's a Kentucky Wonder, maybe some kind of Tenderpod or Blue Lake. The strings are real tender. They're firm and crisp, but they don't hardly squeak when you bite into them. That's how you know they're good and fresh." The others nod in agreement.

The gentleman, Mr. Foster, says in a soft, Southern drawl, "That pork chop tasted like real meat. It looked like those same thin little things we always have, but it had flavor, and I didn't need to wrassle with it while I cut it up this time."

Mrs. Fogel speaks again in her tiny voice. "You can't get pork like we had in the old days. They raise it too lean. It's got no flavor." The seniors nod and agree, and the elevator bell dings again. Three more patients, one in a wheelchair, head toward the kitchen. I nudge Lucinda. "Call Glenn. Or Marissa. I'm not comfortable here. Being surrounded by a crowd of riled-up old people makes me nervous."

I hear a new warbling voice. "How about that cake? That was something else, wasn't it? Like a good old-fashioned butter cake. Dense, you know? Not light as air like those mixes they use. I like a heavy, moist cake. My mother made them like that. Used to be, if you wanted a fluffy cake, you had to spend all day with an eggbeater. Angel food really meant something back then."

A male voice pipes in, "Are there seconds?" The crowd turns to me with eager anticipation. Lucinda is flustered. She doesn't know the rules. There has never been such a request. I'm relieved when Marissa arrives.

She rings a butter knife against a melamine pudding bowl to get everyone's attention. "Folks. Let's all give a cheer to my good friend Kate Linden, and thank her for filling in for Damon today."

The seniors clang together pots and pans and bang wooden spoons against metal bowls. All this for pork chops and applesauce? I am speechless. Marissa okays their request for seconds, and the seniors polish off the leftovers. I stay at the nursing home much longer than I had planned. Good home-style cooking has struck a chord with these people, and they're not ready to go back to their TVs and radios. Lucinda brews a pot of hot decaf coffee, and we herd the growing crowd into an empty activity room near the kitchen. Mrs. Schmidt is still obsessed with her green bean. She and a liver-spotted man without a neck compare stories of their most successful gardens. There is much debate over how to grow the sweetest summer tomatoes and the best recipes for surplus zucchini. Recipes are compared for bread-and-butter pickles and corn relish. I don't say much. I just listen.

One man who looks like he might be a million years old tells us, "One time, way back when I was a kid in Missouri, an early frost wiped out the crops. All we had that year was corn mush. Boiled corn mush, fried corn mush, cold corn mush. It was god-awful, but at least it was food. And then at Christmas, I don't know how they did it, but my folks got each of us kids an orange. One whole perfect orange apiece. Let me tell you, nothing has tasted so good in all my life. That was the best present I ever got."

A spunky old lady speaks up. "You remember bread with cream? You ever have that?"

"You mean milk toast? I always hated milk toast. I had to eat it every time I got sick," says the neckless man.

"No, not milk toast, Carl. I'm talking about bread and cream. Back in North Dakota, when we wanted a snack, Mother would slice us a thick piece of home-baked bread and spread it with cream. Not the kind you get in the store, but the thick cream that settles on the top of farm-fresh milk. Sometimes she'd sprinkle it with sugar." There is a communal sigh.

I swear, I could listen to these folks talk all night. But I leave when Marissa whispers in my ear. "My shift is over, and Steve's out of town. You want to meet up with Iris and grab a drink or something?" I agree, and we leave together. It's time for some quality roommate time.

I met Marissa in college. Back then, she was the one looking for the fairy tale. She said she was going to be a nurse so she could bag herself a rich doctor and live the life of luxury. She almost did it, too. She had this urologist who promised her the moon and stars. But while she was dallying by the pool at his mansion on the golf course, waiting for his divorce to be final, she fell in love with Steve, the greens keeper.

We find Iris at home. She is wired from her recording session. "Rex is just sooooooo amazing. He knows so much about sound and music. He's got me singing all these old songs I never even heard of. It's so cool. I can't wait for you to hear some of our stuff!"

It's great to see both of them so happy. I wish I could share their current enthusiasm. I'm excited by a lot of what is going on in my life right now, but I'm also confused. Iris seems to sense that.

"So how's the Great Gaston Lambert Fishing Derby going?"

"Fishing Derby?"

"You know, catch and release, catch and release . . ."

I whack her with a fringed velvet couch pillow, and we all laugh.

"I'm still working on it. I'm sure I've wreaked a little havoc this weekend, even though I'm not there." I tell Iris and Marissa about this weekend's diabolical dinner plans for Courtney, Gaston and Adele.

"You're horrible! I love it!" raves Iris. We giggle some more. Since I am sharing, and I am just dying to tell someone, I spill the beans about Sam. "And guess what? I had sex last night with Sam."

"You *what*?"

"I kind of had sex."

"*Kind* of had sex? What, are you fifteen? You either had sex or you didn't," is Marissa's professional opinion. "And who's Sam?"

"Did you use your condoms?" Iris sounds panicked as she reaches for my handbag. She is relieved to see my stash is smaller. "I *knew* you had a thing for Sam. I could tell when you were talking about him."

I object. "I don't have a *thing* for Sam." I turn to Marissa and explain. "He's just my mom's studio assistant. It's nothing serious. We were just playing around, and one thing led to another. It just happened." I can feel myself blushing. "You should be happy for me. This is the kind of thing you've been telling me to do for months now."

Marissa grins. "And . . ."

"It rocked!"

Marissa asks for details. Iris approves our choice of condoms, and runs back to her bathroom to cram my tampon case full of half a dozen more.

Chapter Twenty-One

Every time I doze off that night, I'm surrounded by old ladies waving green beans at me. Or, I have these horrible anxiety dreams where I have just a few minutes to clean and cook a boat full of giant geoduck. The clams are huge, with their limp gray necks drooping. Gaston is there. He's in a hurry. I know that if I don't get the clams cooked quickly, or if I burn even one piece, Gaston will lose interest. He'll get into one of his model airplanes and leave me forever. At one point in the dream, Sam shows up, and he just laughs and laughs.

I lie in bed, staring at the ceiling, feeling tense and angry and confused. I had a life plan. I wanted to be a top chef. I wanted my name and picture in glossy food magazines. I wanted to serve innovative creations that dazzled the palates of the rich and sophisticated. I was on that track. I was getting there. What the hell happened? Why isn't that important anymore?

It must be my biological clock. Some time bomb of hormones has gone off and messed with my career goals. I'm just feeling lazy from all this time off. Mr. Wright and Sam messed me up. They've been confusing me with delicious, simple dishes and homespun stories. I want some stories of my own.

I may not feel as drawn to the position of celebrity chef anymore, but that doesn't mean that food doesn't interest me. I think I'm more interested in food and cooking than ever. I wonder why that is. Is it the act of cooking that I need? The creative outlet? Or do I crave the accolades? Do I cook to please people, to give them that moment of contentment that Sam talked about, or do I want people to like me more because I can offer them something pleasant?

My primary goal these days has been to win back Gaston and treat myself to a life of ease, but I understand now that that will never be enough for me. If I put all of the energy and inspiration I had as a chef into being a housewife, people will be convinced I'm on crack. I'll be the PTA mother from hell, demanding the punch be extracted from fresh, seasonal fruits and the spice cookies be made with freshly ground Zanzibar cloves.

I've learned more about food and cooking in the past few weeks than since my first month in cooking school. But what is the most important lesson? That I can survive outside of a top kitchen? That Gaston can love a woman who doesn't cook? That business people are starved for decent, creative and nutritious lunches? That old people get really goofy about fresh vegetables?

I need to focus, to get my eyes back on the prize. I'm tempted to defy Gaston's wishes and call his mom. We can meet up at Le Pichet for baked eggs and fresh baguettes with jam and exchange poisonous chat about Courtney. I call Gaston's number, but there is no answer. I could ring his cell phone, but he might be in the middle of some deep-tissue massage or salt rub. Courtney and Adele are going to have to battle it out on their own. Finally, I realize what I have to do.

When Nancy sees me walk through the restaurant door, dressed in my whites and carrying my knife kit, she drops the clipboard she is carrying and runs over to embrace me. At first, I think she might be crying, but when I look closer, I see that her eyes are red and sore from sheer mental and physical exhaustion.

"I'm just here for the day. I have some time and I thought I might be able to help out," I explain, as she rambles on about how glad she is that I'm back. She tells me about the reservations for tonight and all of the work that needs to be done. She introduces me to the new faces and menu changes. She cut out a few of the more complicated and tedious dishes and fell back on popular items we served before. I'm relieved that there is nothing new or unfamiliar.

"So, what can I do to help?" She points me toward the hot line. I grab a battered tablet of paper and a pen, and start pulling tasks from everyone's prep lists. I am treated like a savior. I have energy, enthusiasm and a sense of humor—all things that have been lacking at Sound Bistro the past few weeks.

It feels good to be an expert again. My knowledge and skills can be tested here. I break down big joints of meat into delicate, lean steaks and chops. I love the feel of my long, sharp Japanese knife as it slices effortlessly through fatty red tuna. I congratulate myself as each salmon fillet I cut weighs exactly six ounces. This is the work I know. This is where I'm supposed to be.

As the dinner hour draws near, I help the line cooks assemble their stations. I can sense their collective sighs of relief as they realize they will finally be able to work on prep for tomorrow instead of trying to pull things together for tonight's service. Nancy feels confident enough to excuse herself to her office and sort through paperwork before the dinner rush.

That's when I get to talk to my old line buddies and hear the real scoop. There is plenty of ego-stroking. They swear it's been hell without me. Frank Sato, as usual, gives me the most honest story. We talk as we wrap thin, long threads of carrot, beet and potato around wooden chopsticks and deep-fry them into crisp vegetable springs.

"It was pretty scary here for the first few days after you left. Nancy was a maniac. She was trying to prove that she was in charge and that she knew how everything worked, when it was obvious that she didn't. God, it was ugly. We ran out of everything, and all these weird deliveries showed up. I don't know what changed, but she managed to pull herself together. I guess she figured out that the ball was in her court, that the work wasn't going to get done magically, like when you were here. I've got to give her credit, she's busted her ass. She hired a few new people and managed to say the right stuff to staff she already had. She streamlined the menu. She took out about six things—a couple of apps, that fussy endive salad, that stupid gratin that went with the rabbit. She eighty-sixed the soufflés, thank God."

Frank looks around to make sure it's safe before he says, "I never thought I'd ever see it, but Nancy served fish and chips the other night. She called it a Northwest 'frito misto' and dressed up the halibut with calamari, shrimp and some fried, paper-thin sweet onions. She made those thin slices of puffy potatoes. Pommes soufflé? Pommes gaufrettes? I can never remember the fancy name for those. And served it all with a ramekin of the fennel aïoli—but it was just a spiffed-up captain's platter. It sold like crazy!"

"Any mashed potatoes yet?" I ask.

"God, no!" He laughs. "She's changed, but it's still Nancy we're talking about!"

"So, things are okay?" I ask.

He shrugs. "Like I said, it was pretty crazy around here for a while, but I think the worst is over. Nancy still has her tantrums. We may lose a

couple of the new guys. But in the end, the food is good, and the customers seem happy. Isn't that what counts?"

I nod. It is bittersweet to hear. I never doubted Nancy's talent; it had
just gone into hiding the past year or so. I'm glad to see that the restaurant is managing, but a little disappointed that the whole place hasn't
gone down in flames without me. I spend a few more hours helping to
plate up, trying to renew the enthusiasm I had earlier, but I am uncomfortable during service. On the hot line, I watch the glorious ingredients
I enjoyed prepping be unnaturally manipulated into culinary showcases
that seem fussy and pretentious. I can't help but see the restaurant
through the eyes of Mr. Wright. What used to look so original and vital
now seems almost ridiculous. Nothing here will ever have the impact of
the dishes I have recently shared—the geoduck, the tamales and posole,
not even those damnable green beans.

When the dinner orders slow down, I excuse myself from the line and
pick through the odds and ends in the walk-in that I recognize as leftover
from previous menus. I cook some of the hearty, homestyle foods I am
now drawn to. I make a lamb and lentil stew, a basic green salad and some
herb scones for a staff meal. Even though they can only manage a few
bites in between orders, the whole crew eats the meal with the same
starved enthusiasm shown at Wheton-Lofton. It's not the food itself that
seems to matter, but that someone has acknowledged that they are tired
and hungry. I watch in wonder as the strung-out servers and hostile line
cooks mellow with each taste.

Just after ten o'clock, Nancy pours me a glass of wine and we sit in her
office to talk. I again think of all that I have learned since I was last here.
I listen as she repeats a lot of what I heard from Frank. It's interesting to
hear her take.

"After you left, I realized that I had spread myself too thin. I was so
busy with PR, you know, getting the Sound Bistro name out there, that I
wasn't able to keep track of the kitchen. I know good press is important,
but isn't the best PR always going to be great food? So, I sat down with
the partners and told them I wouldn't do it anymore. They were asking
too much of me. I'm a chef! They hired me to cook, you know? I told
them flat out that if they need better press, they better hire a better PR
firm. I can't do *everything*! Things are beginning to take shape again. I
swear, I've been *living* here. After about our worst night, that night I first
called you, I realized that the staff just couldn't keep up the quality that I
demand. So, I sat down and slashed the menu. It broke my heart, but I'd
rather serve a few great dishes than a whole bunch of crap. And it made

a huge difference. I still have to push them, but they're keeping up. I think we're through the worst of it. I'm gonna put a few of my new specials on the regular menu next week. I did this new "frito misto" thing that looks like it's really gonna make us some money." She takes a sip of wine and asks the ten-million-dollar question. "So, how are things with you? You still doing the secretary thing, or are you ready to come back here, where you belong?"

"Receptionist," I correct. "I was a receptionist, but I'm not doing that anymore. I'm doing some private chef work. And, to be honest, I'm not sure what's next for me."

"Come back! You can start right away."

I shake my head. "Thanks, but I'm kind of obligated to finish up this gig. Maybe we can talk about it after the holidays?" For a moment, I am tempted. I have a fleeting spark of enthusiasm for my old job. I miss my friends in the kitchen. I miss the intensity and rush, the feeling of doing such finely tuned, very specialized, sensory work. And boy, do I miss the dishwashers! But so many things in my life have changed in the past few weeks. I'm not so sure I could get excited anymore about steamed lettuce wrapped around black bass with curried plantain chips and grilled pineapple. And what if I win Gaston back? Do I want everything back like it was?

"How's Gaston?" asks Nancy.

I flinch, then realize the question is coincidental. Nancy doesn't know anything about Gaston's engagement or my plan to win him back. It's an innocent inquiry. She and Gaston always shared a mutual respect for each other.

"Uh, he's good. Actually, I'm hoping we can get back together again. That's kind of why I'm doing this office thing."

"Of course! *Now* it all makes sense. Tell him hello for me."

We talk about restaurants and recipes until our glasses are empty, then I gather up my stuff to go. Nancy stops me at the door.

"So, how should we do this? You want me to cut you a check? I might have enough money in petty cash."

It is an awkward moment. I don't want a check. I didn't come here for the money and I don't want Nancy to think I'm short on cash. I also don't want to be reminded of how little my time and effort are valued here. I come up with the solution. "How about if you send me a gift certificate? I'll think about your offer to take me back, and if everything works out, maybe Gaston and I can have dinner here to celebrate getting back together." That seems to be a good answer for both of us. Nancy fills my arms with wine samples, and not just the cheap stuff this time.

When I walk to my car, I know that I am leaving Sound Bistro for good. This time there are no thrown potatoes, tantrums or hurt feelings, just the knowledge that I'm ready to move on. And I'm ready to tell Gaston the truth.

Chapter Twenty-Two

So here I am, back where I started. It's late on a Saturday night, I have my feet in the toilet and the phone in my hand. But this time *I'm* doing the calling. *I'm* the one with the shocking news. I'm ready to stop playing games. I want Gaston back. I want his warm arms around me, to hear his familiar voice and kind words. I want him to ask me to marry him again and then get giddy with excitement and tell stories about me at work the way he does about Courtney. I want him to love me like he used to, with all of my quirks and flaws. I want him back, right now.

I call, but there is no answer on either his landline or cell phone. He must still be out at the symphony with his mother. Or maybe he's snuggled up in bed with Courtney, too comfy to bother answering the telephone. I hesitate a moment after the beep of his answering machine before I leave my simple message.

"Gaston, we need to talk. It's important. Call me."

I don't sleep well. I wake early and drink coffee until the clock reaches a suitable hour to call Gaston again. Still, no answer. To keep myself from dialing every three minutes, I bake a dozen carrot-raisin muffins and drive to Mr. Wright's. He's not home either. I sit alone in the car for a moment, then drive to Sam's.

Sam opens the door just as I am reaching for the bell. He is dressed in his biking clothes, his helmet straps waving in the wind. Ziggy barks twice in alarm when he sees me. If I was a thief, there's no chance in hell I would break into Ziggy's home. When I see Sam, I realize I've made a terrible mistake. What am I doing here?

"Kate? What are you doing here?" He pushes his helmet back on his head and smiles. "I'm on my way to the studio." I'm relieved at his warm greeting. We haven't spoken since our romantic night, and this could be a little weird, but he doesn't make me feel awkward or uncomfortable. I hold up the tray of muffins. "I'll trade you these for a dog."

Sam and Ziggy sniff at the tray. Ziggy must like the idea, because he rams his huge head against my side and then walks a little past me and leans in so I can scratch his back. Sam takes a muffin, not sure about my offer.

"A dog?" he asks.

"Yeah. I need to borrow a dog. Do you have one I can take for a while?" I peek in behind him, looking for the pack of critters that belongs to the mélange of yips and barks. He takes the tray and opens the door for me. "Sure. C'mon in. What are you looking for? Ziggy's great for intimidation or muscle. Dirk's getting old, but he still keeps a good pace for short runs. Scoop and Micky are always looking for a couch partner. They're great if you're ever feeling lousy and just want to veg in front of the TV." Sam looks me over like a doctor examining a walk-in patient or a tailor fitting a suit.

I go into the kennels and smother the dogs with attention. I am rewarded with licks and smiling dog faces. I want all of them. I turn to Sam, and in a voice I finally recognize as my own, explain, "I'm just going to the park for a walk and I thought one of your inmates might want a prison break." My deeper motivation involves a desperate yearning for unconditional love.

"How about Scooter?" Sam points to a wire-haired Jack Russell mix that seems to have springs in his legs. "His owners are picking him up tonight after a long flight. He hasn't been getting enough exercise, and he can be a real handful when he's wired. You'd be doing them a huge favor."

I agree, and Sam gathers up Scooter's leash, favorite ball and a couple of scooper bags. He gives me a key.

"Just put him back in the kennel when you're done and drop the key in the mail slot. I'm going to be working pretty late."

I give him the eye. "So, what are you working on?"

He opens his mouth and then catches himself when he sees my look of avid curiosity. "Sneaky one, aren't you?" He pushes his bike through the door, and we walk (well, Scooter actually bounces) to my car. At the car door I lean in and pucker up to kiss Sam good-bye, then realize what I'm doing and pull back. I'm flustered. "Oh, uh. Sorry about that."

He smiles. "No problem. Friends kiss all the time." And he gives me a warm smooch. "See ya." He pushes on his bike and takes down the road.

I drive back to the playfields near Green Lake. After I spend a full hour throwing the ball for the furry little dynamo, Scooter settles into a good walking pace. We walk for awhile, then share an order of French fries. It starts to drizzle and a cold wind picks up, but I'm not ready to part with my new buddy yet, so we drive west to Golden Gardens Park, sit in the car and watch the seagulls soaring in the wind currents. Scooter, tired and full, curls up on the seat next to my thigh. I tell him a few of my problems. He couldn't care less. He's just happy to be near me. It's tough to say good-bye. I spend another hour at the vet's office just scratching and talking to the inmates. I'm proud of myself when I leave the building pet-free.

The phone rings the moment I get home. It's Gaston. He sounds panicked.

"Kate, can you come over? Like, right now? Mom and Courtney, well, this weekend has *not* gone well. I need you."

"I'll be right there." I dash to my car and speed to Gaston's condominium. My heart is thumping. "He needs me! Gaston needs me!"

I walk up the outside stairs to Gaston's condo and am poised to knock when I hear shouts coming from inside. I don't even have to press my ear to the door. Standing in the hallway, I can hear the fighting just fine.

"Stop it, Gaston! Just stop it!" shouts Courtney.

"Damn it, Courtney, you just don't get it! She's my *mother*. We're not talking about a neighbor or a friend here. We're talking about my own *mother*."

"I know that, Gaston. Believe me, I understand. But that's no excuse for your behavior!"

"Why can't you understand? How can you be like this? Argh! Where the hell is Kate? Kate *gets* Mom. She'll understand."

It worked! My scheming worked! Courtney and Adele must be sworn enemies, and Gaston can't stand it. He needs me. Yippee!

"Kate?" Courtney shouts, incredulous. "You think what you need right now is your ex-girlfriend? I can't even believe that. Why can't you grow up? Don't you see? This isn't about your mother, it's about *you*. You're being unreasonable. Gaston, I know what you are saying, I know what you want from me, but I just can't do it. This fight is tearing my heart out. I'm sorry, Gaston. I can't take it anymore. I can't stay a minute longer."

Courtney throws open the door and almost smashes into me.

"Kate? Is that you? He really called you?" She's a mess. Her eyes are red from crying, and there is a tiny tic flicking the left side of her mouth. I almost feel sorry for her.

She tries to explain. "He's being so awful, so, so . . . mean. He's just not listening, and I can't handle it anymore. Tell him I'm sorry. I'm so sorry. I love him, but I just can't take this. I've got to go." Courtney dashes down the stairs, wiping her tears away as she runs. I peek my head in the front door and see Gaston pacing in his living room.

I rap on the door frame. "Hello? Everything okay in here?" My face shows concern, but inside my head the *Superman* soundtrack is playing full blast. Ta ta da! No worries, young Gaston, SuperKate is here to patch up that broken heart and lead you down the road of long-term happiness.

"Kate! Thank God you're here!" Gaston rushes over and pulls me into a desperate hug. "It's been so awful. Why didn't you tell me? Why didn't you warn me what a horrible woman she was?"

I caress his tense back and coo soothing words while I look around. Nothing has changed. The place smells and feels so familiar it's like my second home. This is where I belong. This is where my problems will be solved. "I tried to tell you, Gaston. I tried."

"I can't believe I didn't see it before. How come I never saw it?"

"It's okay. She blew smoke in your eyes for a while, that's all. She seems harmless, but no one can be that sweet and mean it."

"Huh?" He pulls away and looks into my eyes. I guess he doesn't understand.

"I mean, it was great while it lasted, but let's face it. Being with Courtney must have been like dating a Care Bear. I can see how it got to you. It's just too much."

"What do you mean? Courtney is an angel. It's my mom who caused all the trouble."

Oops, I guess he's not quite ready for harsh words against his lil' sugar dumpling. I'll have to be more careful. "Adele might have said a few things, but that's only because she loves you. She's looking out for your best interest. If Courtney can't understand that . . . Well, let's say I don't blame you for setting things straight and sending her packing."

I'm just about to ask where his mother is when Adele storms out of the guest room with her fur-lined coat and designer suitcase. The smoke around her might be from a cigarette, but since I don't see one, it might very well be emanating from her fiery aura.

When she sees me she is livid. "*Now* you arrive? Not when I actually needed you, but *now?* Too late, Kate darling. You can't help me. My life is over."

Gaston has sucked in his thin lips and looks away from her.

"Adele? What's going on?" I am alarmed. I nearly hold up my arms to cover my face. I need a shield to deflect her scathing looks. "Gaston, your mother is very upset. Tell her everything is fine."

Adele stomps to the front door. "*Fine?* You think things are fine? My only son, my beloved child, who has never spoken a harsh word in my presence, tells me he *hates* me? He calls me a *bitch,* and still you tell me everything is fine?"

No! This can't be true. "You must have heard wrong, Adele. He could never have said that!" I can't breathe. This can't be happening. I had urged Gaston to stand up to his mother dozens of times, and the most he could ever rally was a disgruntled "Awwh, Mom."

Gaston speaks. "You're right, Kate. I didn't call her a bitch at all." I am relieved. This is all just a misunderstanding. "I called her a mean, nasty, dried-up wicked old bitch." I gasp. Adele shudders and attacks me again.

"You see? You see what you have done, Kate? You threw my boy away to be brainwashed by that horrible thing. She might as well have poisoned him, murdered my little darling." She gestures toward Gaston. "This is not my son. This is not the boy I love. If you had agreed to marry him, we would all be happy. If you had been here for me this weekend, we could have worked together. Now my life is ruined. There is no taking back the hateful words that have been spoken tonight. No undoing what has been done."

Gaston can't take it anymore. "Mom! If anyone should apologize here, it should be you. You should get down on your knees and beg Courtney to forgive you. Beg *me* to forgive you. You did everything you could to ruin this weekend."

He turns to me as if I'm the judge. Is this why he called me? He wants me to be a mediator?

"At first, it was just the normal, little stuff. She belittled the waiters, criticized Courtney's table manners, insisted I send back my dinner for a new one. I was embarrassed, but no more than usual." He turns to his mother, and there is a new, hard edge to his voice. "But yesterday, I heard what you said. Courtney heard it, *everyone* heard it when you told the spa manager that they had done Courtney's facial wrong. That she looked worse than when she came in, like some kind of drowning victim. You were so mean. Wicked. And yet Courtney kept telling me she was fine, to forget it. She took all your poison and smiled. She kept trying to be nice, to get through to you.

"When you refused to go to the symphony because you couldn't stand what Courtney was wearing, I didn't think it could get any worse."

"But darling, you saw that dress!" is Adele's defense.

"She's a *teacher*, Mom! She's on a limited budget!" He turns back to me to explain. "Courtney was irritated, but she let it go. She even made up excuses for her. She said Mom must be tired from the drive, or not sleeping well in a strange bed. But today, oh, today! That took the cake. Courtney busted her ass making a nice family dinner, and Mom refuses to go. She just refuses. So, can you believe it? Instead of getting mad, Courtney brings the whole dinner here, in a picnic basket, with lemonade and daisies and American flag place mats." He looks so smitten for a moment, then he turns to his mother and shouts. "And you can't find one crumb of kindness in that cold heart of yours. You *laugh* in her *face*. You tell her you won't waste your calories on such trash, then spend the rest of the day talking about Kate!" Gaston turns back to me. He throws his arms up in the air in defeat. "It was too much. She kept talking about *you*, Kate, and what a perfect couple we were. How she hoped we would patch things up and get back together soon. My God! I couldn't take it anymore. I couldn't watch poor Courtney get skewered over and over again. I had to say something."

"But, darling, I'm only looking out for you. I only want the best for you," Adele says.

"Then go back home and stay the hell out of my life!" Gaston shouts.

Adele shoots me one last poisonous glare as if this is all my fault. Then, with as much dignity as she can muster, she brushes a wayward lock of hair from her face and lunges through the doorway. Once outside, she sets down her Louis Vuitton case, and with all the might her chic little body can manage, she slams the condo door closed. The whole building seems to rattle. I am speechless. I stand there with my mouth wide open, looking from the door to Gaston.

"The hell with her!" Gaston shouts toward the door. He paces a few more laps around the apartment, then deflates. He collapses onto the couch and hugs a throw pillow. I go into the kitchen and pour him a brandy. He gulps the first glass. I pour him another, then sit next to him. What can I say? I'm not sure I even understand what happened. I pull him into my arms. I let his head fall into my lap and run my fingers through his hair.

"Why didn't I ever see what a horrible woman my mother can be? Why didn't you tell me?"

I whisper, "Your mother loves you. She wants the best for you. We all do. I mean, I sometimes wonder about this engagement, too. Are you sure everything was your mother's fault? I saw Courtney when she left. She was pretty angry. She wanted me to tell you she was sorry."

"Sorry? Courtney said she was sorry? Typical. She didn't do anything wrong at all. She's just so sweet. It's a habit of hers. I guess it's a pretty common characteristic among abused kids. She says she used to apologize to people when it rained. As if she had any control over that." Gaston looks up into my face. He has a dreamy expression. "She's so amazing, turning all that suffering into such love. Giving so much of herself to kids so they can have a better life than she had."

Enough is enough. I push him out of my lap and try to set him straight. "Gaston, get your head out of the clouds. Are you sure this woman is so perfect for you? Is Courtney going to challenge you? She's just so . . . nice. Is that all you want?"

"You too? Jeez! I thought *you*, of all people, would understand."

"Why?" I demand. "Didn't you call me because you know that when things get tough, I'll be there for you? That I'll be able to handle it? You said it yourself: You *need* me. What we had was amazing, Gaston. We were a team. So don't tell me you called so I would patch things up with your fiancée. That's just nuts. I'm not here to be your relationship cheerleader. I just can't do it! It makes me crazy to think of you two together." It's my turn to pace the room.

"Somehow that prissy little lollypop from Montana has you acting like a completely different person. You get engaged on a whim? You flit around with your head in the ether, talking about second-grade bulletin-board projects and Disney characters? My God, Gaston, in defense of Courtney, you called your mother a bitch—to her face! Who the hell are you? And why didn't you ever do any of that stuff for me?"

He is shocked. "But you're different."

"Exactly. I'm not a fragile flower. I know how to take care of myself. Maybe that's why I don't understand how you can be attracted to someone so completely and utterly clueless."

He is instantly defensive. "Courtney's not clueless."

"Oh, please, Gaston. She's a pansy."

He gets huffy. He stands up and waves his finger at me. "Take that back. You don't know anything about her! Yes, she's nice. But what the hell is wrong with that? It's something we could use a lot more of around here. And, my God, if anyone has a right to be mean and nasty, it's her. Your life's been pretty easy, sweetheart, but not Courtney's. She lived through hell as a kid. Her mom drank herself to death when Courtney was barely a teenager. Courtney figures her mom drank so she didn't feel it so much when the men in the house kicked the shit out of her. Until she could get away, Courtney had to play mother and wife in a ranch shack in the middle of nowhere. She went to school, did her chores and then after the lights went out, put up with whichever family member or ranch hand felt like visiting her during the night."

I flinch and close my eyes.

"Yeah. That's right. Sweet, kind Courtney. Nice, weak and helpless Courtney got herself into town at sixteen and found protection with a family she knew. She finished school, put herself through college and after a lot of counseling, has been able to transfer all of that hate and anger into something productive, something good and real. My mother was raised by a team of English nannies, she spent her summers in the Midi and she can't muster up five minutes of decency. How about you?" He turns, grabs his jacket and heads for the door. "What the hell am I doing here anyway? I should be with Courtney."

I run to him and grab his arm. "No, Gaston. Don't go. I didn't know." I pull him back a step. "I'm sorry. I didn't know. Sit down so we can talk."

He lets himself be led back toward the couch, explaining, "I wanted to see you, to talk to you, because I thought you would understand. You, of all people, would understand what it means that I stood up to my mom. I don't think I've ever even raised my voice to her before. It's like my whole world is turned upside down."

I take a deep breath. Things can't get much worse now, so I spill my guts. "I can help put everything right again. I can fix this, Gaston. I still love you. I really love you. I want to get back together. Forever. I think we should get married."

"WHAT?" he shouts, pulling away as though I just announced I was raised by aliens.

I reach out to him. "I never stopped loving you."

Gaston looks with horror at me, then at the door. He says, "Courtney, I need to be with Courtney. Oh, God, what have I done?" then he dashes out of the apartment without looking back. I stand paralyzed for a while, then lock up his place and drive to Iris's bar. When she sees me, she drops her tray of drinks on the nearest table and runs to greet me. She throws her arms around my broken form.

"What is it? What happened?"

"I just told Gaston I still love him and that I want to marry him."

"Oh, shit! What did he say?"

"He looked at me like I was crazy and then ran away, saying he needed to be with Courtney."

"Oh, Kate, I'm so sorry." And I know she really means it. I bury my face in her shoulder and cry like a baby in front of the whole hip, happening world.

Chapter Twenty-Three

I have never had so much trouble managing a basic morning routine. Everything seems overamplified or slowed way down. The coffee takes forever to brew. I've never before noticed the screech of the hot water faucet or the scratchy metal on metal sound of the shower curtain rings. My hair insists on either sprouting wings or clinging to my scalp. My limbs feel thunderous. It isn't just Monday, it is the mother of all Mondays.

I have no motivation to make a delectable lunch. I'm tempted to take Damon's road. I'll buy a few industrial cans of soup and a couple of bags of gassed lettuce at the Cash and Carry and call it good. But the ingredients I need are already purchased, and some prep work is done. As I chop, dice and simmer, I start to feel human. I make a rich oxtail soup with wild mushrooms and barley. All I can manage for a salad is butter lettuce, assorted radishes and crumbled blue cheese. To compensate for my lack of creativity, I throw together a quick batch of whole-grain rolls.

As I pack up the crates and equipment, I wonder how I am going to face Gaston. I buy a triple shot of courage at the espresso stand before I roll my gear into the office. I almost cry with relief when the receptionist tells me Gaston has called in sick.

After I set the lunch up, I go to see Marsha Lofton. I'm going to quit. I'll go work full time at Cedar Heights or apply at the Olive Garden. That sounds about my speed these days. I peek into Marsha's office. My thoughts are erased for a moment by the beautiful view of the Puget Sound and the snowcapped Olympic Mountains.

Marsha looks up from her computer. "Hi, Kate. Is lunch ready?" She looks at me again. "Are you all right?" She knows in an instant that something is wrong. Her honest concern pulls at my heart. I can't help myself; a tear pushes its way out of my eye. She rises, closes the door behind me and gives me a squishy hug before even asking what the problem is.

I squeak, "I'm fine. I just need . . . I just think . . ."

"It's Gaston, isn't it?"

I nod. I don't trust my voice, and it seems inappropriate to be telling my problems to Marsha, my boss.

"I don't know how you've managed it. He's been acting like a giddy, love-struck schoolkid. If I hear another cute story about Courtney and her adorable students, I'm gonna have to smack him!"

I try to smile. The words gush out. "Last night I told Gaston I still love him. That I want to get married."

"Whoa! What did he say?"

"He said he needs to be with Courtney." I look away and wipe my eyes on my sleeve. I pull myself together and say, "I made a fool of myself, Marsha. I don't think I can work here anymore."

"Aw, Kate. Don't blow this too far out of proportion. It's not the end of the world. You told him how you felt. That's just honesty. Let me remind you that you're not the first person to make a fool of yourself in the office-romance department." She holds up a hand. "Please, don't ask me to explain how I know that. But, trust me, you'll live through this. You once told me you wanted to learn how the white-collars live, how a professional office works. Well, honey—you just stepped in it. You can quit and hide your face in shame, or you can rise to the challenge. Professionalism isn't always about starched shirts, morning meetings and spreadsheets. Sometimes it's about looking your coworkers dead in the eye and talking about fluctuations in the commodities market while your skirt's on fire.

"You're here today. Gaston isn't. Who do you think I have more respect for right now? If things get nasty, you just tell me. I'll cut him off from your lunches. That'll teach him to break up with a chef!" I have to grin.

"I know your heart aches, but I think you're gonna live through this. If it gets really horrible, you can run screaming and I'll understand. But I'd sure like it if you stayed."

I manage a response. "I think maybe you and your dad were born with more than the normal share of common sense. You're both so wise and understanding."

She waves off my compliment. "So, now that we're done with that nonsense, let's talk about something *really* important. The Christmas party!" She dashes to her desk and rifles through some paperwork. "I've got a menu here somewhere. I'd love it if you'd look it over, maybe give me your opinion. I wish I could have hired you to do the cooking, but I booked these guys six months ago. What's done is done."

I know she is talking about the company Christmas party. I've been to two previous events with Gaston. Marsha loves Christmas, and she treats the office to a full-fledged gala.

"You are coming, aren't you?"

"Uh, I don't know. I haven't even thought about it."

"Of *course* you're coming! I hope you don't think I invited you because of Gaston. I consider you an important part of this office now. I can't tell you how much I appreciate all that you have done. Dad was so funny at Thanksgiving. I was right about the vegetables: Since you've been cooking for him, his skin has pinked up and he's full of piss and vinegar again. I swear, he talked all day about you and your good food. He says you're a crackerjack cribbage player. Did you really run out and get a geoduck? He must have loved that."

"I hadn't cooked one before. Did he tell you we ate the whole thing? And it was a big one, too!" The memory has me laughing and smiling again.

"So, think about the Christmas party, Kate. It's a week from Friday. It's so nice to see everyone dressed up, and how often does a cook get a chance to get all decked out? You can go get a sexy dress like you had last year and make Gaston eat his heart out. We'll find you a fine date. Ooh, ooh! I've got it! Give me a few days and I'll have that security guard, Victor, all hot and bothered and dying to meet you. He can be your date! Oh, Lord, would I ever love to see him in a tux. Or better yet, out of a tux! Phew." She fans herself.

When I started here, I would never have guessed that Marsha would be the person I would most bond with. I like her because she works and talks like a chef—with aggressive determination. She gets things done. She is also very persuasive. She has somehow gotten me to agree to the Christmas party. It even sounds like fun. I'll buy some fancy dress and make Gaston weep with remorse and Courtney feel sick with envy. A real dress-up party might be nice.

We are interrupted when the temp at the front desk buzzes Marsha and through the intercom tells me I have a phone call. Marsha and I exchange nervous looks. She suggests I use her office phone, and excuses herself to lunch. I pick up the phone and breathe a deep sigh of relief when I discover that it isn't Gaston or Courtney calling, but Iris.

"I swapped shifts and have the night off. I've decided that you need a special kind of fun tonight—better living through chemistry, if you know what I mean. I called Marissa and told her what happened. She's in. I thought I'd give you plenty of notice, to get you in the right frame of mind."

"Oh, God, Iris. It sounds good, but I don't know. Aren't we getting a little old for that?"

"Too old? Are you kidding? I hope they bury me before I'm too old to have a good time. C'mon! I know you're down, and this always picks you up. We haven't done it in over a year. It's time!"

I drum my fingers on the desk, pondering the merits and risks of a night of sensory decadence. "It sounds good, but you know how crappy I feel the next day."

"So, we'll go easy on the hard stuff. Besides, it's too late to back out. I already did the shopping. I'll have everything ready when you get home."

I am giddy with excitement when I hang up the phone. Iris is right. I do need a night of vice. We've shared both good times and bad, and did a little experimenting when we were young. But as we got older, we discovered the combination of chemicals that really works for us: huge quantities of sugar and a splash of liquor. That is our poison of choice. Every year or so we have an all-out sugar and blended-drink orgy we call "Candyland." We have had as many as ten people at our events, but most often it is just Iris, Marissa and me. Gaston tried it one night, but he left early. He didn't have the stomach for it.

When I get home, the party has already started. Iris has draped the living room with plastic car lot flags. Cibo Matto is blasting its techno version of "The Candyman" on the stereo. Marissa blows me a kiss and continues to hang colorful paper lanterns and twinkle lights. There are bowls of saltwater taffy, cinnamon bears, gum drops and assorted bulk candies everywhere.

Iris runs into the kitchen as soon as I arrive home. I drop my tub full of equipment, grab a handful of jelly beans and go to my room to change into soft and stretchy clothes. Iris hands me a pink, sugar-rimmed martini glass when I reappear. Marissa is near the end of her matching cocktail.

"What's this?"

"I'm calling it a Pixie Shtick. It's kind of a sour cherry martini, but the rim is dipped in Pixie Stick guts! Taste it!"

I take a sip. It is vile, but has potential. I say so, and we all giggle. At one point, Candyland nights were just caloric free-for-alls: pans of brownies, quarts of ice cream, beer, wine, all sorts of dreadful combos. But we gradually established parameters to achieve maximum sugar buzz with less gluttony-induced nausea. First and foremost, there must be no chocolate. I know, it sounds almost sacrilegious to binge on candy and exclude chocolate, but chocolate is a much stronger drug. Like opiates, it needs to be administered very carefully. Chocolate is the candy of love, heartbreak, sorrow or rage. It is best used with dim lighting and soulful jazz, and served with bloodred port or old, smoky brandies. In inexperienced hands, there is always potential danger. Mix good-quality chocolate and gummy worms, and you're just asking for trouble. We'll bend the rules now and then. Chocolate Necco wafers are okay. Callard and Bowser chocolate/black licorice toffees are excellent. M&Ms are frowned upon, but tolerated by novices because of the candy shell.

Homemade sweets are better than store-bought. We discovered this once when we were jonesin' for a sugarfest but were low on the goods and too tipsy to drive. I dug through the cupboards and found the ingredients for divinity. It was, indeed, divine. Now we always like to make at least one kind of candy. It keeps us active, and the added risk of playing with hot sugar while drinking is our idea of extreme sports.

Iris has decided we need sugar-bomb popcorn balls tonight. They are the normal syrup-drizzled popcorn but with the added fun of small colorful candies mixed in—Skittles, SweeTARTS, Nerds, Runts, whatever looks bright and cavity-inducing. We take our positions in the kitchen. Iris assembles tools and bowls. Marissa starts popping corn, and I mix more drinks. I fill the cocktail shaker with ice, pour in some Kirsch, vodka, a dash of Cointreau and lime juice, then shake like crazy. I empty a big plastic tube of sweet-and-sour pink powder onto a plate and frost each glass with pixie stick dust. I pour out the drinks, add a splash of Maraschino cherry juice and pass the glasses around. They are a hit.

I start boiling the sugar and corn syrup. Marissa plays DJ, and Iris keeps us laughing until we have created a mountain of pink, candy-studded popcorn balls. By nine o'clock we are lying flat on the floor, next to the TV. Our teeth hurt, our tongues are multicolored and torn to shreds. We are a little drunk and on the downside crash from all that sugar. I know I won't sleep well tonight and I'll feel like crap in the morning, but right now—I am surrounded by my closest friends and I am happy. Who needs men when women are so much fun?

As expected, I wake up late, feeling like hell. When it is clear that coffee will not cure my poisoned system, I pull on a mélange of old clothes, tie my hair in a bandanna à la Rosie the Riveter and go bowling. I haven't been since I was a kid, but I want to do something loud and violent, and I have a great time blasting the pins into smithereens. I feel better when I get home. My blood is oxygenated and I don't feel as fuzzy. I am on a snack hunt in the kitchen when the phone rings. Much to my horror, it's Courtney.

"Kate? Uhmm. I was wondering if maybe we could get together after work today."

Yikes! Meet with Courtney? After everything that happened? I don't think so!

"I don't know, Courtney. I think I'm busy tonight."

She is silent for a moment. When she speaks again it is with the same little girl voice, but with a slight edge to it. The dumb act is gone. Her words are precise, well chosen and, as always, perfectly enunciated. "I learned some things about Gaston this weekend that are disturbing. I'd like to talk to you." She still sounds nice, but she is all business. I pity the parents of an unruly child called in for a parent-teacher conference. Against my better judgment, I find myself agreeing to meet her at another chain restaurant.

I arrive at the restaurant a few minutes early. I want to scope out the place and get settled in before Courtney arrives. I also want to pick out a seat close to the front door so I can flee, if I need to. I scoot deep into the booth and scan the parking lot for signs of my archrival. I nearly jump out of my skin when a familiar voice comes from behind me.

"Kate? Is that you? I was just in the little girls' room. I saw you as you were sitting down. Gee, your hair looks really nice today."

Damn! My advantage is gone. Not only has she attacked from behind, she threw off the balance of power by starting things with a compliment. I stutter a bit and try to push myself along the seat to stand up, but I'm not quick enough. Courtney sits primly across from me and arranges her napkin in her lap. She cocks her head and smiles. No doubt she flosses twice a day. "I hope you aren't too uncomfortable with this. I've been doing a lot of thinking and need to talk to someone."

And you chose me? I think. The waiter drops off menus and offers drinks. I'm not interested. My system isn't yet purged of last night's sugar and booze. Courtney surprises me. "I'll have a Maker's Mark. Neat." I had her pegged for a strawberry Daiquiri or Lemon Drop kind of gal. My face must betray my surprise.

"I'm not much of a drinker. I'll have white wine now and then, but I just love the taste of good bourbon. It reminds me of my grandfather. Well, not my *real* grandfather—he'd drink gasoline if there wasn't anything else around. I mean my Missoula grandpa. On Sundays, after church, he would sit in his chair by the fire and read to us. He always had a tiny, cut-crystal glass of Kentucky bourbon on the table next to him, in case his throat got dry. Sometimes, when it was really cold out, he would let us have a sip."

When the drink comes she swirls the liquor and sniffs the vapors like a connoisseur. She takes the tiniest of sips.

"I didn't have the greatest family. That's kind of why I need to talk to you. I need you to understand about the engagement."

I flinch. Has Gaston told her about our conversation? Is this a sweet girl's way of telling the competition to back off?

I try to explain my case. "Courtney, I don't know what Gaston told you about the other night . . ."

She holds up her hand to silence me. It is the gesture of a practiced and authoritative teacher. I zip my lips and let her talk. "It's taken me a long time to work through my family issues. There was a lot of anger and resentment. I blamed them for so much."

I clench my teeth, ready for her to spill her guts, to tell me about her horrific childhood in all its intimate details and make me feel bad about my good life. This must be a cheap, emotional ploy to get me to feel sorry for her and leave Gaston alone. I drum my fingers on my seat and brace myself for her sob story. It never comes.

"I've gotten past that. I'm in a good place now. I'm happy with my life and my job and with who I am. That's why I can't marry Gaston. I can't take on that much rage, that much dysfunction. When Adele came into town, I could feel myself falling right back into the darkness I worked so hard to get out of."

I make a cartoon face of disbelief. "You can't marry Gaston?"

She takes another tiny sip of her drink and tries to hold back the tears.

"When we met this summer, everything seemed just so perfect. It sounds corny, but I knew as soon as I saw him that he was someone special. We fell in love so fast. It was like the movies. I'm not the kind of person who acts on a whim. I like to plan things out. Getting engaged after just a few weeks, that is completely out of character. It was crazy! But I never had any regrets or second thoughts until this weekend.

Everything was going so well." She smiles sadly and turns her glass. "Then, his mom shows up, and instead of being happy, Gaston became this angry man that I didn't even recognize. He shouted at her and called her horrible names. Sure, she was nasty and unkind, but he's an adult. He should have been able to maintain his self-control.

"I kept asking him to calm down, to forget about it, but he couldn't. I tried to get him to see the pleasant moments, the lighter side, but that just made him angrier. He shouted at me that I didn't understand. And then he called you, Kate. Instead of working things out with me, he called you."

"But, Courtney, that's not . . ." She holds her hand up and again I am silenced.

"It's okay, I understand. You're probably his best friend in the whole world." She sniffles a bit, but doesn't shed a tear. "I'm glad he has someone in his life who understands him, who he can talk to. I'm just sad that I can't be that person. Today, I think he finally understands. No matter how much I love him, I just can't marry someone with so much rage, so many unresolved issues. I need to protect myself." She swallows the lump in her throat. "I talked to my therapist, and she agreed this is best."

She bites her lower lip and turns to me. Her eyes are filled with love, not hatred or resentment. "I know how much you mean to him. That's why I need you to understand. He is such a dear, sweet man. He needs help, and I'm just not able to give it to him."

Courtney is managing to retain her composure, but I can't. Hot tears are streaming down my cheeks, and it is all I can do to hold back loud, gulping sobs in the face of such honest heartbreak. While I blow my nose in my napkin and dab at my tears, Courtney folds some cash and tucks it under the bread plate. She takes one last taste of bourbon and says, "Thank you for meeting with me, Kate. Thank you for understanding." And she is gone.

When I arrive home, Gaston is sitting on my front steps. He is a cold, broken heap of a man. As I near him, he pulls himself upright, falls into my arms, buries his face in my neck and sobs. "She broke up with me. She left me, Kate. What am I going to do?"

I hold him tight and rock him back and forth, whispering soothing words. "I know, I know. It'll be okay, Gaston. It'll be okay."

I lead him inside and onto the couch. He wraps himself in Iris's acrylic, rainbow-colored afghan and tilts his body against the armrest. There is nothing to say, so I go to the kitchen and start cooking.

How do people handle crisis situations if they don't cook? I chew my nails, pull my hair, compulsively clean, make lots of lists and *cook*. What does the rest of the world do? I can think of nothing more uncomfortable than seeing a loved one in pain. I wasn't blessed with that magical skill of sitting with the afflicted person and sharing their grief. I end up babbling nonsense, making tasteless jokes and fidgeting like a colony of ants has crawled into my underwear. When I cook, I feel like I am doing something constructive, giving, healing while the world is crashing down elsewhere.

I cook at a frantic pace while Gaston lies on the couch, sometimes sleeping, sometimes just staring into space. I take him a bowl of homemade noodles in a creamy cheese sauce and a piece of toast. He moves the pasta around the bowl and takes a few bites of bread. He chews mechanically. I sit with him. Now and then I jump up to refill his water glass or get him more toast. He starts to thank me a few times, but I hush him right up. I don't want to hear any gratitude. I don't deserve any. If I had just accepted his proposals in the first place, he wouldn't have found himself in such a mess. Yes, this is what I wanted, but it's hard, knowing that I am responsible for his broken heart and present misery. When he is finished, I whisk away the dishes. I'm not always such an efficient waitress—I don't want Gaston to go into the kitchen and see the tower of cookies, pies and cakes I have created to soothe his (my?) grief.

I stand and look at him for a while. Finally, I take his hand. "Let's get you to bed." I lead him to my bedroom. We take turns in the bathroom, brushing our teeth and changing into sexless, comfortable clothes. He crawls into my slightly disheveled bed. I slide in next to him and hold him in my arms, and we both silently cry ourselves to sleep.

At about one-thirty in the morning I wake up because Gaston is making that awful clicking sound he sometimes makes when he sleeps. I elbow him in the ribs, and he turns on his side. It works like magic. I haven't lost my touch.

I hear Iris. That, not Gaston's night sounds, is what has wakened me in the first place. I get up, pull on a robe and slippers, and go to the kitchen for valerian tea. She is standing next to my mountain of baked goods with a cookie in her mouth, trying to decide which item to try next.

"Hey," she says.

"Hey, yourself." I put the kettle on and sit down at the kitchen table.

"I'm guessing by the sheer quantity of food in this kitchen that all is not right in Kate's world."

"Gaston's asleep in my room."

"Did you use a condom?"

"God, no."

"Kate! You don't know what he's been up to in the past few months! You have to be more responsible! What if—"

"Shut up, Iris. We didn't have sex."

"Oh."

I get the tea and honey. Iris helps herself to a sliver of raisin pie. I tell her the condensed version of my evening.

"So, I guess that's good. It's what you wanted, right?" she asks.

"Yeah. I guess it is."

Chapter Twenty-Four

Gaston is a zombie. I drive him to his apartment early so he can change into some work clothes, and he just wanders around in a daze, touching things. If I didn't finally pull a suit out of his closet and push him toward the shower, he would miss another day of work. Once I send him on his way, I return home and prepare the Wheton–Lofton lunch. Even though I cooked like a madwoman last night, I can't seem to slow down. In addition to the pot of Mexican *albóndigas* soup and a salad of fresh watercress, jicama, tomatoes and oranges in a spicy cumin vinaigrette, I make fresh corn tortillas and throw some ingredients in pots to slow cook for Mr. Wright. I'm a maniac.

I peek in Gaston's office after I set up lunch. It looks like he's snapped out of his delirious state. His mind has engaged now that he is surrounded by the structure and endless stream of numbers he loves so dearly. I try and keep a low profile at lunch. I'm not sure what I would say to Marsha. I'm not even sure how to talk to Gaston at this point.

After lunch service, I drop the lunch things off at home and make up a delivery for Mr. Wright. I have a feeling he might be a navy bean fan. On a hunch, I have also boiled a corned beef with carrots and little red potatoes. I fry yesterday's homemade noodles in butter with half a head of green cabbage and lots of fresh black pepper. I also pack up some of the baked goods.

Mr. Wright accepts the food with more enthusiasm than I have ever seen before. He has a sparkle in his eye and a bounce to his step.

"Ham hocks and navy beans? Corned beef? Is that pie? Hoo, boy! I must have won the dinner lottery!" He rubs his hands together, then picks at a little of the corned beef.

I pack the food in his refrigerator, but can't seem to share his playful mood.

"Well, I'd better be going."

"What's the hurry? You haven't given me my special instructions. Where are the little containers of special bits and the magic charms to say over the soup?" He's teasing me.

"I'm done with all that. From now on, I'm just going to make basic stuff. It's just like you said, what's the point of putting in all of that extra effort when people like it best plain? Maybe I'll just go get a job at the Olive Garden. Everyone seems happy there. The food is fine. They might even offer a dental plan."

He narrows his eyes and gives me a close inspection. "How about if I make you a cup of tea? You go sit at the table. I'll be right in." It's more of an order than an invitation.

I sit down at the dining room table and deal out a game of solitaire while Mr. Wright fusses in the kitchen. I hear him opening cupboards and clanking silverware. When he comes out, he's not carrying tea, but a tray of corned beef sandwiches and two tall glasses of milk.

"To heck with the tea. I couldn't stop picking at your corned beef, so I made us some sandwiches. You looked like you could use one."

He has sliced the corned beef nice and thin and stacked it up with mayo, sweet pickles and spicy mustard on dark rye bread. I didn't think I was hungry, but after the first bite, I realize I haven't eaten all day.

We eat our sandwiches and drink the milk, and then Mr. Wright leans back in his chair and pins me with a look of concern.

"Let me tell you something, Kate Linden. You have a gift. No, you *are* a gift. At least to me you are. I feel more alive since I met you, and I don't think it's just because I'm eating more vegetables. You got me remembering things. Important things. Not only am I remembering them, I'm smelling them and tasting them, too.

"My sniffer and taste buds are old and tired, just like my eyes and ears. They're not as sharp as they used to be, but they'll stop working altogether if I don't use 'em. And you gave them a good jump start. You know, after Dori left me, I got used to losing things, to living without things. I guess I needed you to come around to remind me of how much I'm missing. How much life there still is out there."

His compliments fill a void in me that I didn't even know was there. A hollow spot in my heart trembles and thumps. I didn't realize how much I yearned for the approval of this intelligent and honorable man. He may not be my father, but he's the closest thing I've had to one in a long, long time. My eyes sting as the tears well up.

"Who knew that you can go out and *buy* a geoduck? I never would have thought of that. I just assumed those days were gone. And you know, I've been buying lunch meat and cold cuts for so long, I forgot there was such a thing as real corned beef. I forgot how good this stuff is." He picks at the crumbs left on his plate and then puts his warm, wrinkled hand on mine and pats it.

"I'm not quite sure what's got you down today. But I hope it's not all that nonsense I said about chefs messing up good food. I want you to know that your cooking has made a difference. It *does* matter. And it's not just because you spoil me, or because you can make all that fancy stuff. It matters because you care about people. That's what I can taste most of all in your food. And it's the flavor I've been missing."

He leans back and waves a dismissive hand. "Go ahead and get a job at the Olive Garden, if that's what you want to do. Why the hell not? You'll have a steady job, and that's good, right? But don't stop cooking what's in your heart. That's where it really counts. You're a good kid, Kate. I'm very glad we met."

I can't hold back my tears anymore, and I know I won't be able to explain them, so I respond by reaching over and giving Mr. Wright a big hug.

He is flustered. "Well, how about that? What was that for?"

I sniff and say, "It's because you make the best damn sandwiches in the whole wide world."

Later, I drive away with a feeling of confidence. I'm proud of my decisions and actions of late. I'm doing all right.

Instead of driving home, I decide to drop off the last of the food at the studio. The music is loud and modern, so I figure Sam is here alone.

I holler "Helloooo," and hear a response from back in Sam's private room. The door is open, so I sneak a peek. Once again, I am foiled by a thick, black curtain hanging in the doorway. Sam smiles when he sees me. His hair has been cut. I was learning to like his wild curls, but the short style looks great. His hair is still thick, with a lot of natural wave and highlights. Now that it is trimmed back, it is easier to appreciate his bright eyes, long neck and marvelous facial bones.

"Who are *you*?" I tease. He is puzzled by my question for a second, then remembers his new grooming. He smooths back his hair, and his eyes sparkle. "Funny. I'm not so sure I'm interested in beauty tips from a woman who used to have orange hair."

I agree. "Where's Mom?" I ask.

"She's showing our new stuff to a couple of stores. It's pretty cool. Have you seen any of it?"

I had seen some new glaze test tiles over the past few weeks, but hadn't put it all together that Sam and Mom had been working on a new line.

"We're calling it Rain Ware. All of the different glazes go with a texture to represent Seattle weather patterns." He shows me various mugs in shades of blue, pearl, oyster and steel gray. "We've tried to make clearly recognizable designs to represent Seattle's famous skies: fat rain splatters, misty drizzle, dripping downpour. This one is like wet, billowing fog."

"They're beautiful. They almost scream to be filled with a comforting hot beverage."

"Is that a hint? Can I make you a cup of tea or coffee?" I decline, but he wanders over to the kitchenette anyway. "Are you here to work? I think we're pretty well caught up."

"No, I just came to talk to Mom for a minute." Now is my chance to announce to Sam that I am a success. My plan has worked, and I have won Gaston back. But I don't want to. I fiddle with my earring instead.

"Everything okay?" asks Sam.

I can tell by the way he looks at me that he knows something is up. It's like he can drill right into my head. Fine! If he can read my mind, I don't need to bother explaining myself. Let him figure it all out. He's the self-proclaimed expert on women, after all.

"I'm great! Couldn't be better. Tell Mom I stopped by, will you?" I leave, not quite sure why I'm mad at Sam. In the car, in the parking lot of Mom's studio, I have a flashback of my original hopes and dreams for a future with Gaston. I remember my fantasies of having romantic dinners together and lazy, loving weekends at the Market or the movies. So far our reunion has involved me spoon-feeding him comforting calories and holding him while he whimpers. Well, starting tonight my visions will stop being fantasies and start becoming reality.

Chapter Twenty-Five

When Gaston gets to my place after work, my hair is fluffed, my makeup freshly applied and a new perfume is delicately dabbed at my neckline. I am at the stove cooking up a spicy pasta *arrabbiata* sauce. The table is set for two, the Barolo is breathing and the lamb chops are trimmed and marinating. I lay out a small plate of salami, olives and dressed artichoke bottoms for a little antipasto.

I smile at Gaston with obvious adoration as he enters the kitchen, and stir the pot with my big wooden spoon. I cool a taste of the sauce with my breath and lift it to Gaston's lips. He shakes his head and crinkles his nose.

"Thanks, but I think I'll pass. That smells pretty spicy, and I've been fighting heartburn this week." He pounds on his chest twice with his fist and lets out a belch. Then he grabs half a bag of corn chips and a soda from the fridge and heads to the living room to watch TV. I stand there, posed with my spoon and silly grin for a moment, then follow him into the living room.

"So, what would you like for dinner then? There are lamb chops marinating."

"Don't go to any bother, Baby. That sole with capers you do is always good. Do you have the stuff for that around?" He thumbs the remote. "I keep forgetting you guys don't have cable. How do you live with only the local channels?" His voice is accusing.

"TV has never been a priority around here," I remind him.

He makes a face of obvious disapproval. "I'll look into it, maybe find you a deal on a big screen and a satellite dish."

I move the sauce to the back burner and wrap the lamb chops tightly.

I'll give them to Mr. Wright. He'll appreciate them. I don't have any sole or the fat, salt-cured capers Gaston likes. I dig around in the freezer and find a couple shrimp and three scallops. A few minutes later, I present Gaston with a nice, mild seafood omelet for dinner. The Barolo isn't right for the eggs, but I'm not about to waste such a good bottle of wine, so I serve it. The way Gaston chugs it down, it might as well be some cheap plonk.

After dinner, Gaston fulfills part of my fantasy. He helps me clear the table. But instead of doing the dishes side by side, he sets his plate on the counter, pats his belly and thanks me for the good meal before he goes back to the couch. I try to hum a little tune to lighten my mood while I find myself resenting still more dirty dishes. I remind myself to keep my eye on the prize. Sex with Sam rocked my world last week. Sex with Gaston should blow my mind. Tonight, we won't just *sleep* in my bed.

After the kitchen is clean, I go to the bathroom, spritz more perfume in private places and brush my teeth. Then I head to the living room to ravage Gaston. He will forget Courtney tonight. He will see that our bodies and souls were meant to be together. We will elope and start planning our family. I sit close to him on the couch and run my fingertips along the inside of his wrist and forearm. He loves that.

He looks away from the TV to say, "That feels good." Then he spins around so his back is toward me. "You know, I've had this pain in my right shoulder. It's been really getting to me. Must be all the stress. Can you work on it a little?" He points to a spot. I readjust myself to give him a shoulder rub, hoping that he will sink into my arms.

"Nope, that's not getting it. Can you feel the knot in there? Here, how about if I sit on the floor and you can really put some muscle into it." He drops onto the floor and directs my hands to the knot in his shoulder and insists that I poke and knead at his back in a very unromantic, therapeutic manner.

"Ah, yeah, that's it. That's the ticket." At least I have him moaning in satisfaction.

Gradually, I lighten my touch and start stroking his neck. He flicks my hands away from his ear a few times, like it tickles, but soon I feel his skin prickle with excitement and his breath slow. I lean over and kiss him behind his ear. He doesn't object. I kiss him again. He turns off the TV and looks at me with hunger and passion. I slide down beside him on the floor. We embrace and kiss like old times.

"What are you doing to me, Katie? I feel like I could explode right now."

"Poor boy." I lick at his ears. "Have you missed me?" I can't imagine Courtney is much in the bedroom; she's just so uptight. I unbuckle his belt, and he moans. My body roars with excitement and sexuality.

"Oh, baby. Yes, let's do this!" He pulls at my clothes, and I help him along as we fondle and taste each other. We've done this a hundred times. We know where all the parts go and how to progress. Everything is moving right along until I open my eyes for one split second. Damned if I don't focus on one of Iris's treasured paintings of sad-eyed children. The waif is staring down at me in obvious disappointment, one tear suspended on his cheek. He's Iris's nagging harbinger of safe sex. I try to shut it out, but I can't. I recall Sam's enthusiastic response to my conjuring of condoms. That worked out pretty well. Very well, in fact. Before it's too late, I pull away from Gaston just long enough to whisper, "Let me get a condom. I'll be right back."

He pulls me toward him again and whispers back, "We're okay."

"No. We need to be safe." I try to peel myself away. He pulls me closer.

"It's okay. We're still good." Then he sits up. "Oh, did you go off the pill?"

Our conversation has become a little less sexy and a lot more clinical. We sit across from each other, questioning.

"No, I'm still on the pill. But you've been . . . uh, away for a while. I think we should take precautions."

He pulls me back into his arms. "No worries. Courtney and I never had sex. It'll be just like old times."

I melt back into his arms for a few seconds until his words sink in. I jump up like the floor has been charged with an electric current.

"You and Courtney never had sex?" I demand.

He shakes his head innocently, as if it's no big deal.

"You were together for what, almost four months? You were engaged to be married and you never slept together?"

"Oh, we slept together a few times. There were some nights I just couldn't bear to leave her, so I spent the night."

"You never had sex?" I know I'm repeating myself, but I can't quite believe what I just heard. Gaston *loves* sex. He *always* wanted to have sex. It was what we did best. There is *no way* Gaston could be in a relationship for months and not have sex. Not with someone who couldn't even cook. It is impossible.

He tries to explain. "I told you about Courtney's childhood. She was terribly abused. And then when she went to college, I guess she was a little wild. She was kind of well, er, promiscuous. When she finally got help, she promised herself a 'second virginity' and vowed she wouldn't have sex again until she was married."

"You never had sex with Courtney?" I am pacing now, waving my arms. "How do you expect me to have sex now?"

"What do you mean? It's a good thing, right? I haven't been with anyone since we broke up. We can have all the sex we want and it will be safe! C'mon, Kate!"

I pull my clothes back on while Gaston pleads with me to get naked again. I can't do it. I can't do any of it.

"Everything is all wrong, Gaston. Don't you see? This is all wrong."

"I thought this is what you wanted?" Gaston sits. He leans his head back on the couch. He is frustrated.

"I thought it was, too." We sit in silence for a while.

"Gaston, I didn't want to marry you last year because I wasn't ready. But last month, when you told me you were engaged to Courtney, I couldn't stand it. I couldn't let you go. I figured it was my job that got in the way of our relationship. I thought I never gave you enough time, so I made some big changes. And now that we're back together, I don't know. Things seem different." I start pacing again.

He looks hurt. "I love you, Kate."

"Yeah, yeah, I know. And I love you, too." The words don't quite drip from my lips in breathy emotion. I rub my temples for a while, looking for words. "When we're apart, I want nothing more than to be with you. I want to marry you." I sit next to him and hold his hand. I stare into his dark brown eyes, looking for answers.

"You're everything a woman can want in a man. You're kind and thoughtful and handsome. It seems so right. It makes sense." There are no answers in his eyes. I look away. "But now when we're together . . . it's weird. We used to talk for hours on the phone. We couldn't wait to see each other, to be with each other. Was it the anticipation, the fact we saw so little of each other that made it exciting? You see me all the time now. Do you ever feel that old thrill?"

Once the words are out, I see the truth. My relationship with Gaston was exciting because our time together was so limited. It wasn't my work at the restaurant or my inability to commit that broke us up. The demanding hours might have been what kept Gaston and me together for so long. Our sexual rendezvous were exciting, but when we spent a lot of time together, it was kind of dull. There weren't always fireworks. He would get preachy, and I would get bored. I look at his tired face. Am I sure this soft man is my one true love? And am I the person he wants to be with? "I guess the real question here is, do you still love me? Or am I just a warm, familiar body to keep you comfortable until you patch things up with Courtney?"

"I love you both." He looks away. "It doesn't matter, anyway. After this weekend, there's no hope with Courtney. I lost her." He looks back at me, almost desperate. "And I ruined things with my mom. I don't think I could take it if I lost you, too, Kate."

I might have Gaston's body back, but Courtney still has his heart. I see now that my dreams with Gaston really were fairy tales. He's not my prince charming. That's why I didn't marry him in the first place. He's just a nice guy with a lot of money who happens to be protected by a dragon woman. Seems like an easy mistake.

I press my hand to his cheek. "I'm pretty sure there's still hope, Gaston. I spoke to her the other day, and let me tell you, she may have been thinking clearly and responsibly, but in her heart she was a mess. She's hurting, and that means there is hope."

I feel sorry for Gaston, so I'm willing to be charitable. "Since I got you into this mess, I'll help you out of it." I reach for his hand and pull him off the couch. "Let's go talk to Courtney and get this straightened out, right now."

Courtney doesn't live in a suburban apartment complex overlooking a strip mall. She has a tiny one-bedroom apartment on Queen Anne Hill, just above Lake Union. Gaston says that if you stand on the toilet and look out the bathroom window, there is a nice view of downtown Seattle. I park on the street and make Gaston promise to sit in the car until I call him. They are both emotional wrecks, and if they see each other, I figure there will be a lot of waterworks, stammering and little progress.

I buzz Courtney's place. She is caught off guard by my arrival, but she lets me in without much hesitation. Newspapers, magazines and spelling tests in big writing cover the counter and kitchen table. A bowl of ice cream and a jar of peanut butter lie interrupted on the coffee table in front of the TV. She has a movie paused, but turns it off when I enter. I get a quick glimpse of George Clooney and approve of her choice. She is wearing a long nightgown and a well-worn terrycloth robe with ducks on the lapel. Her feet are encased in thick socks. I hate to see that her hair and complexion are perfect.

"Hi, Kate. Can I help you with something?" Once again, I am surprised by how much I admire Courtney. She doesn't waste any time apologizing or making excuses for her mess or casual attire. I am, after all, an uninvited guest.

"I won't stay long. I just need to explain a few things. I need to come clean."

She tilts her head in curiosity.

"When Gaston told me he was getting married, I kind of freaked out. I couldn't imagine he could spend his life with anyone but me. So, I've been kind of sabotaging your relationship."

Courtney is silent but interested in what I am saying.

"What happened last weekend, the whole Adele thing—that's my fault."

Courtney bows her head. She must think I'm just trying to be nice and covering for Gaston. I would think, since I've been so horrible to her, that she would know better by now. I go on confessing.

"No, really. I thought I wanted Gaston back. Adele and I talked on the phone and we worked together to ruin things for you. I told you to cook foods I knew Adele would hate. I kept reminding Gaston about how much his mom liked me, about all of the good times we had. I did everything I could to mess up your weekend."

"Kate, I appreciate your honesty. But how can you take credit for what happened when you weren't even there? I won't let you take the blame. There is obviously a deep-seated problem between Gaston and his mother."

"See? That's the thing. Gaston has never said a harsh word to his mother in his life. He's never even raised his voice to her. And suddenly he calls her a bitch? That's not right!"

"Exactly. That's my point."

"No, wait. That's not what I mean. Gaston loves his mother. He adores her. He was just mad that she liked me better than you. He was mad because she was so mean to you."

She furrows her brows. I don't think I'm getting through to her.

"He loves you so much he cursed at his own mother. Don't you understand that? He loves you so much that he was willing to fight her to be with you. He loves you more than anything in the world, Courtney. I've never seen him like this. I mean, you haven't even had sex!"

She is disturbed by my words. She sucks in her lips. "Kate, I know you're an important friend, but I'm just not comfortable talking like this. I understand that you are trying to help, but this is between Gaston and me. It's personal."

"But he loves his mother! He never fights with her. And he loves sex. Don't you see? He's willing to sacrifice so much for you."

"Kate, I'm not prepared to have this conversation with you. I'm going to have to ask you to leave."

"His mother's *always* been a bitch. That's just the way she is. But the important thing is that he stood up to her! He fought for you."

Courtney pushes me toward the door. "You aren't helping, Kate."

"But he loves you!"

Courtney's eyes flash with anger. She pushes me out the door and says, "Then tell him to get some help. Tell him it's time to treat his mother like the intrusive, insensitive, rude woman she is instead of acting like a whiny child. Tell him to stop running to his ex-girlfriend when he wants approval or when things get uncomfortable. And tell him to face me like a man instead of sending you to my door to fix his mistakes!" She slams the door shut in my face.

Yikes! Courtney isn't sweet at all. She's brutal. I stand frozen at her door with my hand raised to knock, but instead I go back to the car.

"What did she say?"

"She's a lot tougher than I thought."

He slumps back into his seat. "I kept telling you that. She still hates me, doesn't she?"

"I'm not quite sure about that, but she sure has your number. She figured you out a hell of a lot faster than I did."

"Whadya mean?"

"You've got issues, Gaston, big issues. And it's time for you to get your shit together. Go get some help. Join a men's drumming group, hug a tree, learn how to tune up a car, do whatever it takes. Then maybe you can go back to that woman and tell her, straight up, what you've done to change. Don't try groveling or begging for forgiveness—that's not going to work for this one. And don't pretend a wedding is going to make everything okay. Stand tall, be strong and honest, and then cross your fingers, 'cause it's going to take a lot more than just prayers to win her back."

"But . . . but . . . you said . . ."

"And you know what else? I'll admit I didn't help you with your relationship. I might have made things a little trickier, but when it came to really screwing things up, you did that all by yourself."

I make sure he has taxi fare to get home and then kick him out of my car. "You're on your own, buddy. Good luck." Gaston stumbles from the car looking dizzy from my barrage of tough love. I go home, eat a couple of cookies and sleep better than I have in a week.

Chapter Twenty-Six

When I was nine, I had beautiful, long hair. When it was washed and smooth, it shone like golden silk. But I wasn't the kind of girl who liked to sit still while my mother brushed my hair a hundred strokes a night. I preferred to climb trees and play kickball with my brother's friends. Combing my hair free of tangles was always a battle of wills. If Mom got her way, she would tie my hair in tight braids and leave them be for a couple of days. If I managed to wriggle free of her grip or wear her out before she was done, my hair would be loose and wild and end up even rattier. I would scream even louder the next time.

Just after school let out that summer, we had both had enough. Mom took out the big scissors she had always threatened to use, and I didn't object. I let her cut off my long, golden messy hair right above the worst tangle. I had a shoulder-length bob, and after the initial trauma, I loved it.

That's how I feel today. I'm a little sad. I know something near and dear to me is gone. I will miss Gaston, but I know it is for the best. I feel lighter. My heartbreak has inspired change, and I am better for it. I have learned how to enjoy my own company again. I am my own woman. I can feel it in my blood.

Today, in addition to being released of my domestic fantasies with Gaston, my life is in order. My customers are well fed and my lunches are prepped. I'm not needed at the studio. There is no scheming to do or landmines to set. The house is clean. I have a fat bank account and a well-rested body.

I ponder my list of recreational ideas with glee and go to the Woodland Park Zoo. The day is overcast and chilly, so there aren't many people around. I laugh out loud at the antics of the otters and orangutans. I creep alongside the slow loris and marvel at the three-toed sloth in the nocturnal house. I buy a hot dog and cup of hot cider and find myself appreciating the exotic pheasants for their plumage rather than their flavor potential. When I get cold and tired, I leave the zoo and go to a nature film at the IMAX theater. I almost choke on a piece of popcorn because I forget to close my mouth watching the stunning scenery on the huge screen.

I make plans for future days off. I'll take myself to the glass museum in Tacoma, go skiing, maybe drive to the coast. This week, I'll go shopping for a ridiculously sexy dress and impractical shoes for the Wheton-Lofton Christmas party, then maybe get my battered nails redone and have a tan sprayed on. I will go out and listen to music with Iris, and let Marissa set me up with rich doctors. Yippee! I'm free!

At about seven the next morning, I'm up drinking coffee and planning my day when Iris staggers in the front door. She looks beat. I check the clock. "Wild night last night?" I ask.

"Hardly. I was at Rex's place, working. He's got a studio set up in his basement, and we just kind of lost track of time."

"You've been playing all night? Your fingers must be bloody stumps."

She inspects her fingertips. "No, they're fine. But my throat is sore. I've been singing."

"Singing? Just singing?" I can hear now that her voice is tired.

"Yeah. Rex is a way better guitar and keyboard player than I am, so he's got me singing all this new stuff. And you know, it's not all that bad."

"That's because you've got a great voice."

"No, it's not that. I mean, my voice is okay, as long as the guitars are loud enough and the crowd is drunk."

Iris has never had a lot of confidence in her singing voice. I've always liked it. She's got a unique sound.

"Thanks to the miracle of modern recording equipment, Rex has been able to make me sound pretty good."

"So, when am I going to hear some of this new stuff? You have a disc ready? Got any gigs planned?"

"Rex thinks I'm ready to play a show, but I don't know. I'm not sure I even want *you* to hear it yet. It would just kill me if you didn't like it. I'm tempted to book a gig out of town and give it a test run on strangers, you know? If they boo me off the stage, I won't ever have to see them again."

"I'll find out about it, you know. I'll follow you," I threaten. "And if I hear someone boo, I'll kick them in the shins."

Iris smiles. "In pointy-toed shoes?"

"Absolutely!" Iris looks small and vulnerable this morning. She says she's just tired, and waves off my concerns for her health.

"You're up early. Did Gaston sleep over last night?" Iris asks.

"No. Gaston's gone. He's out of the picture."

She is incredulous. She lights a cigarette and grills me for more information. I fill her in on the whole story.

"I'm proud of you, Kate. You're so smart when it comes to men. I would never have been that strong. I probably would have slept with him and then clung to any last shred of hope, even though I knew he was in love with someone else. I suck when it comes to men, you know that?"

I know it well, but it was nice to hear her admit it. "What about this Rex guy?"

"He's way out of my league."

"Not likely. You're a catch!" I say. She dismisses my comment. I change the subject. "So Marsha Lofton somehow talked me in to going to the big Wheton-Lofton Christmas party. You want to be my date? It's always a pretty good party, lots of food, live music, dancing. You can wear one of those old bridesmaid dresses you tweaked."

"Thanks, but no thanks. I'll pass. Why don't you invite Sam?"

"I suppose I could, but it doesn't seem like his sort of thing. And it might feel too much like a date. We agreed the other night that we aren't looking for anything serious." I avoid using the term "friends." Iris will accuse me of falling for a cheesy line, and I don't feel like explaining our arrangement right now.

She goes to bed, and I finish up my cooking. I've got the lunch system down pat. Folks are fed and and I'm out of the office by two. I leave my car in the lot and take myself shopping. All in all, I think I try on fifty fancy dresses (three with sparkles) and fall in love with a slinky green and gold number. I dawdle in the jewelry and accessories department, and then splurge on a pair of very high heels that make my legs look firm and sexy and my posture positively rigid. (Maybe there is something about this shoe thing after all!) I rest in the lobby of the W Hotel and nibble warm cashews with a glass of late-afternoon Champagne, then go to Magic Mouse Toys and pick out a bunch of adorable things for little Danny. I run and show Mom my purchases. She loves the dress and shoes, but she already bought Danny the same Thomas the Tank Engine train set. I go back and exchange it for some neat bath toys.

My run-in with Kurt, the cute, produce guy at the nursing home, has made its way through the restaurant grapevine. I get a couple of invitations to interview. A local corporation is looking for an executive chef for one of it waterfront locations. The money is good, but the salary comes with pretty strict menu limitations. While I still like the idea of a more corporate/professional environment in the kitchen, I don't think clipping my creative wings will offer a lot of job satisfaction. I also get an emergency call from an infamous chef who lost half his crew to another tantrum. No, thank you.

Over the weekend, I drive to the coast and check into a cheap beach-side motel near the fishing town of Westport. I take long walks on the cold ocean beach and stroll along the docks. A fisherman in tall rubber boots sloshes through the hold of his boat picking up angry Dungeness crab until I am satisfied I have selected the best three. The grizzled motel owner and his wife point to an outdoor kitchen with a big sink and propane fire ring made specifically for visitors like me who come to town for the crab, oysters and razor clams. We talk about great seafood and compare chowder recipes as they help me cook and clean the crab.

I sit alone at the scratched linoleum dinette set with a bowl of melted butter and a cold bottle of Sauvignon Blanc. I eat one entire crab myself while watching sitcom reruns on the ancient motel TV. (They're all new to me.) The night is clear, and the moon is full, so I bundle up and take another walk on the beach. The sand is smooth from the receding tide, so mine are the only footprints. The moon is so bright I can see my shadow on the glimmering sand. The terrain feels borderless.

I love Seattle, and I know part of the city's beauty comes from the dramatic topography, but you can't go far without banging into a hill or mountain. If you want to gaze at an endless horizon, Seattle ain't your town. Here at the coast, it's pretty flat. The beach runs for miles in either direction. Before me, just past the breaking waves, is the entire Pacific Ocean. I walk to the peak of a grassy dune, and I swear, I can see forever.

On Sunday, before I leave town, I wander through the shell shacks, looking at the shelves and shelves of souvenirs printed with local names but made in distant lands. I buy an old church cookbook from a used-book store. It has a recipe for German sauerkraut soup that catches my eye. I spend all weekend living in the moment. I don't worry about my future, don't fuss over relationships, barely think about food. I just have a good time. I crank up an old rock and roll station and sing all the way to Mr. Wright's house.

"Kate, what a pleasant surprise. Come on in. I'll put the kettle on."

"Thanks, but I can't stay. I just thought you might like a crab. I spent the weekend at the coast. I bought it right off the boat."

"Well, I'll be. Thank you. This will be quite a treat."

"I suppose I should have made you a salad or something to go with it. You know, some vegetables."

"How about if I promise to eat it with one of those packets of broccoli you put in the freezer? Will that fulfill my vegetable quota? I don't want you to get in trouble with my daughter. No, siree. I like this arrangement far too much to mess it up."

I give him a kiss on the cheek. "I'll be back on Tuesday with more food. Any requests?"

"Well, yes, as a matter of fact. Don't make too much, or it will just go to waste. I've decided to take an old rock-hounding friend up on an invitation. I'm leaving in a few days for Arizona, and we're going to take the train down to the Copper Canyon. I'm going to see if a little sun might warm these old bones up enough to do some exploring."

I wish him well on his trip, and find Mom at the studio. Mandy is there too. I hear her before I see her. She is reading Sam the riot act. "Are you crazy? You can't go home for Christmas. Selena will be there."

"God, Mandy, shut up already. I can handle it."

"That's what you say now. But when you see her, you'll go all soft and she'll seduce you again. You might as well just throw yourself in Mount St. Helens."

"I haven't seen Mom in months. I want to get some special oxides and clay base for Lauren. And . . . Why am I even explaining this to you?" I step into the room and can tell by Sam's expression that he is relieved to see me, if for no other reason than to interrupt the argument he is having with his sister.

"Kate's here. Let's drop it," he says to Mandy.

"Kate's here? Perfect! Let's see what she thinks." Sam groans, and his head goes limp on his shoulders. Mandy doesn't even bother to say hello; she just jumps straight into her debate. "Sam wants to go home for Christmas."

"Yeah, so?" I walk over to Mom's desk and hand her the cleaned crab, all wrapped up in plastic and paper.

"Crab? What a treat! Thanks, Honey." She is pleased with her present and dashes off to put it in the fridge. She's obviously trying to stay out of the siblings' argument.

Mandy won't let me off that easy. She looks at me as if I am a traitor. "He can't go back yet! Don't you remember why he's here? Selena still calls him all the time. If he goes, she'll drag him back into her witch's lair. I just know it."

I'm done playing puppet master. "If Sam wants to go home for Christmas and get caught up with that hussy, what business is it of mine? Seems to me that Sam's a big boy. He can make his own mistakes."

Sam gestures toward me. "Thank you! See? Kate agrees. You need to just back off. Why don't you spend all of this energy taking an interest in your own love life for a change, and leave your poor brother alone!"

She tries another tack. "I'm worried about you, Sam. You're alone. You're still vulnerable. And you're forgetting about the history you have with Selena. She's the only woman you've ever loved. Don't you know how much control she has over your emotions?"

I think about pointing out how Mandy is doing a pretty good job of trying to manipulate Sam's emotions. I wink at him as a warning, then step close and take his arm.

"I guess we have to tell her, don't we?"

He looks at me like I'm crazy. I pinch him and look down at my shoes, as if I'm embarrassed. "I made Sam promise not to tell anyone, but since you're so worried about him, I guess we have to come clean. You don't have to worry about Selena anymore. Sam and I are a couple now."

She gasps and then shouts, "No way! That's great! Lauren, did you hear that?"

Mom squeals, jumps up from her desk and hugs us both. She makes all sorts of congratulatory noises. "How did this happen? Why didn't you tell me?"

Mandy turns to Mom. "You were right all along, Lauren. They are *perfect* for each other, and you knew it right from the start."

Sam and I don't have much trouble looking flustered and embarrassed after that comment, but we really ham it up. He nuzzles my hair and makes smoochie sounds in my ear. I coo a little in appreciation and pat his butt as retribution.

Sam finally says, "How it happened isn't relevant, Mandy. What's important here is that you know I'm over Selena. She's old news. I have Kate now." He makes a ferrety face and pokes me in the ribs. "Isn't that right, kitten?"

I secretly pinch him hard for being such a dork, then rub his nose with mine and say, "That's right, Pookie Bear!" Then we both start giggling like naughty schoolkids. Mom sits back, looking very proud of herself. Mandy actually buys it.

"This is just so great! I knew moving to Seattle would be the right thing for you!"

We continue to feign our adoration until Mandy remembers why she is here in the first place. Sam packs up four boxes of the new Rain Ware mugs. Mandy is giving sets away as Christmas gifts. When she has everything in order, she gives us both kisses on the cheek and leaves in a whirl of happiness.

Sam steps away from me and lets out a huge sigh. "Phew! Thanks for that, Kate. She was driving me crazy!"

"No problemo. Sorry for the ruse, Mom. I just thought Sam could use a break."

She is devastated. "You mean, you two aren't . . . ?" We shake our heads. She's a good sport and laughs with us, but there is an odd feeling of betrayal in the air.

Sam must feel it, too. He is eager to leave the room. "Do either of you need anything from me? 'Cause I've got some work to do." He points over his shoulder to his private studio.

"Well, yeah. Maybe you can return the favor. I'm supposed to go to the Wheton-Lofton Christmas party on Friday. I'm okay on my own, but since you owe me one, maybe you could go as my date?"

Sam screws up his face. "Can't I just take you out for a pizza or something?"

Mom sits back in her chair. Her smile has returned.

I shake my head. "That's not good enough. I need a date who looks like he's having the time of his life. That kitten thing might be a bit much, but feel free to act like you adore me. Gaston will be there."

"Are you nuts? No way. Forget it! I'm done with corporate events, remember?"

I shrug and run my finger through some clay dust. "All right then. I understand." I head back toward the door and give him a mischievous grin. "But I might have to tell Mandy you coerced me into lying in order to cover up a clandestine rendezvous with Selena."

Mom smiles. Sam's mouth drops open. "You wouldn't!"

"I might." I feel deliciously wicked. "But not if you pick me up Friday night at 7:30. G'night, Mom!" I holler as I leave the building. Oops. I forgot one last detail. I poke my head in the door and shout back to Sam, "Oh, yeah—and it's formal. You might want to wear a jacket."

Chapter Twenty-Seven

I go back to the studio on Wednesday to pester Sam again about the party. "C'mon, Sam. It'll be fun. There's music and door prizes, and Marsha always orders tons of shrimp." Some of the folks at Wheton-Lofton seem to be most impressed by the abundance of shrimp at this event.

His eyebrows rise with interest. "Big shrimp? I like big shrimp."

"Huge shrimp! Giant shrimp!" I find myself pulling on his arm, pleading.

He laughs. "All right, you talked me into it. I'll go."

I jump up and kiss him on the cheek, then do a little dance. "Hooray! You won't be sorry. I bought this awesome dress and these high heels and new earrings and everything! It'll be fun, I promise."

I'm thrilled that Sam has agreed to go. Once I asked him, it became kind of an obsession. I *really* wanted to go with him. Not just to prove to Gaston and Marsha that I have moved on, but because Sam is so much fun. He'll laugh at my jokes and his eyes will twinkle. And he'll make my dress look even better. It would be a crying shame to wear that dress with no date.

I was very nearly ready to weigh my argument by explaining to him that Gaston and I are through. Thank goodness I bit my tongue just in time. Telling Sam about Gaston might not have swayed him to my side. now, trying to explain things to him. *Well, see, my diabolical plan to break Gaston and Courtney actually worked, so I declared my love to him and told him I wanted to get married, then when he agreed and came back to me, I refused to have sex with him and tried to single-handedly patch up his ruined relationship.* Once Sam heard that, he'd probably leave the state.

When Friday night finally arrives, I find myself marveling at what a few weeks away from commercial fryers and industrial grills can do for your complexion. My skin is glowing, and that, combined with the sexiest dress I have ever owned, my new hair and recent experiments with makeup, have all come together to make me one mighty hot package. I dot a drop of sandalwood oil on my wrist. It is the scent I like the most right now, one I wear for my own pleasure. I look once again at the clock. It's 7:28, and no word from Sam since Wednesday.

I decided hours ago that I would give him until 8:15 and then accept that I was too pushy and go to the party without him. I sit on the couch and curse myself for being too punctual. I wiggle my freshly painted toes, thumb through a couple of food magazines, then face the facts. Sam will never show. Why would he? I check my teeth in the hall mirror for lipstick one last time, grab my beaded evening bag and am bracing myself for a solo night when the doorbell rings.

Sam and I stare at each other with stupid smiles on our faces for a few seconds. He is wearing a tuxedo. Not some funky dog hair–covered tweed sports jacket like in my recent nightmares, but a real tuxedo that fits him beautifully. And grown-up shoes. I'm still not quite used to seeing Sam's new haircut. I stare for a moment at his regal bone structure and clear, tan skin. His blue eyes aren't mocking me, flashing in anger or squeezed shut in frustration. They look kind, and make my own eyes glimmer and shine.

"So. Can I come in? It's freezing out here!" He blows on his hands and stomps his feet. I pull him in the front door and gave him a big fat hug and sloppy kiss of appreciation.

"Careful, lady! You're squishing the flowers!" He hands me a tiny bouquet of aromatic violets. I can't imagine where he found them. I am overjoyed. I breathe in their sweet aroma and decide violets are my all-time favorite flower. "They're beautiful, thank you."

"No problem. Speaking of beautiful, you were right, that's a hell of a dress!"

I smile and perform a dainty twirl, then self-consciously slug him on the arm. "Thanks." I am effervescent.

"So, we better get going, huh?" He covers my shoulders in a new wrap, and we head out for the party. Sam has borrowed the veterinarian's Lexus for the night. I give him directions. Marsha Lofton has rented the Grand Central building for the company party. It is an old brick complex in the heart of Pioneer Square. During the day it bustles with tourists, locals and a lot of Seattle's advertising community, who dash around the wonderful bakery, shops and galleries. At night, with special arrangements, the indoor courtyard is transformed into an elegant party setting, perfect for formal winter events. As usual, Marsha has spared no expense. The old red bricks are dressed with miles of fresh-cut evergreen boughs and ivory silk. A fire in the central fireplace crackles and warms the room with a golden light. A jazz combo plays holiday standards as a team of smartly dressed servers pass Champagne and hors d'oeuvres.

The senior partner, the formidable and rarely seen Russell Wheton, meets us as we arrive. I introduce Sam. We share a few words of small talk until an ebullient Marsha Lofton pulls me away.

"Hello, darling! Merry Christmas, merry Christmas! Isn't it wonderful?" She gestures to the room with one arm while she gives me a friendly pat with the other. I'm guessing she's had a few early eggnogs. She is wearing a sparkly red jacket, black silk pajama bottoms and a huge poinsettia corsage. Her feet are squeezed into a pair of sandals that might have been made by the same cobbler who did Dorothy's ruby slippers. Marsha's hair and makeup look professionally done. She's a big, beautiful woman in real life. Tonight she looks fancy.

She tugs at my wrap. "You look stunning! Take that thing off and show yourself!" I give it up and do an awkward spin and curtsy, kind of like I used to do when my aunt Virginia dressed me up for Easter Sunday. "Marvelous! What a fabulous dress!" My skin electrifies as I feel Sam's fingertips on the small of my back. He has stepped up next to me.

"Oh! Goodness! Who's this?" asks Marsha.

Sam holds out his hand with confidence and gives her the treatment— full eye contact and one of his knockout smiles. "Sam Guerra. Nice to meet you, Ms. Lofton."

Marsha flutters at his greeting and offers her hand as she subtly checks him out from head to toe. "Well, Sam. How nice to meet you, too." She bats her lashes a few times, then comes back to earth. "Ooh, Kate. I'd love for you to meet my husband." She turns but finds only empty space. "He was just here a minute ago, but I guess he got away. He hates these things. I bet he went back into the kitchen to badger the caterers."

Two new couples arrive behind us, or Marsha may never have given up Sam's hand. She pulls me close and whispers, "To hell with Gaston. I'll expect a full report on Sam, first thing Monday morning. What a butt!"

"Dirty old woman," I whisper. She laughs and moves on to greet her new guests.

"Can I get you some Champagne?" Sam offers. I accept. As he crosses the room, I look at him with fresh eyes. I want to see him as a stranger might, instead of as the familiar mud-coated, wild-haired artist I first met. I had been dazzled at the sight of him when he arrived at my door, but I figured that was because he had actually shown up. Or was it? I look again. His posture is strong and confident, and he moves with the liquid grace of an athlete or dancer. He lifts two glasses of Champagne from a passing waiter's tray and turns back. I take my glass, clink it with his, and we share a silent toast.

"That tux fits you awfully well. How did you pull off a rental at such short notice?"

"Why do you assume it's a rental? Can't a gentleman have a tuxedo in his closet in case of emergency?"

"Sure! A gentleman should always have at least one tuxedo."

Sam nods in agreement.

"So, where did you get yours?"

He pretends to be offended and then explains, "I bought it a couple of summers ago when a whole crowd of my college buddies got married. I was kind of glad to dig it out. I haven't needed it in a while, and I want to get my money's worth out of this thing before it goes too far out of style."

I flatten his lapels and straighten his already straight bow tie. Then I give him a kiss.

"What's that for?" He looks around. "Is Gaston nearby? Which one is he?"

"I just felt like it. I don't know if I mentioned it, but I really appreciate you coming with me tonight. As for Gaston, don't worry about him. He's out of the picture."

His eyes go serious. "Out of the picture? What does that mean?"

"We had a long talk last week. I don't want to bore you with the details, but I'm over Gaston. We're all through. I should have told you before, but I didn't quite know what to say."

He can't stop grinning. "So this is a real date? Just you and me?"

I nod.

"That's about the best news I've heard all year!" He leans over and gives me a kiss that makes me dizzy. I smile.

"I have to admit something, too. I wanted to come to this party with you the very first time you mentioned it. But I couldn't stand the idea of being just a decoy or some kind of stooge. It would have killed me if we came here together and you spent the whole night yearning for Gaston. Then I decided I'd rather be here than sitting at home wondering if tonight was the night. If tonight he won you back."

I cock my head, curious if he really said what I think he said.

"I know I told you we would be just friends, and I meant it at the time, but it's been killing me. Last weekend, when we pretended to be a couple for Mandy, I could barely let go of you. I wanted to just hold you and call you pet names and make a complete fool of myself.

"The last few times I've seen you, you've been hypnotizing. You've had this internal radiance, a glow and energy I've never seen before in a woman, and I can't keep my eyes off you." He adjusts a tiny stone on my necklace. His fingertips linger, and my skin turns electric. I don't say anything, just cover his mouth with kisses.

"Now that I know this is a real date, I tell you, Kate, it's going to be tough for me not to tear that dress off you right here and now." My body temperature jumps twenty degrees at the mere thought of it.

"I think good manners require that we stay for at least ten minutes," is my reply.

He kisses me again. "Maybe just one dance?"

He pulls me into his arms and spins me onto the dance floor. I am dazzled by his grace. "Are you kidding? You dance, too? You're really the whole package, aren't you?"

"Sisters, remember? My services as a dance partner were demanded from a very early age. I didn't mind. I liked dance classes, at least until my third grade buddies intervened and informed me that baseball was much cooler." When the song ends he steps back and expertly drops me into a dip. When I stop laughing, I look over and see Gaston and Courtney standing alongside the dance floor, staring at us.

"Oh! Hi!" I straighten up and smooth my hair. "Uh, Sam, I'd like you to meet Gaston Lambert and Courtney Davis. Gaston, this is Sam Guerra." Sam continues to hold me around the waist as if it were the most natural thing in the world. Courtney nods. Gaston looks dyspeptic.

"It's nice to see you together," I say.

They don't look like they're having an especially good time. Courtney stands with her arms crossed in front of her. She's wearing something that looks like a funeral dress with some festive earrings and a brooch. I have new respect for such useful clothing.

Gaston urges Courtney and Sam to speak together, and pulls me a few feet away. "You were right, Kate. It took a lot of talking, but I managed to convince Courtney to give me another chance. Things are going to be different. She agreed to come tonight if I promised to follow some pretty strict guidelines. We wrote out a contract. I have to see a therapist about my unresolved parenting issues and go to an emotional self-defense class that she found was really helpful. I guess you have to learn to attack and bite and kick your demons who are actually these big guys dressed up in protective gear. She's limiting my calls, and she insists that we have one home-cooked dinner a week at her house."

"And your mom?"

"She left me a message last week. She flew to Prague for intensive massage and hydrotherapy. I'll deal with her later."

I'm happy for him. "I hope you can work things out, really." I give him a peck on the cheek, and suddenly Sam appears.

He takes my hand. "Do I see shrimp?" He pulls me away from Gaston, pretending to chase after a waiter. When we are out of sight, he pulls me into a secluded corner and kisses me like he means it. "He wasn't trying to woo you back, was he? He looked pretty intense."

"Sam? Are you jealous?" I tease.

"Jealous? Of Gaston? He's merely the man you have been determined to marry since I met you. He's an attractive guy who was having a very intimate conversation with my date, who happens to be the prettiest woman in the room. Why on earth should I be jealous of Gaston?"

Just to torment him I say, "Did I forget to tell you that Gaston's family is filthy rich?" He groans and slaps his forehead. I chuckle and kiss him sweetly. Then to reassure him, I say, "I could have had Gaston, you know. We could have been celebrating our engagement tonight. But you know what? I wouldn't change a thing. There isn't anyone in the world I'd rather be with than you." And it's true. I'm having a magical night. "You might even get lucky," I whisper in his ear.

"I'm ready for you this time. After Thanksgiving I actually made a run to the pharmacy, just in case you had the urge to ravage me again. We single guys need to be prepared."

"Excuse me, but I seem to remember being on the receiving end of a little ravaging myself."

"Guilty as charged! But if we do it again, I'm not adverse to sitting back and letting you do all the work. I'm a modern man."

"In your dreams!"

We laugh and dance and stare into each other's eyes. When the band takes a break, I am snapped from my reverie by a very familiar voice. It is Iris. She has settled onto a stool in front of the microphone with her guitar. Behind her stands a stringy little guy with a keyboard who I assume is Rex. She introduces herself, gives me a quick nod and then starts singing like I have never heard her sing.

Everyone in the room is mesmerized. At times, she almost croons, but it is nothing like a classic torch singer's voice or a lounge chanteuse's. It is Iris *unplugged*. Like Kurt Cobain when he sang Leadbelly, Elvis Costello doing country western and, of course, her new idol, Marianne Faithfull. Iris combines old and new styles, phrasing each uniquely, without detracting from the original spirit of the music. She sings some old blues standards, some upbeat contemporary songs and, best of all, a few of her own pieces reworked as wailing, heartbreaking solos. Iris isn't just another punk wannabe or garage band singer anymore: She is an artist performing music that is as unique and complicated and beautiful as she is herself. I am so proud of her.

I pat Sam's chest and point to my friend. "That's Iris. Can you believe it? Isn't she amazing?" I lean over to a few people I know from the office and tap them on the shoulder. "That's Iris. We live together. She's my roommate. Iris is my best friend." They look as if they would prefer it if I stopped bothering them and let them listen to the music. When the duo finish their set, I forget for a moment where I am and fill the room with a shrill, two-fingered whistle of approval. I run over to Iris, and we grab hands and hop around like squealing teenagers. (We might have even performed something similar to the dreaded sorority girl greetings we claim to despise.)

"You were incredible, Iris! How come you didn't tell me you were singing tonight?"

She's more animated than I've ever seen her. "Did you like it? It seemed like everyone really liked it. I told you I was doing some new cool stuff." She is talking fast; her sentences run together. "Rex and I have been working like crazy. It's our first public gig. You told me about this party, and I just locked on to it. I figured it would be a good chance to try things out on strangers without like totally humiliating myself at a real club. And I liked that you were going to be here. So, I just called up Marsha, introduced myself, and she agreed to book us after she heard the demo stuff. She's pretty cool, isn't she? You really liked it? I'm so glad! I've been dying to talk to you about it, but I couldn't bear it if you hated it. And you've been going through so much lately. I didn't want to dump on you, too. Is that Sam? He's totally hot."

When she takes a breath, I have a chance to speak. "You were brilliant. Everyone around me thought so." She beams at the compliment and then says, "It's not me, it's Rex. He's just so amazing." She looks around the room for her keyboard player. He's putting equipment away. "He's the greatest. And he's just so cool. He kept handing me sheet music and telling me to sing however I wanted. He played along on the guitar or the keyboard, and we just got into this groove."

I watch Rex grab a beer for himself and a glass of Champagne for Iris. He hands her the drink, then stands very close to her. He's a nerdy kind of guy with big, dark glasses and skin that might not see the light of day much. His face doesn't show a lot of emotion. He and Sam share a few words, then do a neck bob thing, which seems to bond them as fellow artists. I'm getting a vibe by the way he watches over Iris that this Rex fellow is interested in more than just a musical duo. I'll have to check him out. This might be a pretty good match for Iris.

Iris is pulled away by some of her new fans. Sam and I wander to the buffet table. We talk to some folks from the office, sidle to a dark corner to kiss, then dance cheek to cheek. At the next musical break, Sam and I both win door prizes. He gets a $300 gift card from an electronics store; I win a clock radio. Lady Luck is smiling on us.

When the music starts again, he pulls me to my feet. But this time, he leads me away from the dance floor. "How about we go home and have a party of our own?"

"You read my mind."

We go to Sam's place. He hasn't made any arrangements for someone to watch the office, so he has to spend five minutes putting the animals to bed. Afterwards, Sam joins me in his small bedroom. I light a candle and he turns on some soft music. I slip off my shoes and snuggle up to his chest for one last slow dance. He holds me close and strokes the short, soft hair at the back of my neck as we rock from side to side. He gently nudges my dress off my shoulders and I let it fall to the ground.

Our coming together is slow and tender. I don't feel driven for a sensual release or the desire to let everything go. This time, I take Sam in. I want to absorb his every essence. The night seems to last forever. We explore and share our bodies, we doze, we kiss, we chat, and then we start all over again.

It's a marvelous thing, making love with a friend.

Chapter Twenty-Eight

I remember Sam taking care to lock the pets out last night. He must have gotten up at some point, because Cy, the cat, is now curled up, sleeping next to my warm, still form. I pet him, then turn over and snuggle into Sam. He pulls me close, wraps me in his delectable arms and sighs with contentment. Ziggy stands up when we start to move, inspects our embrace and then lies down again with a similar deep sigh. We doze for a few minutes, then Sam and I can't keep our hands to ourselves. We enjoy a few of the highlights from last night's sexual marathon.

"Hmmmmm." A long, contented hum is all I can manage as witty conversation for awhile.

Sam kisses me on the nose. "We still have a few weeks until Christmas. How about if we find a couple more parties, you put that dress and those shoes back on, and we repeat the whole night?"

"You gonna wear that tuxedo again?"

"Sure."

"Then it's a deal. And if we can't find a party, how about if we concentrate on just the dancing and undressing part?"

We manage to let go of each other long enough to perform our morning duties. Sam exercises the inmates while I take a long shower. After I step out of the tub, I find myself in an awkward situation, one that I've never been in before. It's eight-thirty on a Saturday morning and all I have to wear is a skimpy cocktail dress and high heels. I poke through a stack of clean clothes in Sam's bedroom and pull on a pair of his athletic pants and a Wallace and Gromit T-shirt. He comes back into the bedroom and stops short, gaping at me. I am embarrassed.

"Sorry. I should have asked. It's just that I'm not too keen on strapping those instruments of torture back on my feet. And it seems kind of sleazy to be wearing a tiny dress this late on a Saturday morning. I'll change."

"Don't you dare!" He pulls me close and kisses me hard. "You look gorgeous."

I'm pleased that he seems to find me as attractive in sloppy clothes as he did in a designer dress, but a woman can't live on sex alone. "I'm starving."

Sam claps his hands, then grabs his keys and a jacket. "There's a nice café just down the street. Let's go!"

"Er, well, the sweats and T-shirt fit all right. And I'm the first to admit that my feet aren't exactly petite, but . . ." I pull up my pant legs and wiggle my bare feet. "I don't think I'm going to be able to pull off wearing your shoes. Can we go to my house first?"

Sam still has the vet's Lexus, so we drive to my house in style. Neither of us is surprised when we find Rex sitting at the kitchen table in his boxer shorts, reading the paper.

"Hi," I say, grinning. Iris has *got* to be happy about this. Out of her league? Pshaw!

Rex pushes up his glasses and nods. He looks embarrassed. "I'm just making some coffee. I guess Iris isn't much of a morning person."

I snort at his understatement. That's putting it nicely. I don't want to give away too much personal information, yet. If this guy is worth anything, he'll love her for who she is. If he's another jerk—well, it might be better if he learns about her morning demeanor on his own. I suddenly feel very protective of Iris. I know she likes this guy. She seems genuinely happy when she's with him, so it would suck if he turned out to be another asshole. I don't want to see her hurt again. Rex seems all right, but I'm tempted to give him the third degree. I want to find out his personal history, his hopes and dreams, his intentions with my best friend. I manage to resist the urge. I go to my bedroom and change into my own clothes.

When I get back to the kitchen, Sam and Rex are talking about music. Rex is pouring four cups of coffee. He hands one to Sam and one to me. I notice that he makes one of the remaining cups just how Iris likes it, with lots of milk, but no sugar. That's a good sign. I suggest he warm up a couple of maple scones from the freezer. I watch his every move. He is neat and respectful of our space. As he balances his precarious load of coffee cups and scones and starts to leave the kitchen, I can't keep silent anymore. I have to know if this kindness, this generosity, is real.

I blurt, "So, Rex. What are your plans with Iris? You serious about her?" Sam is sitting at the kitchen table. When I see him cover his eyes and grimace, I realize that I might sound a teensy bit like his meddlesome twin sister.

"You asking me what my intentions are, Kate? Whether I'll respect Iris in the morning?"

I squirm. "Yeah. That's about it."

I want Rex to bowl me over. Last night, he was standoffish and kind of geeky. Today, well, I like him okay, but he's a little nervous. I'm sure sitting with strangers in your boxer shorts waiting for the coffee to brew isn't the time to look especially smooth. I'm impressed that when the talk shifts to Iris, he stands tall and looks me dead in the eyes. His energy is focused and his mind engaged. He radiates an aura of strength and competence, and my fears are put to rest. This is a good man.

"Iris is going to be a star. She's going to make it big."

"Yeah." All I can do is nod. I've always thought so, too.

"But music can be a rough business, and let's face it, Iris isn't as tough as she acts. Some smooth-talking sleazeball could eat her alive."

I nod again.

"As for my plans with Iris? Let's just say I'm going to stick to her like glue for awhile. I know of a couple of labels that might be interested in her, and I'm not going to let those vultures tear her to shreds. I'll make sure she doesn't smoke too much, that she remembers to eat and gets some sleep, and that she leaves plenty of time to practice. A lot of people have wanted to work with me in the past, but Iris is the real deal.

"So if it's okay with you, I plan to wake up beside her as often as I can. That way I can remind her the moment she opens her eyes that she's an amazing woman with about ten tons of talent in that skinny little body of hers. In fact, I plan to do that right now before she gets her clothes back on, or before this coffee gets cold." There is a playful gleam in his eyes. "I'd prefer the cold coffee, personally."

Sam smiles into the newspaper. I have to laugh. How can I object to that?

Sam and I walk to my favorite local café for pancakes and a few gallons of coffee. After our plates have been cleared, he leans back in the padded booth, stretches his arms wide and looks around. "Mmm. That was good. If I was going to open a restaurant, this is what it would be. No frills, no pretensions, just good food. Did you ever think about opening a place like this?"

I look around. It has never occurred to me to open a basic café. "I never really thought about it," I admit. Sam doesn't pressure me for answers. He just looks interested in what I have to say. "I planned on being a hotshot chef. I used to think a place like this was below me, a waste of my talents. But now, I'm not so sure. I don't think a neighborhood cafe would be bad."

Sam makes a good sounding board, so I keep talking. "I've been questioning everything these past few weeks. Not just my career and my relationships, but my feelings about food and cooking. Half the time I look at what I'm doing right now and feel like a total loser. The other half of the time, I love it. I feel useful, like I'm doing people a service."

"You feel like a loser?"

"Yeah. I feel invisible, like I'm just another cook. When I told people I was the sous-chef at Sound Bistro, it meant something. Anybody who knew anything about food was impressed. Now, I make soup and salad three times a week for a financial firm downtown. I might as well be working in a cafeteria. I was at the top of my game before. I was getting somewhere. Now, I'm nothing."

"It's impossible to win at that kind of game, you know. You can't win at art."

"Huh?"

"Food isn't just your job; it's your art. And who wins at art? The people who make the most money? The folks who get famous before they die? The person with the most ribbons and medals and magazine covers? Is that what you want?"

"It was. It might still be."

"How many people will it take to tell you that you make incredible food before you'll believe it? I don't mean to sound sanctimonious, but why is it more important for a magazine editor to like your food than your neighbor? You have this amazing skill. If you ask me, the only way you can possibly fail is to limit access of your gifts to rich folks who can get a reservation."

"But that's the business. That's the way it works."

Sam gestures around us. "Uh, excuse me, but what about this place? I just had a great meal with a beautiful woman and I didn't have to wear my tux again. I couldn't be happier. If you don't want to keep doing the freelance stuff, why can't you find a neighborhood place like this to work your magic?"

I look around, thinking about what he has said. "But it's more complicated than that. I'm not adverse to the concept, at least not anymore.

There's a lot of honor in making good, simple food for your neighbors and friends. I guess that's what I've been trying to figure out. I realize I've been trying to impress the wrong people, but lately I've had the feeling I might also have been cooking the wrong food. I made what the magazines told me to make, creating these elaborate showcase dishes instead of trusting my own instincts. But then again . . . if I trusted my own instincts I might serve nothing but peanut butter and Pop-Tarts."

He laughs. "Yeah, right."

I feel so close to Sam, so safe with him, that I'm even willing to tell him about my junk-food secrets. "It's the honest truth! When no one is around, I eat a lot of crap. I like gas station corn dogs with yellow mustard. I like frozen Ding Dongs and Kraft macaroni and cheese, the bright orange kind, with ketchup on it. I like Cocoa Puffs and cherry Slurpees and cheap frozen pizzas. I like all that food I know is really bad, so how can I ever be a real chef? How can I trust my instincts or keep up my standards? Some guy might come in and try to sell me Cheez Whiz in a fancy crock with a French name and I'll buy it because I *like* it."

Sam sits back in his chair and looks over at me, startled. "You're a mess, aren't you?" I let my head fall onto the table with a light bang. He chuckles. I look up and have to laugh. My deep, dark fears look pretty harmless when they're brought out into the sunlight. He reaches across the table for my hand.

"All those years, all that work, and you could be brought down with a little Cheez Whiz. It's a crying shame."

I try not to smile. "This is *important*." I can't manage to maintain a straight face. Sam can't either, but he gives it a valiant effort. We both end up grabbing our full stomachs and laughing until it hurts.

"You need to give yourself a break more often, Kate. You're not a just a chef, you know. You're much more complicated than that. Cooking might be your job, and it's certainly your art, but it's not who you are. Who cares that you eat crappy food when you're off work? Would you expect a professional perfumer to live a life devoid of Band-aids and bubblegum? Are professional musicians only supposed to hear birdsong and lapping waves? I'm going to bet that Yo-Yo Ma has a Madonna CD or two in his collection, maybe even some cowboy yodelers. Your sense of taste is your profession. Of course you eat junk food now and then. You're giving yourself some time off."

I am swooning with love for this goofball across the table. "How come you're so smart?"

"Let's just say I've learned from experience. I've been thinking a lot about work and art and love myself these past few months." He looks over at me with an impish grin. "You want to go down to the studio? See what I've been working on?"

"Your art! Your secret art!" I leap up from the booth and dash out the door. I bounce in the parking lot, a lot like Scooter, the Jack Russell terrier. On the drive to the studio, Sam tells me more about what brought him to Seattle. It wasn't just Selena.

"Remember I told you about when I worked as an engineer? I hated it. I had to put in a precise number of hours, sitting at my desk, talking on the phone or just wandering around the halls working figures in my head. I had worked out a way to streamline things, to make the ordering and shipping more efficient, but my supervisor didn't want to be shown up. He wouldn't use any of my ideas. It was so frustrating, having to fill out these forms and go through these archaic, expensive steps when I knew it could be done faster and better.

"The money was good, the benefits were okay, but I was dying a little bit more every single day. It got so that I would avoid looking out the windows. If I didn't see the wind moving the leaves or the sun bouncing off the mountain scrub, I could almost pretend that the recirculated air and gray cubicle walls were a habitable human environment. Then I caught Selena with that other guy, and Mama Rose died. Going to work became unbearable. So, I quit. I went camping in the mountains. I got my hands dirty again. I got burned skin and sore muscles, and I felt alive for the first time in years.

"I realized that I had been working for Selena's dreams, not mine. She didn't want me; she wanted a certain lifestyle—a husband, a big house with a pool and a cactus garden."

"She wanted the fairy tale," I say, knowing from my own experience.

"I guess so. Mandy doesn't get it, but I'm so over Selena, it's not funny. Sure, she still calls and she tries to get at my heart, but that's because she's getting scared. Sweet, stupid Sam Guerra was always there for her."

We arrive at the studio, and I nudge Sam toward the painted door. "So, what did you decide to do? What's in there?"

"When I asked myself what I wanted to do, this was it." He unlocks the door, pulls back the curtain, and I step into his lair.

"Oh, my God! This is incredible!" I have envisioned all sorts of things behind the door, but an entire Claymation studio isn't one of them. I gawk at the lighting equipment, digital camera and computer all directed at a table. There are sketches and photos of an elaborate desert scene hanging on the wall above a rough framework, and assorted props made of colorful, pliable clay.

Sam sounds like a proud kid as he explains. "I used to put together these five- and ten-second shorts with a couple of my friends back in college. It was a gas. I got to build elaborate sets and roads, fool around with computers and clay, and make people laugh.

"This is what I want to do with my life right now. There's a good chance nothing will come of it. But who cares? I like my job with your mom, and I'm having fun. If things go bad, I can fall back on my degree and get a job with the state or something. The important thing is, I can say I gave it a try. I finally know what it feels like to do exactly what I want.

"Even though she broke my heart, I don't regret my relationship with Selena at all. She was the one who taught me about passion. I spent a lot of my life chasing after the passion I felt for her. In the end, I was able to turn that desire and feeling into something much more important: my own life, my art and now you, Kate. You're my newest passion."

I am drawn to him. I wrap my arms around him. "You're my newest passion too, Sam," I say, and we kiss like teenagers. We kiss until we hear something behind us.

"Ahem." It's Mom. We yank back from our lip-lock as if we were caught doing something naughty. My cheeks and ears are red hot. She smirks. "So, I'm going to guess you two had fun at the party. Or is this just another act?"

Sam scratches his head and looks for something else in the room to focus on. I fiddle with a piece of wire on the table. "Mom! I didn't know you were here. I didn't see your van out front. Did you just get here?" I say in what might be a slightly accusing tone. She pushes her glasses down to the tip of her nose. "My brakes were making a funny sound, so I dropped the van off at Gene's, around the corner. I've been here for an hour or so. I heard you two arrive. I figured you would come out when I turned the music on. I knocked, too, but I see that you've been busy."

I can hear the music now. Sam and I fidget and talk simultaneously. "Your brakes are giving you trouble? That's a shame," he says. I add, "That Gene is a wonder. He can fix anything." We look at each other and then bust out in nervous laughter.

Mom laughs with us. "Well, I don't want to interrupt. I just thought I'd make my presence known. You two kids get back to work . . . or, whatever else you were doing." She drops the curtain and shuts the door. I know Mom is happy for us and doesn't mind one bit that we were fooling around. But it's still embarrassing to be caught by your mom when you're making out in a closet.

When we stop laughing, Sam shows me his character prototypes and drawings. He's been collecting ideas for years. I meet Xavier, the high-stepping kangaroo mouse whose dream is to become the next Lord of the Dance. There is the narcissistic Casper, the current jackalope postcard supermodel. Marvin is a skinny tortoise in a huge shell and necktie. Sam has me cracking up as he makes the tortoise jerk and dance to old Talking Heads classics, just like David Byrne.

"Lately I've been thinking about doing something with spiny desert lizards at the cosmetic surgeon's," Sam says. You know, some lumpy lady gila monster who's trying to achieve the dewy soft skin and lithe figure of the rain forest geckos. Or some loose-skinned lizard looking for a nip and tuck?"

I explode with enthusiasm. "You're brilliant! I can't believe you keep this a secret. Why don't you show everyone how cool this is?"

"Why don't you open the oven door and show off the soufflé while it's cooking?"

"Good point." Suddenly I'm concerned. "Now that you've let me in here, the project isn't going to flop, is it? You're not going to blame me if things don't go well?"

He shrugs. "Nah. Not anymore. I don't think you would have done me any favors here when we first met. That was some seriously bad juju you were giving off for awhile."

"Speak for yourself, Buddy!"

"Yeah, okay. I was in a pretty weird spot, too. Let's just call it a transitional phase. I was dealing with all of that crap back home. And getting this set up has been a steep learning curve. But I think things are really coming along now. Having you know about this will make my life easier. I can bounce ideas off you."

He turns away from the set and drawings and pulls me into his arms again.

I want to get even closer to him and yet we are pressed tightly together. He hugs me and finishes his thoughts.

"I don't want to tell you what to do about work; I've probably done enough of that already. But I will say that, for the first time, I've got my art and my career in balance and I've never been happier. I hope that soon you'll be that lucky."

I lean into him and rest my head on his shoulder. I do love him. It's a different kind of love than I had with Gaston. He's my friend and confidant. There is a trust and warmth we share, kind of like I have with Iris. He kisses me, then moves another stool up against the set. He tells me about the camera and the figure mechanics. We spend the rest of the day sitting side by side, building tiny scrub cactus and mesquite brambles, and playing with voice and story ideas for Nadine, the lipstick-loving lizard.

Epilogue

"Elvis!" I shout. "Leave poor Muffin alone!" I rescue my
tormented pooch by picking up the pesky adolescent cat and tossing him
on the couch. The kitten bounces off the couch onto the side table and
bats at Spike in his tank. Spike puffs up into a threatening pose. Elvis
spins and attacks the couch cushions. He's at the stage where he's still a
kitten, but not quite as adorable. He's lanky and not in complete control
of his limbs. He runs kind of sideways and falls off things. I'm hoping
this phase won't last long. He's a real handful.

Instead of appreciating her liberation from the living room corner, my
scraggly brown mutt, Muffin, runs back to play with her former torturer.
I throw up my hands. They're siblings. They love to torment each other.

Iris brought the kitten home at Christmas, just one day before I was to
leave for Portland with Mom. He was the funniest-looking thing. He has
one crinkled ear, an orange patch over one slightly crossed eye and a tiny
Hitler mustache. Iris said she picked him because he was the ugliest kitten she could find. She knew we wouldn't be so shallow as to base our
adoration on mere physical beauty. We would give him the love he
needed. She named him Elvis to improve his self-image, and it seems to
have worked. This cat is full of himself.

A week after Elvis arrived, Sam brought me Muffin. He found her on
a bike trail under the freeway, huddled in a wet cardboard box. She had
been abused and abandoned. She still flinches at quick movements and
loud sounds, but after several months, of tenderness and care she's no
longer just skin and bones. I think she knows she's safe here, although she
may have her doubts when Elvis gets frisky. She absolutely worships
Ziggy, who is presently asleep in the corner on his braided rug.

I go back into the kitchen, where Sam is cleaning collard greens. He asks, "Am I doing this right? I'm just pulling the leaves off the tough stems." I give his work the okay and pat his butt a few times.

Sam still lives at the vet's office. We spend a lot of nights at his place, but we always cook here. I pull a chunk of salt pork from the fridge and hand it to Sam. "Mr. Foster said we should slow cook the collards with salt pork instead of bacon. He says it's better. I guess it's more authentic." He nods.

I've been going back to Cedar Heights Nursing Home once a week. We started a cooking club. Each week, one of the patients picks a recipe and I help them all prepare it. Then we sit in the activity room by the kitchen to eat and talk about food, recipes, old times and what we might like to try next week. The cooking club is where I got most of today's recipes. It's a great time for all of us. Since Lucinda was promoted to main cook, everyone seems happier.

Mr. Foster is the one who hooked me up with the smokehouse in North Carolina. He says they make the best country hams in the nation. I ordered one, and I've been soaking it for two days, changing the water every four to six hours, just like he suggested. I've never cooked a country ham before. I've been trying a lot of new things lately.

It's Easter Sunday and we're having a genuine dinner party. I bought a tablecloth and candles and everything. I picked a big bouquet of tulips, and Sam and I even dyed a dozen eggs for the centerpiece. They're pretty wild, but colorful and festive. Everyone is coming. Even Iris and Rex are flying in from L.A. He got her a contract with a big label, and I can't wait to hear how the recording is going. She's going to be famous!

Marissa is bringing Steve. That will be nice. I guess the baby is starting to show, and I haven't even seen her engagement ring yet. Mom and Aunt Virginia are picking up Mr. Wright after church. I introduced him to my wacky aunt a few months ago, and they really hit it off. We all get together now and then for dinner and cards. He and Aunt Virginia like to trade stories and compare their visits to the great cities of the world.

Marsha is pleased that her dad has so many new friends. She's coming today, too. Turns out her husband, Don, is from Mobile, Alabama. When he heard about my experiment in Southern cooking, he had to get involved. He's bringing okra and cornbread. He says we Yankees make our cornbread too sweet. He also claims to be able to cook okra in a way that doesn't make it gross and slimy. I'll believe it when I see it.

I'm still doing the lunches for Wheton-Lofton. When Marsha announced to the staff that their lunches were ending, there were threats of a walkout. She worked out a deal with them. They have to sign up and chip in at the beginning of each month if they want to eat, and she'll match their contributions. It's going okay, but the big projects are over, folks have more free time and I think the novelty might be wearing off. There have been more and more leftovers. At least Gaston still appreciates my cooking.

We're still friends, but not so close that I invited him today. He and Courtney seem to have worked things out. His initial therapy sessions unearthed all sorts of issues. He's become a walking, talking commercial for personal empowerment and a self-help seminar junkie. He's even scheduled to walk on hot coals next month. It must be what he's using as a substitute for sex. Courtney still won't agree to marry him. But she has loosened some of her strict relationship bylaws. And Gaston has made a few demands of his own. I guess part of their new relationship contract includes her taking some cooking classes. I haven't heard a peep about Adele. I've been tempted to call her, but I don't think it's the right time. It may never be the right time.

"Okay, the collards are on and I preheated the oven for the ham. Did you make that glaze yet?" Sam asks.

I point to a bowl on the counter. "Right here."

He gives my shoulders a squeeze.

The former headwaiter at Sound Bistro called me last week. He and his partner are opening their own place. It's nothing fancy, but it sounds interesting. It's going to be a used record store with a connecting café that will stay open all night. They want the food to be simple but fun, and the cocktails to be funky. Dishes should be good, but eclectic enough to attract a breakfast crowd, draw some family diners and still appeal to the 3 a.m. munchies set. I've agreed to work with them on the menu and the pricing and to get the kitchen up and running. Sam's eager to help, but I don't want him to spend too much time away from his sets. His stuff is really coming along.

"Kate, where did you put the black-eyed peas?"

I reach for the bowl of black-eyed peas that are resting under a clean towel on the counter. We'll shell them together.

I'm not exactly sure what my future holds, but I don't need to worry about that right now. I've got more important things to do. I'm making the macaroni and cheese.

Recipes

Hazelnut Orange Twists

If you've got frozen puff pastry, you've got the makings for a good snack, virtually any time of the day. Here's a quick breakfast treat.

> 2 sheets frozen puff pastry dough, thawed
>   according to package directions
> 2 tablespoons melted butter
> 2 tablespoons sugar
> ½ cup finely chopped hazelnuts
> ½ teaspoon ground cinnamon
>
> **Orange glaze**
> 1 cup sifted confectioners' sugar
> 2 tablespoons fresh-squeezed orange juice
> 1 teaspoon grated orange zest
> Drop of vanilla

Preheat the oven to 425°. Line two baking sheets with parchment or silicone sheets.

Brush the thawed pastry evenly with melted butter. Sprinkle each sheet with sugar, chopped nuts and cinnamon. Press the toppings into the pastry by rolling with a rolling pin. Cut pastry into eight strips. Twist each strip and arrange on the prepared baking sheets. Bake for 15 minutes until pastries are light brown, then flip and continue baking until they are dark brown and crisp, about 4 minutes more.

While twists are baking, mix together the confectioners' sugar, orange juice, zest and vanilla in a small bowl.

Move the twists to a cooling rack, drizzle with the prepared glaze and serve warm.

Yield: 16 pastries

Walnut Drambuie Shortbread Cookies

It may be too much to claim these are the world's best shortbread cookies, but they're pretty great, and incredibly easy. Whip up a batch in your food processor. Then you can press the dough into a traditional mold, or chill it and roll out your favorite shortbread cookie shape.

1 cup walnuts
1 cup all-purpose flour (for best results replace 2 tablespoons of flour
   with cornstarch or rice flour)
¼ cup superfine sugar
¼ teaspoon salt
4 ounces unsalted butter, cut into small cubes
2 tablespoons Drambuie liqueur

Place the walnuts in the bowl of a food processor and pulse nuts until they are finely ground. Add the flour, sugar and salt and pulse until well combined. Drop the cold butter into the dry ingredients and pulse to combine evenly. The dough should look like moist cake crumbs, but not pull together yet. Add Drambuie and blend just until the dough comes together.

Press the dough into a traditional cookie mold or turn the cookie dough out onto a piece of plastic wrap, flatten slightly and chill for at least 30 minutes.

Preheat the oven to 300°.

Roll the cookie dough out onto a lightly floured surface, cut into desired shape, decoratively prick cookies with a fork and sprinkle with a bit more sugar. Place cookies on an ungreased baking sheet and cook until dry and just barely brown around the edges, about 20 minutes.

Remove the cookies to a cooling rack. When cool, transfer to an airtight container.

Yield: 36 1½-inch cookies

French Onion Soup

I was taught to make a good French onion soup in a family-style terrine instead of individual bowls. I still prefer it that way because it leaves your guests with the option of seconds. The trick to the best soup is to use top-quality beef or veal stock and to be very patient caramelizing the onions. Don't be tempted to use sweet onions. Use good pungent onions or the finished soup will be almost as sweet as caramel.

    4 tablespoons butter
    1 pound pungent yellow onions, sliced
    2 tablespoons flour
    2 quarts good beef or veal stock
    Good-sized bouquet garni (2 bay leaves, a big sprig of thyme
        and 6 or 7 bruised parsley stems)
    1 small rustic bread loaf, sliced one-inch thick
    2 cups grated Gruyère cheese
    Salt and pepper to taste
    Splash of cognac or sherry if desired

Heat a large, heavy sauce or stew pan, and melt the butter until foaming. Add the onions. Cook slowly until the onions are a good even brown, 15 to 20 minutes. Stir in the flour, cook until golden brown, and add the stock and bouquet garni. Simmer the soup for 30 minutes. Season soup with salt and pepper.

Preheat oven to 400°. Remove the bouquet garni. Place the slices of bread in a heavy overproof casserole and pour the hot soup over them. Cover with grated cheese and bake for 25 minutes until the cheese is brown and bubbly. Serve hot with a splash of cognac or sherry.

Yield: 4 to 6 servings

Smoked Chicken and Sweet Potato Chowder

This is a simple but delightful soup, just perfect for an autumn supper. If smoked chicken is unavailable, feel free to substitute smoked turkey, ham or simply cooked chicken.

> 1 cup coarsely chopped bacon ends and pieces
> 1 small onion, chopped
> 2 tablespoons butter
> 3 tablespoons all-purpose flour
> 1½ quarts good chicken stock
> 2 cups sweet potatoes, peeled and diced
> 2 cups smoked chicken, skin and bones removed,
>   chopped or shredded (½ pound)
> ¼ cups peeled, roasted red peppers, diced or pimentos
> 1 cup heavy cream
> 1 teaspoon chopped fresh thyme
> Black pepper
> Salt

Heat a heavy soup pot over medium heat and fry the bacon and onions until they are golden brown, about 8 to 10 minutes. Pour off excess fat if there is any. Melt butter in the pan and stir in flour. Let flour cook, stirring constantly until it is golden brown, 2 to 3 minutes. Add chicken stock and stir well, making sure nothing sticks to the bottom of the pan. Bring the soup to a boil. Add sweet potatoes and simmer until they are tender, about 15 minutes. Add smoked chicken, red peppers, cream and seasonings and simmer 20 to 30 minutes more. Season to taste. Serve hot.

Yield: 6 servings

Toasted Almond and Caramel Mocha
(MARS LATTE)

1–2 tablespoons toasted almond or toffee syrup
1 tablespoon good-quality caramel sauce
2 tablespoons good-quality chocolate sauce
2 shots espresso
8 ounces milk, steamed

Whipped cream
Toasted chopped almonds
Chocolate and caramel syrups for drizzling

Mix the syrup and chocolate and caramel sauces in the bottom of a mug. Steam the milk and set aside while brewing espresso. Mix together the hot espresso and flavorings, then pour on the steamed milk. Stir gently and top with whipped cream and garnishes.

Yield: 1 huge, calorie-packed beverage

Crunchy Duck Salad

Kate would surely roast off her own ducks, but I usually skip that step and buy one at my favorite Chinese barbecue joint. If duck isn't your thing (it falls in the category of cute food), or you don't live near a handy barbecue joint, use a rotisserie chicken, some cooked shrimp or maybe cold roast pork as an alternative. Or just enjoy the veggies alone. For really easy preparation use one of those magic slicer-dicers my dad calls the "banjo" but are actually known as a mandoline.

1 Chinese-style roasted duck, skin removed, meat shredded
4 cups napa cabbage, thinly sliced
1 cup julienned carrots
1 cup julienned English or Japanese cucumber
1 cup julienned daikon radish
1 bunch of watercress, stems removed
3 green onions, thinly sliced

Hoisin vinaigrette
½ cup seasoned rice vinegar
½ cup hoisin sauce
1 teaspoon fresh grated ginger
Pinch of red chili flakes
1 teaspoon toasted sesame oil
2 tablespoons peanut oil

Garnish
Green onions, radish sprouts and crispy duck skin

Combine the vinaigrette ingredients in a small bowl and whisk together.

In a large bowl, combine the duck meat and all of the vegetables. Toss the salad with the vinaigrette and arrange the salad on a platter. Garnish with radish sprouts and duck skin that has been crisped in the oven and shredded.

Do not dress salad until ready to serve.

(Alternatively, arrange each vegetable separately on a plate with the duck meat in the center and offer the dressing alongside for a pretty presentation.)

Yield: 6 servings

Fried Geoduck

No doubt about it, connoisseurs will tell you never to cook a geoduck. Or, if you must, then to merely wave the raw pieces in a hot broth or they will get tough. But the giant clam is mighty ugly and we Northwesterners aren't always that brave. I think it's much more comforting and very delicious if you do it the old fashioned way: fry the clam strips in butter and cracker crumbs or grind it up for chowder.

> 1 small geoduck (1½ pounds)
> 1 cup all-purpose flour seasoned with salt and pepper
> 3 eggs, beaten
> 2 cups finely ground cracker crumbs
> Plenty of butter for frying
> Fresh lemons and sauces for service

To clean the geoduck, cut off the shell and discard all but the neck and yellow body meat. Plunge the clam in hot water for 5 seconds. Peel off the coarse skin from the siphon. Slice the geoduck into bite-sized pieces and toss a few pieces at a time in the flour. Shake off any excess flour. Dip pieces in beaten egg and then dredge in finely ground cracker crumbs. Fry the clam strips quickly in hot butter until just golden brown, about 1 minute per side. Eat with lemon and tartar or cocktail sauce.

Yield: 4–6 servings

Posole

I'm not going to claim any expertise in Southwestern cooking. My friends Jacques and Jamie Guerin from Albuquerque make their posole very simply with red chilies and no condiments. My mom, on the other hand, does a pretty mean green posole that we love to load with odds and ends. I'll leave the final decision up to you.

> 1 pound pork, such as pork shoulder or boneless spare ribs,
>   cut into chunks
> 1 small onion, diced
> 1 clove garlic
> ½ cup diced green chiles or 2–3 red chiles
> 1 large can of hominy
> 1 quart good chicken stock
> ½ teaspoon oregano
> Salt and black pepper to taste
> Juice of 1 lime

Brown the pork lightly in a soup pot. Add the onion, garlic, and chiles and cook until aromatic, about 3 minutes. Add hominy, stock, and oregano and simmer on low until the pork is tender, about 2 hours. Season with salt, pepper and lime juice and serve with assorted condiments and corn tortillas.

Suggested condiments:
Lime wedges
Radishes
Sliced cabbage or lettuce
Diced avocado
Pickled jalapeños
Crumbled queso fresca
Sour cream
Sliced green onions
Cilantro sprigs
Olives
Diced tomatoes

Pixie Shticks

No kidding! Don't expect to find this on a cocktail menu anytime soon, but if you feel like getting the girls together and getting a little crazy, pink drinks are always a welcome addition.

Frost two martini glasses by rubbing the rim with lemon or lime and dipping the rim in Pixie Stick powder.

In a cocktail shaker full of ice, pour in 2 ounces vodka, 1 ounce kirsh, 1 ounce fresh squeezed lime juice and ½ ounce Cointreau or triple sec. Shake thoroughly and pour through a strainer into prepared glasses. Splash in a bit of cherry juice and serve with a cherry.

Or, for a much more sophisticated drink, I found a wonderful French cherry eau de vie that is divine mixed with vodka and lots of ice. The Pixie Stick dust still adds a certain charm.

Yield: 2 cocktails

Wild Blackberry Pie

We're blackberry snobs in the Northwest. The big fat, juicy Himalayan berries that grow like weeds around town are tasty as a snack, but it's the low-growing, tiny wild blackberries that are treasured for baking. They are early and small, but once you try them you will be hooked on the more robust, tart and almost floral flavor.

Two pie crusts

6–7 cups tiny wild blackberries
2 cups granulated sugar
¼ cup cognac or brandy
4–5 tablespoons cornstarch or tapioca flour
2 tablespoons butter

1 egg white, whipped
Granulated sugar

Preheat oven to 425°.

Mix the berries, sugar, liquor, and cornstarch and let rest while preparing the shells.

Roll the bottom crust extra thin and place in a lightly oiled pie tin. Mix the berries again and pour into prepared pastry. Dot the top of the berries with small pieces of butter and then cover with the top pastry.

Bake at 425° for ten minutes, then reduce the heat to 350° and bake for 45 minutes. Five minutes before the pie is ready to come out of the oven, brush the top with whipped egg whites and sprinkle on sugar.

Let the pie cool and serve with vanilla ice cream.

Yield: 8 servings